MW01255083

Country Law

The Shops on Wolf Creek Square

Gini Athey

Enjoy,
Gini Athey

Book Stop

603 S. Military Avenue
Green Bay, WI 54303
(920) 498-0008
www.bookstopinc.info

To Kendra B. —wonderful friend and first-rate supporter.
My books are for sale in her
needlework shop because that's the kind of
person she is.

To Carmen W. —next-door neighbor and special friend
who ordered my book to give
away as soon as it was available.
Thank you.

A Note to Readers...

Welcome to Wolf Creek.

In *Country Law*, the second book in my Wolf Creek Square series, you'll meet new citizens of the Square and enjoy reconnecting with some residents and families you already know from *Quilts Galore*.

Nestled in rich farm land, Wolf Creek is a small fictional town west of Green Bay, Wisconsin. Unique to the town is Wolf Creek Square, a pedestrian-only area where historical buildings surround a picnic area, a stage used for concerts and festivals, flower gardens, and walkways. The Square is a beautiful and safe place for shoppers, children, and visitors to gather for festivals and events scheduled during all four seasons.

While Georgia Winters has a secret to reveal and a plan to reunite her family, she has no idea how to manage the attentions of Elliot Reynolds, her high school sweetheart. I, too, returned to my hometown after years of schooling and employment because there was a special man waiting for me.

You'll learn about the historical town with snippets of history added to the story. Some of the Square's residents can trace their ancestry to the beginning of the town. (You can read the history of the beginning of the town in *Quilts Galore*.)

So, join Georgia as she wonders if this tight-knit community will accept her once her secret is divulged.

Families break apart because of misunderstandings and outspoken words by those we trust. Georgia and her sister, Beverly, must bare themselves to family and friends and tell the whole truth in order to rebuild the trust they had as children. They never believed their past decisions would have such far-reaching consequences.

Please visit my website, www.giniathey.com and sign up for my newsletter and mailing list. You'll want to know what's happening on the Square and with its citizens.

Gini Athey

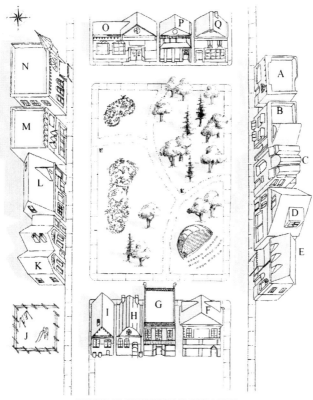

WOLF CREEK SQUARE

A-Farmer Foods
B-Farmer Foods
C-Rainbow Gardens
D-Vacant
E-Country Law
F-Art&Son Jewelry
G-Quilts Galore
H-Vacant
I-Pages

J-Fenced Playground
K-Styles by Knight and Day
L-Vacant
M-Biscuits and Brew
N-Inn on the Square
O-Museum
P-Mayor's Office
Q-Vacant

"It's a funny thing about coming home. Looks the same, smells the same. You'll realize what's changed is you."

—F. Scott Fitzgerald

"Coming home seemed to have started the healing process. No longer vivid and garish, the memories seemed to be covered in gossamer, fading behind a curtain of time and forgiveness."

—Karen Fowler

Prologue

I tried one more time to stop my sister from giving up my great-nephew, her grandson. "Beverly, you can't sell Toby." I stood next to the crib staring at the innocent baby.

"You want him, Georgia?" she asked. "I've taken care of Toby *and* Mom for six months now. I'm done."

I glanced across my sister's dining room where sunlight cast shadows across the floor outlining the hospital bed. To make the long days of caregiving a little easier, she'd converted the room into a combined nursery and hospital room. But she never complained—at least to me—about the burdens she carried.

"You know as well as I do there's simply no way I can take him. I barely make enough money to support myself." My hands trembled as I thought about what would happen to the little boy.

Opening a copy of our mother's will, Beverly waved the sheaf of papers at me. "Not exactly the amount we expected from Mother, is it?" She dropped the papers on the bedside table. "If only she'd told us she'd sold all the land."

Each Christmas, our dad had told us that one day the land outside of Wolf Creek would be ours and we would be able to enjoy the bounty of its richness. But he was gone now. And so was the land.

"I was *counting* on that money," Beverly said, still gazing at the baby.

"Me, too, I suppose." I gently rubbed the sleeping baby's cheeks, then sat on the edge of a small chair next to the crib. "But selling Toby isn't right."

"Look, Georgia, Richard Connor doesn't care how he gets a grandson. When he read Mom's will, he asked right out what would happen to the boy. Remember?"

"Of course, I remember," I said, a sick feeling intensifying in the pit of my stomach.

"Mom left everything to us," Beverly said, "so if you want Toby, he's yours."

"No." I slumped back into the chair and buried my face in my hands. "Better he go to a good home that can provide for him." Still, I couldn't stop thinking that Toby had become nothing more than a piece of jewelry or furniture discarded by the heirs of an old woman's estate.

***

"Since you don't seem to be able to produce a son of your own, I've found one for you."

Chad Connor's father, Richard, spoke from behind the massive teak desk in his office, but, Chad noted, he didn't look at him. Instead, he focused on the view through his wall-to-wall windows. The panoramic view spanned the city's business district and west across the Fox River and the jewel of the city, Lambeau Field, home stadium of the Green Bay Packers.

Sitting in one of the leather visitor's chairs, Chad almost managed to smile inside. At last, his father's detached words no longer inflicted the emotional hit they once had.

"Here's the money," Richard said, tossing the brown envelope on the desk, "and I'll let you know when and where to pick him up this afternoon."

Of course, he wouldn't hand it to me. Chad stood and dutifully picked up the package and slipped it into his coat pocket.

"Remember," Richard said, "that boy will be raised as my grandson. Mine."

March
1

Six years later…

Bright sunlight bounced off the windshield of my car as I pushed my rolling suitcase through the car door and into the middle of the backseat. I glanced at the clear sky. Yes, I'd chosen the right day to leave Milwaukee and return to Wolf Creek.

Once underway, I pulled onto I-43 North, but before I made it through Sheboygan a strong east wind off Lake Michigan blew light snow across the road. That got my attention. I turned off the instrumental renditions of old popular songs playing on the radio. I didn't need distractions, no matter how bland. I grew up with snow on the roads, but I'd never lost my tendency to be cautious. I tucked in behind an eighteen-wheel transport, close enough to see his running lights, but far enough behind to be safe.

A few miles south of Green Bay, blowing snow glazed the roadway and the line of cars and trucks all slowed to a safer speed. Unfortunately, the semi driver turned north toward Door County and I lost the protection that had provided a sense of security. I kept heading to the turnoff for Highway 29 that would take me west.

The extensive road construction meant confronting confusing crossovers and lane closures, which demanded focus. That was for the best. The conditions forced me to at least try to push away the jumble of things on my mind and stay alert for detours and merging traffic from makeshift ramps. With surprising ease, I navigated all of it as I drove farther west.

Even during the most demanding part of the drive, I found myself drifting into questions about my decision to return to Wolf Creek and opening old wounds. But after spending a second or two in that territory, I again stiffened my spine and resolved to see my plan through to the end. No matter who suffered. But could *I* endure the worst?

As I talked to myself, the reality of my decision reenergized me and the miles quickly fell behind me. The snow stopped, but the overcast sky had made the day a dark one.

I turned off the state road leading into Wolf Creek and onto the Square. I'd made a reservation at the Inn on the Square, at least for one night, maybe longer. The receptionist I spoke with on the phone chuckled when I'd hesitated about the number of nights I'd be staying. But she assured me that they weren't full and she doubted the Inn would see a rush of tourists during the last week of March.

I pulled into the parking zone behind the Inn and turned the ignition key off. I'd made it, and I gave the steering wheel a quick slap as proof of my accomplishment.

Many years ago, Wolf Creek Square had been made a pedestrian only area, surrounded by historically correct buildings. At least their façades were reminiscent of the late 1800s, although many had been renovated to include modern conveniences. The Square itself remained a walking area, but the driveways behind all four lines of buildings on the Square accommodated deliveries with parking areas behind.

I lifted my suitcase from the back seat of the car and pulled it behind me as I circled around a delivery truck blocking the walkway to the side entrance of the Inn. The overcast afternoon dimmed the view of the back of the buildings.

"Oh, excuse me." A middle-aged man, at least judging by his graying temples, held the door open, his only expression a reserved smile. "I thought I'd make a quick delivery to

Crossroads and be gone before anyone drove in."

I hesitated, trying to look at him more closely in the dim light. Of course, he looked familiar. And I'd have known that voice anywhere. With any luck, he wouldn't recognize me. I wasn't ready to see him yet.

"No worries. I don't have much." I lifted my small bag as if offering proof, but glanced away, hoping to fade into the shadows.

"Wait a second," the man said. "Georgia? It took me a minute, but even in this dim light I'd recognize those crystal blue eyes of yours."

I wanted to fold back into myself. I'd been in town all of five minutes. And I'd already run into him.

"Hello, Elliot." My heart did a stutter beat when I said his name. "So, you're still in the grocery business, huh?" I wanted the conversation off me and onto something mundane. I started with his store, but the weather would be next, or maybe I could start talking about the sinking sun. Anything but me.

"Hi there, Peaches."

His smooth voice rippled the air around me. And he was as broad shouldered and trim as he'd always been.

Of all the scenarios I'd imagined, running into Elliot Reynolds the minute I parked my car hadn't been one of them.

A car pulled behind Elliot's truck and the driver honked. Not once, but twice.

"Uh oh. Someone's impatient." I took a few steps back. At least the interruption would save me from further conversation with Elliot.

"Um, you back in town for long?" He edged closer to his truck.

Another honk.

"All right, already," he said impatiently. "Geesh."

The car window lowered. "Going to be here long, Elliot? I need to get to the shop and unpack the car."

"Oh, hi, Jessica." Elliot moved to the side of her car and then beckoned me. "Come on over, Georgia. I want to introduce you to Jessica Knight. She and her business partner, Mimi Day, own Styles, the dress shop on the corner." He pointed down the row of buildings. "It's new since you were last in town."

I took a few steps toward Elliot and he made a quick introduction.

"Georgia's family has been part of Wolf Creek for a very long time," Elliot explained to Jessica, while looking at me quizzically. "It's good to see her—for, well, however long she'll be here."

I didn't see the need to interrupt and tell him I'd returned to Wolf Creek to live. He—and everyone else in my past— would find out soon enough. Besides, I allowed myself a sliver of a chance to change my mind and slip away—again.

"Nice to meet you, Georgia," Jessica said with a grin. "And stop in sometime. New clothes for the season are coming in as fast as Mimi and I can unpack them." She glanced up at Elliot. "Uh, about the truck?"

"Oh, sure, sure." He gave me a quick wave. "Welcome home. I'll stop by the Inn later."

Oh, my. I took a few deep breaths before entering the Inn, still thrown by seeing Elliot Reynolds even before I unpacked.

I checked in quickly, and within minutes I unlocked the door to my room expecting to see generic hotel furnishings and maybe a few amenities. I was so wrong. A bouquet of fresh flowers brightened the small sitting area in front of the windows that overlooked the Square. The mint-colored painted walls and white trim gave the room a soft, calm feeling. A fringed lampshade added style, and the white eyelet bed ruffle made me think of the Victorian era. The colors of the quilt on the bed matched those in the room.

I smiled to myself when I spread out items from my cosmetic bag on the counter in the modernized bathroom, thankful that the quest to maintain a quaint atmosphere hadn't stood in the way of modern facilities. Charming was one thing, outdated was something else.

I went back to the window, surprised by how many shoppers filled the Square. Six years ago when I'd come back—albeit briefly—most of the shops closed during the week in the winter months, only opening during the weekend days. How things change, yet not.

Directly across the Square, through the spindly branches of the leafless trees, the lights in Farmer Foods shone brightly. I saw people moving about in the store. And that brought my mind directly back to Elliot.

No!

I unpacked quickly, hanging my coat, a pair of black slacks, and a black and white patterned blouse in the antique armoire. I shook my vest and laid it across the back of a chair to give the folds of the wool fabric time to relax. Since I'd not decided how long I would be staying at the Inn I left the rest of my things in the suitcase.

A light knock on the door interrupted my thoughts.

"Coming." I opened the door, surprised to see a young woman holding a tray. I assumed she had made a mistake because I hadn't ordered anything.

"Hi Ms. Winters. Elliot Reynolds just sent this fruit basket over. And I brought you a carafe of fresh water."

I stood aside while she moved into the room and slid the tray next to the vase of flowers. It was getting crowded in the room already. "We don't use bottled water here, but if you prefer, I can get some for you."

I looked at the etched carafe, filled with ice and water, topped with a matching glass. "No, no. This will be fine…" I noticed her nametag was shaped like the Inn. "…Gwen. Thank you."

"Just call the front desk if you need anything."

She closed the door quietly and I was alone again with my thoughts. And one more reminder of Elliot. I noticed a small note tucked between an apple and a banana. True to the man I remembered, the note simply read: *Dessert and coffee tonight, 7:30, Crossroads.*

As I read the note the lurch in my stomach reminded me I hadn't eaten since I'd stopped for a breakfast sandwich at a drive-through on my way out of Milwaukee. I wanted a simple lunch, nothing to upset my stomach when I carried out my afternoon plans. I had enough butterflies to deal with as it was. I pushed away more nagging thoughts of Elliot.

What was he up to? Sure, we went back a long way, but we hadn't had an actual conversation in years.

I'd noticed a map of the Square next to the telephone and remembered seeing a place called Biscuits and Brew that offered lunches. This was a new business to the Square since I'd left, but it sounded like a perfect place for me. There were other shops, too, that occupied the buildings I remembered as being vacant, and lending a depressed look to the Square. More changes to the small world of Wolf Creek Square—and so far they seemed pretty good.

I grabbed my coat and purse and headed out, ignoring stabbing little fears about who might recognize me.

***

The coffee shop sat next to the Inn and when I stepped inside a world of wonderful aromas hit me, the obvious coffee, the sweetness of baked goods, and the hearty smell of tomato.

"Hello. Welcome to Biscuits and Brew." She pointed to her nametag. "I'm Stephanie, owner and jack-of-all-trades for this establishment." A smile crossed her face. "What can I get for you today?"

The chalkboards listed all the coffee/espresso combinations and flavors, muffins, biscuits, sandwiches, and rich pastries. Hmm…more choices than I cared to read.

"A small cup of soup and an equally small sandwich."

Stephanie grinned. "Tomato Florentine is today's soup and the sandwich special is turkey on rye."

"Sounds perfect. And add a small coffee, too."

"Hazelnut is the flavor-of-the-day."

So many decisions, and I was only ordering lunch.

"That's fine."

After paying and being told she'd bring my order to me, I chose a table near the front window. Lost in thoughts about my plan to visit Uncle Miles that afternoon, I was startled by how quickly a waitress delivered my meal.

The hot soup warmed me and for the first time since I'd pulled into the parking space behind the Inn, my muscles relaxed. And wow, I'd already found a source of made-from-scratch cooking.

It gave me a chance to get my mind off Elliot and focus back on the reasons I'd packed up and driven out of Milwaukee that morning. First, the steadiest job I'd ever had ended. I'd called Uncle Miles a month ago and told him that the reorganization of the firm had meant great things at Merkel & Kline, but for some of the paralegals and secretaries, it meant being given 30-day notice. I was in that group. Then I'd told him I intended to return to Wolf Creek. Uncle Miles had laughed and told me he needed a competent assistant in the office of Miles Owen, Attorney at Law. I accepted his offer immediately and began making plans to give up my apartment in Milwaukee.

Our family situation was more complicated than would seem obvious at first, especially because we were a small family among many larger families with roots in Wolf Creek. Who lived where was one of the issues. I had one sister, Beverly, and after our mother, Uncle Miles' sister, died, we offered Uncle Miles her house. Beverly and I were grateful he accepted our offer, because it meant having another Owen living in our family home, located only two streets south of the Square. One of my fondest childhood memories was racing down those streets and into the Square for an ice cream cone on a summer afternoon. Three years ago Uncle Miles had moved his office from a small building in town to the house.

I finished my lunch and walked to my car, still parked behind the Inn. It took only a few minutes to make the short drive to Uncle Miles' house. I could have walked, but after running into Elliot the first minute I'd arrived, I wasn't ready to be recognized again.

I pulled behind the second of two cars parked on the street in front of the house, assuming my favorite uncle was busy with appointments. Before stepping out of the car, I stopped for a minute to will my heartbeat to slow down, maybe calm the mild fluttering in my midsection. I needed to confide the truth about my return to Wolf Creek and I didn't want to keep piling story upon story. Really lie upon lie.

The front door was unlocked, so I stepped inside. Wow.

The living room was a mess. Boxes of files, yellowed with age were stacked in the corners of the room and along the wall behind the couch. Two piles of newer looking files covered a table set up in the middle of the room. Apparently, the table and chairs had served as a desk.

I was drawn to the two voices in the back of the house, but I didn't recognize either of them as belonging to Uncle Miles. The voices grew louder as the men came toward the front of the house.

"Oh, excuse us. We didn't hear you come in." The younger man came forward. "I'm Nathan Connor and this is Jack Pearson." He gestured toward the man behind him before extending his hand.

Connor. A wave of nausea hit first, right in the pit of my stomach. Then my mind caught up and began offering explanations, starting with coincidence. The Connor name was a common one in northeastern Wisconsin, so it likely had no connection to the Connor family I knew. Since Beverly and I had worked with an attorney named Richard Connor, I reminded myself, and he wasn't here in Wolf Creek.

"I'm Georgia Winters," I said, my voice hoarse. "I've come to see Miles Owen—well, Uncle Miles to me."

The man who'd identified himself as Nathan picked a pile of files off one of the nearby straight-backed chairs. "Would you have a seat, please?"

My anxiety level rose a notch. He hadn't mentioned my uncle yet. Why? I cleared my throat. "Is my Uncle Miles here?" But I lowered myself into the chair he offered and he pulled another close and sat.

"Ms. Winters, I'm not sure how to tell you this gently, but Miles had a stroke two days ago. He's in Memorial Hospital in Green Bay."

"A stroke? Uncle Miles? Why didn't my sister call me? She's Beverly Winters."

Nathan glanced at Jack, who'd remained standing. "Uh, yes, Miles mentioned Beverly, and we talked with her about the law office. I guess I assumed she would—or had— alerted you to what happened to your uncle."

My normally clear mind was suddenly confused. "Who are you, again?"

"Nathan Connor. Mr. Pearson—Jack—and I were, or rather, are in the process of joining Mr. Owen in his firm."

"Was he ill?" I still couldn't grasp that Uncle Miles was in the hospital.

"Not that we were aware of." He paused. "Maybe you'd like a drink of water."

"I'll get it," Jack said, hurrying from the room.

"Ms. Winters, did you have an appointment with your uncle? Is there something Jack or I can help you with?"

"Georgia. Call me Georgia. Ms. Winters is too formal."

Nathan laughed. "Okay, then."

Jack returned with a small glass of water and handed it to me.

I thanked him and took a sip. "You may or may not know this, but I'm a paralegal—I started as a legal secretary many years ago. I came to Wolf Creek to work for Uncle Miles. He said he needed an assistant. And he didn't say anything about other lawyers working with him."

But now everything has changed. That seemed too obvious to say out loud.

Nathan sighed. "To be honest, Georgia, your sister told us that the doctors weren't optimistic about Miles' situation, certainly his ability to return to work anytime soon. They advised us to go ahead with the merger and the move."

So that's why they were in Uncle Miles' home. Jumbled thoughts brought me to my feet. I extended the empty glass and Jack stepped forward and took it from my hand.

"I imagine you want to see Miles," Jack said, his voice low and kind.

"I need to see Beverly. Then I'll head to Green Bay." I moved toward the door. Both men followed me.

Nathan lightly touched my arm, communicating concern. "I'm so sorry. Please let us know if there has been a change in Miles' condition."

"Sure. Sure." I opened my purse to get my keys. "I'm staying at the Inn for a few days. 'Til I make other plans."

I slipped out the door quickly, avoiding the need for more

niceties or a handshake. My hands were shaking as it was, and I chose to hide it.

Glad I'd decided to drive over to see Uncle Miles, I quickly took on a new plan for the afternoon, stunned by the news about my uncle. Sure, he was no longer young, but six years ago, the last time I saw him, he'd been physically strong, his mind sharp as ever.

I drove to the other end of Wolf Creek, usually referred to as the older part of town, because many of the homes were smaller and had been built shortly after the soldiers started coming back from World War II.

Beverly and her husband had bought their house from an older couple, the original owners. Lily had been born soon after, long about the time Beverly's husband had decided the lady serving beers at the neighborhood bar was better suited for him. No matter that he was a brand new father— he hadn't hung around long enough to be a dad.

My heart did a nosedive when I saw the house. Nothing had changed. Same color—white, same window shutters— black, same swag curtain in the front window. Probably the same flowers would sprout in the front garden once the snow melted and the ground warmed. And all this sameness went back more than 20 years. It was as if after Beverly's husband left she didn't care much about anything—even Lily, her only child.

I touched my temples, as if willing those thoughts away. They were linked to another part of the Owen family history, one I wasn't ready to think about at the moment.

I sat in the car debating my next move. It was still early afternoon, so I assumed Beverly would be working, or maybe she was in Green Bay with Uncle Miles. I finally called her, getting the expected voice mail and told her I was in Wolf Creek and was on my way to Green Bay to see our uncle.

So off I went, backtracking through Wolf Creek. Twenty miles later, I navigated through Green Bay and found the medical complex that had been a landmark for generations. I let the valet take my car and checked with the information desk to find out where I'd find my uncle.

As soon as I'd stepped into hospital, my eagerness to see Uncle Miles intensified. I followed directions to the row of three elevators and waited impatiently for the doors to open. My soft-soled shoes barely made a sound as I walked down the quiet halls to Room 537. The door was closed, and for some reason, I knocked before entering, but of course no one answered. Uncle Miles looked like himself, sort of. The tall, muscular man I'd known had withered to a fraction of his size. He appeared vulnerable, although breathing quietly, as if deep in a sleep.

Still, tears streamed down my cheeks. I leaned in and kissed his forehead. Then I pulled a chair up next to the bed and after sitting down, I picked up his hand and held it in mine.

As far back as I could remember Uncle Miles had been a big part of my life. Even after he went away to law school when Beverly and I were just little kids, he called every Sunday evening to talk to us. I would pester him with questions about the law and wanted to know the finer points of what other kids would have deemed dull as toast— contracts, wills, rules and regulations. Uncle Miles never laughed at my questions, but my father, not a warm or open-minded man to begin with, declared that a waste of time, since no one would respect a female lawyer. Uncle Miles came back to Wolf Creek, but he'd never married, usually explaining that he'd married Lady Justice. That had always made me smile.

My musing about the past was soon interrupted when one of the nurses entered his room. "It might help if you talked to him. We don't have time to be in his room much, but he seems more calm when we're around and talking to him."

I nodded and drew Uncle Miles' hand to my cheek.

"We haven't seen any family since he was admitted," the nurse said.

I quickly wiped my face. "I only learned what happened less than an hour ago. It's a shock. So unexpected."

"Sometimes it is harder on the family than the patient." She quietly went about checking the intravenous line, his blood pressure, and temperature. She finished by repositioning his head on the plumped pillow and straightening the covers. She was kind enough to give me her support by squeezing my shoulder as she left the room, adding that I could call Miles' doctor for more information.

"Hi, Uncle Miles. The nurse told me it would be good to talk to you so I'm going to tell you all about my day." I started in Milwaukee and travelogued forward to that moment at his side. I held back only the part about seeing Elliot Reynolds and my school girl reaction to him. But he might have enjoyed that, too.

Every now and then I'd feel his hand tighten on mine. That small gesture brought me a twinge of hope.

I kept my visit short, but assured him I'd be back tomorrow. I needed to see Beverly. Now. Apparently, she'd never visited Miles and she sure hadn't called me. Miles was family. Our family. My family. What little family we had.

Okay, I needed to shoulder some guilt for that. I hadn't been in touch with Uncle Miles nearly enough, and Beverly and I hadn't talked in years.

I checked my phone while I waited for the attendant to bring my car. Since I saw no return message from Beverly, I decided to go to her house, park the car on the street and wait.

And wait I did.

But I wasn't without company or new things to mull over. Two messages had come in while I was driving back to Wolf Creek.

One from Nathan Connor asking me to stop by the office the next day. "Oh, and please don't be mad about my getting your number. I told Gwen at the Inn it was important that I reach you."

The second was from my friend, Virgie, from Milwaukee. She wanted to know if I'd had a safe trip.

After almost an hour, I was about to leave when I saw Beverly's garage door opening. Her car turned into her driveway and she drove it inside. I got out of my car and approached her. Nothing much had changed except age. Her blonde hair, always such a fine feature, had darkened, but worse, it had lost its shine. She was still petite, maybe even too thin now. We'd always presented a contrast, me with my light brown hair and slightly taller with a curvier body. I swear she was wearing the plain brown wool coat I'd seen her in six years ago, while I wore a newer lined raincoat in a shiny black and embellished with a flattering tie sash.

"Beverly, Beverly," I called. "Wait, don't shut the door. It's me. Georgia."

She glanced up briefly and then ducked her head into the backseat and lifted a bag of groceries into her arms. Only then did she look directly at me. "No, I'm not doing this."

I raised my arms in the air. "What happened to hello?"

"Hello. No."

"You're not doing what?"

"I'm not taking care of Miles."

"Uncle Miles? Who asked you to?"

She pushed her overly long bangs off her face, then eyed me suspiciously. "Isn't that why you're here?"

"No thanks to you, I only learned about Uncle Miles this afternoon. Which begs the question, why didn't you call me?"

"They said he wouldn't get better." She shifted the bag to rest on her hip, but made no move toward the door. And I wasn't being invited in. "Why are you here?"

I yearned to deflect her question, but my resolve to clear my past and make Wolf Creek my home again gave me strength.

"I lost my job in Milwaukee, some firm restructuring plan that pushed out a bunch of us. So I came back to work for Uncle Miles. It was all arranged. He was expecting me today."

"You want to live here? In Wolf Creek?"

"Yes."

She looked away from me when she said, "Bad decision."

My impulse was to argue, maybe explain my plan, but my phone rang and interrupted us. I rummaged in my purse to turn it off, yet didn't want my conversation with Beverly to end. I moved so I stood between her and the door into her house.

"The phone call can wait. I want to talk to you about my return to Wolf Creek. I don't want my move to change your life."

She laughed. "Can't avoid that with you here. People will remember what happened six years ago."

"Let them talk."

She moved to the side, then forward to the door. "Goodbye, Georgia. You handle Miles, leave me out of it, and we'll both be happy."

She unlocked the door and went inside. Slam, the door closed. My sister, more like a stranger than family, never suggested I come in or even asked where I was staying.

Now what?

I walked back down her driveway and as I opened the driver's door of my car, Beverly's garage door closed. I got the message.

I retrieved my phone from the depths of my purse to check the call that had come in while I talked with Beverly. It was from Nathan. Not knowing if it was about Uncle Miles, I rang back immediately.

"Hi, Georgia. Thanks for calling back. I asked you to stop by Miles' house tomorrow, but Jack and I wondered if you could come by now. Or, are you too busy?"

I looked at Beverly's buttoned up house, then glanced at my watch. The day had passed quickly and it was late afternoon. But that left me plenty of time to grab some dinner. And meet Elliot.

"I have time right now."

"Terrific. Come on over and walk right in."

2

Some things never change, and Wolf Creek covered a small geographic area. That meant no destination in the small town was far away. So a few minutes after ending my call with Nathan, I parked in front of Uncle Miles' house for the second time that afternoon.

Unlike Beverly's home, I noted that Miles had upgraded the exterior of Mom's house. For one thing, he'd put a small lamp post in the middle of the flower garden. He'd also installed a Miles Owen Law Office sign by the front door. Even amidst the dreary remnants of winter the house looked cared for. I'd always loved the house Beverly and I grew up in. I sighed inside thinking about telling Nathan and Jack about every secret corner and where to step to coax a squeak in the floors. I still wanted to live there some day.

Before memories took me too far back, I went inside the house. With my hand still on the door handle I called out, "Hello? It's Georgia."

From the kitchen I heard, "Back here."

I closed the door behind me and walked toward the back of the house.

I hadn't noticed earlier that even though the living and dining room were cluttered with boxes, the walls had been painted a soft ivory and new curtains hung on the windows. They were light and airy, lacey ones which surprised me, but they softened the starkness of the rooms and probably added to the relaxed atmosphere Uncle Miles liked to establish with his clients.

In the kitchen, Nathan sat at the table with a half-eaten

sandwich in front of him. He didn't keep me guessing, but put his fork down and motioned for me to sit down.

"How would you like to work for Jack and me starting tomorrow? We're moving the business to one of the vacant buildings on the Square and need an assistant on board immediately. And…" He held up his hand as I was about to answer. "And, would you like to move into this house for the time being? There are a lot of files here and we don't want the house to be empty for any length of time."

He stopped to take another bite of his sandwich, giving me time to think about his offer.

Without weighing the pros and cons, or even discussing the salary, I said, "Yes. To both."

Maybe I'd left behind the analyze-everything-before-deciding person. She was still back in Milwaukee and a new, more spontaneous lady had arrived in Wolf Creek. I'd have to think about that later. But while it happened so quickly, I decided I liked that new woman already.

We talked about my responsibilities for the Owen, Connor & Pearson Law Office. Before we'd finished, Jack returned from having dinner with his wife and joined us at the table. It was a friendly, casual conversation that left me knowing this was the right place for me. And it was the kind of opportunity that didn't come often in life. At least not in mine.

The meeting lingered into the evening, and with dinner forgotten I rushed to get back to the Inn. When I walked in—well, almost ran—Elliot was waiting. As much as I was looking forward to my evening with him, I'd wanted a few minutes to touch up my makeup, maybe change my clothes. But nothing in my return to Wolf Creek had gone according to my plan. Why would my evening with Elliot be any different?

Elliot waved from a small table by the window and rose halfway out of his chair. As I slipped into the chair across from him, it occurred to me that we could have been meeting like this in the evening every day for the last thirty years. But we hadn't. I had to keep reminding myself of that.

The darkness outside reflected our images on the window,

like a mirror. I saw the two of us together, looking the same as any other middle-aged couple enjoying an evening together. As a young girl I had dreamed of being with Elliot Reynolds, but his family had harbored other ideas.

"Earth to Georgia?" Elliot waved one hand up and down in front of my face.

"Huh? Oh, sorry. My mind is racing from everything that's happened today."

"Only good things, I hope." His soft smile relaxed me and brought my attention back to the moment.

"Yes, no. Some of each, I guess." I explained what had happened to Uncle Miles and that he was never far from my thoughts. "I still don't know the extent of the damage caused by the stroke. But then, Nathan Connor and Jack Pearson hired me without even asking for a resume. They're Uncle Miles' new partners." I left Beverly out of my rundown, more or less pretending she hadn't been a part of it. I leaned forward on my elbows. "So, that's the short version of my day."

"Quite a day for you, Peaches. I hadn't heard about Miles. He's a good man, handled many issues for my family for years. I'm glad to know someone is taking over for him so we can keep a law firm here in Wolf Creek."

"I have a lot of experience," I said, leaving it at that, "so I can be useful to Nathan and Jack. And that feels good."

"Just don't get any ideas about leaving again." He reached across the table and took my hand.

Good grief, where had that come from? Elliot's touch jolted me to attention, just like hearing him call me Peaches. And he hadn't bothered to ask if that was okay with me, either. Sure, his touch felt nice—more than nice. But I pulled my hand away.

"I don't know what I'm going to do, Elliot. My plan has only taken me so far." I stared into the restaurant, but not focusing on anything in particular. "I have a wrong I have to right. Or, maybe I should say I have to untangle a mess I made years ago."

Elliot's face darkened and I spotted a flicker of sadness in his eyes, but he quickly shifted in his chair, changing the subject to the new happenings on the Square.

Glad he backed off, I asked him about what looked to me like a Wolf Creek renewal, starting with the Square. Crossroads was a beautiful restaurant and the Inn looked like it was thriving, maybe even a bit upscale compared to a generation ago. Biscuits and Brew was a lively sort of place.

"We have a lot to be proud of around here," Elliot said, "and we can give a fair amount of credit to an old friend of yours. Sarah, Sarah Hutchinson. She's our mayor now."

"That's terrific," I said, grinning. "I haven't seen Sarah yet. She doesn't know I'm back." I swatted the air in frustration. "No time today, not with trekking to Green Bay and seeing Uncle Miles."

"You'll have time," Elliot said, his soft voice reassuring. "You'll enjoy talking to her. She's become our resident historian, too. She's written up a history of the town, starting with the first families—and she included yours."

Family history? Nice for Sarah, maybe, but not so good for me.

I forced a light tone in my voice when I said, "I can say one thing for sure about the Wolf Creek renewal, as you call it. The coffee is tasty, and I never had mousse pie this good in Milwaukee." I popped the last bite into my mouth.

"It's a Crossroads specialty," Elliot said, his eyes teasing and fun, "so you can have it any time your little heart wants it."

"How's Eli?" I asked, not nearly as interested as I attempted to sound. But an unexpected yawn caught me by surprise. I flushed, embarrassed when it was clear Elliot had seen me force the yawn back.

His amused smile made it okay, somehow. "Time to let you get upstairs. You're a working girl tomorrow."

Girl? Right. I hadn't been a girl for many years, not since Elliot had been a boy. Forty had thrown me but good. Now, approaching fifty, I wasn't sure if Elliot saw me as an "older" woman. I'd prefer a "mature" woman getting a second chance at life, but didn't want to debate that issue with him.

"Yes, it's been a long day." I pushed my chair back,

feeling an awkward tension about ending the evening. "Oh, I'm moving into Uncle Miles' house—I don't think I mentioned that."

"That sounds fine," Elliot said getting to his feet. "Nice as it is, the Inn isn't home." Backing toward the door, Elliot waved. "Glad you're back."

I returned the wave and hurried up the stairs. I don't know if he watched me or not. But I knew that no matter what else I'd come back to accomplish, I had to deal with Elliot Reynolds, too.

As soon as I let myself into my room, I started getting ready for bed, but the past kept intruding into my thoughts, making me both tired and wakeful. But it wasn't just any part of the past. My thoughts were all about Elliot. We had a bond, he and I, and it went back to high school and was as changeable—even volatile—as a rolling wave. Like most teenagers, I suppose, at least most of the kids we went to school with, Elliot and I would ride a wave of happiness right up to its crest and then a misunderstanding or jealousy would send us sliding down until the wave crashed on a beach of our own making. Through it all, though, Elliot called me Peaches. So corny, yet the word still sounded like music when he said it.

Not that I didn't spend many dreamy hours fantasizing about my happily-ever-after life with my first love. How quickly I let myself be detoured. I shook my head, so many years later still wondering how it was that I had so little fight in me. I could blame "youth," but that didn't mean I was without my share of regrets.

A single incident had changed everything, and through the years the memory of it never strayed far from my thoughts. One afternoon at the grocery story, Mom and I overheard Martha Reynolds tell her neighbor that I wasn't good enough for Elliot.

Mom's response was swift and certain. "Better off learning this now," she said, "than after you became an unwelcome member of his family. They'd never treat you right."

Earlier, sitting with Elliot in Crossroads, I sensed that he

31

wanted the same thing in those moments, to go back and talk it all through. Yet here I was, climbing into bed and pulling the blanket up around my chin, having let one more chance to tell Elliot the truth slip away. What would I have said? That I accepted my mother's platitude as wisdom?

As it stood, I doubted Elliot ever understood why I broke up with him. Just like I never truly accepted my mother's supposed wisdom about my narrow escape from a family who would never accept me. But I did nothing about it. That's the part that still ripped through me, and maybe it's why I left town, not just once, but three times without ever explaining any of it to Elliot.

With sleep not likely to come, I climbed out of bed and sat at the table by the window. Elliot's fruit basket and the flowers failed to lighten the mood that had come over me. I felt like such a coward—and not for the first time in my life.

Rather than see the hurt in Elliot's eyes when I walked away from him, and allowed myself to feel it in my own heart, too, I left Wolf Creek after high school and worked at a large retail store distribution center south of Green Bay. I moved into an apartment with two girls I worked with, and my life looked pretty good, at least from the outside. I was young and part of me enjoyed that first taste of independence. Plus, finding dates was never a problem. Finding another Elliot was a different issue.

I might not have had the steel spine to stand up to Elliot's mom, but I didn't lack for ambition. I wanted to do better than my parents expected of both Beverly and me. After a couple of years, the vision of spending my life working at the distribution center loomed, and not happily. When I saw a notice about a paralegal program at the university, I signed up and started night classes. I was close, so close, to finishing, but when my roommates quit their jobs and left town for other jobs, I couldn't handle the rent alone. Feeling defeated, I headed back to Wolf Creek.

What a low point it was to unpack my boxes in my old room, down the hall from Mom. No, maybe the lower point was working at a local daycare, hating every minute of it, but not wanting to go home to Mom at night either.

I stared out to the Square, thinking that 25 years earlier, the town had almost abandoned the Square—one contingent wanted to tear it all down and bring in an assortment of big box stores to revitalize Wolf Creek. What a crazy idea. The Reynolds brothers, young as they were, plus Sarah Hutchinson and her family, had the gumption to join with others to fight that awful idea. I smiled to myself thinking of my old friend, Sarah. Mayor Sarah Hutchinson. I'd have known that if Beverly and I had been in touch.

I drew some satisfaction, too, when I thought about Mom assuring me she knew Wolf Creek was not the right place for me. She never stopped encouraging me to find a job far away—move on and with any luck, move up. Mostly, she wanted me to forget Elliot. No luck there, Mom.

But I wondered what she'd think of Wolf Creek now, its Square so popular with locals and tourists alike. A day-trip destination the brochure said. From the foot traffic I'd seen and the business at Crossroads, I could see that was true.

For the first time since I'd checked in, I turned on the television. I needed distraction, not more thoughts on the ups and downs of Wolf Creek Square, or on the pettiness that had been part of our small town when I was young. Maybe some of that had changed, too.

Even distracting myself with TV news and a so-so weather report couldn't push away another memory, the day I saw an announcement in the *Wolf Creek Gazette*. Mrs. Reynolds got her wish for Elliot, all right, when Mary Beth Stratton, whose father was President of the Wolf Creek Bank, an institution long gone now, announced that she and Elliot were engaged. Big news in town, and bad news for me. It pushed me out.

In that same newspaper under the classified section of employment, I saw that the Merkel & Kline Law Firm in Milwaukee was hiring entry level document processors—secretaries really. On a whim I applied and, much to my surprise, and Mom's too, the firm hired me. Mom helped me pack and, with tears, sent me off to the big city. She'd given me more than enough money for an apartment and to get some things I needed to live on my own. At the time, I hadn't known how to thank her.

Fortunately, I thrived away from the watchful eyes of a small town. My life grew in small steps. I never had expected much of myself in the past, but whatever the lawyers wanted done, I happily did. My paralegal classes had given me a basic knowledge of legal terminology and a small understanding of the legal system. I upgraded my skills as technology became an ever changing part of the job.

I was still young when I left town for good that second time. That was that. I'd had the one three-day visit six years ago, the visit whose consequences I'd come back to untangle, but here I was. Home.

3

The next morning, with the sun shining brightly and my mood upbeat, I grabbed a carryout breakfast sandwich and two large coffees from Biscuit and Brew on my way to Uncle Miles' house. The same two cars were already parked on the street by the time I arrived.

Juggling the contents in my full hands I was able to open the unlocked door without spilling or dropping any of my breakfast. I used my foot to close the door, perhaps a little more forcefully than necessary, but it did announce my arrival.

"We're in the kitchen," a voice called out.

I recognized Nathan's voice and hurried to join him. Jack was also at the table, with a woman at his side.

"Morning, Georgia," Jack said. "I'd like you to meet Liz, my wife who…"

Not waiting for Jack to finish his sentence, Liz jumped up and grabbed one of the coffee cups from my hand before it tumbled. Her fast action sent us both laughing.

"Thank you, and it's nice to meet you." I set my sandwich and coffee in front of the only empty chair at the table.

"As I was saying," Jack said with a grin, "Georgia is going to organize the office and keep it running smoothly."

"We'll see if I can do everything they want done," I said, shrugging out of my coat.

Nathan pointed to the chair for me to sit, just as he'd done the previous afternoon. He never stopped eating the large omelet on his plate. With his free hand, he passed me a manila envelope before I'd even tasted my coffee.

"Keys and contract." Nathan stopped eating long enough to add, "Liz has offered to help get the office ready for business. You two put together a list of the equipment we need. Miles' computers are seriously outdated, so new ones are first on the list."

We waited for him to say more, but he went back to his breakfast.

Finally, I let out a loud hoot. "Well, if things had gone according to plan, I'd have bought a computer first thing, too. I always knew Uncle Miles was behind the times. But I imagined he'd hired someone to create documents on the computer for him."

The others at the table laughed along with me.

"Fortunately, we have our personal laptops or we couldn't have created an employment contract for you," Jack said.

"I have a computer, too," I said, "although not with me. Besides, it's very old. What I used at the firm was the latest version of everything." By that time, I wasn't sure what I'd gotten myself into, afraid I'd fall into the rabbit hole of chaos any minute. On the other hand, I enjoyed the notion that I'd have the freedom to make the job my own—and get a new firm off the ground. This was so different from my job in Milwaukee, where each day had become a repeat of the days before.

Liz broke the silence. "Let's go to the Square first and see if Charlie's finished one room so we can have the office supplies delivered directly there and not have to move it twice."

I'd taken a bite of my sandwich and chewed as fast as she talked. Her body vibrated with energy making her dangling earrings swing. Of course, the purples and reds of her bright geometric patterned jacket added to the vibrancy that almost bounced off of her.

"Good idea," I said.

I quickly finished the rest of my breakfast and then gathered the plates and cups from the table and set them in the sink. "Does this coffeemaker work?" I reeled from the black scum in the bottom of the pot. "Whoa!" I'd asked the question in a general way. No one answered.

I opened the refrigerator door and found food from who knew when. I closed the door. There was no doubt in my mind that Uncle Miles hadn't been well for some time before his stroke, but he'd put on a good front when we'd talked on the phone.

The disarray explained his reasons for so readily wanting me to come work for him. The Uncle Miles I knew was a man with meticulous habits with his clothing, his health, and, of course, his work. He always put the client first, but never forgot his own wellbeing. Somehow, I'd have to find the right time to talk to Nathan and Jack about the real Miles Owen. Based on the state of things, my uncle couldn't have left a good impression.

Chairs scraping across the floor jolted me back to the work ahead. I'd deal with the house when I moved in and the law firm contents had been moved out.

Liz and I took my car to the Square and parked behind the vacant building on the southwest corner. As we walked around to the front door, I didn't need to say much, because Liz was like an encyclopedia, quickly telling me about a cleaning service in the next town. They'd fly through the house and make it livable after such a long period of neglect. Then she told me about how glad she was to have moved to Wolf Creek, and then there was her granddaughter, Andrea.

Sounds of men remodeling greeted us when we opened the door and stepped inside.

"Hello?" Liz raised her voice to get the man's attention above the high-pitched sound of a saw cutting wood. An audible click and a winding down of the noise was a welcome relief. How could men work with that intense sound all day? My question was answered when the man took off the ear protectors and safety glasses.

"We're looking for Charlie Crawford," Liz said, walking toward the man.

"Last room down the hall." He pointed toward a hallway on the far side of the room. "Might have to yell at him, too."

We navigated around stacks of lumber, boxes of nails and sundry tools I wasn't familiar with. My knowledge of tools began and ended with hammers and screw drivers. The noise of the saw started again behind us.

We passed three rooms on our way to the end of the hall. Surprising to me, they were all the same size. No hierarchy in this firm, no corner office. My decision to work for them boosted my mood even more. The last room, empty of furniture and slightly larger than the others, was either the conference room or the storage room. There was no way of telling without furniture or shelving.

"Good morning, Charlie," Liz said to the man on a ladder. He was installing a light fixture and had parts of it in his mouth. He finished and bounced to the floor. Oh, to be that young and agile.

"Hi, Liz. You're here early today."

"Busy day. I'd like you to meet Georgia Winters. She's going to be the glue that holds this office together."

Charlie wiped his hand on his jeans before reaching out. "Georgia."

I returned the greeting and handshake, noting his name. Crawford. Another Wolf Creek name from the past. I went to school with a couple of Crawford kids.

"The boys are getting anxious to move. They're boxing up more stuff today," Liz said.

"Going to be tight. We had to put extra reinforcements in the basement before we started changing walls up here. It took longer than I'd planned."

"Is this room ready?" Liz asked. "Georgia and I are going to the office supply store to buy one of everything."

Charlie and I laughed at her casual take on the buying trip. But maybe she wasn't wrong. I'd never put an office together before and there had been an office manager at Merkel & Kline, so I didn't even know where the pencils came from.

"Seriously. Can we have them deliver the order tomorrow and store it here?"

"Sure. Just a few details to finish in here, but nothing we can't work around. Nathan's first of April opening is pushing us into some evening and night work, but consider it done."

I liked Charlie's attitude and work ethic. If I needed work

done at Uncle Miles' house, he'd be the man I'd call.

"Call Nathan if you have questions. I don't want Jack worried about the opening."

"Got it."

We said our goodbyes and headed to the front of the building. Once outside the door, Liz touched my arm, stopping my steps into the Square. She told me about Jack's heart attack the previous summer, and explained that Nathan and Jack had worked together in the Richard Connor law firm in Green Bay. It was a difference of opinion between father and son that prompted Nathan to leave and join Uncle Miles. Jack hadn't been able to handle the stress on his health with the time required for the new corporate cases, so he, too, joined Miles and Nathan.

Richard Connor…so much for coincidence.

Reeling from this new information, I sensed there was more to the story of Nathan and the man I now knew was his father. But it wasn't my place to ask, much as I wanted to wring every drop of information out of Liz. But I was conscious of carrying a secret, and the name Connor was all over it. While I could only wait so long before talking about my plan, telling Uncle Miles about it first was no longer possible.

I'd become ensnared in a complicated situation, but I'd accepted a job and now had to do it. I took a deep breath and forced a smile when Liz suggested making our list over a cup of coffee at Biscuits and Brew.

"Well, well," Liz said, her face breaking out in a grin, "look who's out and enjoying a morning stroll."

Her bright smile told me Liz knew the couple we were approaching. When she exchanged a warm hug with both of them, I concluded she knew them well.

I was beginning to understand her jump-right-in personality, although it had unnerved me at first. But nothing about her seemed the least insincere, and that made me like her even more.

She turned to me. "I want you to meet my best friend, Marianna Spencer. She owns Quilts Galore." Liz pointed to the shop at the end of the Square. "And this is Art Carlson."

Liz slipped her arm through his. "He owns Art&Son Jewelry, next to the quilt shop."

They both shook hands with me. Since leaving Wolf Creek years ago, I hadn't spent much time with people who were as warm and friendly as these three. Even with my good friends in Milwaukee, hugs weren't part of our greeting.

With quick, choppy sentences Liz told me about Art's son, Alan, and Marianna's stepdaughter, Rachel, and Rachel's infant son, Thomas, and how Art and Marianna were together—the new couple on the block.

Whew! Two days in Wolf Creek and I'd already met four shopkeepers. I had to laugh at my plan to remain as invisible as possible and just accomplish what I came back for. Somehow, it didn't matter. I was drawn to the feeling of being part of a tight-knit social community like the Square.

Suddenly, Liz checked her watch and then grabbed my arm. She wished Art and Marianna a good day and almost dragged me to Biscuits and Brew.

We spent over an hour making lists. She'd brought a catalog from the office supply store and as we paged through it we jotted items on our notepads. One list was marked "Immediate," one "Soon," and the third we called our "Wish List."

On our drive to Green Bay, Liz told me about her son and his family and how good she felt about the decision she and Jack made to move to Wolf Creek. She stopped describing her recent life changes only when we pulled into the parking lot of the store. But I wished I could have learned more about this dynamic woman. I could already see that Jack was quieter and although friendly and kind, he didn't exude the same kind of energy. From what little I'd seen of Jack, Liz stood out as his polar opposite.

Shopping with Liz was an adventure and we chatted and laughed as we compared prices and brands. By the time we'd finished, the trip had almost amounted to a buy-one-of-everything-in-the-store extravaganza. We finally rolled our two loaded carts to the checkout line, having saved our wish list for another day. The way Liz talked, though,

I sensed we'd be shopping for those items soon. We took the three laptops with us, but we arranged for delivery of everything else, and then we were off.

We drove passed Uncle Miles' house, but not seeing any cars in front, Liz told me to continue on to the Square. I parked behind the new office next to Nathan's SUV. With the computers in our arms, we entered by way of the back door.

The sound of men laughing greeted us. What a wonderful sound, so unlike the whispered conversations I was familiar with in the Milwaukee firm I'd so happily left behind.

"Men in a good mood. Nice to hear." Liz smiled and walked into the room.

"Well, the shoppers have returned. Is there any money left in the office fund?" Jack asked.

"Weren't we supposed to spend every last nickel?" She tried to keep a straight face, but a flirtatious smile broke through.

"Whatever we need, Liz. Hard to run a business without equipment and supplies." Nathan absently checked his watch. "Where did the time go?" He checked the time again. "I have to pick Toby up in twenty minutes."

"Go, go." Liz pushed him toward the door.

My stomach twisted as a dizzying wave forced me to grasp the edge of the counter to steady myself, all the while hoping I'd covered myself.

But Toby? How many Connor-Toby combinations could there be? Was Nathan his adoptive father? Had I foolishly taken on more than I'd planned by agreeing to work for Nathan?

As much as I needed answers to all my questions I turned my attention back to the group and listened in as Liz told Jack about establishing an account with the office supply store. As if delivering a report, she let him know that the tech crew at the store would be coming to set up the electronics. I heard my name attached to the state-of-the-art photocopier we'd chosen and took that as a cue to chime in.

"They even provide classes to get the most from the copier. That might come in handy if you need to hire some part-timers eventually. And the same goes for the computers," I added. "These programs update all the time, and everyone involved will need to learn the system, too."

In the back of my mind I realized that if the firm attracted more and more business, as Nathan and Jack hoped it would, I would end up being more paralegal than secretary, and they'd need computer savvy staff.

"We'll keep this office competitive one way or another." Jack lazily put his arm around Liz's shoulders. "Enough work for today. Another big day again tomorrow, especially with the office supplies arriving."

"Are you staying at the Inn tonight, Georgia?" Liz called out the question as she walked out from under Jack's arm toward the door.

I nodded. "I'm too tired to think of moving tonight."

Liz left, but then I remembered Nathan's comment about leaving Uncle Miles' house unprotected. "Or, were you expecting me to stay at Miles' tonight?" I asked Jack.

"No, no. One more day won't matter. We told the police that it was empty and they're keeping an eye on it. Might be best if you let them know when you've moved in, so they'll expect to see lights on."

I grabbed my purse off a pile of lumber and turned to leave.

"Peaches, wait."

I'd recognize Elliot's voice anywhere, even before he entered the room. Besides, no else called me Peaches.

I had to stop this nonsense.

Jack's eyebrows reached his hairline. "Peaches?" he teased.

"Careful, man, she's mine," Elliot said, walking into the room. Fortunately, his playful challenge was obvious.

Reacting to the joke, I joined their bantering. "No fighting, boys."

"Jack?" Liz called from the end of the hallway. "Charlie has a question for you."

Jack tipped a wave to us and left the room.

"Ready to go, Peaches?"

"Go where? And why?" That escaped before I could

censor my mouth. Oh, dear. What happened to that sensible woman when I was around him?

"To eat. Bet you haven't had anything since you left Biscuits and Brew this morning?"

"You saw me there? With Liz?" This was all too much. First the Peaches business and commenting on whether I'd eaten or not. But watching me? Okay, that sounded paranoid. His store was on the Square after all. Still. Elliot had no idea what my mission was in coming back to town. If he did, he might not even like it. Or me.

"It's no big thing," Elliot said. "A couple of people, including Eli, recognized you. Some people in our old crowd work on the Square—a few are shopkeepers." He paused. "You have to eat, and so do I. So, let's go get some dinner."

When he put it like that, what could I say? "I need to tell Jack I'm leaving so he can lock the door."

"You go on. Drive over to the Inn. I'll tell Jack and walk across the Square. We'll get there about the same time."

He left me by the door and headed down the hallway to the front of the building.

Now what? My lack of an answer told me my big Return to Wolf Creek Plan hadn't included Elliot Reynolds or my feelings for him. How had I missed that?

Even though my drive to the parking area behind the Inn only took minutes, my mind raced back to Nathan and Toby. Was it possible Elliot knew some of that history, and my part in it? There had to have been talk back then when a baby disappeared and his great-grandmother died. But I hadn't stuck around long enough for the questions.

I'd considered leaving a note at the front desk of the Inn, asking for a rain check on the evening, but, again, Elliot was waiting for me when I walked into Crossroads. Or was it Eli?

When we were in school together most people had difficulty telling the Reynolds twins apart. I understood that. Physically they were typical of identical twins, tall and lean in their build, with nearly black hair, now salt and pepper. As kids, even I occasionally made the mistake of calling them by the wrong name. But I always knew Elliot by the way he spoke, his voice soft, gentle, more serious. Eli's personality expressed a trait of spontaneity, humor, and the touch of the jokester. Eli never called me Peaches, though, even when he tried to fool me. That nickname from long ago was between Elliot and me.

"Hello, Georgia."

"Eli. How nice to see you again." Fortunately my voice remained even.

Silence. An uneasy silence.

"Uh, is there something I can do for you?" I asked, my voice a little shaky.

"Yeah, there is. You can leave my brother alone."

With that, he turned on his heel and left. I raised my hand, wanting to tell him to stop. But nothing came out. Eli disappeared across the Square. I stood, frozen, about to give in to my urge to run to my room. But before I could decide, Elliot came through the door, greeting me with a big smile.

April
4

I looked on as Nathan turned the calendar on my desk to April. Then he cast a happy grin my way as he unlocked the front door. We'd made his deadline. The Owen, Connor & Pearson Law Office was officially open for business. Even better, Wolf Creek had a viable law firm, and it was no April Fools' Day trick.

That didn't mean any of us planned to sit around and wait for business to walk in, although, any would be welcomed. Plus, Miles' clients needed attention, too.

The more I was around Nathan and Jack the more I began to relax and enjoy the work. In spite of knowing at least a part of the truth about Nathan and Toby, I began to let his identity settle in the back of my mind, as if it wasn't so important after all. We started the enormous job of finding the files of the cases Uncle Miles had been working on before his stroke. Regrettably, they were not together, nor in any order for that matter. We started using the dog-eared and faded look of old files as a way to sort them, but soon found that he'd reused some yellowed folders for new cases, too. That told us we faced a slow process, but I approached the task as I would a puzzle and began with the excitement of finding the keystone piece for my plan.

As much as I needed to help bring order to the chaos Miles left behind, I also, more than Nathan or Jack, needed to see to Miles himself. Not long after our two-minute conversation the day I arrived in Wolf Creek, Beverly had called the hospital and had listed me as the contact person for Uncle Miles, with all decisions about his care transferred to me. That meant making all the arrangements, too. Of course, Beverly neglected to tell me what she'd done, so I was surprised when the nurse called with her latest update on Uncle Miles' condition.

In those first days I fell into a pattern of daily visits to Uncle Miles, sometimes rising early and visiting Miles before work, hoping to catch the doctor making his rounds. Sometimes I'd make an early evening trip to the hospital, where I'd tell him the stories of my day. Somehow, I wanted to believe he could hear me tell him that his law firm was in good, capable—and ethical—hands. That would mean something to him. Maybe, I realized, if he wasn't destined to get better, he could die in peace.

On one visit with him I'd boldly asked if he'd heard anything from Lily. She was Beverly's daughter, after all. What was I hoping for when I asked? A sign? A hand movement? I couldn't even be sure he'd remember my niece, but I'd delayed telling him about my plan long enough. If he understood any of my explanations, that would be a bonus. If not, it wasn't any loss.

A few days later I noticed he appeared weaker and a quick conversation with the nurse confirmed my observation. The last time I'd asked the doctor about Uncle Miles' recovery, he'd only sadly shaken his head. I'd visited before work that day, and when I realized what the doctor was really telling me, I broke down and cried. I'd lost six years of being with him because of *my* embarrassment, *my* guilt.

And without any help or support from Beverly, of course, I made all the arrangements for Uncle Miles' transfer to the long-term care facility connected to the hospital. A nursing home. Say the words, I told myself, bleak as they were. On the day a bed became available, I called Nathan a little after 7:30 in the morning to say I'd be in after I made sure Miles was settled in his room.

As he had before, Nathan told me to take my time, that family always came first. Jack was like that, too. He and Liz seemed particularly concerned about Miles, maybe because Jack had been through a crisis himself, and he was much younger than Miles.

The attitude about family the two men showed was so different from the Milwaukee firm, the kind of place that no one even used all their vacation days, mostly from fear of being viewed as not committed enough to the success of the firm.

Over the next two days, on the drives back and forth from seeing Uncle Miles and at night when I was alone, Elliot filled my thoughts. And Eli. The night we had dinner, before I could even think about how to respond to Eli's veiled threat, Elliot had found me shaken. To say our Crossroads dinner was awkward was an understatement. He sensed that I was restless, and I sensed he wanted me to talk to him, explain myself. The early, casual, "Hi, Peaches" greeting couldn't last. Both of us focused our remarks on the Square, the Farmer Foods' expansion, and Uncle Miles. Safe topics.

Through his many emails and text messages, Elliot made no secret of wanting to see me, but Eli's warning had confused my desire to see him.

But in the back of my mind I kept asking myself what Eli thought was going to happen? Did he really think he needed to protect Elliot from me? A part of me burned in bitter realization that Elliot's mother wanted to protect him from me, and now his twin was going down that same path. And how had things turned out for Elliot? Not well, as far as I knew. Mary Beth had sought greener, the color of money greener, pastures. No, Elliot hadn't been good enough for her, after all.

No matter what would happen between Elliot and me, we were both old enough to take care of ourselves. Neither of us needed Eli interfering.

***

Shortly after Miles was moved to the long-term care facility, I focused on getting ready to open the office on the Square. Our space was shaping up nicely, and I looked forward to the day—coming soon—that we'd have only one office. That would make it easier for all of us to breathe new life into the now updated law practice. Uncle Miles was a great lawyer, but it was up to Nathan and Jack to modernize the office, a big commitment and not much leeway in terms of time to do it. As I unlocked the door I spotted Liz and the woman from the quilt shop approaching our front door.

Oh, dear. What was her name?

Liz waved before I could turn away, so I stepped outside into a clear, crisp spring day.

"Lock the door and come with us," Liz said in what I now recognized as her take-charge voice. "You need to meet more of the Square people." She let out a quick laugh. "Let me revise that. You need to see more of the people on the Square."

"Maybe you were right the first time," I said wryly. I held up one finger as a signal to wait for me. I ducked back inside the office and grabbed my purse and locked the door behind me. Being with Liz would start the day on a good note.

"Marianna and I often go for coffee to talk about upcoming events for the quilt shop," Liz explained.

Marianna, of course. Marianna. I said the name to myself two or three more times and knew I had it nailed.

"Nice to see you again, Marianna."

"It's good to see you, too. But don't let Liz fool you. We start out talking about my store, but most of the time we end up chatting with other shop owners and employees from the shops on the Square and don't get any business done."

As we walked along, I noted Marianna's muted earth-tone colors and tailored clothes, a sharp contrast to Liz's bold colors and her trendy flowing style. But I'd seen Marianna's window displays and knew they benefitted from her artistic touch. Her own subdued appearance let the bright, vibrant design of her shop windows stand on their own as creative pieces sure to draw the eye of even a casual shopper.

"You'll have to stop and look around inside," Marianna said. "Liz told me you were moving into Miles' house. Maybe you could use a quilt for one of your beds."

I nodded. Between the law office on the Square and checking in on Uncle Miles I hadn't even thought about making Uncle Miles' house into a real home for myself. I'd barely had time to walk around the Square and introduce myself and the law office and tell everyone we were open for business. I had to laugh, though. What happened to my plan for a quiet return? That had quickly evaporated. In fact, I found myself settling into my life on the Square and giving less thought to why I'd come back in the first place. But, in the back of my mind, I hadn't changed my mind. No matter how at home I felt back in Wolf Creek, I still had to right a wrong.

"My things are due to arrive from Milwaukee in a couple of days," I said, nodding to Marianna, "so I'll be able to think about settling into the house after that."

We arrived at Biscuits and Brew at the same time as Elliot and Eli showed up, with their sister making them a group of three. Once again, my memory failed me and I couldn't pull up her name.

"Hi, Peaches," Elliot said, moving to the side so the six of us didn't block the door. "It's good to see you joining the morning bunch."

I forced myself to keep looking at Elliot, which enabled me to ignore Eli's piercing glare. But it threw me and I found myself searching for a reply to Elliot's greeting.

"Do you remember our little sister, Megan?" Elliot asked, pointing behind him and apparently unaware of Eli sidestepping away to distance himself from the group.

"Little sister?" Megan playfully jabbed Elliot in the ribs. "Welcome to the Square. I own Rainbow Gardens, the flower shop two doors down from you."

I shook her outstretched hand. "I'm Georgia, by the way. Do you provide the bouquets for the Inn? The flowers in my room were beautiful."

"Yup," she said, her mouth widening into a brilliant smile. "It's been a great way to let people know I'm here. Marianna calls it soft marketing. Like those brooches of Art's she wears all the time."

I looked at Marianna, and, sure enough, a beautiful flower shaped brooch made of pastel colored stones sparkled on the lapel of her jacket. Hmm…seeing her made the wheels in my mind turn. Virgie, my closest Milwaukee friend, wanted to leave Merkel & Kline and market the one-of-a-kind vests she designed and sewed for her clients. I had a couple of gorgeous vests she'd made for me. Unfortunately, the inevitable cash-flow, or more accurately, the lack of it, had kept her at her desk. But maybe if I wore her vests, others would want one and I could send the business her way.

We filed into the coffee shop and became part of a noisy exchange of greetings from those already gathered.

"I'll get coffee for us, you two grab a table," Liz said, gently pushing us farther into the room.

I looked at one large table filled with women laughing and talking over each other, finishing each other's sentences as they debated an issue of some sort.

Marianna tugged my arm. "Come on. Let's join them."

By the time we'd reached the table, the women had shuffled the chairs around to make room for us in their already tight circle. Introductions took only a minute or two and then the conversation continued on as if there hadn't been an interruption.

Marianna reached across for one of the coffees Liz had brought. She turned to me, "A little overwhelming isn't it? Don't worry. A year ago I was the new kid and felt the same way you're feeling now."

New kid, huh. Hardly. But Marianna had no way of knowing that my family had a long history in Wolf Creek. Growing up, I thought I'd never leave. Then, once I did, I had more or less accepted the idea that I wouldn't come back. Now, here I was, in the midst of a group of people with Wolf Creek roots and likely an equal number of people who were the town's new folks. None of that mattered at the moment, though.

Not wanting the conversation to focus on me I listened as someone asked how Marianna liked her remodeled shop. When I heard that Charlie Crawford had done the work it only reinforced my decision to have him do needed updates at the house.

I sipped my coffee and listened, and before long, the Biscuits and Brew morning bunch, as Elliot had called them, gathered their empty cups and went on about their day. Likewise, I nodded to Liz and touched my watch. She smiled and understood that it was time for me to open the office. I fell in line with the rest of the group. Then, just outside the door, I saw another woman from my past. And I so wished I hadn't run into her. At least not yet.

"Georgia, I'd heard you were back." Sarah frowned. "Elliot mentioned it the other day."

"And I was going to call you or stop by your office," I said, my cheeks growing hot. Sarah Hutchinson was no stranger, but more than any of the other people I'd seen so far, except Elliot, Sarah was a friend.

"And I hear you're the mayor of Wolf Creek now—and a popular one, too."

Sarah beamed. In Wolf Creek, the role of mayor had usually been more like being a good will ambassador and town booster, and from the happiness in her face, the role suited her. "As I'm sure you've noticed, the Square has changed a lot while you were gone."

"And for the better," I said with a nod. But Sarah hadn't changed, except for adding a few years like the rest of us. Her thick hair, cut fashionably short, had some gray strands mixed with her natural brunette, but that only added to her striking looks.

Sarah turned away and opened the door of the coffee shop. "I'll stop by soon to see you—and Nathan and Jack, of course. I want to make sure they know I appreciate what they're doing for the Square."

"Please," I said, "make it soon." Seeing Sarah made me realize, deep inside, how much I needed a friend—and not just any friend. I needed her. And I owed her an explanation.

"Oh, and Georgia, say hi to Miles when you see him. I always enjoyed my visits with him," Sarah called before disappearing inside the café.

"I will," I called back. Would he respond when I used her name? Maybe, maybe not. It wasn't predictable day to day.

Halfway across the Square I checked my watch again, shocked at how much time had passed. I hurried the rest of the way and found the door unlocked. The bell jingled its greeting as I pushed the door open.

A little boy sat in my desk chair twirling around and humming a tune I didn't recognize. He stopped suddenly and slipped out of the seat. He hunched his shoulders as if trying to make himself invisible as he hurried away.

"Good morning," I said. "Are your parents in a meeting with Mr. Connor or Mr. Pearson?"

"Nathan's in his office." The boy's voice was soft, almost weak.

And he hadn't answered my question.

As if saying his name summoned him, Nathan came into the reception area.

"Heard the bell jingle. That sure is a happy sound." Nathan positioned himself behind the boy and rested his hands on the boy's small shoulders.

"Georgia. I'd like you to meet Toby. Someday I'll tell you the long version about why he's with me, but for now, let me introduce Toby Connor."

I steeled myself to stay open to meeting this little boy, to control my reaction, to reveal nothing. *Good Lord. Toby was my new boss' son.*

"Hello, Mr. Toby Connor. My name is Georgia Winters. I work for your dad and Mr. Pearson." Was my voice steady? Sufficiently nonchalant?

"Toby calls him Jack," Nathan said. "We're informal with names all around."

"Then call me Georgia," I said with a nod, "and you can sit at my desk anytime I'm not using it."

I was rewarded with a big smile that crossed a small, sweet face dominated by big dark blue eyes. Familiar eyes.

I reached across the desk and held out my hand. Nathan nodded and then Toby put his hand in mine.

I rested the fingers of my left hand on the desk to steady myself. I'd held this boy's tiny hand before, shortly after Mom died. It was the same day Beverly and I decided to let Richard Connor take him. The identical sickly churning in my stomach I'd had that night came rushing back. The magnitude of the mistake played out in my mind. Huge. I could almost see the mistake itself waving an accusing finger in my face.

"Okay, young man," Nathan said, "if you're not well enough to go to school, then it's back to the conference room." Nathan lightly twisted Toby around and swatted his little butt. "Go on now."

Nathan turned back to face me. "He can rest on the couch in there 'til we go home."

I cleared my throat and stiffened my shoulders to help me focus. "Is there something he needs? Water, milk, snacks?"

My concern for Toby's needs surprised me, but at the same time, my feelings sat right. The little boy was family. Even if no one else knew that, I did.

***

Alone that night, I let the reality of Toby sink in. It had happened so much sooner than I imagined—if at all. Meeting the little boy, that is. But it woke me up, too. I'd come back home with a plan to reunite our family, but that was Miles, Beverly, Lily, and me. As for reuniting Lily and Toby, that was something else again.

For a few years now, having our family be a family again was so important to me. But now, Toby was with Nathan, a puzzling situation in itself, but I had no right to ask about it. I didn't even know where Lily was.

Was there a woman in Nathan's life? I hadn't heard about one, even in a jesting man-to-man kind of way. The foolishness of my thoughts hit hard. They confused me, too. I shook my fairytale thoughts out of my head. What? Did I think that somehow I could reunite Lily with Toby by way of Nathan?

Real life intruded into my thoughts and forced me to think about what I could manage. Maybe find Lily, or do what I could for Uncle Miles.

5

Although we'd declared April 1 as opening day, little details kept Charlie and his crew on the job through the next Friday and the cleaning service had to wait until Saturday to finally make the front windows of the new office gleam in the morning sun.

Early Monday morning, I fixed toast and made coffee for the first time in my new coffeemaker. I went about my morning whistling random nonsense notes in my typically slightly off-tune tone, which distracted me from everything in my sight, from the appliances to the floors. Every inch of the house needed the Clean Sweep crew, another sign of Uncle Miles' inability to keep up with life's ordinary demands over the last few years.

Nathan, Jack, and I all agreed that working in small batches would be the efficient way to make our way through the stacks of files Uncle Miles had left behind. We started with the most recent papers and worked back through past dates. Maybe we'd luck out and find the current documents we needed to update the small firm's clients. So far, clients had been patient, but that wouldn't last.

As for me, I hoped I'd come across something that related to Lily. I'd seen a number of files with "Owen" on the tab, giving me hope, but so far I'd turned up nothing helpful.

That wasn't surprising, since Mom had used the Connor Law Firm in Green Bay for her will and other estate documents, rather than going to Uncle Miles. That had troubled me for years. As the executor of Mom's will, Beverly might have an explanation, but that didn't mean she'd tell me. I hadn't seen or heard from Beverly since my first day back in Wolf Creek. Sadly, I didn't expect her to reach out.

If I started thinking about the state of my family, my heart would grow heavy. Instead, I put my cup in the sink, ready to head to the Square. Then I jumped when the doorbell rang. Who would want to talk to me this early? I peeked out the front window before opening the door. There stood Elliot with a bouquet of flowers.

Now what? There, I'd said it again.

I opened the door wider.

"Elliot? What brings you by?"

He held the flowers out for me to take. "Just something to brighten the house."

Should I invite him in? I wanted to. But what meaning would he take from that? What did I even want him to think?

"Uh, Elliot, I was about to leave for the office on the Square, but thank you for the flowers."

"I'll walk with you. Too nice a day to drive."

None of this made sense. Not Elliot showing up, nor me trying to pretend there was nothing between us. Was it fair for me to act like Elliot had been waiting for me to come back? He had a life, or so I wanted to think. Well, no, that wasn't true either. I wanted to be with him.

I glanced at Elliot, who stood patiently on the porch, peering into my face. The only polite thing to do was to open the screen door to welcome him in. "Come in while I put these in water."

With my back to him and leading the way to the kitchen, maybe I could settle my heart.

There may or may not have been a vase somewhere in the cupboards, but I didn't have time to look. Instead, I grabbed the ice tea pitcher sitting on top of the refrigerator and filled it with water.

He stood behind me. Close behind.

I struggled to keep my mind on the flowers and my hands busy filling the pitcher, all the while keenly aware that if I turned around he'd be close enough to…

No!

I cleared my throat. "That'll do until I get home and find a proper vase, or I can stop and get one from Megan." I quickly folded the flower cuttings into the paper wrap and shoved them in the trash.

He took a step back and laughed. "She said I should take a vase for them, but when does a guy carry a vase when he takes flowers to his lady?"

I'm not his lady.

"Elliot, please, you can't keep talking this way. We can't go down the wrong path again. I'm back in Wolf Creek to take care of something personal—something in my family that needs to be addressed."

He leaned against the counter and crossed one foot over the other. "If you just tell me what it is maybe I can help."

"No, I need to do this on my own. But I need time, too. I've started a new job, I want to spend time with Uncle Miles, and I need to settle into his house."

Leaving him standing at the counter, I walked to the front of the house and picked up my jacket and purse. He followed only when I held the door open, as clear a signal as I could send that it was time for us to leave.

"Peaches, listen to me." He stepped onto the porch, but turned to face me, more or less blocking my exit. "I'm *not* walking away."

Was that a figure of speech or was he referring to my clandestine quick trip in and out of Wolf Creek six years ago? When I hadn't contacted anyone. Not him, not even Sarah. Yet they all knew I'd been in Wolf Creek. Either way, I had no time to worry about it now. Nor did I have time for romance and a relationship. Not even with Elliot.

"But I can't tell you anything about why I'm here." I stared down the street, trying to make sense of my thoughts. I wanted to grab his hand and sit on the top porch step and tell him what I carried in my heart. Impossible. For now, anyway. "I just can't."

"I hear you, Peaches. You don't believe me, but I do. Maybe you don't believe in yourself." He grinned. "But I meant what I said. You take the time you need. I won't call, I won't text. But I'm not going away."

Elliot hurried down the stairs and crossed the street. He took off in the direction of the Square. And then in my mind, I saw Eli, whose warning continued to loop through my head.

***

I'd resolved to spend a couple of hours each day organizing the file boxes in the storeroom, but my progress wasn't even or steady. And it wasn't for lack of effort on Charlie Crawford's part. He'd done a superb job building floor to ceiling shelving in the storeroom that gave us plenty of space to store Uncle Miles' files. But on the days I had too many interruptions to make much progress I'd come back to the office and spend a few evening hours alone bringing order to the chaos.

I spent more time than I cared to on the phone, repeating information about Miles and talking up Nathan and Jack. Plus, with the news the office had moved to the southwest corner of the Square, we were in the thick of things.

Then there was so much courting to do. Courting new clients, that is. I managed phone calls, took endless messages, searched for critical documents Nathan and Jack needed for their cases, all the while adjusting to their working style. Similar in philosophy, each managed both time and tasks in his own way.

When I'd sit with Uncle Miles, I felt so much affection spill over. Somehow, without him fully understanding the reasons, he'd given me a chance at a new life. "If only you could tell us what you've been working on," I'd whisper.

Uncle Miles knew how to listen, and apparently, Elliot was a lot like him that way. And also like Miles, Elliot had done exactly what he'd said he'd do. No calls, no texts. No surprises by the front door. I'd taken it upon myself to stay away from Biscuits and Brew, ceding the ground that had been such a big part of his life, but also because I was afraid to see him—or Eli.

That's why my heart skipped a beat when I unlocked the front door of the office one morning and saw him sitting on a bench across the walkway. *Cut it out…this is ridiculous!* Clearly, this was a case of first love, and at almost fifty years old, I needed to grow up.

I waved and called out, "Morning, Elliot."

Long strides carried him to the door, and me, in short order. Like the hero in a romance novel.

Nothing heroic seeped into his voice, however. "I need to talk to Nathan or Jack about the building."

He kept his distance, and I got the message.

"Nathan should be here shortly. And Jack's coming in after lunch." It wasn't easy for me to reveal Jack and Nathan's schedule so casually. At Merkel & Kline, everything was done by appointment, tightly scheduled, okayed by the attorney, and then confirmed. But Nathan and Jack wanted our clients to know their business was important to us and we'd be readily available to them.

"Did you have an appointment?" I asked.

"No. But I need to see one or the other. Doesn't matter which one."

"Have a seat and I'll call Nathan." I pointed to the reception area where a sofa and two winged-back chairs circled around a low-rise coffee table.

Fortunately, Nathan arrived through the back door a couple of minutes later, so I didn't have to work at my desk conscious of Elliot's presence across the room.

Nathan came right to my desk and after I explained the situation, he met Elliot halfway across the room for a handshake and a quick greeting. "So, what can we help you with today?"

I expected Elliot to follow Nathan into his office, but instead he blurted out the issue. "Before his illness, Miles was working on the sale of the building next to Farmer Foods. We'd like to announce we're moving the store into the larger building. We were planning to go public with it at the business association meeting next week. On the other hand, if it's not all squared away, we don't want to be premature about it."

"Good thinking," Nathan said with a nod. "Come on back to the office—you, too, Georgia. You can take some notes so we're all clear on what needs to be done."

the house would relieve some of my loneliness. Despite meeting new people on the Square and being welcomed into the new law firm, not to mention being needed and valued there, I was still alone. And alone with my secrets and my plan, which might or might not come to fruition. Hard to admit, I couldn't control everything going on around me.

In passing, I'd told Jack I planned to make some changes to Miles' house, and taking me at my word, he arranged for a final move early the next Saturday morning. And he assured me I wouldn't be alone, and as I'd come to learn, he was true to his word.

What a group Jack assembled! He showed up with Nathan and Toby, along with Charlie and his whole crew. Alan Carlson, the son part of Art&Son Jewelry, heard from Jack that I needed help, so I met Alan, a twentyish man, for the first time that morning. I immediately liked him.

In full take-charge mode Liz arrived with a box of muffins and sweet rolls from Biscuits and Brew. I grabbed coffee mugs and filled them so I could start another pot brewing. I added a carafe of orange juice and glasses at the end of the table.

"Treats first, then the work," Liz announced.

"Should be work first, then the reward," Charlie countered, grinning. "At least for my crew."

We all laughed, especially Charlie's crew, as we each picked out a muffin or roll from the box.

Toby stood up tall and peered into the box on the table. "I want the donut with the chocolate frosting."

"Eat fast, young man," Nathan said, lifting the donut out of the box and putting it on the plate. "You have a big job as door manager."

"Door manager?" Toby's eyes were open wide with curiosity.

"That means you'll hold the door open for us so we can have our arms free to carry the boxes." Nathan flexed his biceps, and that brought on a giggle from Toby. The boy turned serious again when he sat in the chair Nathan pulled out for him and enthusiastically nodded when asked if he wanted a glass of juice.

My mind shot to a memory of Lily sitting at the same table eating pancakes her grandmother made only for her. Mom had dropped chocolate chips into the small silver dollar sized cakes and shushed Beverly when she started to object. The image, so clear, so crisp, threw me off balance. I grabbed the counter to steady myself and glanced away to keep from staring at the little boy's sweet face and marveling at the traces of his mother. For one thing, those deep blue eyes had traveled through generations of the Owen family. And when Toby smiled at me, it was like Lily casting a little girl's grin my way.

Having left Wolf Creek at such a young age, I had so few memories of Lily, but I cherished them all. And I had the good fortune to be her aunt from far away, so any birthday card or small gift I sent, or every phone call, too, was considered special, at least when Lily was a little girl.

Fortunately, the coffee maker bubbled and sputtered announcing the brewing was done, so I was forced to transfer my attention before anyone noticed I'd taken a trip down memory lane. Not an easy trip either—not with such a confusing mix of emotions rushing in. I grabbed the pot and while the conversation in the kitchen continued, I filled a mug for Liz and Nathan, and me, and topped off the rest.

"You okay?" Liz asked as she put plates and mugs in the sink.

"Sure," I said, resigned. Apparently, Liz never missed anything. "Something brought up a quick flash of a memory of my mother making breakfast. That's all."

Obviously, there was so much more, but I had no intention of talking about Toby and Lily. Liz had no way of knowing about that part of my past—my family history. Still, when she lightly touched my arm, I wondered if there was more than simple empathy in her response. Could she know more than I thought, and if so, who would have told her?

Proving true the stereotype that hard-working men eat fast, Charlie's crew downed their coffee and pastries in a matter of minutes. Then, off they went to haul the remaining boxes out the front door to the waiting trucks. Liz followed them around the room with a vacuum cleaner, and then directed two of Charlie's men to move some of my furniture from the second bedroom to the living room.

The whole operation took less than two hours, but in that time, the space turned from an office to a home. With Toby still working hard at his big job of manning the door, I thanked everyone as they filed out of the house.

What a satisfying morning. And all because I wasn't doing everything alone.

The task of rearranging the house had an aura of sadness about it, though, knowing that Uncle Miles would likely never return home. To make the house mine, really mine, then, I decided to move my uncle's things to the smaller bedroom and take the more spacious one and convert it into a room I'd claim as mine.

Alan Carlson had mentioned that when he wasn't designing and making jewelry with his dad, he volunteered to help out people on the Square. "Really," he'd said, "I mean it. You can call on me whenever you need a hand."

Eyeing the beds and dressers, I realized it was only a matter of time before I took him up on that offer. Not only were these pieces awkward, I had to admit they were too heavy for me to muscle around.

My plan called for spending the weekend days at the new office organizing files, but since the last few boxes I'd gone through dated back so many years, I didn't hold out any hope of finding information about Lily. Maybe my chances were better if I rummaged deeper through what Uncle Miles had stored here at the house. I held out hope I could find Lily simply by uncovering information about her whereabouts hidden within Miles' things.

Somehow, the basement, which I knew would take both time and effort to clean and organize, loomed as a gold mine of Owen history. My grandmother, and I'm sure the women before her, had been nothing if not savers. Saving for a "rainy day," wasn't just an adage, it was a mantra in my family.

Before diving into my to-do list, I cleared away the remains of breakfast, chuckling that every last donut, muffin, and sweet roll were gone. Then I was off and running. So many details to cover. I couldn't give away some of Uncle Miles' suits and take over his closet until I'd checked every pocket for odds and ends, each of which held some kind of surprise, from old twisted metal paperclips to a half-consumed roll of his favorite butterscotch lifesavers, and his collection of handkerchiefs—cloth ones, too. I smiled at that. Who even owned those nowadays? And were there still people in the world who savored butterscotch lifesavers the way Miles did?

My careful search turned up nothing of value except for 71 cents in pennies, nickels, and dimes. Sadly, the dresser drawers I tackled next were a tangled mess of odds and ends clothing. It looked as if he'd more or less scattered his socks and T-shirts in the large dresser. Like the boxes and files in the office, no system or pattern emerged to help me make sense of it all. What had happened to my organized-to-a-flaw uncle?

Since Uncle Miles was still alive, it wasn't right to give everything away, but I picked out a collection of useful items and put them in piles to take to the resale shop associated with the shelter a couple of towns west of Wolf Creek. The rest I packed in boxes and transferred to the basement. Is this what happens to us all? Our things become burdens and someone is left to sort, sift, and store? That thought brought tears to my eyes. Uncle Miles was much too proud to want anyone spending afternoons reorganizing things he'd likely never use again.

A wave of sadness that felt at once familiar and new washed through me. Six years had passed quickly, and because of my weakness I'd lost that time with the most important man in my life.

I groaned when the doorbell rang, just as I was fighting back tears. I considered not answering it, but Mom's schooling propelled me to the door, all the while telling myself to be polite.

I peeked out the front window, half expecting to see Elliot. But it was Sarah who'd come visiting. Happy to see her, I quickly unlocked the door and invited her in with a sweep of my hand.

Sarah stepped inside and scanned the room, nodding with approval at the obvious progress. "I don't have any plans for dinner and since you've obviously been working hard all day, I thought you might like to join me for dinner at Crossroads."

The mention of dinner made my stomach growl. Too focused on my quest for the day, I'd forgotten about lunch. I grinned at my old friend. "Guess my body is saying yes. The thought of cooking isn't appealing either."

"What are you up to around here?" She craned her neck to take in more of the living room and into the dining room.

"Dealing with stuff all day. Files, storage boxes, and just now, I finished boxing up Uncle Miles' clothes. I doubt he'll be coming home or wearing any of them again."

Sarah thrust a bottle of wine in a carry-bag from one of the better-known local wineries in Door County. "I'm so sorry, Georgia," she whispered. "I remember how special he was to you. And I have to say he was special to me—to all of us, really." She waved at the bottle I now held. "Let's crack that open and have a glass. We'll toast Miles."

"Okay," I said, pulling myself up to stand a little taller. "Let's offer a toast to his life."

Sarah followed me into the kitchen. "Have a seat." I nodded to the collection of plates and glasses and mugs on the counter. "Early this morning, Jack and Nathan had Charlie and his crew move the rest of the boxes destined for the office. Between the coffee, juice, and the goodies Liz brought from Biscuits and Brew, it was almost a real breakfast."

Sarah nodded. "Can't beat B and B's sweet treats." Then she knit her brows in thought. "You probably don't know this, but letting Country Law open on the Square stirred up some controversy. I think it will be a valuable addition to the Square, but others disagreed."

"Really? Why?" Odd that Nathan or Jack hadn't said anything.

"It meant granting a waiver of one of the bylaws. The merchants on the Square had agreed to reserve the storefronts for retail shops, and they meant selling products and not services. That's why you don't see a salon or a day spa."

Liz had mentioned that Country Law broke new ground on the Square, but she hadn't gone into detail. "I suppose I didn't know there were actual rules, well, bylaws."

"Oh, yes, these are clear, specific rules, not just preferences. But I argued for an exemption in this one case, because an up and running service business was better than the eyesore of a vacant building." Sarah shrugged. "Besides, Country Law might bring in more foot traffic on the Square. Who knows? It's too soon to tell."

"Apparently, the dissenters came around," I said, turning the corkscrew one last time before pulling the cork.

"They did. Well, most did."

I brought out my mother's favorite stemmed wine glasses and filled each with the rich, dark red merlot.

"Mom's holiday glasses," I said. "I found them on the top shelf in the cupboard over the refrigerator. I doubt anyone's opened that cupboard for years, but they bring back Christmas and Thanksgiving memories for me."

"I'll bet," Sarah said, lifting her glass. "Let's toast her, too."

"She'd have enjoyed sipping a glass with us this evening." We held our glasses suspended in the air. "Okay, then," I said, "to Mom and Uncle Miles." We clinked glasses.

Something didn't feel right.

"And to the future of the Owen family," I said, "as small as we are."

Sarah smiled and clinked again.

Only I knew that without Toby, or rather, without the truth about Toby coming out, the Owen family wasn't likely to have much future.

I had a quick shower and when I came out of my newly fixed up bedroom ready to go, I saw that Sarah had washed the dishes from the morning. I sputtered some words of protest about her doing them, but she playfully pushed me toward the front door.

"Nonsense. I'd have sat on the porch and waited for you. I'm hungry, let's go."

How did anyone ever argue with her and win? No wonder Country Law got its waiver.

We walked the couple of blocks into the Square, and got to Crossroads just as the dinner crowd gathered. Warmed and relaxed from the wine, Sarah and I both indulged and feasted on the special, Shrimp Alfredo, made with whole wheat linguini and fresh local cheese and milk.

When the waitress brought the salad included with the special, its bright colors were enough to lift anyone's spirits. I dipped my fork into the ramekin of raspberry vinaigrette dressing, a house specialty, according to Sarah. Sweet with raspberry, subtly sharp with vinegar, I let out a quick, "Wow…no wonder you recommended it."

"I won't lead you astray," Sarah said with mock seriousness. "But I hear the chef may be leaving soon, so enjoy as much of his cooking as you can."

Feeling mellow, our dinner conversation consisted mostly of food talk. Like me, Sarah considered herself more of an appreciator of food than a cook herself. Between the atmosphere, the food, and the company, I hadn't found myself so at ease since coming back to town.

"I hate to think of the chef leaving," I said, "not when it's so easy to come here for a meal. What a loss."

"I've tried to convince him to stay," Sarah said, "and give us at least one more summer season. He's made Crossroads one of the major draws of this whole Square." She punctuated her words with her fork. "Losing him could affect all the owners."

I'd started to ask Sarah what she'd done during the years I was gone when the waitress brought us wedges of Crossroads signature chocolate mousse pie and decaf coffee, which came with the special. So much for questions. We'd have time for that later.

When we were done and we had our check, Sarah, known to the waitress—of course—teased her about having at least one table as easy as, pardon the pun, pie.

We all groaned, even Sarah.

With freshly filled coffee cups, we leaned back in our chairs, content. I'd known Sarah for years, almost my whole life. She was Beverly's age, but our paths often crossed and as young people, we'd developed a strong bond. Best friends, more or less. We took for granted that we'd always tell each other the truth.

I'd broken that promise, not only when I left the first time, but later. Sarah knew Elliot and I had a history, and she sensed my need to leave and forge a different life. When I'd avoided her six years ago I assumed our bond had cracked. I'd never expected to be having dinner with her again.

I needed to tell her my real reason for returning to Wolf Creek. Did I come right out and tell her the whole story? This part of my plan had been fuzzy. Not fuzzy soft, but fuzzy blurred. In that gray area where guilt and embarrassment lived.

"Miles was so excited about your coming back and working for him." Sarah spoke with her fork again, this time making little air circles.

"Do you know if he'd been ill recently? He'd never mentioned feeling anything but his typical tip-top way— that's what he called it. 'I'm in tip-top shape,' he'd say."

Sarah shook her head. "He always seemed just the same to me. I didn't see him every day, but he enjoyed Crossroads just like the rest of us. So, I'd see him on the way in or out now and then."

I scanned the room to be sure no one I recognized was sitting nearby. "I'm not going to talk about this to other people, but I can tell you the man's house and his clothes were a mess. Disaster, really." I shook my head. "This is certainly not the way I remembered him. A couple of generations ago, people would have called him dapper."

"Whatever happened inside his house, he didn't show it on the outside. No one mentioned any concerns about him to me." Sarah swallowed a mouthful of coffee. "But when the stroke happened we were all surprised." She fidgeted with her napkin. "I called Beverly to see if she needed help."

The mention of my sister churned my stomach.

"Yes, she was there to admit him to the hospital," I conceded, "but then, nothing." This emotional hit surprised me, especially the tears that formed quickly and fell just as fast. I wiped them away with a quick swipe before they traveled the length of my face.

Sarah reached across the table and took my hand. I'd never felt alone when we were together as kids. I'd missed our friendship, and I hadn't even known it.

"As long as I've unleashed," I said, "I might as well add that Beverly turned Uncle Miles' care over to me. She made it all too clear she doesn't want to be bothered."

"Well, good for you. No interference. You can handle this anyway you want." A huge smile crossed Sarah's face. "Welcome home."

I squeezed her hand. "Thank you."

Sarah made a quick segue to briefly updating me about two men, one of whom was interested in her, but too narrow-minded to make him a serious contender for a relationship. The other man was more of a heartbreaker. She'd really liked him, but small-town life wasn't for him. And Wolf Creek was everything to her. She couldn't imagine leaving it for anything—or anyone.

She didn't ask about Elliot and I stayed mum on that topic. But we talked as if there had never been a break in our friendship. Oh, that felt so good.

"Let's have dinner again soon," I said.

"Absolutely," she said, "but I'm not waiting for another shared meal to get an answer to my question. I expect you to tell me why you really came back. It can't be a layoff. Milwaukee firms always have job opportunities for skilled people like you—or you could have taken off for a bigger city or a warmer climate. But you didn't. You showed up here, even after cutting all your ties."

Inside I ruffled at her subterfuge. All that warm "welcome home" talk. She'd become even better at breaking down barriers through the years. What a terrific advantage that must have given her as mayor of this little town with its popular, friendly, but gossipy Square.

"Busted," I said with a shrug and cynical laugh. "But, and I repeat, but, what I'm about to tell you is for you only. No one else can know this, for now."

"Fair enough," Sarah said with a nod.

"I want Nathan and Jack to continue believing that the office—and Miles—are my focus. Which they are—sort of."

I'd stepped on my own story somehow. In the first line I'd made the truth sound sneaky and deceitful. I could see that from the pinched look on Sarah's face. It would have been a good time to fade away into the wallpaper.

But I couldn't do that. I sat up straighter, looked her in the eye and said, "I have my reasons, and it's not about hiding anything. I'm here to find out where Lily is and convince her to come back home."

Sarah dropped her fork.

6

The next morning, a thud against the door startled me awake. I opened one eye and figured the sun was coming up and the fat Sunday edition of the *Wolf Creek Gazette* had just been delivered. Instantly, I was wide awake, glad that my life was moving forward again. And maybe dropping my guard with Sarah and talking about the past left me feeling lighter, even a little buoyant, and certainly deserving of a leisurely Sunday morning. I rolled onto my back and stared at the ceiling of what had been my parents' bedroom and tried to remember Dad before the tractor accident had killed him. Oh, how Mom must have struggled to raise two daughters. Neither Beverly nor I had made it easy for her either, always complaining about one thing or another.

My train of thought was not only running backwards, it was heading toward regret, so I jumped out of bed to shift my mental gears.

After coffee, breakfast, and the paper, it was almost noon before I walked over to the Square.

Now that I was living in Uncle Miles' house—well, my house now—it looked more like a home than an office. To further that transformation I had a mission for my trip, which was to buy my first item from a Wolf Creek Square shop. I'd enjoyed listening to Marianna describe the new fabrics arriving for the summer season and telling Liz and me her plans to make samples her customers could see. Since Liz made samples for the shop, too, they tended to get on a roll with their excited conversations. Given all the work they put in, Quilts Galore was as good a place to start shopping as any.

I was walking past Art&Son Jewelry when Art himself stepped out the door.

"Nice to see you, Georgia. So, Nathan finally gave you some time off so you can enjoy the Square?" His baritone voice rolled into a laugh.

"Good to see you, too, Art."

He pivoted to check his front window display so I stepped forward to get a closer look at his hand-crafted jewelry.

I pointed to a small pin that reminded me of a brilliant sun or a starburst. "Oh, I like that one."

He waved his arm. "Come on in. Have a look around. You might find something else you like."

My plan was to upgrade the furnishings in the house first, but maybe a new piece of jewelry would boost my spirits. Art held the door open and I walked through, nearly laughing out loud. Wow. I immediately became immersed in a pirate's bounty of gems and stones artfully displayed on royal blue velvet. Scattered amongst the pins and necklaces were blue boxes with Art&Son Jewelry embossed on the top. A few boxes were open, and he'd casually draped the necklaces and bracelets across them, drawing my eye even more. Some boxes were propped up at an angle and pins and earrings sat in their cotton nests.

As I circled one of the counters Alan stepped into the store from a doorway that led into what I assumed was a workshop in the back.

"Hi, Alan. Having a good day?" As I spoke, an idea came to me. When he helped move files from the house to the office, he'd spoken about his willingness to help shop owners and others in the Square.

"Every day's a good day. Even when you have to work." He smiled at his dad. I didn't detect any teenage attitude with his comment.

"How long are you working today?" My blunt tone even surprised me. "Oops, excuse me, I should explain. You see, I'm switching furniture at Uncle Miles' house and need some help. Since I heard you say you help people, maybe you could help me. And I'd certainly make it worth your time, too." I sure didn't want to press him into doing anything he didn't care to do. "Only if you want to and have the time," I added.

"I work 'til three," Alan said, "and then I can come help you."

"Works for me." I nodded goodbye to both Carlsons and left.

I smiled to myself. So much for my plan for a leisurely visit to Quilts Galore, but that would have to wait for another day. I headed back home, thinking about all I had to do to get ready for Alan. Between stripping the beds and moving the smaller pieces of furniture around, I'd be ready to manage the larger ones by the time he arrived.

A few minutes after three, Alan arrived. "Wow! Place looks like a house," he said, scanning the room. "Nice."

"Thanks, but the beds and dressers are too big for me to muscle around."

I led the way in and out of the rooms, explaining what I wanted. "So, what do you say we start by moving this bedroom set into the dining room?"

"You think you can handle your part?"

I immediately saw that Alan had the same teasing eyes that made his father so appealing. But I wasn't going to let a young guy just out of his teens—maybe—make me feel like I was too old to move my own furniture. "I can."

We emptied the room, one piece at a time. The door bell rang just as I finished vacuuming the empty spaces we left behind as we shuffled the furniture. I stuck my head out of the room and saw Alan approaching a young girl and a toddler standing in the living room.

"Hi, R. Thanks for coming," Alan said cheerfully, as he lifted the toddler into his arms and immediately tickled the baby's belly.

The girl grinned. "Your dad thought you might need some help and sent me over rather than wait for you at the store."

He nodded to me. "G, this is Rachel Spencer–I call her R. And this squirmy little guy is her son, Thomas."

"The G is for Georgia," I said before Alan had a chance to explain. Besides, Thomas had his full attention and he carried him off into the kitchen. "And it's nice to meet you, Rachel. But what's with the 'R' and 'G'?"

"Oh, that," she said, grinning. "Alan calls everyone by their initial. I'm "R," Marianna's, M.A. Now, you're "G."

"Okay. And your son? Is he "T"?

"Well, he usually calls him Buddy or Big T. Alan hasn't settled on which yet." She paused. "By the way, I'm Marianna's step-daughter. Thomas and I live with her in the apartment above her shop."

"Do you work on the Square, too?" I asked.

"You'll see me at Biscuits and Brew and I work at Marianna's shop, too. She's teaching me everything I need to know about sewing and fabric."

"You sound like a busy Mom."

"She is," Alan said, coming out of the kitchen with Thomas on his hip. "She takes classes at the community college, too."

Before I had a chance to say yes or no, Alan plunked Thomas into my arms.

"Now that R is here, we'll get the rest of it done."

And so they did, making short work of it, too, even zipping the seven drawer dresser into place in a matter of minutes. That left only a large, solid-sided low-rise table. Uncle Miles had put a soft, deep-cushioned chair next to it, along with a floor lamp. The chair and lamp I'd moved into its new place earlier, but the table had been too heavy and awkward for me.

While the duo of Alan and Rachel worked—and laughed a lot—I entertained Thomas from our perch on the sofa in the living room. There I was, a total stranger, but the delightful little guy accepted me and was even amused, apparently, by my attempts to get to know him.

"Hey, G, you'd better come here," Alan called from the bedroom.

His shaky voice gave me a jolt. I picked up Thomas and his stuffed animal and went to the room.

"We didn't mean to do it," Alan said, pointing to one side of the six-sided table that had opened up. "When we tipped the table, that panel fell like that."

74

I glanced down and saw that a door had formed one side of the table and nothing serious had happened to it. It simply had fallen open. I hadn't seen a piece of furniture like that before.

"Looks like it was built with a hidden door," he said, his voice still showing his nervousness. "We didn't break it."

I shifted the baby so I could touch his arm. "Alan, calm down. I know you didn't break it. Don't worry about it."

When I passed Thomas to Rachel, she stepped in closer to Alan, as if closing ranks.

Trying to make light of the moment, I rubbed my palms together. "Okay, let's see what's inside." I knelt on the floor next to the open door. The space inside had two shelves, both filled right to the top. "Wow, look at all this stuff."

I began to pull out papers and files and asked the kids to grab some empty boxes in the corner of the dining room.

"I can get them," Alan said, bouncing from the room, all signs of anxiety gone.

I sat back on my heels and gazed at the piles surrounding me, stunned. This could be just another bunch of stuff to be sorted. On the other hand, it was possible I'd found a gold mine of Uncle Miles' personal papers. Not the kind of files and paperwork I wanted Alan and Rachel to see. When Alan came back with the boxes, I asked them to move a couple of heavy pieces and they left Thomas with me. While using a storytelling voice to describe to Thomas how exciting it was to organize Uncle Miles' things, I transferred the papers and files to the boxes. At that point Alan and Rachel moved the cabinet and the remaining furniture.

The job done, I pulled some money out of my purse, thanking the two for their help. But Alan waved me off, saying the operative word was "volunteer." Grinning, Rachel picked up her tote and slung it over her shoulder. She coaxed Thomas to wave goodbye, which made Alan and Thomas both laugh. That gave me an opening to stuff the bills in his jacket pocket.

"Buy everybody a treat at Biscuits and Brew," I said, playfully hiding my hands so he couldn't give the money back.

Once the front door clicked shut, I rushed back to the bedroom. Where would I begin? I quickly scanned the yellow-edged files on the top of one pile, but most were outdated. But near the bottom a bright pink box announced itself. How could I have missed it earlier?

I knew that box. I'd helped Lily make it for Valentine's Day when she was ten years old and I'd come home for a weekend visit. Surprised that the memory returned in such vivid detail, I closed my eyes and inhaled deeply.

She'd asked Uncle Miles to be her escort—using that formal word—to the father-daughter luncheon at school. He'd accepted with great fanfare and even bought a new suit for the occasion. Since Lily had never met her father either before or after he'd divorced Beverly, she'd accepted Uncle Miles as the man in her life.

I opened the box. In his meticulous lettering, he'd even dated the letter, as he'd done with all the correspondence he saved. There, on the envelope was Lily's address and phone number.

I'd found my treasure. With tears streaming down my cheeks, I pressed the letter to my chest.

***

Sarah had called a Wolf Creek Square Business Owner's meeting for the last Tuesday of April, to be held in the large private dining room at Crossroads. Nathan and Jack insisted I be there. "You're the first person people see when they come through the door," Jack had said.

I wanted to meet everyone, put faces to names I had heard. And, for sure, to let everyone know that Country Law was open for business. Sometimes I still preferred a quiet evening at home with my thoughts about the unavoidable challenges of my plan. But the two lawyers, my bosses, after all, had used their persuasive talents until I'd agreed to attend the meeting.

I spent three days deciding what to wear, which was not a sign of the confident Georgia shining through. I settled on black slacks and matching wool blazer, set off with a white blouse. Professional, but as long as I was going to be at what could be a long meeting, I wanted to be comfortable, too, so I could enjoy the evening.

From the way Sarah took my arm when I arrived and led me around, introducing me as her old friend to the gathering crowd, it was as if she'd been waiting for me to arrive. So many people. Did they all work in shops on the Square? It was exciting, somehow, knowing I was a part of this community, which was more than welcoming. I already knew how talented these men and women were, too. Sarah soon had to leave me on my own to convene and run the meeting. That was okay, because I was enjoying my conversation with Megan Reynolds, Elliot's sister.

When a wave of sadness hit, I knew why. I'd pushed Elliot away, but seeing him in the room, it hurt to know how much I would have enjoyed being with him. Maybe now that I'd located Lily—a start, anyway—it was time for me to confide in Elliot, tell him the real reasons I'd come back to Wolf Creek.

I spotted Jack and Liz across the room. They already knew most everyone in the association. But I didn't see Nathan. When Jack happened to glance around and saw me, he made his way through the crowd to come to my side.

"So glad you're here," he said. "Nathan called and said that Toby wasn't feeling good and he didn't want to leave him with the baby sitter."

"Oh, well, I hope it isn't anything serious." Once again, Toby wasn't well—and it all sounded vague. Was this a trend? Something I needed to worry about?

When Sarah stood at the podium, her first job involved adjusting the mic to a lower position. She'd always been petite and looked even smaller behind the podium. She tapped the mic to get everyone's attention. "Will you all take a seat, please? I'd like to get the meeting started."

Liz buzzed across the room to join Jack and me, pointing to chairs where we could easily see Sarah.

Sarah had such an easy way about her, quickly welcoming everyone, the established folks, as she called them, and the newcomers. That was Jack and me, but I assumed there were other recent arrivals.

"Okay, all you shop owners, please stand up and introduce yourselves. Let's make sure we all know each other."

Surprisingly, I either knew or had been introduced to most everyone. Those whose names I didn't know were still familiar faces, mostly from being around the Square or from mid-morning jaunts to Biscuits and Brew. I still tried to avoid Elliot early in the morning, but I often went out for a muffin or donut by mid-morning.

Jack did a fine job for Country Law, introducing me as their right hand person. When I stood, Elliot waved in subtle acknowledgement of me. Jack apologized for Nathan's absence, but didn't offer a reason he wasn't there. Instead, he invited everyone present to stop in and meet Nathan and chat with all of us.

Sarah asked a couple of people to hand out a schedule for the summer festivals and activities. I scanned the list, wondering who was supplying the energy for all the events. Between the Memorial Day commemoration and the Founders' Day Festival, and those were only the beginning, the next several weeks were going to be busy around the Square.

I couldn't stop thinking about how different my life was now that I was back in Wolf Creek. Being in Milwaukee hadn't brought out this desire, this yearning, to change my life—and change myself—for the better. I hadn't known how much I needed a community to call my own. My life had been so limited in Milwaukee, although it wasn't something I thought about much during those years. My job there had kept me busy—I'd made sure of that—but it had also kept my mind off Wolf Creek and what might have been.

I sat in the meeting listening to Sarah and considered my sense of loneliness and isolation, not brought on by anyone else, but because I was being secretive. I thought about Toby and Nathan, and, of course, Elliot. Yes, I needed to move my plan along.

The day after the meeting, I visited Miles and stayed longer than I'd planned. But it took a while to tell him about moving his office to the Square, and with so many scheduled events, how busy we all hoped the Square would soon be. Then I had to tell him about moving the furniture and meeting Rachel and Thomas. Finding Lily's pink box was big, very big.

I wanted Uncle Miles to understand my goal was for Lily to come home and be with her family. I held out hope that she and Beverly and I would find our way back to each other and once again be a family. Besides, I whispered to Uncle Miles, I didn't want Lily to repeat my life, and from the look of it, that's exactly what she was on track to do. Like me, she apparently thought that staying out of sight meant no one would think about her either.

I expected that Miles might become agitated with my news. Yet, when I said Lily's name, he seemed to exhibit a calmness I hadn't seen on previous visits. Finally, I was done talking. I'd worn myself out. I patted Uncle Miles' hand and made the long walk down the hall to the exit and the parking lot, dreading the trip home.

I thought I was too tired to think anymore about Lily and my plan. But on the drive home I made a decision, and it felt right. My next step was to ask Nathan about Toby and how their relationship came to be.

May
7

Itacked Sarah's summer schedule onto the cork board we'd hung above the coffeemaker. Since it was my job to keep the office running smoothly I figured that was the best place for it since we all trekked to the coffeepot to fill our cups. I'd learned one thing about both Jack and Nathan. Like me, the two liked their coffee.

With the schedule staring us in the face, no one could offer a feeble excuse about not knowing that this or that meeting was scheduled or that lines would be longer at Biscuits and Brew because of a festival or other event. Well, we'd try it, anyway, and see what happened.

I tried not to laugh at Jack and Nathan's expressions in response to my announcement that I'd be posting notices on the board regularly. Oh, so very different than Milwaukee, where a notice of an event was viewed as an opportunity to see and be seen and maybe advance a career. But days passed when I never once thought of that big office in that big city. The transformation was nearly complete, and I was becoming the hometown girl coming home.

The next morning a soft rain fell from a layer of pewter colored clouds hanging over Wolf Creek Square. Rivulets of large water drops traveled down the panes of the front window. Although it was a month late the adage of April showers bringing May flowers made me smile. Out of nowhere, some short stanzas of the old song "Singing in the Rain" popped into my head and I sang like pro.

While I didn't usually mind a short walk in the rain, I was

meeting Sarah after work for dinner and didn't want to walk home alone after dark. I'd never been afraid of the dark, but after living in Milwaukee and hearing nearly daily reports of attacks and robberies, I'd learned to be cautious. One of my colleagues at the law firm had been mugged when she'd found herself isolated on a dark street. She hadn't planned to end up in a dangerous situation, but it had happened all the same. I felt pretty secure in Wolf Creek, but I didn't want to become a statistic either.

Sarah had invited me to her apartment above the Mayor's office. I was happy about that because I wanted to see how my friend lived. I knew she didn't spend much time shopping or cooking. She laughed and nodded when I said that going out for meals was becoming an everyday event for me and I wondered why I even moved my pots and pans and baking dishes.

I drove the two blocks and parked my car in the lot behind Country Law. I prided myself on coming in a few minutes early to start the coffee brewing and arranging the files that Nathan and Jack would need for the day. My days offered such challenges and excitement that it occurred to me I hadn't enjoyed being at work and focused this much in a long time—years, actually. Plus, they needed me, and I'd managed to turn the once chaotic office into a smooth-running machine. But maybe I was the only one who consciously noticed the change.

Only yesterday, Jack complained that the senior partners from the Richard Connor Law Firm in Green Bay still contacted him about leaving and wasting his expertise in corporate law. Nathan refused to be drawn into the conversation. I, too, withheld my comments. Nathan probably said nothing because he wanted to stay silent about his own life. He still hadn't explained why he had left the Green Bay firm, but anytime I mentioned Toby and his grandfather Nathan became very quiet.

In my car at the end of the day, I rounded the corner by the new Farmer Foods store and parked behind the mayor's office. The familiar mix of emotions came back when I was saddened that the back of the new grocery store had no windows, but relieved that I could avoid seeing Elliot, or him seeing me. Nothing, it seemed could stop my mind from traveling directly to Elliot. Where did I want him in my life? I knew I couldn't wait until Lily came back home to see Elliot again. That was fool's thinking, especially since I had no assurance that Lily would agree to come back to Wolf Creek again. My happiness to be home for good didn't mean our small town was the right place for her. I had to face that reality.

After parking the car, I took the time to walk by the front of the buildings on the east end of the Square. The Wolf Creek Museum was the first building kitty-corner from the Inn. I peered in the window and found rows of displays of heritage items that piqued my interest. I needed to take an hour off and visit this historical place soon. I walked past the mayor's office toward the last building on that end of the Square. I remembered it being vacant when I was a youngster and the older kids, always looking for ways to scare the younger ones, spun tales about it being haunted. We even indulged in bets as a way to entice other kids to go into that house on Halloween. I smiled to myself. If my memory was correct, no one ever took the bets. I wondered if anyone had rented this building or if it had remained empty all these years.

I walked back to the building on the Square where Sarah's office was located. The small bell jingled as I opened the door. I'd noticed that each shop, at least those I had been in so far, had a similar bell. As Nathan said, the bells made a "happy sound."

"Oh, Georgia, welcome to my small part of the Square," Sarah said, grinning and looking exuberant. "I was just confirming *three* bus tours of day trips to the Square in July." She came out from behind her desk and wrapped her arms around me. "Isn't that wonderful? To see the Square so popular again?"

"We'll be busy at Country Law, too. That's for sure." I paused. "At least I hope so." I didn't really know if the small firm would be busy. As she'd mentioned earlier, we had no product to sell, and buses bringing flocks of tourists probably wouldn't have a huge impact on us.

Sarah moved to the front door and turned the lock. "Enough for today." A few clicks of the light switches left the office space in a soft glow from the antique street lights outside. She opened a pocket door near the back of the room that revealed a stairway. With a swoop of her arm she invited me up to her "humble abode."

The flight of stairs ended at the opening to her apartment.

"Oh, Sarah. This is beautiful." Antique furniture—family heirlooms, I presumed—gave the room a historical feel, but not in a museum-like or stuffy way. In her unique, feminine style, she'd mixed the old pieces with present day amenities, like her television and an open laptop on a small desk. Her microwave and coffee maker nestled in the corner of the kitchen-dining area. I continued to walk around the small apartment to see what made my friend's home comfortable.

Two closed doors were probably the bedroom and bath. I didn't want to ask to see her bedroom, but I'd bet there was an antique suite in there, too.

"When did you move up here? And, for that matter, when did you become mayor? I've wanted to ask you that before, but every time I thought of it we were talking about something else."

Sarah grinned and put her finger on her temple. "Hmm... let me think. It must be about five years ago now."

"That's a long time in elected office," I said, also thinking that she'd taken office shortly after I'd left.

She shrugged. "No one wanted to take on renewing the concept of the Square in order to keep the town vital. But then I thought, my family started the town, so why not me?"

"And look where you and the town are now?"

"Yes, I love every minute of it." She laughed and rolled her eyes. "Well, almost. There's always someone or something trying to mess up the works."

As she set the table she continued to describe her first couple of years as mayor, stopping only to pour a generous amount of wine into extra tall stemmed glasses.

"Seems like we both enjoy our wine, don't we?" I held the glass up to the light. "Family crystal?"

"A few years ago I made a promise to myself. If I have to store the family heirlooms I'm going to use them. The museum is full of family stuff and there is no relative on the horizon who is the least bit interested in them."

"No one?" I asked in surprise. "Your family is huge."

"Truthfully, I have cousins and nieces, grown women now, but they're not interested, at least at the moment. When I point out they could have their pick, they just keep saying 'maybe later.'"

I'd seen a Crossroads bag on the counter earlier and smelled a delicious aroma escaping from her oven. She started brewing a pot of coffee and then pulled individual salads from the refrigerator, one for each of us. She motioned for me to sit and pulled out a chair for herself.

I unwound from my day as Sarah and I brought up old times and mixed the conversation with talk of things going on in town and the busy season ahead for the Square. We laughed as we traveled back to the time when we'd both liked Bob Sawyer. And that led us to reminiscing about our crush on the science teacher, Mr. Colbert. Sarah exchanged our salad plates for dinner plates and served chicken cordon blue and a baked potato. Green beans with almonds added a touch of color to our meal.

The more we talked, the more we laughed, and the safer I felt, which led me to conclude that we'd renewed our friendship to the point where I could tell her about finding the pink box and Lily's address and phone number. We'd made it past the break I'd created with my runaway behavior six years ago. I trusted her now and when I was ready to tell it, my story would be safe with her.

Suddenly, a smug grin took over Sarah's expression. She rose from her chair and picked up a thick folder from the top of her desk.

"I probably know the most about the history of Wolf Creek, so last year I decided to write a book about our town," she said, putting the folder on the table between us.

"I've read the brochure you did. The one that's available at Biscuits and Brew. Very nice."

She pushed the folder toward me, shyly. I'd noticed

a reticence about her when we talked about her writing. It surprised me because she was usually so bold about expressing her ideas.

"I know you like history," she said, "and I'd like you to read this section for me. There's no rush. I'm far from being ready to organize the different sections."

"Oh, that will be fun." I held the folder close to my chest before resting it in front of me. I rubbed my hands together to show how eager I was to get started. And it was time for me to head home. It had been a long time since I'd felt so at ease with anyone that my emotions got the better of me, to the point I ended up stammering when I said good night.

A few minutes later, I was home, checking messages on my phone. I was always a little apprehensive when I pushed the "playback" button, never knowing when the nursing home would call about Uncle Miles. I was surprised that Nathan had called and asked me to come into the office an hour earlier the next day. What could he want?

I readied the coffee maker for morning, finished my evening routine, and then settled into bed anxious to begin reading Sarah's manuscript. I wanted to learn more about my community and who could ask for a better teacher than the mayor.

***

1851
CRAWFORD FREIGHT LINE

For three years Asa and Eleanor Hutchinson had encouraged travelers that rode their stagecoaches to consider relocating and becoming part of the growing community of Wolf Creek.

Their efforts were rewarded.

Each summer more homes and businesses enlarged the small community. Residents and shopkeepers alike waited patiently as crews of workmen built their homes and stores—or added on rooms and space to expand.

The Crawford family was at the center of all this construction. John Crawford, his wife, Mabel, and their sons, Keith, Sam, and Jacob worked tirelessly to bring lumber from sawmills in Wausau and building materials from the surrounding communities to the new town. Quarried stone for fireplaces and bricks for homes came from Green Bay.

Everyone agreed that the Crawford Freight Line, with their wagons and teams of draft horses had been instrumental in making Asa's dream—the community of Wolf Creek—a reality.

JOHN CRAWFORD—FATHER

John was at the freight office long before dawn to check each team that would be pulling a load that day. A loose shoe or weak harness could delay a shipment or injure an animal. The Crawfords' pride centered on good service for a fair price and prompt delivery.

As darkness faded into a bright sunrise the boys arrived to begin another day of hauling.

John addressed his sons. "Sam, Asa's going to ride with you to Green Bay and he asked if you'd help Eleanor with her horses when you get back."

Jacob jabbed his brother's ribs. "You'd rather work for her than us anyway."

"No argument from me, little brother." Sam punched Jacob's shoulder.

"Jacob, quit stalling. Get this grain to the miller in Wausau. There's a load of lumber at Pittman's sawmill to bring back."

"Sure, Pop." Jacob climbed aboard the wagon and clicked his team to start them pulling the heavy load of wheat.

Sam waved to his dad and turned the team pulling his wagon to head east. He'd stop at the relay station for Asa and let Eleanor know he'd be back later in the afternoon. Maybe she'd have one of her sweet biscuits for him this morning.

"Keith, come inside. We need to talk." The son followed his father into the small office of the freight station. John poured coffee for the two of them and motioned for Keith to sit. John sat in the chair at the small desk.

"Son, one of you boys needs to learn more about this business than hauling." He stopped for a swallow of the strong, black brew he'd poured. "You're the oldest. I think it should be you." John leaned back in his chair. "I'm old and tired, son."

Even Keith later said he wondered if his father sensed what was coming. The following winter, John Crawford died; the next summer Mabel followed him. John from pneumonia and, some said, Mabel from loneliness.

The Crawford Freight Line continued for many years. Their descendants continue to live in Wolf Creek today.

***

I set the pages aside and wondered if the Charlie Crawford who'd done the remodeling at Country Law was part of that same family. It seemed likely so. Maybe when I read the next section I'd find out. But satisfying my curiosity would have to wait. I wanted to be rested for tomorrow's early start. I had trouble relaxing, though, thinking about Nathan's call. For all the sleep I got, I might as well have stayed up and read more of Sarah's book.

***

Nathan was already in his office when I arrived the following morning. Jack sat across from him in one of the client's chairs, and both had their favorite cups filled with the dark roast blend we all enjoyed.

"Get yourself some coffee, but don't unlock the front door yet," Nathan said. "Better not to have interruptions this morning."

My insides tightened. What could be so serious that we needed a special early meeting? I hurried to fill my cup and get another pot brewing. As I passed my desk I grabbed my notepad and pen. Jack had moved to the other visitor's chair so I sat in the one closest to the office door. The warmth of the coffee in the mug brought a degree of comfort, but not enough to settle my nerves.

Nathan looked directly at me when he took a breath and spoke. "When I first talked with Miles about partnering with him in Wolf Creek I didn't know how my life was going to change so dramatically in the months to come."

I cut my eyes to Jack to catch his reaction, but if had one, he didn't show it. His passive expression was so lawyerly. Maybe he knew what Nathan was talking about or maybe he, too, was hearing this for the first time.

"Let me give you a short version of a very long, unpleasant story concerning my family," Nathan said, frowning and sending the chair on an almost imperceptible nervous swivel. "It's important to me that you understand why I asked you to come in early this morning."

I nodded in acknowledgment.

"You know my father, Richard Connor. But what you might not be aware of is his desire to control everything, his family as well as his business." He tightened his mouth. "He even controlled my mother to the point that she didn't seek further medical treatment after her leukemia diagnosis." He paused. "It's hard to say this, but he sent her off to an institution to die."

Nathan's memory sent a chill through me. I fought the urge to reach across the desk and make a physical connection to show my support. But the way he sat back in his chair and avoided looking at either Jack or me, told me such a gesture wouldn't be welcome, at least not at the moment. As he took a swallow or two of coffee, I wondered if he was going to tell us more, maybe about Toby.

"My father had two sons," he said, as if reading my mind, "and neither fulfilled his expectations. He wanted a grandson, but my brother and his wife couldn't have children. I wasn't married, and my father was an impatient man, so he arranged to get a child for them."

Oh, Nathan. If you only knew.

"Last November, my brother and sister-in-law were killed in a car accident during an early November ice storm."

Someone knocked on the front door, and we all looked at the Nathan's office door. But no one made a move to answer it.

Nathan continued as if he hadn't heard the interruption. "Richard expected to become Toby's legal guardian, but to everyone's surprise, mostly mine, my brother had made me his legal guardian if anything were to happen to them. And against the odds, something did happen and took them both."

Jack must have known some of this story because he got up and returned with the carafe from the coffeemaker and refilled our cups. Then he left again, but when he came back, he had a legal pad in hand.

"My father hasn't been careful about talking in front of Toby," Nathan said, "and that's led to confrontations. That's partly why I wanted to leave my father's firm."

"I understand," I said. *Did I ever.*

"My greatest concern was—and is—Toby's health. He became withdrawn and listless. I thought it was grief from losing his parents and his insecurity. I mean, with his parents gone, who could he count on?"

Nathan stopped to take another swallow from his mug.

"Yesterday his doctor called and wanted to see him in the afternoon. That's why I left early."

He explained this while looking at me as if he had to account for his time.

I tilted my head. "Well, then, time off excused." My remark broke some of the tension that had built, but Nathan checked his watch, took a huge breath and got back to his story.

"This is the worst of it," Nathan said, half-closing his eyes. "Toby has a genetic disease called polycystic kidney disease. The kidney gets filled with cysts, which keeps it from functioning properly." He stared at his hands, obviously needing a minute with his thoughts before continuing. "It'll only get worse. He's looking at dialysis and…I've learned that he may need a transplant—soon."

"Transplant?" I echoed.

Nathan nodded. "Toby's illness explains his listlessness, but sudden sadness or dreams wake him in the night. He misses his mother still—and his dad, too. He talks about both of them less now. Maybe the memories are fading, but some nights, he wakes up asking where they are."

"I'm so sorry he's gone through such a trauma." I shook my head. "And now he has to cope with an illness, too. It's too much."

Jack stood again and walked behind my chair and circled to the back of the desk. He put his hand on Nathan's shoulder. "Whatever you need, Nathan, we're here to help. Georgia, we know you have taken on a larger role in this office than we first described, but we'll need you even more now. Nathan's focus has to be Toby."

"I'm not leaving. I wouldn't even consider it." *And for reasons I can't even talk about.* I checked my watch and stood. It was past time to open Country Law for the day.

Nathan rose from the chair, too, and extended his hand. It seemed formal, but we shook hands like we'd made a deal.

"Thank you, Georgia."

I was sure Nathan could have told me much more about Richard and Toby. But did I really need to know more? What mattered was getting Toby the medical help he needed.

And locating Lily.

I hurried to unlock the office door, spotting Elliot sitting on the bench at the end of the Square. My insides jingled like the bell on the door. The man took my breath away. That's all there was to it. He stood and came across the walkway.

"Another beautiful day in Wolf Creek, isn't it?" Did my

voice reveal my bad case of the jitters?

He hung back on the top step, almost as if he'd changed his mind. "Are…are you free for lunch today? I want to show you the new store before we open it to the public."

"Why?"

He backed down one step and that put us eye to eye. A tinge of pink circled his neck.

I almost laughed. But I didn't. Instead, my body moved forward and with Elliot a step below me, we were closer to standing directly face-to-face. Giving no thought to where we were or who would see us, I kissed him. And no little peck on the cheek either, but a full-blown, I-love-you kind of kiss.

"Do we need a new ordinance about public displays of affection on the Square?"

I'd recognize Jack's voice anywhere and now it was my turn to blush.

Elliot bounced down the steps—all three of them—and yelled back over his shoulder, "I'll pick you up at noon." He took off in a quick jog down the walkway toward Farmer Foods. Now I did laugh—to myself. With his lean, athletic build, he looked like a teenager taking off down the Square, and I felt like I'd been caught in the act of kissing a boy.

Without looking at Jack, I stepped back into the office and took a deep breath. "Okay, Mr. Pearson, you have Mrs. Wilson coming at 10:30. I have her file ready for you." I walked to my desk and handed the folder to him.

I'd never tried to deny the reality that I still carried deep feelings for Elliot, not that I'd say that out loud, especially not to Beverly, and not even to Uncle Miles. But, oh, how I wished our past had traveled down a smoother road. When I kissed him, I'd followed an impulse dictated by my heart. But now what?

I had no time to answer my own question, and the morning passed quickly with phone calls, emails, clients coming for meetings and the three of us rescheduling appointments to make Nathan's workload lighter. As work-oriented as I'd always been, I was able to stay focused on the day's activities, but inside, my body danced with excitement about my lunch date with Elliot. I must have been smiling like a Cheshire cat because Jack frequently glanced at me and shook his head, and I think he was trying very hard not to smile.

As noon approached the jingle of the doorbell drew my attention. Since I expected Elliot to show up any minute I was surprised to see a woman come inside. I'd seen her once or twice at Biscuits and Brew, but couldn't place her or her name. If I was going to be the "face" of Country Law I needed to do better about matching faces with names.

This time I was saved from having to greet her and introduce myself and hope she'd do the same. Instead, she barreled into her purpose for coming in before I could say anything.

"Last year it was Marianna Spencer and Art Carlson showing their…their affection on the Square. Now it's you and that food man."

My mind raced in its search. Who was this woman?

"I'm sorry, but I haven't been here long, so I don't know you." I turned away and took a couple of steps toward the chairs in the reception area and extended my hand to indicate she could take a seat. "Would you like some coffee?"

She didn't sit. "I don't have time for that. My name is Doris Parker and I own Pages." She turned to point toward the location of her store, on the corner beyond Quilts Galore.

I finally put the face and the name together, also recalling Liz and Marianna mentioning Doris' frank and loud disapproval of Rachel having Thomas. But they laughed it off, too, assuring me that Doris didn't approve of much of anything.

"The Square is a place for business, not courtship…if that's what you want to call it. Just so you know, I'll be talking to Sarah about this."

"I apologize if I offended you." Now it was my turn to suppress a smile. I tried to be contrite knowing that Sarah had given Country Law a special waiver to be on the Square. But I doubted my old friend would see the kissing incident as critical to the integrity of the Square.

"See that it doesn't happen again." With that, she opened

the door and sent the bell jingling. When she left, she pulled the door closed with a little extra force than needed.

Whew! One little kiss and the whole Square was abuzz. Well, okay, it wasn't so little. More like a kiss that promised a little romance. Definitely not a peck…*stop this!*

The bell jingled again with Elliot's arrival. "Ready, Peaches?"

"Did you see Doris just now?" My cheeks warmed. "She *scolded* me for kissing you in public. Can you imagine that?"

"Yeah, I sure can," he said with a smirk. "So, do you want to upset her again?"

I laughed at his cocky reply.

"Doris is the thorn of the Square," he said with a shrug. "She's always complaining about something, but at least she's not vicious or hurting anyone."

As we walked past Rainbow Gardens I waved to Megan working on a Memorial Day display in her front window. So far, it had red, white and blue flowers and patriotic bunting.

Elliot's stride became longer the closer we got to the building at the corner of the Square, where a temporary banner announcing the "New Farmer Foods" hung in the window. Alongside it was another sign saying "Opening Soon."

I wanted to ask him a million questions about the expansion. When did they decide? Why? Did Eli agree? But when he opened the door for me to enter, none of that mattered. I was with Elliot and he beamed with excitement and pride. He was about to show me his new store.

"You are the first non-worker to be here, Peaches." He switched on a bank of overhead lights and brought the store to life. I could picture the fruits and vegetables enhanced by the spotlights placed over the produce bins, the bright light sure to entice shoppers to buy.

His enthusiasm bubbled as he gave me a tour around the store, describing each area in detail. He explained the way he planned to display the various items, how the store was designed so that each area flowed into the next, and that one section was created solely for locally grown and produced foods.

Elliot slipped his hand in mine as we circled back to the front door. "I'm glad you're back, Georgia. We've been apart way too long. So, whether you're ready or not, I'm going to be part of your life."

Then it was his turn to be bold, giving me a million butterfly kisses as I melted against his strong body. This was where I belonged.

I heard the door behind me open and I stepped back and looked over my shoulder. There stood Eli, his expression as icy as the freezers in the storeroom.

I grinned at Elliot, but quickly glanced away. "It's time I got back to work. Never a dull moment at the office."

Once out the door, I almost ran back to the safety of Country Law. I got right to work and spent a fairly quiet afternoon organizing files that Jack would need the next day. Nathan had already planned to stay home with Toby, which left Jack with a jammed morning schedule, mostly appointments with old clients of Miles that were being transitioned into the new practice.

So far, we'd been successful in contacting everyone connected with Miles' current cases. Most expressed gratitude that Nathan and Jack had jumped in so quickly to give them the kind of service Country Law needed to become known for. The firm would never be able to compete with larger city firms, so personalized service, and even the atmosphere on the Square, were the elements we needed to tout.

By the time I went home, I was weary, but oddly content. My emotional battle about Elliot was over, for the time being anyway. He was going to be part of my life. What part remained to be seen. A few kisses didn't make us a duo, or that's what I told myself.

Regardless of what Elliot said, I wasn't ready to let him dominate my thoughts. Not when Uncle Miles needed me. Every visit, I noticed Miles showing increasing signs of decline. Although his day-to-day care was in the capable hands of the nursing home staff, he was always in my thoughts. Meanwhile, I'd taken pride in organizing the

Country Law office. I had to keep Elliot separate from all that—and more.

I'd come to Wolf Creek with a plan. Now I needed to take the next step. Toby's serious illness reinforced my determination. Despite the pleasant day I'd had, one word kept coming in my mind and I couldn't shake it off... *transplant, transplant.* Sitting alone in my bedroom, the work day behind me—and without Elliot or anyone else around—I retrieved the small piece of paper from the pink box. Then I dialed Lily's phone number.

8

A soft feminine voice answered with a simple, "Hello?" I didn't have a response. I'd expected the call to go to voice mail. Hearing her voice made my heart stop and stutter into the next beat.

Oh, Lily. I've found you.

"Hello. Uh, please don't hang up. I'm not a telemarketer. I'm looking for Lily Winters. I'm her Aunt Georgia."

"What's my uncle's name?" she shot back.

"Miles. His name is Miles Owen." I couldn't get the words out without stumbling on them. I swallowed hard. "Miles Owen…from Wolf Creek, Wisconsin."

"And my mother's name?"

"*Beverly.* Oh, Lily. I've really found you." The tears gathered ready to spill.

"Is it really you Aunt Georgia?" Her tone had changed from flat to breathless. "And how is Uncle Miles? It's been so long since I talked with him."

"Uncle Miles is sick, honey. He's had a stroke. I think you should come home to see him."

First, the click, then the dial tone.

Frantic, I redialed her number. She didn't answer, nor did her voice mail activate.

Now what? I mentally kicked myself for rushing it—pushing her too fast.

I had to search for her. I got this far, and I wouldn't let it go. But with all I had going on at Country Law, especially Nathan and Toby's situation, I couldn't ask for time off to drive to Madison to begin a search for Lily. And I admitted to myself that I didn't want to leave Wolf Creek. Yes, I'd reconnected with Elliot, but if I left again, especially without explanation, could I ever again mend things between us?

I decided I'd keep calling with the hope that she would eventually answer.

***

A few days after reaching Lily, I sat in my car across the street from Beverly's house. I took the chance that she would see me even though I hadn't called ahead. As her car approached I took in a breath and left my car, timing it so I would meet her in the driveway.

I doubted she would agree with or lend support to my plan, but I was done with family secrets. We were sisters, after all, not strangers.

She surprised me when she wordlessly opened her house door and gestured me to follow her inside. But she didn't ask me to sit down. She folded her arms across her chest and said, "What do you want?"

Nothing like gracefully easing into the conversation.

"I want to tell you about our family." My fingers drummed on the counter and to settle them I clutched my purse to my chest. I'd debated a long time on what news I would tell her first, and somehow, going down the generational line seemed the best way.

"Miles? Did he die?"

Surprised by her flat tone, I said, "No. Why would you ask that?"

"Why else would you come here?"

I ignored her rhetorical question and an angry tone that sounded forced to me. She looked sad, defeated. It broke my heart. "Uncle Miles is weaker—and getting weaker every day. But he's getting good care at the nursing home."

Staring into the space of the living room, Beverly sighed. "I'm tired, Georgia." She paused, looking deep in thought as she stared past me. "But tell me your news. Then you can go."

"Okay then," I said, my spirit lifting a little. Maybe she

was softening, willing to admit her interest. "You should know that my boss, Nathan Connor, is Toby's guardian."

So much for making a plan.

Beverly froze in place, her eyes wide open, like a frightened animal. "You've seen him? Toby?"

"Yes, and he's quite a little boy," I said softly. "But he's sick, Beverly. His kidneys are failing."

I saw her eyes instantly soften, but she lifted her chin and tightened her mouth. "And how does that concern me?"

Oh, please. Ignoring her *supposed* lack of compassion or even curiosity, I went on. "I found Lily's phone number and address in Uncle Miles' house. You see, I'm living in the house now. I found a box with all the letters Lily had written to him."

Beverly still hadn't moved, so I kept talking before she changed her mind about my presence in her house.

"I called her, but she hung up when I asked her to come back to Wolf Creek. I never got a chance to tell her about Toby. But, Beverly, she absolutely needs to know what's going on with her son."

"He's not her son anymore. She ran away. Remember?"

What nonsense. And look where it got us. "As I remember it, you made it too miserable for her to stay."

"Dumped her kid on Mom is what she did."

I raised my arms in frustration, finally letting it show. "What else could she do? You wouldn't help her."

Here it was again, the old argument we'd had so many times. Always with the same result. Neither of us would, or could, back down from our entrenched position, although Beverly's expression was less hostile than I'd seen since I'd been back. This news about Toby could open the door that our mistakes had slammed shut long ago.

I stared at the carpet, old and worn out, just like our fight with each other. "Look, I just wanted you to know that I contacted Lily and that Toby is sick. He may need a kidney transplant."

One part of me wanted to suck the words back into my mouth, knowing I might have overstepped Nathan's confidential information about Toby. But I also doubted

Beverly would tell anyone. Isolated and secretive as she was, who would she tell?

I turned toward the door. "I'll leave you alone now."

I walked down the driveway with a heavier heart than I'd come with.

***

The frustrating conversation with Beverly stayed with me, along with an underlying sadness over the state of my family. Then, under a bright blue sky dotted with fluffy clouds, many citizens of Wolf Creek, including most of the Square's shopkeepers, gathered with a purpose tinged with a different kind of sadness. We had come together to honor one of our own, a local young man killed in Iraq. Sarah had made a point of asking the owners to be present for the memorial service, and I'd volunteered to purchase small flags for us to carry during the ceremony. Nathan planned to bring Toby, and Jack added that Liz would be coming to the Square, too, because she planned to help out at Quilts Galore during the busiest shopping hours of the holiday weekend.

I'd whined a bit—only to myself—about having to show up alone, but Elliot called and rescued me. We agreed to meet at the ring of flagpoles by the stage set up for Saturday morning's event. Although the new Farmer Foods would officially open its doors to the public on Monday, Memorial Day, they delayed the planned grand opening celebration, so they wouldn't pull attention away from the soldier's memorial.

I pulled on a cardigan sweater to keep out the chilly morning breeze. The sun was great, but it was much cooler than expected for late May. Still, I don't think Elliot held my hand throughout the ceremony to keep us warm. He got too big a kick out of antagonizing Doris, even waving our clasped hands at her when she walked past us.

Weeks ago, I'd given up any attempt to stay quietly in the background, but on the other hand, I didn't want to flaunt my relationship with Elliot at such a solemn event. I jabbed him in the ribs and told him to behave. He kissed my forehead in response to my reprimand—or maybe he was reacting to Doris' sour look.

We all settled down when the young soldier's dad, a tall, broad-shouldered man, spoke in a proud, resigned voice about his son and the family's sacrifice. And most of his words expressed the joy his son took from serving in the military. He nodded to acknowledge the honor guard representing every branch of the military, and he noted the local high school band that provided the opening music—rousing Sousa marches. I smiled at Toby, sitting up on Nathan's shoulders and clapping to the rhythm of the melodies. Well, sort of to the rhythm. He wasn't half-bad for a six-year-old.

When the ceremony ended, people wandered away to various locations in the Square, many off to grab coffee at Biscuits and Brew. The only people in an obvious hurry were the shopkeepers who scurried this way and that toward their stores. This weekend marked the official opening of Wolf Creek Square's summer season.

I shooed Elliot back to Farmer Foods after he'd rattled off the million little ends to tie up before Monday. After organizing Country Law, I knew that small details, like arranging file drawers that no one saw, were as important as obvious things like the reception area and even new clients' first impression of me.

I'd made no plans for myself for the day except to do some people-watching and enjoy the atmosphere. And I intended to become a Square shopper myself.

Since Beverly had agreed—and without hesitation—to transfer ownership of our old house from Miles to me, I was free to get some things to make the place feel like my home. I still felt like a visitor somehow and I wanted to change that.

On the day I arrived in Wolf Creek, Jessica had invited me to come to Styles and have a look at the clothing she and her business partner, Mimi, offered. So feeling upbeat, I headed that way, and in the mood for a new blouse or a summery tunic, if one caught my eye.

With Country Law up and running and Uncle Miles' situation settled for the moment, I was enjoying a little time to myself. I left Elliot to tend to his details, and headed to Country Law to grab my purse and start my trek around the Square. As I approached what I'd begun to think of as Elliot's bench I saw a young lady sitting there.

My heart soared. I knew.

It was Lily.

I ran the last few steps. I had to be sure it was her. When she looked up, those dark blue eyes—Owen eyes—removed any doubt.

"Lily?" I fought the impulse to rush up and hug her and tell her all the news in one breath. But I held back. We'd been separated for so many years I didn't know if Lily would welcome that kind of approach.

When she saw me, she stood and slowly inched back, as fear and doubt flashed in her eyes.

"Lily?" I tried again. "It's Aunt Georgia."

Ah, at last, a smile emerged. That same quirky smile that had pulled love from my heart and sent it her way. That was true even when there had been so little love coming from her mother.

With a sweep of her arms she gathered me into a hug, holding on a little bit longer, and tighter, than I'd expected.

"I'm sorry I hung up on you," she said. "I just couldn't handle the bad news about Uncle Miles' stroke."

"Want to tell me about it? Have you eaten today? What has kept you in Madison?"

I wanted to know everything all at once. How she lived, where she lived, friends, girlfriends, boyfriends. Her fingers were free of rings so I jumped to an assumption that no special man had claimed her heart at the moment.

I hustled her across the walkway. I doubted any shoppers would need a lawyer on a Saturday, but with Country Law new on the Square shoppers might stop in. Nathan and Toby planned to come back to the office, and so did Jack. No doubt Liz would stop in before heading to Quilts Galore, so I needed to get Lily off the Square in a hurry.

"Why don't we go to my house and talk? I've got the

makings of pasta salad and a couple of sandwiches." I stopped and stared at her. "Oh, Lily, I can't believe you came home."

"I want to see Uncle Miles."

I tapped my temple with my fingertips. Of course she'd want to see Miles. "He's in a nursing home in Green Bay. We can leave now, stop for lunch, then go see him."

I'd been smiling since I'd seen her on the bench and now my cheeks hurt. But I could handle a little hurt like that every day. I longed to tell Elliot my good news, but I hadn't yet explained Lily and Toby and my part in Toby becoming a member of the Connor family. But if Elliot and I were going to continue our relationship, he had a right to know the story—and my part in it.

I ushered Lily into Country Law and hurried her down the hallway past the offices and out the back door. Only Nathan's and Jack's cars were in the parking area.

"How did you know I'd be at the Square?" I asked, genuinely curious.

Lily shrugged. "I didn't know, but I took a chance. Life doesn't change much in Wolf Creek, Aunt Georgia." She said that in the wise tone the young use when explaining the obvious. "By the way, when did you come back?"

"The end of March. I'd lost my job at the firm in Milwaukee, and Uncle Miles asked me to come help him with his practice."

"Was he ill back then?"

I thought for a minute. "Not really. Didn't seem to be. So far, no one I've asked says he seemed frail or sick before his stroke. And he sounded like himself on the phone."

"Will he know me?"

By now we'd reached my house. Lily had parked her older Ford Focus on the street, close to the same place I'd parked no more than nine weeks ago. How quickly my life had changed.

I passed over her question. Not so much avoiding an answer, but because I didn't know what to say. The doctors and nurses weren't sure how much Miles understood what people around him said. I updated him with town news and various stories, but nothing gave me much indication of what he did or didn't understand. None of the medical staff spoke in encouraging terms either.

We were soon underway and stopped for lunch at the Allouez Café, a big family restaurant near the hospital that never had a long line. After we ordered salads, a Taco for her and a Cobb for me, I explained it was best not to arrive at the nursing home around lunchtime because that was a busy time for the staff.

Once we'd dispensed with pleasantries, our conversation slowed down and became more guarded, and by the time we dug into the salads the waitress delivered, we'd reached an awkward phase. I sighed to myself, resigned to the idea that getting reacquainted would take some time. Lily kept talking in generalities about the drive to Wolf Creek and the cool summer we'd had, again reminding me of the little girl in her grandmother's kitchen and then the young woman telling her family she was pregnant.

"Have you seen my mom?" Lily asked.

She asked. Finally. "I saw her last week." That was that. Never in a million years would I tell Lily about her mother's lack of interest in her. "She hasn't changed much."

"I didn't expect she would have." Lily sat up a little taller in the booth and squared her shoulders. "Guess you'll have to be my mom." A small smile crossed her face.

"Being your aunt is enough for me."

Her smile faded, her expression went blank.

"Oh, Lily, that came out wrong." Another internal sigh. Why had I responded so fast? "What I meant to say is that Beverly is your mother. You can't simply assign that title to someone else."

I paused, noting her expression reflected renewed interest. "You see, hard as it is to accept, I've come to believe that my sister doesn't know how to be a mom. But someday she might change her attitude."

Lily set her fork down and pushed her half-eaten salad aside. "I don't know why I keep hoping."

Food didn't interest me anymore, either. I signaled the waitress for the check. Maybe seeing Uncle Miles would make Lily feel like she was part of a family.

***

Uncle Miles was the same, in bed with a light blanket covering his hospital gown. I didn't know why, but every time I'd entered his room I hoped to see something different.

Lily grabbed a straight back chair and dragged it to his side. If she was shocked by his pale skin, she never let on, but planted a kiss on his forehead before sitting and taking one of his hands into hers. I think I'd been much more surprised by Uncle Miles' appearance than Lily was, and I'd seen the deterioration over the weeks. She spoke to him easily, too. It was as if she visited every day and his diminished capacities didn't change anything.

Every now and then I noted his fingers twitched, but I couldn't tell if it was in response to her presence or was simply an involuntary movement.

Lily's dialogue—or monologue, I guess—with her great-uncle never touched on personal events or feelings, like losing Toby or her mother's lack of interest. Maybe she would have said more if I hadn't been in the room. But she stumbled for words only when she recounted memories of the two of them together. Finally, after almost forty-five minutes, her conversation winding down, Lily glanced at her watch.

"Time for me to leave, Uncle Miles. It's a long drive home." She stood and bent over to kiss him goodbye. "You keep those nurses on their toes."

"You're going back to Madison?" I asked, because I thought I must not have heard her correctly.

She shrugged. "I think it's best."

"For who?"

"For all of us." She looked down at her great-uncle, her only uncle.

Uncle Miles made guttural sounds and tightly held her hand until his knuckles turned white. This was new to me. I'd not heard the sound, nor seen him reach out during any of my visits.

"I don't think he agrees." I moved to his other side and

patted his arm, murmuring assurances that everything was fine.

"You want me to stay?" she asked, looking from Miles to me and back again at Miles.

"I think he gave you your answer," I said. "He thinks you'll leave town again, disappear. But you can stay with me."

"Well, okay. I did bring my toothbrush." She smiled and those dark blue eyes danced.

I sensed Lily's life was about a lot more than she'd told Uncle Miles, but I didn't care. I was determined to convince her to at least consider returning to Wolf Creek for good.

"Can you stay for a couple of days?" I pressed.

No answer.

On the drive home, I stopped to pick up a few groceries. Lily, who had been quiet during the ride, chose to stay in the car. But not being ready to answer Elliot's questions, I purposely avoided Farmer Foods. Still, it was up to me to tell him, and Sarah, too, about Lily's return. I needed to do it soon. If Sarah could see me stocking my house with food, she'd tease me about our eating out pact.

As I tossed items into my grocery cart, thoughts of Lily and her future ran through my head and jumbled with images of Toby. And then Beverly entered the picture. But where did I fit in?

Later, sitting out on the porch over coffee, Lily and I talked like roommates. I honestly answered her questions about her grandmother's illness and death, and eventually the conversation came around to Toby.

"I didn't have the means to take care of Toby," I said. "I had to work and support myself. That didn't leave daycare money or any of what a baby would need."

"Mom wasn't of much use, I guess," Lily said.

"She'd taken care of *our* mother for months," I responded, somewhat defensively. Strictly speaking, Toby wasn't my responsibility or even Beverly's. "She was ready to live her own life."

I didn't tell her Beverly and I had received money for Toby. That would have been too shocking, even cruel.

I changed the subject again by linking Uncle Miles' stroke to my new job opportunity with Nathan and Jack.

"I'd like to meet them sometime," Lily said.

I was surprised that she spoke of a future relationship with me. Oh, how that made my heart sing. But then, there was the matter of Toby. I couldn't keep Lily in the dark about him for long.

After settling Lily into bed for the night and watching her nestle under a soft blanket, I called Elliot. I told him a shorthand history of Lily and her weekend visit to Wolf Creek. He didn't press for more detailed explanations. When I asked about the store opening, though, he chattered like a squirrel. My memories of the quiet, reserved man he'd been didn't mesh with this animated, enthusiastic person on the other end of the phone.

He rambled on for awhile before telling me I should get some sleep. "Good night, Peaches. I love you."

All I heard was the dial tone. I tried to calm my racing heart and follow his directions.

***

Over cups of vanilla flavored coffee and store bought muffins Lily and I enjoyed a leisurely Sunday morning. We went from the kitchen to the living room and talked until it was time to head back to the kitchen for a pasta salad lunch.

Earlier, I'd regretted not having plans for the three-day weekend. Not anymore. Lily's arrival had given me renewed energy to convince her to connect with her family. If not with her mother, then at least with me.

By Monday morning Lily had turned my mind into a whirlwind of racing thoughts. Lily had told me about her boyfriend, news in itself, but then she'd found him in bed with her roommate. Now she didn't want to go back to Madison. I liked hearing her talk about wanting more for herself than a low-level job at a tax preparation company and waitressing at a hotel on the weekends to make more money. Without a roommate to share expenses, her money issues would loom even larger.

Years ago, I'd invested my share of the money Beverly and I got for Toby. I'd never used any of it even when at times my own expenses exceeded my salary. I'd decided to save it all to give to Toby someday, if I'd ever found him. That's why it didn't seem right to offer the money to Lily. Instead, I offered another solution to her situation.

"Move to Wolf Creek and live with me. There's plenty of room in the house for both of us. I've heard about two or three shopkeepers on the Square asking around for summer help. That would give you time to think about your future."

"Really? But Aunt Georgia, you don't even know me—not anymore."

My stomach jolted hearing those words. The truth, sadly. "You're family," I said, giving her a mock sidelong glance. "And I bet you don't have a police record or date guys with guns in their waistbands."

A burst of laughter confirmed my assumption.

I scooted to the edge of a couch cushion and extended my hands. "Look, I came back to Wolf Creek when life threw a basket of lemons at me. So why not you?"

I got up to refill our cups from the second pot we'd brewed. "Then you don't have to go back to Madison today or can you wait until after the holiday?"

"I don't need to go back today," she said with a shrug. "Not really."

"Good. We can check the newspaper and the community board and see what jobs are available either in Wolf Creek or right on the Square."

Lily glanced away. "I don't know about this. It's happening so quickly."

"Nonsense." That's what I said, but she had a point. I admitted that my plan was moving ahead faster than I'd prepared for or even hoped.

Two key people still didn't know the truth of my return to Wolf Creek—Lily and Nathan. Oh, that wasn't true. Elliot and Jack, even Sarah deserved a full explanation. And, of course, Toby.

I had a lot of people to talk to and soon.

It was mid-afternoon and the Square was filled with

tourists and shoppers. I took in the sights as I made my way around the shops. I think I burned off some nervous energy by whiling away a couple of hours going in and out of shops. I didn't know exactly how or when, but with Lily's return, many lives were about to change. Not just mine. Maybe I'd been celebrating Lily's homecoming a bit too soon.

The traffic on the Square was winding down when Lily called. She'd made the phone call from her car and sounded excited when she reported that she was on her way back to Madison to give notice to her employers and landlord. I hoped she'd follow through and not change her mind.

June
9

At Country Law we knew many bus tours were scheduled to visit the Square, but we'd assumed that wouldn't have much impact on us. That's why we were surprised by how many casual shoppers took the time to stop in. Only a few people went as far as to ask about our services, but I handed a business card to everyone who came in. My attitude could have been summed up in the phrase, "You never know."

Wolf Creek had a way of growing on people, at least according to what Sarah and Jack had told me. Jack and Liz spoke from experience, of course, being among the newer residents. The town attracted a fair number of retirees who'd found their way to town and had settled right in. No telling when they'd need a lawyer to handle a real estate deal or an estate plan, or new wills and power-of-attorney documents.

As for Elliot, with the opening behind him, he called on Tuesday morning and started the conversation with, "We should have made this move to the bigger space years ago!"

Toward the end of our happy call, I asked him to come to my place for dinner after work. He was busy, but it was truth time. Still, all day, I found myself doing some serious second guessing.

When he arrived, I poured us each a glass of red wine, a good match for the meatloaf dinners I picked up at Crossroads. No muss, no fuss. I didn't want anything to interfere with telling him about my past, and it had to be done before Lily came back.

"This is great, Peaches," Elliot said, grinning. He'd polished off the dinner in no time and leaned back in the chair.

I grinned back, but quickly looked away. I couldn't meet his eye, not yet. "The thing is, we have to talk."

"Hmm…sounds ominous." A crease appeared between his brows.

"It's not just my story, I need to tell," I said. "It's Beverly's and most of all, it's Lily's." I started at the beginning, with Lily seeming like a lost teen, fending for herself.

When I got to the difficult part about agreeing with Beverly to send Toby to a good home, Elliot picked up my hand. He had no idea how painful it was to talk about keeping this kind of secret, how it limited my life. I had trouble looking at him, but he kept his warm fingers holding my hand. Only later, when I explained why I had taken the money and run away was my humiliation complete.

Elliot let go of my hand, at some point. My heart sank when he leaned back in the chair and folded his arms across his chest. I tried to ignore that gesture and keep the story moving forward, desperately getting to the present time, when I had to make a decision. "I have to tell Lily and Nathan."

"You do," he said. "You can't keep these secrets for much longer. Especially not with the boy so ill now." He shook his head and sighed.

"I don't think you could possibly judge me more than I judge myself," I said.

"Ah, Peaches," he said, picking up my hand again, "I'm not judging. It's just that lives are going to change once the information is out. You didn't create this mess all on your own."

I managed a sad smile in response. But then, to think straight, I gave the table a light slap and got to my feet. "Dessert time," I said, pointing to a box on the counter.

I wanted him to understand.

I *needed* him to understand.

But I had a feeling that wouldn't happen all at once.

I slid pieces of strawberry pie onto two plates and sat at

the table again. Then I changed the subject. "I swear this town has more holidays than a greeting card company. So, tell me all about what happens on Founders' Day."

"Big doings around here, Peaches. You and I need to grab a wagon ride. And music all day, and lots of food. And those lawyer guys of yours need to dress up like frontier lawyers."

I laughed at all of Elliot's descriptions, agreeing that I'd certainly be up for a wagon ride, but I resisted the idea that I'd need to look like a prairie lady in what passed for a business suit in the nineteenth century. Nathan probably knew nothing about Founders' Day on the Square, but Jack could probably fill him in.

When we finished our dessert, Elliot carried our plates to the sink and continued to clear the table while I put the food away. Without saying anything, we fell into the rhythm of washing the dishes. I hung the damp dish towel on the rack, but Elliot made no move to leave my side.

"Let me stay close to you, Peaches." His voice was low, almost a whisper.

My throat closed and tears gathered in my eyes, Elliot circled me in his arms and held me tight against his strong body. The muscles in my neck and back eased as a sense of security washed over me. It was as if I'd relaxed for the first time in days—maybe weeks. We didn't need to talk. Our bodies talked for us.

When he left, my house felt empty.

***

Nathan raised an eyebrow when he saw my name as one of the appointments for the day. "Okay," he said, turning to Jack, "will you handle phone calls and walk in clients while Georgia and I talk."

Jack nodded, and I followed Nathan into his office. I closed the door behind me and sat across in the client's chair.

"Uh…what can I do for you today?"

Seconds passed as I stared at my tightly clasped hands. This was going to be much more difficult than I'd imagined. "I have something…what I mean is, I *need* to tell you about

111

my family's relationship to Toby."

His expression darkened, his eyes flickered in fear. "Toby."

It was a statement, not a question.

"Yes. I'm Toby's aunt. My sister, Beverly, is his grandmother."

Nathan leaned forward and rested his arms on his desk. "And that means his mother is…?"

"My niece, Lily."

Nathan jerked his body back, as if needing to widen the distance between us.

"You need to know the whole story."

He gestured with his cup for me to continue.

In as linear—and lawyerly—a manner as I could manage, I relayed who was who in the Owen family and how these relationships involved Toby. Nathan's expression didn't change as he patiently gave me time to explain how I was involved in Toby becoming part of the Connor family.

"It's probably not my business to tell you this, but I hope you'll reconsider your relationship with your father. Richard needs to know about Toby's illness."

He dismissed that idea with a flick of his hand, but I didn't take that seriously. He needed time. We all needed time.

"Here's something else. I contacted Lily and invited her to return to Wolf Creek and live with me. The thing is, this was part of my plan when I came back here. I didn't have any idea about what Miles had arranged with you and Jack."

Nathan turned away, suddenly distracted, or so it seemed. "I see."

Did he?

"There's one more piece of information you need."

Nathan pushed his chair back from the desk, needing even more space separating us.

"Yes?" His voice was low, almost a whisper.

"There was money involved when Richard got Toby." Suddenly I wanted to run from the room, from Country Law, from Wolf Creek.

You did that once before. Remember? And where did that take you?

I expected him to say something. Yell at me? Warn me to stay away from Toby?

"Thank you, Georgia."

His flat tone let me know things had changed between us.

I rose to leave.

"Georgia?"

"Yes?" I waited expectantly, while Nathan stared at the floor.

"I need to be clear with you about something." He cleared his throat. "You said that you were Toby's aunt, and Beverly is his grandmother, and Lily...well."

I frowned, puzzled and eager for him to make his point. It was excruciating to be in the same room with him.

"But Toby is *my* son, not Lily's. You're biologically his aunt, but he doesn't know that and it doesn't matter anyway. You—and your sister—are *not* his family now."

As I listened, I was conscious that this was a dad talking, but he was a lawyer, too. In my best lawyerly voice, I responded. "You're right, Nathan. My family gave up our right to be Toby's family, and yes, he's your son."

I turned to leave, but stopped short of turning the doorknob and opening the door. I gave into the urge to say one more thing. "Your brother and his wife must have loved him a great deal—and now anyone can see how much he means to you. I know it's true, because he's such a special little boy."

I hurried out of his office before he could respond. I spent the rest of the day with a renewed focus on doing my job as efficiently and responsibly as possible, maybe because I didn't know if I'd have my job much longer. Still, if I lost my job, so be it. At least the truth was out. I busied myself sorting through some of the remaining boxes, ultimately bringing order to the chaos of Miles' files. The air was thick around me. I periodically took deep breaths in an attempt to shake off the heavy atmosphere. Nathan spent most of his day behind his closed office door. We barely exchanged another word all day.

Despite staying busy, the hours crawled by, and Nathan and Jack were in Jack's office when I locked the front door and left for the day through the back entrance. I waved to them as I passed Jack's door.

Not wanting to be alone I wandered around the Square debating whether to pick up a sandwich at Biscuits and Brew or get carryout at Crossroads or get in the car and drive to Green Bay and hide out at a movie. I did none of that, but ended up in Sarah's office.

In my mind, I kicked up my resolve to tell her the truth, too. But when I asked if she were free for a quick dinner, she shook her head. "I've got appointments scheduled until 7:00 and a dinner meeting after that."

"Well, then, another time. It was a spur of the moment idea." I forced a grin and waved goodbye.

Late afternoon shadows slanted across the Square. I set out for home.

Alone.

***

When I arrived at the office the following morning I saw Charlie's C4 truck in the parking area. I chuckled to myself when I thought of the explosive C4 and if he'd intended the pun with his company's name, Charlie Crawford's Construction Company.

The door to the upstairs was open when I entered. Men's voices echoed down the stairway from the vacant space above. I recognized Nathan's voice and I assumed the other was Charlie's. I heard footsteps as they walked to the front of the building. I'd occasionally ventured upstairs to the second floor, mostly when I wanted to store the copious empty boxes that once held electronics and other office equipment we had installed. It was one large, empty room. I climbed the stairs to join them, knocking on the wall to let them know I was there. Best not to scare the boss.

I was surprised Nathan walked toward me, coffee cup in hand. "Now that Charlie's done with Farmer Foods I asked him to check out this space and see if he could make an apartment for me and Toby."

"Really?" Toby here in Wolf Creek. Apparently, our conversation yesterday hadn't fractured our relationship. At least for now.

"Charlie's done some work on the apartments above Art's and Marianna's shops and when I looked at their places last week I knew this was the right decision."

"Won't be too bad of a job," Charlie said, staring at the ceiling. "Lots of noise, though. Just so you know." Charlie took steps toward the window, where he grasped the frame as if checking the wood. "Maybe I can get the guys to do some of it in the evenings or weekends."

"Won't matter. Our client's aren't stuffed-shirts that need glass towers."

I'd never heard Nathan say anything about the Connor firm in Green Bay, but I remembered lots of glass windows in the building when Beverly and I had listened to Richard Connor read our mother's will.

"Besides, I'm tired of driving back and forth to Green Bay every day. How soon could you start?"

"I'll have the crew stop and we'll block out the room and open space. Then you can take a look." Charlie reached for his phone. The conversation was the abbreviated jargon of working men and meant nothing to me. "They're coming now."

"Can't ask for more." Nathan shook Charlie's hand and headed for the stairway. "Have Georgia look at it when you're ready. Women have a good eye for that stuff."

Charlie smiled when I turned back from watching Nathan depart. "I don't know what he's talking about. You did a fine job downstairs without having me around."

"Always good to have another opinion," Charlie said. "Sometimes I get tunnel vision."

How diplomatic.

Less than five minutes later the crew of three men of varying ages arrived. They were the same men who had moved file boxes from Uncle Miles' house to this office. I listened to Charlie explain Nathan's idea before I left the men to their work and went downstairs to begin mine.

My first call of the day was to Marianna Spencer at Quilts Galore. Without explaining that the remodeling upstairs would be for Nathan I boldly asked if I could see her home above the quilt shop.

She agreed, but cautioned, "You have to understand that we have a toddler and two adults living here. It's messy, but I make no apology for that. We live a busy life."

"A mess of any size is fine with me," I said with a chuckle. "As a matter of fact, I'd met that other adult and her son the day I'd asked Alan to help move some furniture. Rachel and Thomas were both as nice as they could be."

"Come around 1:00. Usually there is a break right after lunch time."

Mornings were our busiest, too. The local people seemed to avoid the Square in the afternoons when the bus tours and vacationers filled the shops and restaurant. I mentioned to Jack that I'd be gone around one o'clock for about an hour.

"Say hi to Liz for me. She's working with Marianna today."

"How'd you know I was going there?"

"Nothing is secret on the Square, Georgia. Remember Doris? We are the new kids on the block, so to speak, and everyone is watching."

"I'll remember that."

***

When I arrived at Quilts Galore, Marianna mentioned she'd called Art so I was able to see how the two apartments were similar—living area overlooking the Square—and how they were different. After walking through both, I preferred Marianna's open space where the kitchen area flowed into the living room. There was a small half-wall that separated the kitchen from the living area in Art's apartment. That may have been a structural requirement, I wouldn't know, but in any case, neither place felt small or confined and that surprised me. Instead, they were cozy.

On my way back to Country Law I realized I could comfortably live in either place. I returned to a group of men laughing upstairs. The jingle of the bell on the door must have alerted them that someone had entered. The pounding of footsteps on the stairs confirmed my hunch. It was Jack.

"Nathan's anxious to get this project going before Charlie commits to other work so you'd better hurry up and give your opinion."

I walked up the stairs to see lines on the floor for two bedrooms, a bath, kitchen, wall closets and even a corner electric fireplace.

How did he know I wanted a fireplace?

Whoa, whoa. I curbed my enthusiasm. This was Nathan's apartment, not mine.

Charlie walked me through the plans. A couple of guys pretended to be walls so I could visualize the spacing. I suggested more kitchen cupboards and an apartment size dishwasher. I didn't know if men liked to do dishes, but, at least they could put the dirty ones in it. Charlie made additions and subtractions on his clip board. I was surprised he didn't use a calculator on his phone or some other device. We laughed about getting the lumber ordered before Nathan exploded. There is was again. That reference to C4.

"Tell Nathan I'll bring the contract by tomorrow."

All day I'd been able to avoid the obvious questions about this plan of mine, which was unfolding. So far, I hadn't had much part in the way it was being formed. But that evening when I was back home and reconsidered my plan, I realized I hadn't anticipated the new twists and turns that had occurred since my return to Wolf Creek. When and how would Lily see Toby? How should I forewarn her? Besides, I wondered if she'd follow through and actually return to Wolf Creek and live with me. Maybe she was having cold feet. Either way, she wasn't with me, and meanwhile, life on the Square went on.

When I'd been in Quilts Galore earlier, Marianna— and Liz—insisted I join them in the morning at Biscuits and Brew. I'd been there a couple of times, but I'd stayed away because of the unsettled situation with Elliot—and especially because I didn't welcome running into Eli. But now, more so than before, I wanted to be part of this unique community that made the Square special. So, I put thoughts of Eli aside when Liz turned on her persuasion mode and wouldn't take no for an answer.

The next morning when I showed up and ordered my coffee, the place was abuzz with talk of the Founder's Day celebration scheduled to start on Friday. Period clothing was encouraged by Sarah, but most of the women at the table declined for one reason or another. Sarah called those reasons mere excuses. Other women pointed out that the docents and those running the activities stood out in their period clothes and that was enough. I only shook my head no when she looked at me.

Sarah explained that the previous year the stagecoach rides were the featured attraction. This year I'd seen posters and flyers for the Crawford freight wagons. Sarah told us that Charlie had restored two wagons similar to those his family had used during the building of the town. He'd arranged to have a local Amish family bring their teams of field horses to pull them, so they could offer rides through the streets of Wolf Creek. The two wagons would accommodate many more people than the single stagecoach.

I had my answer. Charlie was a descendent of John and Mabel.

Sitting at the next table, Elliot and Art carried on their own animated conversation. Soon Jack and Nathan joined them.

"Hey, Peaches." Elliot raised his voice for me to hear. And everyone else, too. "I bought tickets for us to ride on the wagons." He'd obviously overheard Sarah talking about them.

What would that man do next?

Doris turned her icy stare on him. I laughed inside, a bit embarrassed at how public Elliot was. I was saved from further embarrassment when Sarah's watch beeped. That beep was her way of reminding everyone that it was time to open for business. In unison everyone at my table stood and went outside. I didn't look back at Elliot, although I was tempted to. I had to talk with him about discretion. Somehow, that seemed like a concept he hadn't heard of.

A sticky day was predicted, hotter and more humid than usual for early June. The damp air cloaked me as I stepped outside. It was already warmer than when I'd gone inside

Biscuits and Brew. And it was only 10:00 in the morning.

At the office, my day started to the sounds of sawing and pounding upstairs. So, Charlie and his crew were already at it and a blinking red light on my desk phone signaled the start of another business day for Country Law.

Early that afternoon, Nathan left with Toby for another doctor's appointment. I didn't want to intrude, but the strain on Nathan's face was evidence that Toby wasn't getting better. I wanted to tell him that I cared and hoped I could help, but I lost my chance. Nathan didn't come back to Wolf Creek that afternoon, but took Toby home instead.

My day at the office ended with the joy of Lily calling to say she'd be in Wolf Creek by suppertime. She'd stuffed her car to the gills and sounded a happy tone when she said she'd wrapped up everything in Madison. She was free to come and stay with me. My heart sang a little tune.

Since my refrigerator was nearly empty, I called Crossroads and ordered two of the day's specials to go. I still needed some essentials from Farmer Foods and in my rush through the aisles I ran into Eli. Literally. The man was as tall and solid as his brother, and their hair seemed to be going salt and pepper in exactly the same pattern, but I felt none of the excitement that happened when I was next to Elliot. I stepped back quickly and tried to mutter a quick apology.

"It's okay, Georgia. Glad to have you shopping here."

"How do you like the new store?" I asked as I edged farther down the aisle, opening the distance between us.

He ignored my question. "Just don't hurt my brother again."

"*Again?* You think *I* hurt *him?*"

He screwed up his mouth in skepticism. "Don't pretend you don't know. What do you think happened when you ran out of town after your mom died?" He inched closer to me.

"Mom?" I couldn't think straight, but for some reason, I knew I had to understand what Eli was saying.

"You know, vanishing." He snapped his fingers in the air. "Poof. Off you went, and Elliot thought he was the reason you ran away."

I never considered my leaving would affect anyone, certainly not Elliot. At the time, all I was concerned about were my own feelings. I only wanted to escape. Why hadn't Elliot told me this at dinner? Why did I have to hear it from Eli? What else hadn't Elliot told me?

My mind was crowded with questions and what ifs. Tears welled up in my eyes. The middle of Farmer Foods was not a good place to start crying, not if I didn't want after-work shoppers as witnesses.

I deposited the items I was carrying into Eli's arms and brushed past him and out through the door. I crossed the Square, yearning for home, but then I remembered the carryout dinners I'd ordered. I headed for Crossroads, managing to control myself—and rearrange my features. Still the hostess' frown revealed her concern. I forced a bright smile and thanked her for being prompt.

Lily had already arrived by the time I got home. Focusing on her and unloading her car distracted me. We were soon laughing ourselves silly trying to dislodge a suitcase wedged in the backseat of her car.

"We can unpack later," I said. "Let's eat first." And so we did, sitting down to a plateful of colorful roasted vegetables served over spicy rice noodles.

Lily grinned and picked up a fork. "Well, well, Wolf Creek has gone gourmet."

I shrugged. "Things change."

10

With two of us under its roof, my house had taken on a "lived in" look. I'd lived alone for so many years that I was acutely—and painfully—aware of Lily's things in the odd places they landed. Was that a sweater draped over the back of the sofa? What had been inside that bowl left on the coffee table? I couldn't identify its remains. The pairs of shoes by the front door weren't too bad, but good Lord, the house was a mess.

Oh, the sin of pride. I'd been so proud of myself for keeping my Milwaukee apartment neat and clean. Just like the sages say, if we do something long enough, it becomes a habit. Or maybe a rut. In any case, I didn't want to criticize too much for fear that Lily would leave—for good. It had been a long time since I'd shared space with roommates, and I could only imagine that Lily and her housemate hadn't been the neatest duo. Whatever the explanation for her messy ways, I needed to lower my expectations. Lily hadn't said much about her life these last years, other than to recount her financial difficulties.

My concerns took a back seat, though, the afternoon that Lily bounced into the house, kicked off her shoes and ran to give me a huge round-about hug.

"I got a job! Can you believe it? Already? After only two days of looking?"

We finished whirling around and she flopped on the couch all smiles and beaming with pride in herself.

I sat on the edge of the nearest chair. "Are you going to tell me where?"

"At Crossroads. At the Inn. I told them about being a waitress at the hotel in Madison. Do you know what the manager—Melanie—did while I was sitting there?"

No use trying to edge a word or question in. Lily was on a roll.

"She called the hotel and asked what kind of employee I was. Can you imagine that? I was about to sneak out if the manager in Madison had said anything bad about me."

"Why would they do that?"

"Sometimes I was late," she said with a shrug. Then she abruptly stood and left the room.

Wasn't she dependable? I'd already begun to second guess my decision about having her move to Wolf Creek. I really didn't know anything about Lily Winters. This Lily Winters, a woman of 24. It seemed like such a good idea when I was mulling it over months ago in Milwaukee. But that was before I found myself in the unlikely situation of working for Nathan and learning about Toby's health problems.

Lily returned with a glass of juice for herself and a glass of water for me.

"I read an article that said older people don't drink enough water."

What? "Hey, I'm *not* old. And don't even *think* about arguing over that."

A quick burst of laughter followed as she went back to her spot on the couch. "So let me finish."

I scooted back in the chair and impatiently tapped the arms with my fingertips. "You're the one who stopped talking."

"I start tomorrow. Lunch and supper. And, according to Melanie, I'm going to be tested by fire. She wants me to work all the hours I can during Founder's Day weekend."

"That's this weekend, you know."

"She said something about that, but I was too excited about being hired to absorb the information." She hugged herself, relishing in her good fortune. "Then I can pay my share of living here."

With that statement I'd confirmed that Lily was willing to

work and didn't expect me to support her. Although I'm not sure why I'd thought she might be looking for a handout. After all, years ago she left Wolf Creek with nothing more than a few clothes and had never called for help. At least she'd never called me. Maybe Uncle Miles had sent her money through the years. I didn't know and it didn't matter, anyway. She'd survived and was apparently ready to begin a new phase of her life.

Despite some of the red flags ahead, I could justify feeling a little like a hero when I realized I'd brought Lily back, at least to me and Miles. It was a start.

***

It seemed that every day since I'd pulled into the parking space behind the Inn, I learned something new about all the changes in Wolf Creek. Now, in June, I discovered that the Memorial Day celebration was a mere trial run for the shopkeepers, making sure they were on their toes and ready for the much greater influx of visitors arriving in Wolf Creek Square for Founder's Day weekend. Crowds of people were everywhere. I laughed to myself when I saw Sarah smiling at the long lines at the stalls of vendors trying to keep up with the demands for food and drinks.

I felt like a schoolgirl when I slipped my arm in Elliot's and we walked to the loading area for Charlie's wagons. My body tingled as we were jostled by the crowds and pushed closer together, but Elliot's firm grip secured me next to him. I wanted to stay there all weekend.

Forever.

As if he sensed my thoughts he squeezed my hand and pulled me tighter to him.

And I couldn't keep the butterflies inside from dancing.

We slowly moved up the line and as our turn to ride the wagon approached I saw Jack working as the ticket tender. Dressed in casual shirt and slacks, his cowboy hat was the only vestige of the period clothing Sarah had suggested we wear. As he accepted their tickets, each woman received a tip of his hat, another amusing reminder of an era long past.

"Hello Georgia, Elliot. Enjoy the ride." He punched our tickets and returned them to Elliot.

"Have you seen Nathan and Toby?" I asked.

"I thought they'd be here by now, but I haven't spotted them yet." He paused and glanced down. "We never know what to expect anymore, what with Toby's condition."

That was all Jack had time to say, though, because the crowd behind pressed forward. We moved on and got out of his way so he could get back to his job.

"Are you worried about Toby?" Elliot asked, frowning.

I looked around to see if I knew anyone in the crowd, wanting to be careful about what I said. "He's sick." Years of training in law and confidentiality made me uncomfortable talking about Toby not only in public, but in private, too, even with Elliot. I didn't know how much Nathan had shared about Toby's situation with anyone else in town.

A few minutes later, as we started our ride through town, I forced Toby—and Lily and my need to tell her about her son—out of my mind and focused on being with Elliot. Charlie had bags of candy for us to throw to the children on the side of the street. With their arms waving and their faces all smiles, it wasn't hard to enjoy the atmosphere. The ride took us down Beverly's street, and past her house. Even on this warm summer day, her doors and windows were closed. She might have been gone for the day or the weekend, but I doubted it. Unfortunately, I didn't think she'd take any pleasure in the festivities on the Square.

Still, I never gave up hope that someday we would be sisters in the real sense of the word. Fortunately, I wasn't waiting for that day to come. I had Elliot, Sarah, and Lily, not to mention the rest of the people I'd met on the Square. My world was getting bigger every day. That was all to the good, but while I celebrated my good fortune in returning to Wolf Creek, my struggle with a way to unite my family continued.

Content to be shoulder-to-shoulder with Elliot as we rode through town, I pushed back thoughts of Beverly, but also the more delicate situation of Lily and Toby.

Lost in my thoughts, I was surprised when the ride came

to an end. But I was at full attention when Elliot kissed my cheek. "So, Peaches, I have to get to work. Lots of customers at our snack stalls today."

"Thanks for the ride," I said, wishing he didn't have to go.

"One of many, Peaches, one of many."

I watched him weave through the crowd and disappear into Farmer Foods.

***

From the window of Country Law, I watched Lily walking around the Square window shopping—again. The last few days Lily had stopped in all the shops and now she was making the rounds. She was like a sponge taking in the sights of the town she'd left behind. She never stopped in at Country Law, though, which was probably my doing. I made such a point of talking about how busy we were that she got the message and thought she'd be interrupting if she came in. That's as I'd wanted it. I wasn't ready to talk with her about Nathan or Toby, but I couldn't keep this kind of information private long, especially not in the face of the need for a transplant. As I watched her, I couldn't help but fret about the possibility that someone would recognize her and ask her about her son.

During the three months Mom took care of Toby before she fell ill, she hadn't been at all secretive about our family's situation. To Mom, it was straightforward: her granddaughter had left town and her great-grandson was staying with her for awhile. When I talked to Mom back then, she was excited that Lily had entrusted her with Toby's care. She paraded him around town like he was the best part of her life.

Maybe he was.

When a heart attack had left her weak and bed-ridden, Beverly converted her dining room into—of all things—a combination nursery and hospital room. Beverly never complained about the responsibility—at least to me.

I turned away from the window, putting my attention

back to the pile of work on my desk, but it was difficult to concentrate. Thoughts of something Sarah had said during one of our dinners kept intruding. Some of her relatives had come to Wolf Creek for the Founder's Day celebration and while in town they'd finalize plans for a family reunion in August. I had to assume some of those relatives already lived in town or maybe spent weekends at their family's cabins on the lake. Among them, surely there would be a few who might remember Lily and the mystery around her baby and the fact that both mother and son had left town without explanation—or a trace.

I wasn't worried only about Lily. I knew for sure it was time to tell Sarah about Toby and my part in his adoption before she heard it from someone else.

I didn't want to rush through the story, though, and Founders' Day weekend was not the time for a long conversation with Sarah. Fate granted my wish late Sunday afternoon after the last vendor booth had packed up and left the Square, essentially bringing the Founders' Day festivities to a close. Sounding eager to rehash the successful weekend, Sarah's call started as a friend-to-friend chat, catching up on news and life on the Square over the hectic weekend. I soon steered the conversation about family and the reunion. That's when she mentioned her plan to meet them in Green Bay for a late breakfast the next day.

"I'm planning to go to Green Bay early myself. Why don't you and I meet for coffee? Then I'll visit Uncle Miles and you can join your family."

"Works for me," Sarah said.

We settled on meeting at Perkins on Oneida Street at 7:00 AM.

"Looking forward to seeing you, my friend," Sarah said, her voice warm and cheerful.

After our call, I wondered if she would still call me friend after I told her the whole truth about Toby's adoption.

***

The next morning, I arrived at Perkins first, and followed the waitress to a booth in the quieter section of the restaurant away from the front door and the server's station. I told her who I was waiting for and described Sarah enough to make sure she'd be led to the right table. My nerves had built to a frenzy, with my hands showing it. I spilled some of the freshly poured coffee and had to ask the waitress for extra napkins to mop it up. I kept checking my watch wanting Sarah to hurry, yet not wanting her to arrive at all.

Appearing at the table right at our agreed upon time, Sarah slid into the booth and asked the waitress for a large carafe of coffee. "We'll be here a while," she said, "but not for food. It's coffee and conversation we're after."

The waitress grinned. "Just let me know if you change your mind."

After a couple of minutes of small talk, Sarah said, "So, what's doing with Elliot?"

My cheeks warmed as I told her he'd become important to me. Knowing I was blushing, I admitted, "I'd like our relationship to, you know, move forward."

She flashed a knowing smile, but didn't push for more information.

Since I didn't want the conversation to be about me, I changed the subject. "What do you hear about the chef at Crossroads? Is he leaving?" Lily worked at Crossroads and as often as Sarah ate there their paths would cross soon, if they hadn't already.

"Melanie convinced him to stay—at least through Christmas," Sarah said, a happy lilt in her voice, "plus she encouraged him to try some new dishes. And she's willing to feature them in the special-of-the-day section of the menu."

"How wonderful for Crossroads and the Square." I grabbed the carafe and topped off our cups. The rich aroma calmed me somewhat. And Sarah's presence contributed to that, too. She had that effect on people.

She also read people pretty well. Reaching across the table she took my hand in hers. "What has you so nervous this morning? Miles?"

I sighed. "No, it's not Miles. His condition hasn't changed.

Not that I know of, anyway." I pulled my hand away and put it in my lap with the other one. "But I need to tell you something. It's about what happened when Mom died."

"Your mother? That was, what, six, seven years ago?"

"Yes." The exact time wasn't important. "Do you remember Lily's son, Toby? Mom took care of him before her heart attack. Then Beverly took care of both of them."

"I remember, but I don't know what happened to the boy after Hattie died."

I avoided her eyes when I said, "It's difficult to talk about, but we gave Toby up. He was adopted." I looked up. "You see, he's…he's Nathan Connor's son now."

Sarah's head jerked back in surprise. She sat silent, though, apparently waiting for me to say more.

"And the thing is, he's sick. His kidneys are failing, Sarah." I couldn't keep my emotions from breaking through my voice. "He may need a transplant." I quickly knuckled tears away. I didn't want my reaction detracting from the bigger picture.

Sarah leaned against the high leather back of the booth. "How terrible—for him and everyone around him." She took a deep breath. "I wanted to ask about Lily and the baby, but I didn't want to probe. Your family seemed kind of…oh, scattered, I guess is the best word."

I nodded. "I came back here to try to pull us back together. And now, Lily's back in Wolf Creek. She's living with me and working at Crossroads." I'd hurried through the facts, but we perched on the crest of the waterfall. Sarah deserved to hear the rest of the story.

"Crossroads?" Sarah said in surprise. "I don't think I've seen Lily. But lately I've done mostly take-outs, so I've only been there for a minute or two." She shrugged. "I'm not even sure I'd recognize her, though."

Unknowingly, Sarah had given me an out, but it was important I stay strong. I only nodded at her comment. "I don't know how everyone involved is going to handle the truth. Especially when they all meet each other."

"Oh, you're saying Nathan and Lily haven't met yet? That hasn't happened yet?"

"No," I said, shaking my head. I explained that once I knew the truth, I'd told Nathan and Jack. "I've told Elliot and now you—in confidence, of course."

"Thank you for trusting me."

I heard the words but couldn't look at her. I kept turning my spoon over and over on itself. "There's…there's more."

"Oh?"

Staring at the table I said, "Beverly and I, well, we received money for Toby from Nathan's father, Richard."

I raised my eyes to face her reaction. I got it, too, fast and to the point.

Sarah grabbed her purse, slid out of the booth, and stalked off.

I closed my eyes and sat there—alone. Would Sarah ever speak to me again?

The fallout had begun. I changed my plans about seeing Miles and returned to Wolf Creek.

11

I got through the rest of the day and Tuesday, too, but that evening Lily and I visited Miles. It was a sad visit. Lily tearfully murmured concern that he was getting weaker and less responsive to our presence. I agreed, but there was nothing more to say.

At the time, we didn't know that the unsatisfying visit with Uncle Miles would be our last and that he'd pass away sometime before dawn on Thursday morning. When the nursing home staff notified me, and the funeral home, I was told I could come and get his personal belongings at my convenience.

I first texted Nathan and Jack to tell them what happened and that I'd be in later that morning. Then I called Beverly, but the call went to voice mail.

I no sooner sent the text than a flood of tears started. My mind quickly began the "what if" questions. What if I'd stayed in Wolf Creek instead of slinking out of town? What if I'd kept in touch with Lily all these years? What if I'd raised Toby instead of agreeing for him to go to the Connor family? What if I hadn't run away?

I heard Lily at my bedroom door and motioned her to come in. I told her about Uncle Miles and we held each other for a long time before Lily broke away to start the coffee. I took those few private minutes to call Elliot and with his comforting voice on the other end, I cried my heart out.

Later that morning, I called the funeral home to make arrangements for Uncle Miles and was surprised to learn that only a few months ago, he'd done this for himself. I stumbled through a response, because what I'd planned to discuss was irrelevant now.

"You see, Miles didn't know if there would be any family willing to do this for him," Stu Benson, the funeral director said. "Uh, for that matter, he didn't know if any family members would be attending."

That hit hard. To think, my favorite uncle didn't know if he could count on family when it mattered. Again, my guilt surfaced, hard—my hands even trembled.

Stu suggested I arrive early the afternoon of the service, for what he called "family time." Right. Our little family of three: Beverly, Lily, and me. Four, if we counted Toby, which, of course, we couldn't do publically. Yet, in my heart I thought of him as the future of our family.

I acknowledged Stu's words, but I doubted we'd need much time to say our goodbyes. I knew I'd be saying goodbye to Miles in private moments over the coming weeks and months. He'd been an important part of my early life, and more recently, I was back in Wolf Creek because of him.

Stu had referred to the service as a celebration of Miles' life. "Your uncle didn't want people standing around a coffin whispering and crying."

"No, I don't suppose he would," I said.

"From what he said, he wanted people to laugh and recall stories of his life and how he'd made their lives better," Stu said, smiling, "and Miles wanted someone to lead what he called the festivities."

"I can hear Miles saying that word," I said with a nod. And he would have meant it. Miles might have been married to his work, but his bond was with Wolf Creek and the people.

Sarah popped into my mind. As soon as the funeral director and I ended our call, I texted her—before I had time to lose my nerve.

Her reply was quick and sharp. "Yes, I'll be there out respect for him. Nothing more."

That was it...the call ended.

What had I expected? Condolences? How are you? Can I

help in any way?

Before last Monday's conversation, this would have been a much different call. Sarah would have been at my side as my friend. But I had to accept the friendship was over. Losing Sarah was as sad as losing Miles.

Stu had made a point of telling me that Miles had specified that his celebration be held late in the day on Sunday, so no one would miss work on his account. Right to the end, Miles cared more about other people than himself.

Later, I left voice mail messages for Beverly about the arrangements, and confirmed them with a text. She never called back. Even by Sunday, I had no idea if she'd show up at the funeral, but I'd reached out and done my part.

Lily and I were the first to arrive at Bensen's on Sunday afternoon. No other cars were in the parking lot, but we were early on purpose. We'd come to say our private goodbyes.

As soon as I walked into the building, I stopped to let me eyes make the adjustment from the brilliant sunshine to the subdued lighting inside. In those seconds, I heard two familiar voices, Elliot and Beverly. They must have walked the few blocks to Benson's, which took up a large corner lot a few streets off the Square. Their soft laughter told me they seemed to be enjoying a moment. Really? I held Lily's arm—either to keep her from bolting or as support for myself—I couldn't say which.

After six years Lily was about to see her mother again.

We walked farther into the building, into the room chosen for Miles' celebration. Beverly and Elliot were standing by the casket, closed as Miles' had instructed. I made a small cough to announce our presence.

I watched Beverly as she took in her daughter. Those dark blue Owen eyes had been passed from mother to daughter. Anyone looking closely could see other features passed on through our Owen genes, from their arched eyebrows to the shape of their ears to their expressive hands.

I nudged Lily forward and cast a quick glance at Elliot, whose small nod reassured me. I spoke up in a strong voice. "I think it's time you two got reacquainted."

Lily raised her index finger in the air and said, "In a

minute." Taking charge of herself, Lily moved away from me to the casket and rested her hand on the lid, splaying her fingers as if wanting to cover as much of it as possible.

In unison, the three of us turned away, giving her privacy with the one man who had always been there for her. Earlier, she'd insisted on stopping at Rainbow Gardens to get a rose for Miles, and when she came to the car with it in her hand, I startled at how closely the pink hue of the rose matched the pink box from years ago.

We waited in silence until she joined us a few minutes later. When I introduced her to Elliot, he put his arm across my shoulders making it plain to Lily and Beverly that we were more than casual friends.

I relaxed under his touch, painfully aware of how much I needed his support. I also knew that many people showing up for Miles' celebration would likely be meeting for the first time. For some, that might turn out well, but for others, the outcome could be questionable. I thought of Nathan and Lily specifically.

I'd almost completed my plan for everyone involved to know the whole story of my part in Toby's adoption and the money I received. Of the four of us standing there, only Lily didn't know about the money part or about Nathan and Toby. Maybe that was for the best right now, but eventually I needed her to know that part, too.

I stood back for a moment while Beverly and Lily exchanged small talk, as if trying to cover their discomfort around each other. Their casual, chatty tone sounded stiff, overly formal. The doubt and fear I carried for years washed over me. The wound between Beverly and Lily was more fallout from letting Toby go permanently.

Elliot edged away from the three of us and began greeting the townspeople as one after another, they came to pay their respects. All around me, the rise and fall of laughter and low murmurs started, dwindled, and rose again. All the tones were sweet and lovely—I could hear in the sounds permeating the room that no one had a harsh tone for or spoke a critical word about Miles Owen.

As people moved into the room in clusters, a few took

their turn to come forward to say goodbye to Miles and talk with us. Soon we were surrounded by a crowd of people with stories to tell about Miles. How he'd helped them or their families. In a few cases, he'd recognized a tough spot when he saw one, and that led him to show his delight in being invited to Sunday dinner in lieu of payment.

Of course, even before seeing his files and old ledgers, I knew Miles had been generous with his time and money. The stories that came at me one after the other were more than I'd heard before or even imagined. In the middle of one person's story, I was distracted by a man's voice becoming louder as he approached. The voice belonged to Nathan, who held Toby's hand. Jack and Liz were with them and all four headed directly toward me. I eased away from the man who'd been telling his Miles story, thanking him for sharing it with me and admitting that his family hadn't known about so many of his kindnesses.

After the man left, I reached out to Beverly and Lily and made the introductions, starting with Jack and Liz. Then I took a deep breath and said, "And this is Nathan Connor and his son, Toby."

Beverly weaved forward, as her face lost all its color. Without Jack's arm quickly steadying her, she would have fainted then and there.

Lily made the connection immediately, and unlike Beverly, her face reddened. In the moment, she seemed to forget that Toby didn't know her. She crouched and hugged the little boy, but held on a little too long and Toby wiggled out of her arms. Nathan lightly, but protectively rested his hands on Toby's shoulders.

"Did you know Miles, too?" Lily's voice shook.

Toby nodded.

"Toby had a chance to meet Miles back when your uncle and I decided to become partners," Nathan said.

Toby slipped his hand back in Nathan's. "He gave me some of his butterscotch life savers."

"He gave me those lifesavers, too," Lily said, inserting a note of intimacy in her voice. "That was years ago when I was a little girl just about your age."

I glanced at Nathan watching Lily. His smile was faint, but he hadn't taken his eyes off of her.

When a woman touched my arm I turned away and was soon drawn into another conversation about Miles.

I made the rounds of the room for the next hour or so, but my mind was back to Lily and her brief encounter with Toby. Nathan was pulled away, too, by never-miss-an-opportunity-Liz who'd begun making her way around the room with Nathan in tow, periodically stopping at the clusters of people to introduce him.

An hour later, an attendant quietly asked everyone to take a seat. Immediately, Elliot was at my side. He ushered me, along with Beverly and Lily to the front row. Jack and Liz and Nathan and Toby slipped into the row behind us.

I looked on as Sarah took her place at the small stand with the microphone at the front of the room. In spite of the rift between the two of us, I smiled to myself at how great she looked in a taupe linen suit made colorful with the addition of a scarf dominated by reds and blues.

"In his own words, Miles Owen called today a Day of Celebration," Sarah said, "and he lived a life worth celebrating. He was a quiet man who worked each day so others could move ahead and create and enjoy better lives."

Sarah stopped to take a small sip of water from the glass at her side. As steadfast as she appeared, I guessed that strong emotions churned within her. She'd been a friend of the Owen family her whole life, but last week I'd told her the truth and that broke the bond. Maybe for good. I couldn't say.

"He believed in honesty and integrity," she said, her voice strong and firm. "Some of us here today have tried to follow his example. Many times we have failed, but knowing him gave us strength to keep trying."

She glanced in my direction, but quickly looked away. I wondered if she'd meant to be so obvious. Not that it mattered. I knew very well her words were directed at Beverly and me. Especially me. After all, I'd failed at both integrity and honesty. I grabbed Elliot's hand. I needed his strength.

Sarah spoke of Miles' belief in the community of Wolf Creek and the way its citizens had always made the community unique, right up to this day. Sarah then recognized the extensive list of various organizations Miles supported throughout his lifetime. What was going on between Sarah and me slowly faded away as I became more lost in my own thoughts about all Miles had done in his life.

As Sarah was ending her eulogy, I heard Nathan's voice. "Please sit down, Toby."

Then I heard Toby's little voice. "Grandpa, Grandpa."

Although low and quiet, Nathan's voice was stern when he said, "Toby, be quiet now. And sit down."

I turned halfway around in my chair. There was Toby running down the aisle to the back of the room, directly toward Richard Connor.

All eyes turned to see what was unfolding. Richard had aged in the years since I'd seen him, but he was still an imposing figure.

I lightly touched Lily's arm while she stared at Toby and Richard, her mouth slightly open.

When the room quieted again, Sarah ended with, "I think I've said enough about this gentle man. We all know he won't be forgotten." With that, she gathered the papers she'd brought to the small podium and left the room by the side door. As much as I wanted to run after her and ask her forgiveness I needed to stay. A room was filled with those who had come to pay their respects to a member of my family. I would not run out on them again.

No matter how many hands I shook or expressions of thanks I spoke, Sarah's two words, honesty and integrity, continued to loop through my mind.

In a quiet moment, I scanned the room and quickly realized how many people were new acquaintances from the Square. Uncle Miles had been part of that group in his way, and now I was becoming close to them, too.

Off to the side, Richard and another man, perhaps a law partner, were talking with Nathan and Jack. Toby stared up at them, stepping back and forth between them as they spoke. Lily had stayed close to Beverly, moving among the guests. It appeared that mother and daughter were doing fine. But both followed Toby's movements with Nathan.

Were they wrestling with questions from the past or were they jumping into the future? They certainly had trouble keeping their eyes off that little boy.

The funeral director was soon gently herding the group into the next room where the caterer had laid a spread of finger-foods and hot and cold drinks.

As the room gradually emptied, Elliot stood by the door, as if guarding against any unwanted intrusion.

I turned and stared across the room at Beverly, who was standing with Lily. With her shoulders drooping, she looked tired. Maybe I did, too. But my sister and I were the family elders and if the values central to Miles' life were going to be passed on, it was up to us to do it. Were we up to the challenge?

After checking in with Stu I went to the reception room expecting to see Elliot waiting for me. And I did, but I also found Richard and Nathan face-to-face and in the midst of a dispute, albeit a quiet one. So, they hadn't exactly set aside their differences.

And Toby was taking it all in with worry written all over his face. As I stepped closer I saw a sheen of tears covering the little boy's eyes.

"Can whatever this is wait 'til later?" I tried my best to sound uncompromising. Not easy, considering I was facing two top-tier lawyers.

"He needs a wife," Richard said, jabbing his finger toward Nathan. "He needs a woman who can be a mother to Toby and see him through this illness."

Richard looked at me like I was the answer to his request. The mother part, I supposed.

My heart soared. So, Nathan had told Richard about Toby's condition, after all.

"I agree." The words slipped from my mouth, and I quickly turned and headed straight across the expanse of the large room to join Elliot.

The rest of the celebration went by quickly. Elliot was my support system, even if I had to periodically leave him to talk to other people. I hadn't seen Eli, but he arrived after Farmer Foods closed for the day. He greeted me from across the room with a chilly nod. No change there, not from the first second he'd seen me in town. I hoped Elliot wouldn't find himself forced to choose between his family and me. Even thinking about that possibility felt like a heavy weight had descended on me.

Right behind Eli, Doris Parker filed in. I turned away, almost without thinking. As much as I enjoyed both reading and walking through bookstores, I'd kept my distance from Pages, or more to the point, I'd avoided Doris. That bothered me, though. Had I fallen back to my old habit of allowing other people's opinions to keep me from enjoying all the things I liked? Sarah's words looped through my mind again, prompting me to boldly step forward to greet Doris.

"Thank you for coming to celebrate Miles' life, Doris. How well did you know him?" I couldn't imagine Doris allowing anyone to help her.

"Miles was very kind to me when my husband died," she said. "He helped change the names on the titles and deeds and gosh, all the bank stuff and government forms. He was so patient with me and my grief." Tears welled in her eyes as she talked. "I still miss Ralph."

Who would have thought that sour-faced Doris had a soft side? Maybe lonely? I filed her words away in a folder in my mind, so I'd take care not to share her private words with everyone. I added a note to stop by her shop soon.

As we talked more about Miles and the Square Lily approached and came to my side.

"Hi, Doris. Did my book come in yet?"

Lily knew Doris? And had ordered a book?

"Should be in on Tuesday. I'll text you when it arrives."

"No need for that. I'll stop in on Wednesday before work. And we can talk about that project."

Before I could ask about their project I felt a hand on my elbow and turned to hear a woman I only vaguely recognized from town say that she and her husband were leaving and wanted to say goodbye. I walked to the door and never got back to Doris to continue our conversation.

An hour or so later, the room was nearly empty. Wanting to keep Lily and Bev and my new friends close for awhile longer, I invited everyone to the house. Liz thought that was a terrific idea and hurried off to ask the caterer to box up the remaining food for us to take along.

I hadn't invited anyone to the house since I'd moved in. I didn't count the evening with Elliot, which wasn't a social occasion. I couldn't remember if we'd left it in a mess, I had no time to worry about that now. If a lived-in house was going to bother some people, they could leave. I doubted anyone would judge my clutter.

So in convoy fashion we traveled the short distance from the funeral home to the house. *My house.* The words warmed my heart.

I'd loved the house as a child, but never expected to live in it again. Maybe it's better we don't see the big picture before we live it.

When I unlocked the door the stream of people entering continued until the house seemed to bulge at the walls. Liz asked everyone to move aside so she could bring the food through.

I hadn't seen some of the people from the Square earlier, but Jack said he'd called and invited them, too. As an afterthought he'd asked if that was okay with me. I laughed for the first time since the funeral and assured him that it was. Today was about remembering Miles, nothing more.

When Alan and Rachel, along with Thomas, came through the door, their eyes immediately went to Toby, who'd curled up in the corner of the couch. But he soon slipped off the couch and moved closer to Rachel, who was staking out a corner of the living room. She upended her tote bag and toys scattered on the carpet. Toby stood back, but desire was written all over his face. Noting that, Rachel picked up a truck and with a friendly smile spreading across her face, she held it out to Toby.

He not only took the truck, but inched closer to her. I listened as she told Thomas about their new friend and sharing all the toys. Smiling to myself at how such gestures could go such a long way to establish comfort and trust, I turned my attention to the growing crowd. When I looked back a few minutes later, Alan had taken Rachel's spot on the floor, and now she was heading through the dining room and toward the kitchen, where Liz was arranging more food on platters. Empty places on the array of trays were evidence that people were enjoying the leftovers.

I was about to move closer to thank her when a woman I didn't recognize approached me.

"I only met your uncle recently, but when Stephanie, my niece from Biscuits and Brew, told me of your loss, I wanted to offer my condolences."

"Thank you. But I don't think I've met you."

She waved her hand in the air as if admonishing herself. "Oh, I do that all the time. I think everyone should know me by now. I'm Sally Johnson, and the proud owner of the daycare center just off the Square." Sally nodded toward the kitchen door where Rachel was balancing two trays of food and heading to the dining room. "I take care of Thomas when Rachel works. And, boy, does she work."

"So, I've heard," I said.

"Your uncle guided me as I navigated all the applications and inspections needed to be licensed by the state."

"I'm glad he was here to help you."

Sally dug in her huge purse and withdrew a business card and handed it to me. "I see another young boy that might need my services now and then. Would you introduce me to his parents?"

True enough, with Nathan and Toby moving into the apartment above Country Law, I could see the need for backup daycare.

"Sure. His father is here. Uh, he doesn't actually have a mother."

Difficult words to say.

"Well, let me backtrack," I said. "What I mean is, she died. A while back now."

We maneuvered toward Nathan when I noticed Richard standing nearby. Maybe this wasn't the best time to introduce Sally to Nathan. But then, what would I tell Sally?

I acknowledged the men, noting that Art Carlson had

joined the group. Art knew Sally, and nodded to her, which seemed like a natural opening to introduce Sally to Nathan and Richard.

Handing Nathan her business card, I said, "Sally owns a day care center and takes care of many of the children whose parents work on the Square. I think she's someone you should know."

Nathan glanced down at the card, but Richard spoke first. "Day care? You can make a living doing that?"

Sally tilted her head as if she knew he couldn't possibly mean that as a serious question. In a voice oozing charm, she said, "You'd be surprised what a joy it is to take care of children."

Hmm…smart lady. She ignored the little dig about the money.

Richard cleared his throat. "I'd like to see your place." He was deep into his take-over mode, or his everyday mode, based on what Nathan had told me and I already knew about him.

"Dad, Toby's my responsibility," Nathan said, his voice firm. He turned away from Richard to Sally. "But, yes, I would like to bring Toby for a visit. We'll be living above the office soon."

"When did you decide to move?" Richard seemed to have lost some of his steam. Maybe with Nathan and Toby moving out of Green Bay he realized he'd lost more control of his grandson.

The sound of the front door opening and closing distracted me, and I turned to see Jessica and Mimi from Styles enter. I went to greet them, and the door opened again and Megan came in, followed by Sarah.

I didn't know if I should scream or cry. After walking out of the restaurant, and then saying her piece about honesty and integrity at the celebration, I'd assumed Sarah and I would keep a professional distance. Maybe she thought paying respects to Miles was all about business.

I was wrong.

Before I had a chance to consider how I would act around her, Sarah drew me into a tight embrace, a true friendship hug. "Forgive me," she whispered, speaking into my ear so no one else could hear. "I was wrong to have left you at the restaurant."

Surprised by her apology and unsure of how to respond, I sought the safety of numbers and guided Sarah toward the back of the house. We passed the food in the dining room, and I smiled to myself when Sarah grabbed a small carrot stick and a piece of celery.

The din of women's voices surrounded us, and I knew it wasn't the right time to talk with Sarah about what had happened.

With Sarah by my side, I edged over to Megan and thanked her for the spray of flowers she'd sent for the casket. Since the card read, "The Reynolds Family," I assumed Elliot and Eli were included.

"Seemed like a small tribute, considering all he did for the Reynolds family over the years," Megan said.

I didn't know the particulars, but when I'd gone through the files when we'd set up the office, the name Reynolds appeared on many.

"Well, I hope you'll trust Nathan and Jack to continue serving your family."

"Of course," she said with a shrug as she began wandering back to the cluster of people in the front of the house. "By the way, Eli said to say hello. He had to get back to the store. Something about a cooler not working."

I turned to the sound of Sarah laughing. She'd found herself a job washing glasses, pairing up with Marianna who was busy drying.

Suddenly, my head was spinning with all that was going on—just the number of people milling about in my home astounded me. Six months ago I was locked in a dead-end job in Milwaukee and had one person I'd called a friend. Now, I was surrounded by people who accepted me. Even those who knew I'd made some bad choices accepted me anyway.

As I stood still, feeling almost lightheaded, someone, I didn't know who, turned the lamps on in the living room as dusk began to infringe on the day. Tomorrow would be another busy day for the Square and that meant for everyone in my house. With the exception of Richard Connor, they were all connected to the Square.

As quickly as my house had filled a few hours earlier, it emptied with the same speed. Alan scooped Thomas onto his shoulder. The sleepy toddler rubbed his eyes, but watched Rachel gather up the toys, leaving the truck behind with Toby, who grinned shyly.

Conscious of Lily watching the scene unfold, I followed her to the door, where we waved our farewells. Filled with contentment, I put my arm around her shoulders.

I stiffened when Richard approached. He still left me uncomfortable. Maybe he always would.

"Thank you for including me today," he said, extending his hand. "You may not know this, but Miles and I were friends years ago. Even talked about opening an office together. But he wanted a small, hometown practice and I wanted the bright lights and money of a bigger firm."

I nodded, but drew may hand back. He'd held it too long.

"In all the years I've been in business, I don't think I made this many friends, true friends," he said. He turned and walked away. Alone. I had known that feeling, too, but, like me, he had made his choices and now lived with the consequences.

"Want to tell me what that was all about?" I recognized Nathan's voice coming from behind me.

"I think your dad is reevaluating his life." I smiled at Toby, who stood next to Nathan. The little boy's eyes were dark with fatigue. I bent down to give him a hug and said, "Wow. That truck was a nice gift from Thomas. Wasn't it?"

Toby nodded and leaned into Nathan's leg. A thin smile crossed his face.

"I need to get this little boy home," Nathan said. "See you tomorrow, Georgia."

I walked out the door with them, followed by more people leaving. I delivered hugs and thanks all around. I stood for a moment and looked at the blanket of stars emerging in the sky. For me, one shone brighter. That was Uncle Miles, I decided, and I waved goodbye.

Back inside, I was feeling reflective, but I still had things to do. Beverly and Lily sat on the couch chatting, and I left them to their time alone. In the kitchen, Liz had a sponge in her hand, vigorously wiping down the counters. Elliot was tying up a very full garbage bag.

"What would I have done without your help, Liz?" I pulled a chair out from the table and sat. My feet ached from standing all day in dress heels, so I toed them off.

Elliot put a glass of red wine in front of me. "Have some merlot. It's good for what ails you."

"Absolutely nothing ails me today," I said with a grin. "Did you see all those people coming in and out at the funeral home and here? Miles would have so enjoyed himself."

"That's true," Elliot said.

Liz grinned when Jack sidled up to her and took the sponge out of her hand. "Time to go."

The two waved goodbye, and Elliot and I were alone in the kitchen.

Elliot peered through the archway toward the living room. "Hard to believe your sister and Lily are still talking."

I nodded. "I know, but they have years to catch up on. I figured they'd stop after polite hellos, but something must have clicked."

"Maybe both grew up," Elliot said. "Now, with Miles gone, they see how fragile life and family are."

"Yours, too?"

"Mine?" He'd poured some juice for himself and leaned against the counter.

"You and Eli, anyway. You know, the way he seems to be watching out for you. Especially where I'm concerned. He made it plain that I'd better not hurt you."

He straightened up. "When did he say that?"

"A few weeks ago. He said outright that I wasn't to hurt you, again. What did he mean, Elliot?"

That sent Elliot pacing from one end of the counter to the other.

I knew immediately, this wasn't the time or place to have this conversation. Then again, why not? I needed to know.

Elliot sat down across the table from me and took my

hand in his.

"When you were here when your mom died, you never called to let me know you were in town. You didn't even have a funeral for her so those of us who knew her—or you—could say goodbye. It was like a big secret. When I asked Beverly about it, all she said was that you had left town for good. She wouldn't even tell me where you'd gone or give me your phone number. It seemed pretty plain that you didn't want to see me again."

He let go of my hand and sat back in the chair, and took a couple deep breaths. He tried to look at me, but quickly glanced away.

"I went into a black hole," Elliot said, swiping his fingers across his forehead. "The doctor called it depression. Nothing much mattered to me. Not the store, or friends, even family. Nothing." He extended his hands palms up in front of him. "Eli took the brunt of it. No matter what he tried to do to help, I didn't care. He worked all the time to keep the store going, doing my job as well as his."

I cleared my throat. "Uh, tell me then, how did you recover?"

Lacing his fingers, he rested his hands on the table. "Time, Peaches, time. As the months passed, I gradually realized you wouldn't be coming back to Wolf Creek and I needed to get back to living."

I closed my eyes, as if I could will away the sadness in his eyes. "Oh, Elliot, I'm so sorry. After you married Mary Ellen I thought *you* had moved on. Then I heard about the divorce, but I'd made a life for myself by then."

"Kind of like ships in the dark, huh?"

"Something like that."

"But you're here for good, right?"

The question was always there. He needed reassurance that this time I'd stay put and wouldn't be leaving again.

"Wolf Creek is my home. This is my house." I flashed what I hoped was my best sexy smile. "And you are my man."

I knew it wasn't quite that simple. We still needed to clear the air about what happened to us in the first place, back when his family had written me off. But that could wait.

Elliot shot up and came to my side of the table. He took both my hands and drew me up from the chair and gave me a kiss that curled my barefoot toes.

"Excuse us?" Beverly knocked on the door frame. "Elliot, were you still planning to give me a ride home?" She glanced at Lily. "Or, maybe Lily wouldn't mind doing it, if you'd rather stay here."

"Don't give me that option right now." Grinning, he backed away from me. "I picked you up. I'll take you home."

"You picked Beverly up for the funeral?" I asked, not concealing my surprise.

Elliot shrugged. "You had Lily to go with you, but Beverly would have had to go alone, so I told her I'd pick her up. Didn't give her a chance to refuse either." With his tone so matter-of-fact, he clearly thought this was all very logical.

My, my. That explained why Elliot was already at the funeral home with Beverly when Lily and I arrived.

My mind was still spinning and reeling, but Beverly took my mind off everything when she stepped forward and opened her arms. I stepped into them and went back in time to when, as sisters, we'd done everything together and told each other our wildest dreams.

My emotions were about to break through my calm façade when she stepped back and hurried to the front door. What? Was she walking away from Lily and me?

She turned back. "I'll call you tomorrow."

Lily quickly followed her to the door.

"Guess that's my cue." Elliot held me in an embrace that felt like a promise we'd be together soon.

Then he was gone. I heard him say goodnight to Lily.

A few second later, she came back in kitchen heading for the open bottle of wine on the counter.

"Enough left to top us off," she said, dividing it between us and refilling our glasses. "A toast. To Uncle Miles, to our friends in Wolf Creek, and to family."

"Yes, yes, yes." I took three quick sips.

We wandered into the living room and each settled on

opposite ends of the couch.

"You seemed to get along with Beverly today." I wanted to know the who, what, and why of their conversations.

"Mom. She asked me to call her mom." She bunched a pillow in front of her. "Can you believe it? After all these years?"

No. I didn't believe that Beverly had changed that quickly. I recalled many years back, when Lily had started referring to her mother and addressing her by her first name. It was odd, but I never challenged it. Right now wasn't the best time to question Lily's reunion with her mother.

"Mom said she made a lot of mistakes in her life," Lily said, squeezing the pillow tightly against her body. "And she also said she envied your strength about leaving home and making a life for yourself."

Really? I always thought Beverly was the strong and determined sister. How could I have been so wrong about how she saw me?

Lily stared into the room. "I got on a roll with her today and finally asked about my dad. I always wondered why she used the Winters name instead of his. Do you know what she said? 'If I wasn't good enough for him, then his name wasn't good enough for me'. Can you believe that?"

It still didn't answer all my questions about Beverly's poor parenting while Lily was growing up. But tonight wasn't the right time to tell Lily about my lingering questions about her mother. It was time, though, to show Lily the pink box.

I drained my glass. "Time for a refill. I'll open another bottle."

"I'll do it," Lily said, bounding off the couch and hurrying away.

When she was out of sight, I went into my bedroom and picked up the box. By the time she brought the open bottle back, I'd put the box between us on the couch.

"I remember this." Lily gently touched the lid. A corner of the pink paper had lifted during the years in storage. Lily gently pushed it back into place.

"Do you remember giving this to Uncle Miles?"

"Sort of. I remember being little and we went to a party."

147

"You asked him to go to a father-daughter Valentine's Day school luncheon because you didn't have a dad, but you wanted to go." I reached out to lightly touch the box, as if connecting with Uncle Miles. "He even bought a new suit to wear."

Tears spilled from her eyes and ran down her face. "He kept it." Her fingers trembled when she lifted the lid.

I tried to be apologetic about reading her letters to him. "When I was trying to locate you, I looked through the letters."

She walked her fingers through the thick pile. "Nothing secret in them, at least not that I remember. Just general news and terrible boyfriends." She stopped when she came to the envelope where her name and address appeared in Miles' writing.

I pointed to the envelope. "That's how I found you."

"I'm glad you did. Now I wish I had saved his letters to me. I was too young to know how special they would be one day."

"We all carry regrets." I reached across the span of fabric and took her hand. "Uncle Miles was a special man to a lot of people, including us."

We sat quietly for a few minutes, each sipping our wine. Fatigue came over me suddenly and fast. I eased up, too tired to carry our glasses or the newly opened bottle of wine to the kitchen. "Let's just leave all this," I said. "It can wait 'til morning. I'm heading to bed. Tomorrow is a working day."

Lily patted the box. "I think I'll stay here for a bit. I want to go over the day, all of it."

I smiled to let her know I thought that was a good idea. I turned off the lamp on my end of the couch leaving the room in a soft glow from the lamp at Lily's end. Yes, she needed alone time to travel the years of memories contained in the pink box.

Tomorrow, though, I would tell her all about what happened when Toby went off to his new family. I wouldn't mince words about the money, either. Maybe she would think differently about her aunt and mother when she knew the truth about her son.

12

I'd fallen asleep quickly and slept well, but when the alarm rang the next morning my mind was cloudy, fuzzy, like I'd had too much merlot. I knew that wasn't strictly true. I'd had three small glasses of wine, or maybe four over the whole event. Not that I knew for sure, but it didn't matter. My head felt like I'd consumed the whole bottle.

I pattered to the kitchen to start the coffee, adding an extra scoop of the ground beans for good measure. I needed a richer and stronger brew than usual in order to face Country Law's busy Monday schedule. I left the sounds of the coffee pot behind when I went to finish dressing, still trying to shake away the fog in my brain. My phone buzzed to alert me a text had come in. I saw it was from Liz, asking me to meet her and Marianna at Biscuits and Brew.

Did I want to go? Not really. I didn't feel like facing so many people. But after nearly everyone from the Square had taken time to join in my family's farewell to Miles, I needed to let them know their presence was much appreciated. The decision to head out made, I took a few fast swallows to soothe my throat, dry and scratchy from the hours of talking I'd done the last few days. That's what I assumed, anyway.

So, like the good soldier, I grabbed my purse and headed out.

As I passed Lily's closed door, I noted the silence and assumed she was still asleep. She'd probably stayed up late looking through the pink box and remembering everything from the funeral and these first steps to reconnecting with her mother. We often worked such different schedules it wasn't unusual to leave without seeing her. When we did connect our conversations picked up and continued on as if no interruption had occurred. When I'd made the decision to find Lily I never expected it would be so easy to have her in my home.

Then, too, I'd wondered if she'd wanted to return to small town life after being in the excitement and atmosphere of Mad Town, Lily's moniker for Madison. Or, maybe, because of her financial situation, she grabbed the chance to get back on her feet before leaving again.

After parking behind Country Law and starting across the Square, I spotted Liz and Marianna enter the coffee shop. Good. I'd never been the first of the group to arrive for morning coffee and, even though I now knew everyone, I still didn't want to be the first. It would happen one day, but I didn't want it to be today.

I walked into the morning hang-out to a cacophony of sounds, the din of multiple conversations which mixed with the ongoing sounds of orders for muffins and drinks and the occasional full breakfast, coffee of various flavors poured into cups, the rattle of plates and silverware, and the door opening and closing.

Rachel was doing a fine job of dashing between tables delivering orders, and behind the counter Stephanie multitasked with the ease of a dancer.

I nodded and listened to the organized chaos, but my raspy voice made it clear I was talked out. The topic of the morning centered on the upcoming Fourth of July celebration and the tourists and day-visitors expected to flood the town over the weekend.

"And don't forget the bus from Small Town Tours coming on Friday," Sarah added, taking a second to nod to me when I joined the large table.

"What are your plans for the weekend, Georgia?" Marianna asked, pulling out the chair next to her she'd saved for me.

"Not much planned, at least as of today. Elliot talked about going to the fireworks."

"Plan to sit with us." Liz, the proverbial organizer, made

sure no one felt left out. "Tell Lily she's welcome, too."

"I'll do that." I wanted to add more, but instead, I drained my coffee cup and then reached for my purse on the floor and stood. Whoa…I grabbed the edge of the table to steady myself.

Of course, Liz noticed. "Are you okay?"

"Just the aftermath of yesterday I think." I slowly turned away and waved goodbye to the rest of the group. Once outside, I stood in the sunshine for a moment and took a deep breath. I wanted to feel as good as the weather, because it was shaping up to be a gorgeous Wisconsin day. I decided to stop at Farmer Foods for some throat lozenges and maybe a quick hello to Elliot, who was no doubt on hand, since he'd mentioned Monday was delivery day.

I was disappointed when the only person I saw was the cashier. She wasn't wearing a nametag and I hadn't seen her often enough to remember her name. Next time I saw her I'd make a point of asking and repeating it to myself in order to permanently add her name to my memory bank. Megan, her arms full, fell in line right behind me. I waited by the door for her to check-out so we could walk to our end of the Square together.

I was about to leave Megan at her shop door when I remembered Marianna wearing one of Art's brooches all the time and the way she engaged in soft marketing of all the shops. "Do you have a small flower arrangement that would work in the office reception area?" I asked. "We need something bright and cheery there."

"Let's see what's in the cooler." I followed her inside and she moved to the glass refrigerated case that showcased premade arrangements. She held out one that had bright red carnations, white daisies, and small irises with a tinge of blue. "Red, white, and blue." She swept her other hand to encompass the refrigerated case behind her, which at the moment were filled with flowers in those colors.

I nodded in approval. "I'll take it. And give me one of your business cards to place next to it."

"Why, thank you, Georgia." Megan clipped some extra daisies to add to the arrangement.

Watching her, it occurred to me how much the three Reynolds siblings still resembled each other. I hadn't noticed that before, but the three shared the same dark hair. While Eli and Elliot had sprinkles of gray, Megan's was still dark and styled in a flattering pixie. It occurred to me that she was a woman who'd always be considered cute at any age.

Moving at a snail's pace I carried my patriotic vase and flowers on down the walkway to Country Law. Even if no one else noted the colorful flowers, at least I'd enjoy them. As sick as I felt, I needed something to cheer me up.

The sounds of construction assaulted me as I went inside. The loud voices and thuds of footsteps over my head told me Charlie and his crew were in full work mode. I groaned when my head buckled at the noise.

Jack entered through the back door and headed straight for the coffee, as usual. He'd limited himself to four cups a day, not much for a coffee lover, but the limit for a man who had to accept that his heart was no longer 100% healthy.

"It's the first taste that's the best," he said with a grin after the first swallow.

He'd drawn a straight-backed chair to the edge of my desk and sat looking at the open space of the reception area.

"That's wasted space." He pointed with his cup to the other side of the building.

"We need chairs for…"

"No. I meant the extra office."

Was he talking about the space they'd made for Miles? Even his diplomas and certificates had been hung on the walls in anticipation of his return.

"So soon? You want to remove his stuff now?" I couldn't believe Jack would be so insensitive.

"Well, I've been talking with Nathan about changing the office."

I didn't respond, but my already cloudy mind refused to take in his words. The energy drained right out of me, leaving me weak. After all I'd done to get this firm organized and running smoothly, he and Nathan were ready to make changes.

Jack turned toward me. "Are you not feeling well?"

No, I'm not, and you're not helping. I cleared my throat, wincing at the soreness that had settled there. "Like I told Liz and Marianna, I think it is the relief of Miles no longer suffering, maybe coupled with such a long day and talking to so many people yesterday."

Maybe it was best that I barely had a voice. If I were as strong as usual, I might have told him that if he'd been waiting for Miles to die before taking over and changing the mission of Country Law, I'd be gone. I'd returned to Wolf Creek to be part of a hometown legal firm that put its clients' needs first, not those of its lawyers. Our mission read: *Helping regular folks with the legal side of life.* Kind of hokey, but it was true, and Miles had spent decades living up to that.

"If you need to, go on home. We can cope."

"I'm okay for now."

Jack waved into the reception area again. "Nathan and I thought you should move into that office and focus on doing the kind of work you're trained to do. Most of what you've been doing is secretarial. Um, I guess they're called assistants now."

He stepped over to the coffee maker and brought the carafe to refill my cup, topping off his, too. Sly guy.

Jack shook his head, pinching his mouth in frustration. "With Nathan busy with Toby, I've got way too much to do. If I wanted to work this hard I could have stayed in Green Bay." He grinned sheepishly. "That's classified information. Don't you dare breathe a word to Liz."

And continue working for Richard Connor? I don't think so.

He readjusted the chair to take in a different view of the office.

"The flowers are a nice touch. From Megan?"

I nodded. "We needed to brighten it up in here a bit—to match the beautiful summer days we're having."

"Okay, then, let's have her do a bouquet or some kind of decoration every couple of weeks. She supports us, we support her."

"My thoughts, too," Jack said.

But Jack had strayed from what he'd said at the beginning of our conversation. If I'd heard him right, Jack and Nathan wanted me to act less as office manager and more as paralegal. And move to an office of my own. I liked the sound of that. I'd also jumped to conclusions and seriously misjudged Jack. Wow, he hadn't been talking about removing traces of Miles, but making room for me to expand my role in the firm.

"Now, about shifting the offices," Jack said, inching away and heading toward his office. "Give it some thought and we can talk more when Nathan is available."

Minutes later, the Taylors arrived for their appointment with Jack. The day had officially begun.

***

I dragged through the morning, popping throat lozenges and draining one glass of water after the other. Around noon Elliot stopped in with a box lunch, but the thought of food wasn't appealing. "I'm not hungry, but I'm glad to see you."

Elliot grinned and braced his hip on the corner of my desk. "That's good news. But I stopped to see Megan a minute ago and she said you seemed tired. After the string of days you've had, it's no wonder." He frowned and pointed above his head. "And that noise. It's no wonder you don't feel good."

"I think it's more than the noise and brain fog." My raspy voice had turned into a full blown sore throat.

"I hope it's only a cold. You know, and not the flu." His take-care-of-me mode surfaced. He'd become the male counterpart of Liz, and I loved him for it.

"I'm going home to crawl into bed right after work."

"Call me when you get there. Okay?" He checked his watch. "Gotta run. Another delivery."

Then, poof, he was gone.

By closing time, I was desperate to get home. I locked the front door, waved goodbye to Jack as I passed his office door, and then hurried to my car. It was a warm, almost hot day, but I felt shivery and weak. What a relief to escape the constant pounding and sawing from the upstairs construction.

I couldn't help but laugh over this puny two-block drive home. For the life of me I couldn't remember why I'd driven my car this morning, but I was happy I had. I shed my blazer the minute I got inside my house and within minutes I'd dragged my biggest, loosest T-shirt over my head and pulled on billowy cotton pants. Flopping on my bed, I called Elliot like he'd asked. I prided myself in remembering to make the call, but his box lunch sat lonely and forgotten on my desk.

"Go to bed and sleep, Peaches. It's what you need most. I'll talk to you later."

"I'm already in bed."

"Shouldn't have told me that," he said, his voice low and teasing. "You know how I love you and want to be with you."

A frog-sound laugh escaped. But I, too, wanted to be with him, for the rest of my life. But a history of hurts needed to be brought out in the open and dealt with—soon.

***

I startled awake. Was someone in my house? Or had my disjointed dream become too real? Voices came from the front of the house, the living room. As I became more alert, I discerned two voices, but not the scattered kind voices that came from the television. And there was music. Soft, instrumental jazz. Was I still dreaming?

Then a burst of laughter came from the front room and I recognized Beverly's voice. Beverly? In my house again? I got out of bed and pushed my hair back off my face and went to investigate the voices.

I never expected the scene in front of me. Beverly and Sarah sat in my living room sipping wine. Ugh. Even the sight of the bottle made my stomach twist. I made it to the couch, grabbed an afghan off the back and wrapped it around my shoulders as I sank into the corner cushion.

"Why are you here?" My voice had turned to gravel.

Beverly sat on the other end of the couch next to the soft, plush chair that almost swallowed Sarah up.

"Elliot called Lily and told her you were sick," Beverly said, "but she had to work and called me. She figured I'd know what to do for you. I'm your sister after all."

I shook my head and closed my eyes. That assumption was way too much for me to absorb. How did Lily think Beverly would know what I did to recover from annoying colds and flu? We hadn't communicated in years.

"Lily got carry-out soup ready for you and asked me to pick it up at Crossroads and bring it to you."

"I was waiting for my own take-out when Beverly came in." Sarah picked up the explanation as if these events were all par for the course. "Beverly told me you weren't feeling well and…"

I waved my hand for her to stop. I didn't need this long story of who, what, when, and where. "So you both came here."

"Lily gave me her key to get in," Beverly added.

"Let me heat some of the soup for you." Sarah was already part way out of her chair.

"Later. Not yet. I'm going to rest." I scooted down on the couch, and Beverly straightened the afghan over me. "Keep talking. I want to hear what you're talking about." My mind still couldn't put Beverly and Sarah together for an evening.

I never heard their conversation, and, later, when I woke up, it was dark outside and Lily was sitting in the chair Sarah had been in earlier. The reading lamp was on and Lily had an open book in her lap. Someone had turned off the music.

I sat up and stretched my arms over my head. "Hi. When did you get home?"

"Fairly early, around ten. Mondays are usually slow."

"Sarah and Beverly?" I looked around the room and over my shoulder into the rest of the house for them.

"Sarah went home when I got here and Mom stayed about an hour later."

"What time is it?" I'd taken my watch off earlier and had no sense of how many hours had passed since I'd come home.

"Close to midnight." She put her book on the chair-side table. "Mom said you hadn't eaten any of the soup. How about now?"

I considered the offer and decided I was hungry. "A small bowl, and how about a few crackers."

Not wasting a second, Lily headed to the kitchen.

After being on the couch for so long I stood, stretching my arms over my head. I needed to move around. "I'll meet you in the kitchen," I called, detouring to the bathroom to splash water on my face. I shouldn't have looked in the mirror.

Lily kept her back to me when I entered the kitchen and sat at the table. She'd been quiet, more reserved than I expected since I woke up in the living room. It was late, though, so maybe she was just tired. She'd been working regular hours for lunch and dinner during the week and then longer hours on the weekend. Since she'd started working at Crossroads, she'd taken time off only to attend Miles' funeral. So far, she hadn't mentioned friends in Madison or reconnecting with high school friends that had continued to live in Wolf Creek after graduation. Was it possible she was having second thoughts about returning home?

As ill as I was, I still sensed something had changed for Lily. "Honey, what's the matter?"

"Nothing." She opened the cupboard and brought out the crackers.

"I thought we agreed to be honest with each other."

She turned around and I saw tears streaming down her face. "How could you sell Toby?"

A million thoughts rapidly tangled in my mind. I wasn't well enough to discuss this clearly and, for sure, I didn't want to make any more mistakes. Of all the people I had told about Toby's adoption, Lily hearing the truth had made me the most worried. My plan to pick the perfect time and gently explaining all the circumstances to Beverly's and my decision to let Toby go to a good home hadn't happened. I regretted that now. I'd kept putting it off because I didn't want to see the look of reproach in her eyes. Nor did I want to admit that at the time, I'd agreed with our decision.

Reluctantly, maybe, but I'd gone along

"Who…how did you…when?" My words became a jumble of sounds. I wanted to be next to her, to give her support if she'd accept it, but I stayed seated.

"Mom told me. After Sarah left."

"Why didn't you wake me?" And as an afterthought, "Why didn't she stay to be with you?"

"I asked her to leave." She put the soup in front of me, then opened the drawer for a spoon.

"Please sit down, Lily." I glanced at the bowl, no longer interested in any food, but I didn't want to say anything either. "Tell me what she told you."

Lily didn't accept my invitation to sit. Instead, she leaned back against the counter. But she retold their conversation, keeping it short, but complete. In the spirit of credit where credit is due, Beverly had stepped up and told her daughter the truth. Maybe all of us needed to relive the past in order to enjoy the future. If the Winters women had a future, we had to resolve that no secrets would be left untold.

"You never told me Gram was sick." She looked at me, but only for a second. She'd taken a seat across from me, though. A concession I welcomed.

"Where would we have called? Mom said she didn't know where you were. We believed her." I pushed the soup aside. "She said you never called her, either."

Painful as it was, if we were going to be honest, then Lily couldn't be free of her responsibility to Toby and put all the blame on Beverly and me. "If you were concerned about Toby, you wouldn't have left and not come home."

"To a mother who made it plain she never wanted a daughter? A grandmother who lived in her own 'everything's wonderful' world? A Pollyannaish view of life." She swallowed tears back. "A son I couldn't take care of?"

"I wasn't here to help you either." I reached across the table for her hand. "But I am now."

She picked up the bowl of soup and dumped it in the garbage. The clock on the stove read 1:27 AM. I wondered if either of us would sleep anymore that night. I'd passed beyond fatigue to total exhaustion and another day would begin soon.

I went to her, pulled her into my arms. I wanted her to know that now that I'd found her I'd be by her side in the future no matter what. She could choose to stay in Wolf Creek or make her life elsewhere, but I'd be her support system.

13

Over the next few days, even though I felt much better, my heart wasn't into the clients or the activities on the Square. I'd come to the point where the daily routine of phone calls, appointment scheduling, and emails frustrated me, because I was usually right in the middle of preparing documents for Nathan and Jack. And usually at a moment's notice. I began to agree we needed another administrative person in the office.

I'd called Beverly to talk about Lily and their conversation. She insisted it had been her responsibility to tell Lily about Toby. I didn't have a good answer for that. Yes, I'd wanted to be the one that told Lily about Toby, but I also thought that mother and daughter needed to understand each other's actions.

A surprise intruded on all my thoughts about the past. Lily called Country Law to make an appointment with Nathan.

Not allowing my fluttering stomach to distract me too much, I behaved as I would with any client and asked the nature of their meeting. With a note of confidence in her voice, she said, "Private."

Now what? I faced a dilemma. Did I need to keep Lily's knowledge of the money exchanged for Toby confidential? Did I give Nathan a heads up about her appointment with him? Because Toby was in the middle of all this, and because I hoped the meeting would benefit all three, I called Nathan, who was working at home again. Toby was too sick to be left with the babysitter, so that meant Nathan stayed with him.

In his usual way, Nathan listened without interrupting. Then he said the words that must have torn through him. "Tell me the truth, Georgia? Does she want to take Toby back? Does she think she has a claim on Toby?"

That threw me, although his flat lawyerly voice was typical of Nathan. I'd never considered Lily wanting to reclaim Toby. She'd barely talked to him. So my first thought was to blurt no. I hesitated, though, considering if that had become Lily's plan once she'd seen him? Was it fate that Lily and Toby reunited in Wolf Creek? In my own mind, I'd never entertained such a notion.

"Truthfully, I don't know, Nathan, but she's certainly never mentioned anything like that to me."

"Thank you for calling," he said formally, keeping me at arm's length so to speak. "I know it means a great deal to you that no one gets hurt further." That was that. He said a quick goodbye and ended the call.

The next day at the office, Nathan was his usual self. But I couldn't get it out of my head that I should have told Lily that Toby was sick. It's as if I was holding on to another secret. But on the other hand, I had no idea how much Nathan wanted Lily to know. I simultaneously believed I'd overstepped my boundaries and perhaps not disclosed enough. Talk about confused.

My nerves wouldn't settle the day of Lily's appointment. She'd scheduled a one hour time slot between the lunch and supper rushes at Crossroads. For her sake, as well as Nathan's, I hoped that she wouldn't cancel.

She arrived on time, looking fresh and pretty in a multicolored sundress and sandals. Definitely not her waitress uniform. I assumed she'd gone home to change or had brought clothes with her to work that morning.

I asked if she'd like coffee or tea or just water. She shook her head, so I announced her arrival by phone to Nathan. He stepped out of his office to greet her.

"Hello, Lily. Come in." He smiled when he greeted her and walked by her side across the reception area and on to his middle office.

Almost half an hour later Nathan called out my name from

his office door and asked me to join them. My heart started pounding. I was standing in front of my desk, comparing files of financial data with Jack. But without fanfare, Jack nonchalantly stepped behind my desk and claimed my chair. Nathan still stood waiting by his door.

"Have a seat, Georgia," Nathan said when I entered his office. He closed the door and sat down.

I took the visitor's chair closest to the door and sat. Lily watched me settle in, and then extended a hand for me to hold. I returned her offer and gave her fingers an extra squeeze.

Nathan grabbed a pencil and began bouncing it on the desk surface, about the only sign of nervousness I'd ever seen from him. "Lily has something to tell you."

I held my breath.

Lily hung on to my hand. "Nathan told me something I didn't know before. His father wanted a grandson to carry on the family name so when he read Grandma's will he saw an opportunity to get a child for his son Chad."

"Chad?" I had known Richard had sons, but I never remembered him mentioning their names, which was why I didn't immediately make the connection with Nathan when we'd first met.

"My older brother." Nathan qualified, once again nervously fidgeting with the pencil as he pulled his gaze from Lily and focused on me.

Nervous movements of any kind were so unusual for the self-contained Nathan, but I supposed it was to be expected. After all, this was an innocent child we were discussing.

"So *you* let him take Toby." Lily held my hand so tightly I was forced to pull it away.

"He was going to a good home that would give him love and opportunities we couldn't." I heard the defensive quality of my voice. As weak as it sounded now, it hadn't felt that way at the time Beverly and I made our decision.

"For money." Her voice broke.

"Yes." Without knowing exactly why, at that moment Sarah's honesty speech came to mind. "I haven't spent it."

Lily shrugged. "Mom hasn't spent her share either."

"I didn't know Beverly had made that decision, too." Did that explain Beverly's frugal ways?

"Chad and Nancy were killed last November and they'd assigned Toby's care to me," Nathan added, again turning his attention to Lily. "My father thought—assumed—he'd be Toby's guardian. But Chad, and Nancy, too, had a different idea about what was best."

"Richard must have been furious." I glanced at Nathan for confirmation, which I got with a nod.

Lily clasped her hands in her lap and let out a long, slow sigh. "I told Nathan that Toby belongs to him." She looked directly at him. "And I won't challenge that. I don't deserve him."

She sounded forlorn, and I needed her to know she wasn't alone. "Oh, Lily, don't…we all made wrong choices with Toby."

Ignoring my reassurance, Lily said, keeping her gaze fixed on Nathan. "I told Nathan I want to get to know Toby, and…he agrees." Tears welled in her eyes when she looked back at me. "Toby's sick and it's my fault."

Despite all the complications and Toby's uncertain future, relief rippled through me. The fewer secrets, the better. It had always been my philosophy, despite the evidence to the contrary.

Our conversation was interrupted by a knock on the door and Jack's head appearing through the opened door. "Your next appointment is here, Nathan."

Lily checked her watch. "Oh, no." She raced from the room.

Hmm…she must be late getting back to work.

"I'll talk to you later," Nathan called out after her. He spoke in a louder than normal voice, as if flustered. The remark about calling her had a more personal tone than he usually used to address clients.

Lily waved to acknowledge him and headed out the front door.

Forcing myself to focus, I went back to my desk and pulled out the file Nathan needed for this appointment with a couple. He could view it on his computer screen, of course, and I knew that was becoming standard practice. But both Nathan and Jack liked to have print copies of everything in front them, mostly because it allowed them to focus on the clients and not stare at a screen.

Still shaky, almost lightheaded, I grasped the files and I cleared my throat to steady my voice when I offered them a cup of coffee or water. But, like most of our clients they'd arrived with business on their minds and declined. I'd come to realize that clients in the small town firm were the same as those I encountered while working in Milwaukee. All were busy people and trips to an attorney's office were not social calls.

Back at my desk Jack handed me list of messages that had come in while I was with Nathan and Lily.

"Everything okay?" he asked.

Regret still surged within me, but at least now I knew more details about what had happened to Toby. Plus, I'd weathered my greatest fear. Lily hadn't run away from me. At least not today.

"Better than okay." I sat behind my desk and looked up at Jack. "Maybe I'll write a book about this someday."

Jack laughed and grabbed the folder he had been working on. "All I can say is leave me out of it." He chuckled again on his way back to his office.

All afternoon I stayed busy, mostly because I had so many interruptions. At the end of the day, I passed Jack's office on my way out, ducking in long enough to tell him I'd come in early and assemble the documents he needed for the next day's clients.

"Wait. Please." He lifted the phone and buzzed Nathan's office. "Got a minute to talk?" Jack held his finger up as if to keep me from leaving. "Now."

He returned the phone to its cradle and motioned for me to sit down. A couple of seconds later, Nathan came in and sat down in the other client chair.

"Okay, you two, we have to face a few facts here," Jack said. "This office got much busier much faster than either of us anticipated. Georgia stays busy all day fielding phone calls, running the office, and keeping track of all the documents we need every day. I don't know how we thought one person could do all the work for three lawyers—because we're still handling Miles' cases." Jack focused on Nathan. "And you're busy with Toby, which you should be, but Georgia can't continue at this pace without help. Frankly, neither can I."

Nathan leaned forward and braced his forearms on his thighs. "I know I'm not doing my share. But I'm listening. What do you suggest?"

"Hire a secretary—oops, an assistant. That would free up Georgia to use her paralegal training to support us. She could use Miles' office."

"Know anybody who might be interested?" Nathan asked, turning to me. His eyebrows were raised in anticipation.

In a flash I thought of Virgie, my friend at Merkel & Kline. "As a matter of fact, I do." I stopped to consider what Virgie might say if I offered her a chance to make a major life change. "I'd have to call and ask a friend in Milwaukee if she'd want to leave her job and come to live in a small town."

Jack pointed his pencil at me. "Call her tonight. Let's get this underway. We need to get this done. *Now.*"

"Whatever you two decide, I'll support." Nathan looked back and forth between Jack and me, then he settled his gaze on me. "Remember when I said you'd be the glue that would hold this office together? You've done that and more, and we—both of us—thank you."

We heard thumping on the steps coming down from the apartment. In a minute Charlie stood in the doorway. "Glad I caught you before you left, Nathan. I wanted to let you know your apartment will be done in two weeks. The crew and I can help you move in if you need us." He turned to leave, then twisted back. "Thanks for the job." And he disappeared as quickly as he'd appeared.

***

I was eager to reach Virgie, who, as it turned out was just as anxious to reach me. She had a two-week vacation coming up with no firm plans in place, so she was hoping to arrange a get-together with me. We laughed at the synchronicity of our calls. I wasted no time and described the job at Country Law.

"The thing is, Virgie, I can't guarantee anything, but frankly, Jack and Nathan trust my judgment and if you decide you want the job, I'm almost certain it will be yours."

Virgie laughed. "You've about sold me, you know, but you'll understand that I can't commit until I meet Nathan and Jack."

"Of course," I said. "You can't make this kind of change on a whim. But I'll say one thing—you'll love it here in Wolf Creek. And, in no time, you'll meet some really wonderful people that are part of the Square."

"I'm overdue for a change," Virgie said, her tone somber. "This big city no longer holds my interest—and that's been true for too long."

We chatted for a few minutes, mostly about why I enjoyed my work at Country Law and her latest vest designs. I let her in on what was going on with Elliot. Apparently, she saw right through my casual tone.

"I want to meet him," Virgie said. "Any man who wants to do so much for you must be special. But you're special, too."

"Oh, he is, Virgie, he is."

We both laughed and ended the call. Virgie and I hadn't had too many conversations that ended on that kind of upbeat tone.

Lily arrived an hour later, all smiles, and carrying her dress and sandals. That wasn't the mood I'd expected after our meeting with Nathan.

"Hey, you're up late," she said.

"I wanted to make sure you were okay after meeting with Nathan."

"He called." Her smile broadened.

"Nathan?"

"Yup." With her cheeks reddening, she said, "He invited me to go with him and Toby to the fireworks this weekend. I'll get to see Toby—I know he's Nathan's, but I'll get to see him."

Lily's eyes shone brightly. I soon caught some of her contagious happiness. Wow, this was a gift for Lily, unexpected but welcome. Just as fast I saw a fly in the ointment. "But on this weekend of all weekends, don't you have to work?"

Lily shrugged. "I'm scheduled, but I asked Julie, one of the part-timers, if she'd take my shift on Saturday." She smiled. "She agreed because she needs the money, and she knows Saturday's a good tip day."

"I'm glad you can get the time off for some fun," I said, knowing fun wasn't exactly what I meant. For Lily, this wouldn't be a casual, devil-may-care event. "Liz invited Elliot and me to join their group at the lake and she made a point of inviting you, too, just in case you were free."

"I'll pass that on to Nathan." Lily stared off into the middle of the room, focusing on nothing in particular. "Maybe it wouldn't be so awkward this first time for me with Toby if other people are around. People who Toby and Nathan know. I mean…what I guess I'm saying is that this isn't a date. Nathan asked me so I could see Toby. He was being kind."

I understood, but there was something about the way Nathan had acted around Lily, and now she was trying to clarify what this outing at the lake was and wasn't. I brushed aside my curiosity about what was going on inside either of them. It wasn't any of my business.

"Why don't I ask Marianna if Rachel will be there with Thomas?" I asked, deliberately changing the subject.

"Thanks, but I'll stop and see her at the coffee shop and ask her myself."

A few years separated them, but this was the first time since she'd been back that I'd seen Lily connect with a person close enough in age to become a girlfriend.

I told her about Virgie coming for a visit in a few days, but I didn't mention the possibility of her moving to Wolf Creek or working for Country Law. Lily and I had become a twosome of sorts, and I didn't want Lily to think I would move her aside for an old friend. On the other hand, I wanted

Virgie to stay at my house. With only two bedrooms, that meant someone would need to sleep on the couch.

"I'd like Virgie to stay here with us rather that at the Inn—and I'm not sure they'd have a room available this time of year. Do you—"

"I can stay at Mom's," Lily said, waving off my question. "No problem."

Really?

"Don't you think you should ask first?"

I was still far from feeling close to Beverly, but ever since Miles' funeral she had made small attempts to be around Lily and me. Maybe we could, with compromises on all sides, start acting like a family again. Maybe we'd even become close sisters.

Lily nodded. "I know it won't be a problem, but, yes, you're right. I need to ask."

"Good. Let me know what she says. I'll call Virgie back then."

***

Within twenty-four hours it was all settled. Lily arranged to stay with Beverly, and Jack was only too happy to hear that Virginia—Virgie—Saunders would be in town.

I was happy, too. Virgie and I were known to talk for hours, including devoting time to complaining about our jobs. But I didn't realize how much I had missed our conversations until I knew I'd see her soon.

I had fun getting ready for company, happily filling the cupboards with soup and snacks, although I planned to take Virgie to Biscuits and Brew some mornings so she could meet the people that had become important to me. I also asked Sarah to plan to meet us for dinner one evening at Crossroads. Sarah was the best ambassador for Wolf Creek Square I knew, so if anyone could convince Virgie to move, it was her. Besides, with Virgie as a buffer I hoped Sarah and I could move even further past the bump in the road in our friendship.

Was I hoping for too much? When Elliot called one

evening, I asked him the same question.

"Take it slow, Peaches. If it's going to happen it will. Don't forget, I want to meet her, too."

I heard a hint of anxiety in his voice. "What is it?" I asked. "Is something wrong?"

"Not exactly. You and I agreed to take it slow. But you seem to take care of everyone else, from Nathan to Lily— even Sarah and Beverly—and if there's a little time left, I get those remains."

I laughed off such a thought and changed the subject. Later, though, when we'd ended our call, his words came back to me. Could he really feel that insecure? Then I recalled that earlier in the call he'd suggested dinner at a restaurant in Green Bay and maybe a movie afterward. Preoccupied with Virgie's visit, I'd brushed him off with a quick, "We'll see."

Not the best move to let Elliot—or any man—know I wanted to be with him. But I found excuse after excuse to justify my comment. They all sounded petty and empty, even to me.

July
14

The Fourth of July weekend celebration began in grand style on the Square. The fact that the actual date for the 4th landed in the middle of the week didn't diminish the excitement. Around mid-morning the high school marching band did maneuvers on the pedestrian walkway within the Square. Their intricate footwork and instruments flashing in the bright sunshine encouraged folks to clap their hands and tap their feet to the rhythm. Most of the visitors and shopkeepers paused to step outside and acknowledge the students with hoots and applause. Jack and I had both come in to finish up some work, but when the band started, we both went outside to join the crowd and have a look.

Most of the buzz around us centered on the fireworks scheduled for Saturday night on the shore of Wolf Creek Lake. I needed no reminder, because for two days Lily had been moaning about not having the right clothes to wear to the lake. She didn't think a sundress was casual enough, yet faded blue jeans with holes in the knees didn't seem right either. I suggested she go on a mission to Styles to see what she could find.

I hadn't considered how nervous Lily would be about an evening with Nathan and Toby. I knew she didn't want Nathan to think of her as an irresponsible kid, and she probably wanted Toby to like her, too. Maybe this preoccupation about how she looked had something to do with trying to get a second chance at a first impression. Something about it seemed overdone, though, because Toby

170

wouldn't care what she wore. Maybe this was more about Nathan than Lily would care to admit.

Regardless, Lily acted on my suggestion, and that evening, she'd come home with three different outfits from Styles, including some casual khaki pants and a deep blue T-shirt, a longish swirly skirt and a peasant blouse, and a more conservative silky golden hued blouse and white slacks. I smiled when it hit me that that all three highlighted her hair and her dark blue Owen eyes. Then the debate started all over again.

"I know it's not a date," she said, a little defensively, "but I'll have these nicer things for other occasions. I can wear these outfits lots of places."

As I watched her, I thought back on a conversation I'd had with Jack earlier, after we headed back to the office after watching the marching band. He'd passed on the information that Richard Connor would be joining the group at the lake.

I'd held my breath. "Is that a good thing?"

"Could be, or not," he said. "We'll just have to wait and see what happens."

"Talk about a noncommittal answer," I teased. "But I can tell you this: I'm not getting in the middle of that family. I've got more than enough problems in my own."

"I understand that, Georgia." He hesitated, as if gathering his thoughts. "But prepare yourself. Looks to me like the two families are merging—and fast."

"Huh? What do you mean?"

"Well, I suppose it's not my place to say this," Jack said, letting out a quiet laugh, "but Nathan can't stop talking about Lily. And I don't think he knows how much he's doing it. But when he talked in that man-to-man way a guy might talk to a friend, he admitted she intrigued him. But you didn't hear that from me." He paused as if rethinking what he'd told me. "Now I feel like dope. I shouldn't have mentioned it at all. It would never occur to Nathan that I'd repeat conversations he meant to be kept private—and it was just a moment, if you know what I mean."

"I would never say *one word* about it," I said, thinking

back on how different Nathan seemed when Lily was in his office. I wrote that off to the uncomfortable issue of Toby's biological mother suddenly showing up. Of course, he'd be nervous about that. I hadn't considered that Lily had a different kind of effect on him.

"Well, sorry, anyway. I don't gossip about people, but Nathan has always claimed he planned to be a lifetime bachelor. So, he's surprised me lately. I don't want either of them hurt."

For a man of few words Jack had put a new twist on the Nathan-Lily-Toby relationship. And he'd given me one more reason to think about the way Nathan looked at Lily and her almost amusing insistence that Saturday night's get together was "not a date."

Jack started back to his office, but I could see from his expression that he was still mulling over Nathan's feelings. Meanwhile, I tried to fit all the pieces together. I sure couldn't see Nathan using Toby as a pawn if he was playing a game with Lily, but even more, I couldn't see him playing a game at all, with anyone, for any reason. Nathan lived his life, at least the part I'd seen, like Miles, with a level of honesty and openness that didn't allow for toying with anyone's feelings.

***

When I suggested that Lily might want to take a sweater to the lake, she rolled her eyes and said, "It's *July.* "

But, unlike Lily, I stuffed a sweater in my tote and then watched for Elliot's truck to pull up. But he was full of surprises. Rather than arriving in his pickup, he rolled up to the curb riding a flashy red tandem bike he'd rented. As I approached laughing, he sang the old song about Daisy and the bicycle-built-for-two.

"It even has a basket for that tote, Peaches," he said, dramatically sweeping his hand toward the front of the bike. "Oops, I'll have to call you Daisy today."

"Do you know how long it's been since I rode a bike?"

He lifted his shoulders in an exaggerated shrug. "You

know what the adage says—it's something you never forget." He put the kick stand down to support the bike and secured my bag in the basket. "You ride in front and steer. I'll be the strong man behind you." He flexed his arms to show off his muscles. I didn't have the heart to tell him that it would be his legs providing the power, not his arms.

The adage was true, though. We hadn't gone more than a block when we pedaled our way into a comfortable in-sync rhythm and soon turned onto the road that gave us a straight shot to the lake. The closer we got, the more the cars began to move slower and slower and we passed them by. We rolled into the park, leaving everyone else in the dust, because traffic had come to a standstill. I felt a little sorry for latecomers because parking was already scarce.

"Good planning on your part, sir. I don't want to miss the beginning."

Elliot held my hand and carried my tote bag as we walked toward the lakeshore and scanned the crowd. I heard Liz yell before I turned and saw her waving her arms to get our attention.

"Here. We're over here." Her strong voice carried above the noisy crowd.

Elliot waved back as we cut an angle across the grass toward our group.

Just as Jack said, Richard was there, looking different in what seemed to be stiff new jeans and a polo shirt instead of his suit and tie. He sat on the ground moving dirt with the toy excavator Toby must have brought along. Nathan and Lily sat nearby talking with Art and Marianna. A stranger might have thought them a chummy foursome. I smiled to myself looking at the outfit Lily had settled on, the khaki pants and deep blue T-shirt. Perfect the occasion.

Alan, Rachel, and Thomas soon arrived. The baby entertained us by making a beeline toward Toby and plunking himself in Richard's lap. Richard's warm smile made it hard to turn away and engage with the other adults.

In the background, mixed with the din of the crowd, I heard Richard and Alan entertaining both boys with their sound effects, mostly engine noises and whistle sounds. A perfect picture, almost. To make it so, they needed Nathan with them.

With Jack passing out paper plates and napkins, Marianna and Liz passed around containers of snack foods, sandwiches cut in quarters, and fruit cut in squares and stuck with toothpicks for easy eating. Elliot went to the popcorn vendor and brought back bags of salty popcorn to share among us. I pulled two bags of oatmeal cookies from my tote to add to the feast. Jack then played host at the couple of coolers filled with juice and water and soft drinks.

I sat next to Elliot, letting my head rest on his shoulder. Soon dusk gave way and the fireworks began. The darker the night became, the brighter the bursts of color shown. The loud rockets brought rounds of cheers and reminded me of Charlie and his C4 company logo.

Watching the fireworks, feeling so comfortable under Elliot's protective arm, it occurred to me that I needed to read the next section of the Crawford family history—that history was all about Wolf Creek and led to the traditions and atmosphere that had developed right up to that moment at the lake. Sarah entrusted me with her writing, but I'd put her pages aside when we'd hit the rough spot in our friendship. I needed to get over it.

As the continuous bursts illuminated faces in the crowd, I noticed Lily paying less attention to the fireworks than to Toby, who still sat with Richard. But if her eyes were on Toby, I smiled at the sight of Nathan gazing at her. Maybe Jack was right. Was it possible Nathan was smitten—seriously interested in Lily?

We all stood when the show ended and the fireworks display of the American flag sparkled in its beauty. We gathered the blankets Liz had supplied and helped carry the coolers back to the cars. With so many of us with flashlights and lanterns we must have looked like a group of worshipers on a pilgrimage.

In front of me Richard carried Toby, who was obviously fighting to keep his eyes open. Thomas, in Alan's arms, had given up the fight.

The night sky shone bright with stars that faded only as

we got closer to the lights of the town. After an easy ride home Elliot and I sat side by side on the top of the stairs to my porch. I'd poured us each a glass of cool white wine and as we sipped, I told him that I was surprised by my own excitement about Virgie's visit. "She was my only real friend in Milwaukee," I said.

"You have lots of friends, here," he said, "but don't go forgetting about me." His voice was heavy with longing.

"I won't," I whispered. "In fact, if Virgie comes to Wolf Creek and works for Country Law I'll have more time for you."

He carefully took my face in his hands and brought us together. I smelled popcorn with him so close. Heady when it's on the breath of the man you love. Not any man, my man.

He prolonged the anticipation with feather kisses around my eyes. After a quick nose touch, he plunged in. The kiss became hot, steamy. I couldn't get enough. We made our own fireworks.

"Excuse me." Lily did her best to step past us and into the house.

I immediately thought about Nathan and Lily and how their evening had gone.

Sensing my quick change in focus, Elliot moved away from me and released his hold. "Someday, Georgia, you'll have to decide where I belong in your life. I won't be an afterthought."

"Elliot, I...I..."

"Not tonight." He went to the bike, got on it and peddled away down the dark road.

I had let myself believe that I could unite my family and have Elliot, too. One happy package. It was a nice dream, but maybe not reality. On the other hand, surely Elliot could understand that an interrupted kiss wasn't the same as rejection.

15

That night, as Saturday night turned to Sunday morning, I tossed and turned more than I slept, my mind filled with scattered, disjointed thoughts. The past bumped into the present, and I was troubled by Elliot's inability to understand all the things working together to grab my attention. Yes, I was preoccupied with my family—and with Nathan and Toby. Why wouldn't I be?

I hadn't remembered Elliot as being a demanding man, but things change. We were no longer kids. Besides, I wasn't looking at the situation through his eyes. Even when I did, though, it still came back to my need to focus on my family—and developing my role at Country Law. Elliot or no Elliot, I'd still have a job and a family.

As dawn broke I threw back the sheet and left my bed. Maybe a cup of my favorite roasted blend would help. Knowing I wouldn't be going back to bed, I started the coffee brewing and traded my nightgown for clothes. Then I folded the pages of Sarah's Wolf Creek history that I'd left on my bedside table. I put them, along with a notepad and pen, into my purse. Back in the kitchen I pulled out a to-go cup from my cupboard. I needed to get away for a few hours and rethink what had happened since my arrival in Wolf Creek. And I wanted to read the rest of Sarah's history, too.

So many things nagged at me, even haunted me. During the night, Lily's last comment in Nathan's office had rolled over and over in my mind. Did she really believe she was the cause of Toby's illness? Moving quietly so I wouldn't stir Lily, I folded a lawn chair off the porch and put it in the backseat, just in case I found a secluded spot and wanted to sit and read or just rest.

I settled in my car, put my coffee in the cup holder, and checked my purse to make sure I'd turned off the phone. I didn't want interruptions. I twisted around and saw the sweater I always left in the car on the backseat. It was sticky warm at the moment, but I had no idea what was predicted. It could be a day of thunderstorms for all I knew. But for the moment, I wanted to be like the puffy clouds in the sky that were blown at will by the wind. I had a purpose for the day, but no particular destination.

I weaved my way through the quiet residential streets to the south end of town. A group of four joggers waved as I moved into the other lane to safely pass them. For a small town that became a tourist haven during the day, Sunday mornings allowed shopkeepers time to recover and renew themselves. The retail shops opened every day, no exceptions on Sundays for them. Every sale was important to their livelihood and for the good of the Square, every shop had to be open for customers all weekend—Country Law being the only exception.

When I turned the corner, I realized I'd steered myself to the entrance to Wolf Creek Cemetery. Lately, I'd missed the guidance Uncle Miles was always willing to share with me. Mom, too, in her own way, had encouraged me to leave Wolf Creek and experience a bigger world. I was too young when Dad died to have any memory of wisdom he might have shared.

Miles' grave still showed signs of its newness. The planted grass was thin with a few brown spots on the edges. The parched ground all around me spoke to our recent dry spell. Miles' marker had been installed since I'd stopped in the last time. The engravings on the black granite stone shown white and crisp as the morning sun rose over the nearby trees. Remnants of a small bouquet remained, but the dry petals had browned.

I stood in the morning stillness and absorbed the silence, broken only by a few birds happily beginning another day of foraging. A calmness I hadn't felt in a long time worked its way through me. Strange as it seemed, I needed to stay there a while, in the quiet, by my family.

When I lived in Milwaukee many days would go by that I talked only to co-workers during the day, and my evenings were rarely shared with anyone. I came to accept that private lifestyle and thought I'd done well. But moving to Wolf Creek showed me that was existing, but not the way to be alive.

I unfolded the chair in front of my family's headstones and sat. It was like sitting in front of a type of history book, and Miles had been an important part of the life of the town for many years, just like Sarah's parents and my mother. Maybe I'd write Uncle Miles' history one day and ask Sarah to add it to what she'd already penned about the other families that had built Wolf Creek.

With coffee, birdsong, and a brilliant sky I began to worry less and ponder more. Working for lawyers for years, I'd developed logic and discipline. Moving into the frenzied world of Wolf Creek Square I'd lost that perspective. I reached into my purse. It was time to catch up with Sarah's history.

***

KEITH CRAWFORD—Oldest Son

The early spring weather caused the citizens of Wolf Creek to clamor for goods and supplies. Following the death of his father, Keith hadn't yet found a replacement driver when he'd assumed the management of the office of Crawford Freight Line. Even though his brothers were willing to take extra loads, he knew the only way to keep the legacy of his father's business—honest, prompt service— intact was to take a load himself now and then.

That decision would change the roadway system between Wolf Creek and Green Bay.

The sun rose earlier each day as winter

gave way to spring forcing Keith to leave his home before dawn and check the horses and harnesses as his father had done. This morning he sat by the fireplace of his home, its warmth welcomed as was the steaming coffee his wife prepared.

"Goin' to be a long, slow trip home tonight. The wagon will be stacked high and overfull. So don't you go to worrying," he said.

He stood and gave his wife, Amelia, already making soup for the day, a farewell kiss. He did the same to each small child as they continued to sleep on their pallets. His son, Caleb, stirred at the touch; his daughter, Naomi, never moved.

"Keep those youngens' safe." Keith turned to the door. "Sam and Jacob will stop by when they return."

Amelia pulled her shawl closer and stood on the small porch watching her husband fade into the pre-dawn darkness.

Keith's trip to Green Bay gave him time to consider the future of the freight line. The railroad would be passing to the north of the town soon and bringing many of the items he hauled quicker and cheaper. Yes, goods still needed to be transported from the rail stop to town, but he knew that those short trips wouldn't support him and his brothers. He needed to find another type of work and leave the hauling to Sam and Jacob.

The day had turned warm. On his return trip a combination of melting snow and the ground warming changed the hard packed roadway to mud. Soft spots caused the wagon to lurch and, without the extra ropes he had insisted on, the load would have broken loose and crashed to the ground. The valuable wares would have been lost.

He approached the treacherous crossing of

the Duck Creek River with caution.

Rivulets of melted snow had begun running down the bank, forming a layer of water over the ice. Keith stopped the team and went to the edge of the river to test the strength of the ice and the safety of taking his wagon across.

"Get on with it, man. You can't stand here all day." He looked up to see the sun already in its afternoon arc. He wouldn't get home 'til after dark. He checked the rigging on the horses, the ropes tying the load and climbed aboard. A flick of the reins and the horses pulled hard to get the wagon rolling.

The ice by the shoreline buckled when the last wheels moved from the ground to the ice. Midway across a large split in the ice made Keith rethink his decision to cross, but there was no turning back now. With extra determination and trust in his animals Keith urged them to the other side and up the low bank. He'd made it, the most difficult part of the trip. Or so it seemed.

No more than two wagon lengths down the road he encountered a mud hole. The back wheels of the wagon sank to the axle and brought the forward motion to a halt.

The wagon was stuck.

He got down to survey the situation and slapped the top of the wheel. He remembered Sam complaining many times about this part of the road and now understood his frustration.

There was nothing to do but unhitch the horses and ride them back to town. It was going to take many men to dig the wagon out and at least a day's delay on the rest of the scheduled hauls. He felt like he was letting his father down because of his poor judgment.

A small light greeted him as he came home. He was cold and tired and so many decisions weighed on his shoulders. He gathered strength from Amelia when she handed him a bowl of soup and pulled off his boots.

"We need to build a road, Amelia." He emphasized his decision with a slap to the arm of the rocker. "It'll keep us hauling during spring break up."

Within a week the men of Wolf Creek had come together with their axes, saws and horse teams and built a plank road across the swamp area that had created problems for the Crawford Freight Line for years.

For many years thereafter Keith Crawford was in charge of building roadways around the community of Wolf Creek and bringing year around commerce to the area. He still drove a load now and then for his brother to check on his road system.

***

I smiled to myself thinking of the Crawford family. My own seemed troubled, but those families faced obstacles, too. I had known, deep inside, that returning to Wolf Creek and revealing my part in Toby's adoption wouldn't be easy. But on the flip side of the coin, I'd never expected so many of the shopkeepers on the Square to be new to the area. They knew nothing about the Winters family drama, or, if they knew, it was old news. I'd told the people that mattered to me the events and my part in it. It was time to close that subject and that part of my life and move forward.

So what was the problem that had kept me awake and restless most of the night? Really, what was *my* problem?

I weighed the events of the last weeks and they made my head spin. Everything happened so quickly—Miles' stroke, bumping into Elliot in the first few minutes after driving into town. Nathan and Toby and the realization that I was working for the man who was raising Lily's child, even though he'd never planned any such thing. Then I reconnected with Sarah, and Lily returned, planning Miles funeral, and through everything, Elliot was there. I'd misunderstood our past, and it looked like we could have a future. I hadn't had time to plan and prepare for any of it. All I'd been doing was reacting.

My dear Elliot. My heart wanted to be with him, but did I hold him at arm's length because I was afraid of being hurt again? Or did I worry about hurting him, apparently for a second time? He'd made his position clear to me—and everyone—that I was his chosen.

I laughed at that thought. "His chosen." How romantic it sounded. A real life relationship wasn't a fairytale or a romance novel. It was about give and take and compromise. It wasn't a matter of saying, "I'll put you off until I deal with this crisis, and then I'll invite you to come back."

I'd done that to Elliot. When I looked at the headstones in front of me the names blurred from the tears. I'd asked Elliot for time to deal with Miles and he'd waited. He called and told me funny stories to ease the pain of the days. He held my hand at the funeral and too many other times to remember.

Not remember them? Had I been so self-centered I couldn't remember his presence in this roller-coaster of time since my return?

Even last night he'd made the evening special with the bicycle for two. The memory of it brought me to smile through falling tears. What a fun evening.

That thought reminded me of Lily, who had lived many years on her own, yet I thought I needed to know about and understand everything she did. Sure, I'd persuaded her to come back to Wolf Creek, and to justify taking that risk, I'd decided it was my job to protect her.

From what?

For so long, I'd thought of Lily as little more than a child, yet I'd seen signs that she was moving forward in her life. She was patching things up with her mother, working hard, and spending her money carefully. She interacted easily with the shopkeepers and customers. She didn't know how often I'd heard her name mentioned at morning coffee at

Biscuits and Brew. Always in a positive way, too, even from Doris.

My concerns always circled back to Lily and Toby, and now Lily's relationship with Nathan. Jack's comments had stuck with me and made me think about my role in their lives and what it would be in the years ahead. But I had to face the fallout from my decision to search for Lily. She'd seen Toby and nothing would ever be the same.

I heard a car approaching, its wheels crunching on the gravel driveway, stopping close by. I turned to see who might be visiting a loved one. Parked behind my car was Lily's. How did she find me?

She approached carrying a small bouquet. I made the connection from those she carried to the shriveled ones on the ground. Busy as she was, she hadn't forgotten her family.

"Hi, Georgia. I didn't think I'd find you here." She edged closer to the headstones and laid the new flowers next to Mom's stone. She picked up the dried bouquet and rubbed it between her hands. When the flowers and stems were no more than small pieces she threw them up into the air. "Next time I'll bring two bouquets."

I scanned the area around me. "I needed a place to think— this fits the bill pretty well."

"Me, too, sometimes," Lily said. "My life has changed so much since I came home." She bent down in front of me and gave me a hug, awkward, even clumsy, but that didn't matter. The feelings behind it were all that mattered to me.

"And it's all because you cared enough about me to find me." She sat down facing the markers, her legs folded Indian style. "Isn't it beautiful here?" She stretched her arms to reach for the sun and held that pose for a minute or two.

It seemed obvious that this hadn't been her first visit to the cemetery. Despite her pleasant demeanor, she still seemed troubled, even a little melancholy.

"Lily? Do you want to tell me about your evening? Where did you go after the fireworks?" Was it really my business? No, but I asked anyway.

"To Nathan and Toby's apartment. Toby wanted to show

me and Richard his bedroom. So we all went."

"Toby's pretty excited about moving I hear." I shielded my eyes from the sun so I could look directly at her.

"More than excited, I'd say." She laughed in her clear, joyful way that I remembered from when she was a little girl.

"You still seem troubled. What is it?" Now that we were talking I wouldn't let my question remain unanswered.

She turned away before I could read the emotion on her face so I wasn't prepared for her reply.

"When Toby and Richard were in Toby's bedroom, Nathan asked if I wanted to live there with them." She put her face in her hands.

What could I say?

"Wow, Lily, I don't know what to say. That's quite an idea."

"He doesn't even know me," she said harshly as she got to her feet. "He just wants someone to take care of Toby."

That made no sense at all.

"I don't think Nathan's that kind of man."

"You weren't there."

"No, I wasn't. But…"

"I made Toby sick, so now Nathan wants me to take care of him."

Her stark statement left me lightheaded. I touched my fingers to my forehead, as if I needed a reminder to focus. "You've said that before. But Lily, what do you mean you made him sick?"

"Do you know what's wrong with him?"

I shook my head, although I knew more than I was letting on. I hadn't wanted to add to Lily's self-blame. "Not really—I mean I know his kidneys are failing."

"He has a genetic disease called polycystic kidney disease." Her tone told me that I certainly should be familiar with the medical terminology. "He got it because I carry the gene, and The Jerk carried the gene. Toby ended up getting the gene from both of us. He had a twenty-five percent chance to develop it. And Toby lost."

I got to my feet, too, so I could address her face to face.

"You have to look at that as history, water under the bridge so to speak. His future is important now."

She lowered her head first and then crumbled to the ground and sobbed.

I imagined she was crying over things that had happened years ago that brought about the situation we faced today. I could try to talk her out of her guilt, but that would be futile. And I couldn't simply make it all better.

***

I waved goodbye to Lily as she backed her car out to the narrow road and left the cemetery. I wanted to linger a bit longer, but she'd gathered herself and rattled off the things she needed to do before her lunch shift at Crossroads. Breakfast, a shower, dressing for work, all basic things that would help her navigate the day, even with her mixed and changing emotions about Toby and Nathan. Maybe even her questions about being back in Wolf Creek.

I knew the Square would bustle all day, with visitors arriving mid-morning and staying until late afternoon or early evening. I doubted I'd see her before tomorrow, if then. But it wasn't unusual for us not to see each other except in passing for days on end.

Next week would bring more of the same. Sarah had issued a revised event schedule for July, and it now included three bus tours arriving on separate days. This didn't change much for Country Law, but I could see the smiles on Marianna and Art's faces, and Jessica over at Styles, and many others. Elliot and Eli enjoyed the bus tours, too, because they sold specialty foods tourists bought as gifts. Local honey and homemade jams had always been my fallback hostess gifts and I was sure I wasn't alone.

Country Law wasn't completely left out of the frenzy. In fact, every day a few tourists wandered in for no other reason than curiosity about the new business on the Square. I'd begun to wish I'd kept track of the number of business cards we'd handed out since April 1st.

After Lily's car disappeared toward the main road, I sat a

while longer. The sun felt warm and soothing on my face, a pleasant change from the heat and humidity so common in July. More people had driven into the cemetery, probably on their weekly visit following their Sunday morning church service. With the arrival of the cars, the quiet atmosphere transformed. Soon kids ran in the roadway playing tag, and their parents yelled at them to stop. I stood and folded my chair and gathered the rest of my things. My silent retreat was no longer a good place to ponder the past or the future.

With everyone else, including Elliot, busy at the Square all afternoon, I was at loose ends, but I didn't feel like traipsing around the shops. But since I didn't care to go home to my empty house either, I pulled into a parking space behind Country Law and let myself into the office. I could get a head start on the week. I often wondered how Miles, being all alone, had managed all the work involved in tending to his clients. I had to face, though, that in these last years, Miles' pace had slowed, and with that, he wasn't particularly efficient either. Now, Nathan and Jack had revitalized the law office, and being part of that made me proud.

Finding work to fill the afternoon hours wasn't a problem. Not all of it was challenging. I left the photocopier to do its work of producing ten collated copies of a 40 page document, and turned my attention to preparing folders of information that the coming week's clients would take home after their appointments. Drafts of wills, living wills, financial and powers of attorney. Jack had once laughed and said that the paperless office was an urban legend, kind of like the alligators in the New York sewer system. But I was at home amidst forms and papers, like being on solid footing doing a job I loved.

This mechanical work gave me time to think about Virgie, due to arrive at the end of the week. We'd planned her visit over the phone and by exchanging emails. I had to stop myself from hoping she'd make a decision about moving to Wolf Creek and working for us before it was time to return to Milwaukee. I had leads on some other women who might be interested in the job, my backup plan in case

Virgie declined. I didn't know any of them personally, but based on the feelers I'd put out, they were qualified for the job and might be open to making a change.

Late in the afternoon, with my work done, I stood at the window and watched groups of shoppers moving along the walkway from one store to the next. At that moment I felt alive and decided to go outside to join them. I grabbed my purse before locking the door behind me. Seemed I felt like doing a little shopping after all.

Quilts Galore was my first stop. I spotted a summer quilt in colors that matched Lily's room and bought it. I hoped she'd consider the gift a good surprise, not something her aunt was foisting on her. Marianna and Rachel were busy with customers, so we didn't have time to talk. But seeing the shoppers in the store gave me a lift.

I waved to Doris through her store window, but quickly turned the corner to Styles. The clothes on display in the windows were cute for a day at the lake or for a stay at a resort. But they were better suited for women Lily's age. Marianna had assured me that she'd found clothes for herself there, so I went inside. Maybe I'd find something, too. I had an ulterior motive for checking out Styles. I wanted to see if Virgie's vests could complement the kind of clothing they carried. If they did, then I'd add another selling point to convince her to make the change.

An hour later, I left with a shopping bag in each hand, and in my mind, a new market for Virgie's one-of-a-kind vests.

16

Busier than ever at the office, Monday and Tuesday flew by. On Wednesday, I looked up from the file I was working on to see Toby running to my desk. I'd created a corner in my bottom desk drawer to stash some candy. After the first time I'd shown him where I'd hidden the treats, all he needed was a nod from me before opening the drawer and taking one piece—Nathan's limits.

That day, Toby had a gauze bandage wrapped around his arm.

"Toby? Did you get hurt?"

"Dialy." He picked up miniature chocolate bar and examined the wrapper, but then put it back and chose another, only to put it down, too, in favor of one wrapped in red paper.

That was a jolt. Toby had started treatments—dialysis. Why hadn't Nathan told me? Would Nathan give me updates in the future? Or more to the point, had he told Lily what was going on?

Months ago we'd planned a donor match party, but when Nathan suggested it to the medical team they wanted to keep the pool small at the beginning. More donors could be included later if no match had been found. Testing the family would be first. Of course, I'd thought about that before.

From down the hallway I heard Nathan's voice calling Toby's name. "Leave Georgia alone, kiddo. She has work to do—and what did I say about candy before supper?"

Toby undid the snap on the pocket on the outside of his

cargo pants and winked at me as he slipped the bar into the pocket. Then with a wave he scurried to Nathan's office.

A six-year old who winked. No wonder my heart melted. It melted *for* him, too. He'd already experienced two tragedies in his life, the deaths of the only parents he knew and, now, a life-threatening illness.

After Sunday's reevaluation, I decided I'd take a step back from trying to take care of everyone and take a different approach. All these people I loved had their own lives, and who was I to think I knew what was better for them? Sure, I'd always agree to help, but only on the condition that they step up and ask me. Short of a request, I wouldn't become involved. My resolve made me chuckle inside. It was going to take conscious restraint not to jump in and try to take over, at least when I jumped to the conclusion that I knew best.

The next couple of days passed in anticipation of Virgie's arrival, which happened as planned. She showed up at Country Law minutes before closing on Friday. When the bell jingled on the door, my heart sang with it.

"Welcome to Wolf Creek," I said, hugging her tight. Then I stretched my arms to take a closer look at her. Wow, I was taken aback by her lack-luster appearance. She immediately reminded me of the first time I'd seen Beverly.

"Are you okay? Is something wrong?"

Oops. I was falling back into my help everyone mode. But still, she didn't look like herself.

"You can't know how wonderful it is to see you." She pulled me back into another hug.

"Let's go home," I said. "There's a bottle of wine waiting for us and a whole evening to talk." I turned off my computer, whisked the files into a desk drawer and locked it. Virgie watched as I went through my closing ritual, finally bolting the front door and leading her to the back of the building. I turned off the lights, leaving only the security ones on.

Since I'd walked from home that morning, I climbed into the passenger seat and gave her directions for the two-block drive.

"Not exactly like our commute in Milwaukee," she said,

her tone dry.

"And I like it that way," I said, looking closely at her again. I didn't recall Virgie ever being so careless with her clothes and hair. Okay, faded jeans and an old T-shirt were okay for the drive, although the Virgie I knew would have dressed better even for a long drive. She surely had other clothes. But her hair hung limp and ragged, as if she'd cut it herself.

I was relieved Jack and Nathan hadn't been in the office when she arrived. We were going to have to make some changes before her appointment with them on Monday. At this point she didn't look like the professional I knew she was—and she didn't match the image we'd created for Country Law.

Even in the casual atmosphere on the Square, a law office was different, and I dressed professionally, usually in a suit or a blazer and slacks. I carefully styled my shoulder-length hair. If Virgie began working at the firm, she'd be the first person the clients saw when they walked into our office. Even more than the job issue, though, I was worried about her.

We each carried a bag up the walk, but Virgie stopped by the flower garden, abloom with marigolds, dusty miller and impatiens. "What a lovely garden to go with your quaint little house."

"I grew up in this house." I unlocked the door and gestured her inside. "Then my Uncle Miles lived here before he passed away last month."

Virgie nodded. "I know what he meant to you. His death must have hit hard. I'm sorry I didn't come for the funeral."

I waved her off. "On a Sunday? I never thought you would even consider coming all this way for a couple of hours. Follow me." I led the way to Lily's room with its new quilt on the freshly made bed.

Virgie smiled as she scanned the room, brushing her hand across the quilt in silent admiration.

"It's time for a glass of wine," I said. "Let's go in the kitchen."

Remembering that Virgie liked red wine, I opened a

bottle and poured the rich, garnet-red liquid into the same stemmed glasses I'd used when Sarah stopped by months ago. My hands shook a little thinking of Sarah. Oh, how I missed seeing her.

"A toast, to you and me, and maybe a new adventure for us." I raised my glass to her.

She tipped her glass for a quick clink.

The first swallow tasted heavenly. "Come on, we'll visit awhile before dinner. Lasagna and salad."

Back in the living room, she chose the soft chair and I nestled into a corner of the couch. A small end table and lamp separated us.

"Ah, lasagna. That sounds delicious."

"It's takeout from a restaurant on the Square," I said. "To be honest, I rarely cook anymore."

Virgie rested her head back and her gaze traveled the room. "You like living here, don't you? I hear it in your voice."

I didn't hesitate, didn't have to. "Yes. Yes, I do."

"And Elliot?"

I was surprised that she'd ask about him, well, at least so soon. As much as I'd wanted to get another woman's perspective on Elliot's and my relationship, Virgie hadn't met him. She'd only heard about our past, all my highs and lows over him going back to high school.

"We're good," I said, tilting my head from one side to the other. "It's hard to see each other with the Square so busy, but we keep in touch."

"Doesn't sound like the blossoming romance you described on the phone."

"It's complicated," I said, knowing I sounded defensive.

"They all are."

Restless and uneasy with the direction of our conversation, I got up to bring the wine bottle from the kitchen to the living room. I topped off our glasses and sat back in my corner. "This reminds me of our Friday nights in Milwaukee. Pizza and wine. Cheap wine. I don't think I've had pizza since I moved here."

"I envied you when you left," Virgie said, toeing off her

shoes and pulling her legs up under her.

"I was in a rut, going nowhere." I shook my head, disbelieving of the way I'd let myself stagnate. "Turns out, being let go was the best thing to happen to me in a long time."

Virgie frowned and gulped down a mouthful of wine. "At least you had somewhere to go."

"Maybe you will, too, come Monday."

She put her glass on the end table and leaned forward. "Are they nice people, Georgia? Nathan and Jack? Or are they demanding like the office manager at M and K?"

Years back, we'd begun referring to Merkel & Kline as M and K and it stuck. We even laughed about mistakenly referring to it that way when other employees were around. The partners looked unfavorably on any abbreviation.

Was that apprehension in her voice, maybe a little fear seeping in? But, of course, I understood her wariness about making such a major change, especially at her age.

I extended my hands toward her, closing the distance. "Bluntly, they expect quality work. Like Miles, they're here to help people with the legal side of life. That's our mission statement at Country Law."

I wanted to be clear that her job wouldn't be a go-through-the-motions kind of thing. "You'd be handling daily scheduling, fielding phone calls, that sort of thing. Reception combined with secretarial. But you'd likely be asked to help in other ways, too. Nathan and his son will be moving into the apartment above the office soon. You may be asked to pick up Toby, Nathan's son, from daycare if Nathan is busy."

"Really? That's on the personal side."

"True, but it's different here. I've done it, and Jack has filled in, and so has Jack's wife, Liz. In this firm, we don't really have job descriptions that limit what we do. We all work for the clients doing what needs to be done—and I work for two lawyers with the same attitude, which is why the daycare run occasionally comes up." Later, I'd tell her about Toby not having a mother, and being so ill. Besides, that information wasn't important now.

Virgie's mouth curled up in a faint smile. "Sounds interesting."

Glad to see her smiling, I decided against approaching her about her appearance. It was too soon. She'd only been in town for just over an hour. But it needed saying eventually.

"Here's the most important question, Virgie. Do you want to leave M and K and move to a small town where you don't know anyone?"

Virgie laughed. "Nothing like getting down to the nitty-gritty."

"No reason not to," I said. "Let's talk about it."

"Okay," Virgie said. "I know you. And I assume you'll introduce me to your friends. Right?"

Again, I could see—even feel—her apprehension. "Of course. You'll meet all the shop owners on the Square, and their employees, too. It is a small community of people that support each other."

"Well, I could see myself enjoying that," she said.

"I have an idea, too, that might intrigue you. There's a store called Styles. Two women, Jessica and Mimi, own it, and for weeks now, I've been thinking that they might be interested in your vests—they like the one-of-a-kind accessories. You can wander in there and have a look."

Virgie shrugged. Not the reaction I'd expected.

"I don't sew much anymore."

"Oh, well, you never mentioned that." Was this another way she neglected herself or did it involve money, the lack of funds to buy supplies? "Why? You always seemed excited about your original designs and your customers."

"It's complicated," she said. "Turns out a woman in our office starting copying my designs and selling them for less money." She raised her hands in air. "I couldn't believe it. Even some of my best customers started buying from her. I couldn't compete."

I swallowed back some wine, stunned to hear this. "When did this happen? You worked for a law office, for Pete's sake. Didn't you protect your designs with copyrights or branding?"

"I tried," she said. "I asked one of the lawyers to help me, but he brushed the whole concept off as a hobby and not worth the time or money."

"I don't believe that—it's awful." It was a terrible development, but I had to listen to the little voice inside that told me to quit challenging her and what she'd done or not done for herself. I wouldn't, couldn't, become her caretaker.

She only shrugged and didn't defend herself.

Something inside surged and I couldn't help myself from letting loose. "Listen, Virgie, I can tell you right now that if you don't show anymore self-confidence than what you've shown me since you walked through my door, Nathan and Jack won't hire you. Do you want this job?"

She stood up and stared at the front door. It occurred to me that she was poised to walk out. Instead she stepped closer to me.

I held my breath, feeling astonished all over again at how broken my friend looked. The job aside, my lectures were over. More than anything, Virgie needed compassion and support.

"Oh, yes, *I want this job*. I can't live in Milwaukee any longer. And I can't work for M and K, not after that nasty lawyer wrote off my creativity, almost sneering at me about *hobbies*. But I need your help, Georgia. Please help me."

I rose from the chair.

But the door bell rang.

17

I considered ignoring it. I really did *not* want the interruption, so if I did nothing, the person would go away.

I sighed. I couldn't hide from whoever was on my porch. My car—and Virgie's—were in the driveway and lights were on all over the house. I went to the window and pulled aside the curtain, surprised to see Beverly waiting. I turned the lock bolt and swung open the door.

"Hi," she said, her smile warmer than I'd seen in years. "Sorry to bother you, but Lily forgot her cosmetic bag. She said they're crazy busy over there, and it would be too late for her to get it after work. She asked if I'd pick it up for her."

I opened the door wider. "Come on in."

Beverly stepped inside and into the living room, but hesitated.

I gestured for her to come deeper into the room. "Come meet my friend, Virgie—Virginia Saunders."

Virgie inched forward on the couch cushion. "Nice to meet you, Beverly, but please call me Virgie. I'm not sure I'd answer if you called me Virginia."

"Uh, we were having a glass of wine before dinner and catching up on our lives since I left Milwaukee." An understatement, considering what had gone on before the doorbell rang. "Sit down and join us. I'll get you a glass."

Still looking tentative, Beverly perched on the edge of the seat at one end of the couch.

Grateful for the interruption, but still acting as if Virgie and I were simply passing time on the first evening of her visit, I went to the kitchen to grab a glass. But I took my time. I needed to think about how to respond to my friend's dilemma, her need for help—the fact that she asked for it. Surely, this couldn't simply be a matter of wanting advice about her appearance. Virgie might have fallen into a rut, but she knew what to do. But, if I could persuade Beverly to join us for supper, I'd be able to gather my thoughts. Maybe she needed only a nudge to stop her downward slide. But I knew myself that sometimes it's a struggle to climb back up. I slipped the pan of lasagna into the oven, satisfied there was plenty to feed three.

Glass in hand, I returned to find the two chatting about Wolf Creek and how long our family had lived in the area. I filled Beverly's glass from the open bottle on the coffee table.

"Don't let me interrupt," I said. "Beverly's lived here her whole life and knows more about Wolf Creek than most of us."

"I'm the one that interrupted." She stood and put her still full glass next to the wine bottle on the coffee table. "I'll get Lily's bag and be on my way."

"Do you have plans for supper?" I blurted.

"No…no, but I didn't plan to stay. Virgie just got here and I'm sure you have plenty to talk about."

Beverly had worked her way around the couch toward the bathroom.

"But there's more than enough food for the three of us. The lasagna's in the oven and I picked up a huge salad from Crossroads." I reached out and took hold of her shoulders and turned her back to face the couch. I picked up her glass and handed it back to her. "Here, sit down and relax. No argument."

"Well, Virgie," Beverly said, talking behind her hand. "You've seen a determined woman at work."

Laughing, I said, "I heard that." I snuggled into the soft corner of the couch opposite Beverly.

"Where do you work, Bev?" Virgie asked, picking up their conversation as if there'd been no interruption.

"I work in the office at Neenah Paper. I've been there

196

close to thirty years now."

Virgie's eyes popped open in surprise. "Didn't you ever want to move or change jobs?"

Uh oh...she bumbled into a tricky subject. Beverly's inertia puzzled me, too.

"Years ago, sure. I had all kinds of notions about a new job. But then, Georgia left, so I thought I should stay in town to be nearby if Mom needed help."

Well, that was blunt. "That's exactly what happened. Our Mom needed help and Beverly provided it." I'd never been sure about her reason for staying in Wolf Creek or her sense of responsibility to our mother. Was I so self-centered that I never considered supporting my family in ways other than money? But did the money I sent to Mom free me from the guilt of not being there?

I was saved from further talk about the past when the timer on the oven buzzed. Eager to get dinner underway, I hurried away to take the lasagna out of the oven. "Grab your glasses and come to table," I said.

When Beverly and Virgie stood in the doorway to the kitchen, I wondered if I should have set the table in the dining room. Too late, though, and the kitchen had the homier atmosphere.

I told the two of them to sit, while I topped the salad with Crossroads' specialty Italian dressing. Within minutes we were ready to enjoy a meal that I'd always considered comfort food.

The conversation traveled back and forth, easily, the way chats between old friends do after a long time apart. Beverly added stories about Uncle Miles and our Wolf Creek childhood, noting the biggest bonding experiences the two of us shared. "We drove our mother nuts with our antics, especially all the teasing. We'd come home from the lake with tall tales about Uncle Miles catching the biggest fish we'd ever seen. Miles didn't even like to fish, but somehow the two of us managed to convince her we were telling the truth."

Later, with the leftovers wrapped and put away, we jointly washed up the dishes and went back to the living room with our refilled glasses.

As I settled into the corner of the couch, I was smacked in the face with my new resolution to only help those who asked for it. It seemed like days ago, rather than mere hours, that Virgie was opposite me, almost pleading for help.

I brushed away that memory and tuned into Beverly's question to Virgie about her vests. "Do you plan to wear one for your interview?"

Good call, Sis. I was glad it was Beverly who broke the ice of that conversation.

Virgie lowered her gaze and stared at her hands in her lap. "I have no idea what to wear. It's been years since I've looked for a job. All my clothes are so out of style." She reached up to pat the side of her head. "And this hair! I've been trimming it myself for awhile now—too long."

I understood Virgie's appearance now, sort of, but that begged the question about why she'd let herself become so out of style. She had rich, ash brown hair, with a blunt cut that wasn't quite a bob, but not exactly a pixie either. I wonder what had happened to her confidence. She was over-qualified for the job at Country Law. Maybe I could help that situation, and I could give her a few pointers about clothes, too. But, really, Virgie had a good eye for clothes, so she didn't need advice so much as a boost in her confidence.

Beverly moved to the edge of her cushion. "I'm free tomorrow. Let's all drive to Green Bay and go to one of those walk-in beauty shops. I certainly could use a trim and style myself."

Beverly looked at me for agreement. I nodded—enthusiastically. Beverly hadn't bothered updating her look either. And I always felt better about myself after a hair appointment. Maybe Virgie would, too. But what about finances? I decided to bring that up later after Beverly left. I certainly could loan her money if that was an issue.

"Works for me. How about it Virgie?" We'd made it difficult for her to refuse, but a makeover was in her best interest—whether she agreed or not. Long seconds passed, but finally, Virgie nodded yes.

"Now, Virgie, show me your vests." Beverly folded her

arms across her chest, feigning a stern stance.

I laughed to myself. My sister was like a dog with a bone. She was on her own mission, but I don't believe Beverly realized that in showing interest in Virgie's hair and clothing had sparked a renewed interest in her own. Like Virgie, Beverly herself had been stuck in the past for too long. Their growing enthusiasm was catching, too. Maybe I'd find something new and unique at the mall for myself. Before I arrived in Wolf Creek, I'd been in a rut, too.

So much had changed since my first days in Wolf Creek, back when Beverly had spoken as few words as possible to me. Like Virgie, she hadn't updated anything in her life. Now, something I never expected was happening. I was in the midst of planning a ladies' day out with my sister and my friend. Haircuts and shopping, all of us together. I liked these new twists in my life.

Virgie hurried to the bedroom and minutes later, brought out vests in three different styles. Beverly couldn't contain her excitement at seeing them. Almost hesitantly, she reached out to touch the fabrics.

"This is the one to wear Monday." Beverly held up a silky vest in deep jewel tones of purple, red, and gold. The design was more like a shawl than the standard sleeveless vest cut, making it unique and so eye catching. "And with your petite figure, you can pull off a flowy look."

"Wow. This reminds me of the clothes that Jack's wife wears," I said. "Liz is always in vibrant colors—no wonder she always seems so full of life." I glanced at Virgie. "You'll meet her soon, and if you're wearing that vest she may buy it off your shoulders." I wanted to try it on, but Beverly was already on her feet and had put one arm into the sleeve opening.

"Match this with a white blouse and black slacks and you'll feel terrific." Beverly showcased the vest by turning side to side for us to see.

"And sandals," I added. "This is Wolf Creek, not Milwaukee. Nathan and Jack wear dress shirts and ties, but rarely suit jackets. Professional, but more casual than a big city firm."

I saw Virgie's expression relax. I should have made it clear that her interview wasn't going to be formal, not like the three-step applications larger firms used. Still, Country Law was professional, which is why her appearance had alarmed me.

Virgie grinned, but then swallowed a yawn. Beverly saw it and looked at her watch. "Oh, my, look at the time. Lily may get home before I do."

"Don't forget the cosmetic bag," I said.

"Wouldn't that be something?" She laughed and headed into the bathroom.

"Thanks for being so enthusiastic about my vest," Virgie called out as she stood and stretched her arms to her sides. I knew how she felt. Good food plus good wine added up to relaxation.

"Why don't I drive?" Beverly suggested. "I'll pick you up about 9:30," Beverly said, going straight from the bathroom to the front door. "How about hair first, then clothes shopping, then lunch?"

She grabbed her purse off the floor. "Off I go. Thanks for dinner, Georgia. And, Virgie, I wish I'd met you years ago. I can see why your friendship means a lot to my sister."

And then she was gone.

"We have our marching orders," I quipped as I locked the door.

I turned around and walked into a hug from Virgie. When I slowly stepped back I saw a huge grin appear on her face.

"I'm going to like living here," she said. "If everyone is as friendly as Bev I won't have any trouble meeting people."

I smiled to myself, thinking about how good it was to have my sister back. And Beverly had always quickly corrected anyone who called her Bev. Apparently, Virgie would have that privilege.

***

"Ooh, look at you," Beverly said, lightly touching Virgie's hair, short now, a true pixie cut framing her face in a flattering way.

"You're not so bad yourself," Virgie said, eyeing Beverly's freshly cut bangs.

"You both look like new women," I said. Of the three of us, I was the only one who left with the same cut I'd come in with, although the stylist had given my shoulder-length hair more volume than I managed on my own. I didn't say much about it, but I'd undertaken a minor makeover just before we opened Country Law's doors in its new location on the Square. Brighter lipstick and new clothes had given me a lift then, just heading off to the mall with Beverly and Virgie had been exciting and fun, like a bit of an adventure.

We happily started our long trip through the mall, where we all found clothes we wanted. Beverly spotted a crisp white tailored shirt she declared perfect for Virgie to wear under her vest. Between the new narrow-legged slacks that showed off her petite figure and the new shirt, I knew she'd look great for a Country Law interview, although I still wasn't convinced she'd project the confidence she needed. I quickly shook off those thoughts and refocused on the positive.

By the time we'd circled back to our starting point, hungry but happy, we each carried four shopping bags and complained about our hands hurting from grasping the handles.

"But it's such a good hurt," Beverly said, laughing.

Seeing the bags holding all the new things Virgie bought—and with cash—I was convinced that her self-neglect wasn't about money. A couple of hours later, she picked up the lunch check at Olive Garden without any hesitation.

"This is my treat," she insisted.

"How about one more stop before we head home?" Beverly asked.

"Where?" I asked.

"The fabric store? There's one on the other side of the parking lot."

Virgie's eyes sparkled. "I'd love it. Maybe we can find fabric for a new vest for you, Georgia. I'll make you one as my thank you for giving me this vacation, not to mention a new opportunity." She reached across the table and touched my arm.

"You don't need to do that." True, but I liked hearing this new Virgie, so different from the one who'd arrived yesterday.

"Maybe not, but I want to," she said.

"And there's no need to rush home," I said, "so let's be on our way to another adventure."

"Road trip," Beverly declared, as we all piled into the car to drive the equivalent of a block or two to a parking spot in front of the fabric store.

Sewing on a button or hemming a pair of pants were the limit of my skills with a needle and thread, but seeing Virgie's excited expression going into the fabric store, I looked forward to browsing around. Although I had no interest in learning to sew, Beverly and Virgie had found their common ground. As I walked behind them, they talked in that special language of fabric and threads.

Why hadn't I known about my sister's interest in making clothes? From what I could tell, she was practically a seamstress. When had all this happened?

I claimed the back seat for the ride back to Wolf Creek, leaving Beverly and Virgie free to talk on about sewing, sounding like they'd known each other for decades. A wave of sadness washed over me, though. Beverly and I hadn't spent a day like this since we were girls in high school. Now I wondered what prompted her quick change of attitude. Why was she acting so different towards me? Or, was I the one who'd looked at her with tainted eyes? I took responsibility for part of our distance, but not all of it. She'd changed, too.

I wanted another perspective and I knew exactly where I'd find it. When Beverly stopped for gas, I slipped my cell phone out of my purse and called Elliot. I needed to describe our exhilarating, fun, but slightly strange day. Besides, I missed talking with him. But my call went to voice mail, so I left a short message to let him know I looked forward to a good long talk.

We pulled in front of my house, where Beverly said goodbye and wished Virgie well on Monday. "Maybe we can do it again soon."

"If Jack and Nathan offer her a job and she accepts," I said, "I'll have more time for friends and family."

"And Elliot? What about him, Sis?"

I grinned. "Elliot, too."

Sis? Beverly hadn't called me that in years.

18

As our lazy Sunday came to an end, I waited for Elliot to call. Meanwhile, Virgie grew quiet. I'd been afraid that yesterday's upbeat mood wouldn't last. She had her clothes and a new hairstyle, but something was off.

"Nervous?" I asked after we'd polished off our Cobb salads and turned on the television to catch the national evening news.

"Very." She twisted a button on her blouse. "I know I can do the job you described, especially the computer part. I've turned into a techie of sorts, good at updates and the new terminology."

"That sounds promising," I said, quietly. "We need someone with those skills. Computers more or less bore Jack, and even as young as he is, Nathan isn't that interested in technology beyond his phone that can do everything but wash the dishes."

Virgie smiled at my lame joke, but her face quickly turned serious.

"It's the people-person part of the job that has me jittery. I'm not sure about meeting clients and making them feel welcome. I haven't done that since I was a very young receptionist." She let go of the button and began tapping the arm of the chair. "I've been working alone in a cubical for so long that I sometimes chatter all through lunch to anyone who will listen."

I frowned, trying to gather my thoughts. "After watching you and Beverly yesterday I don't think you have anything to worry about. You acted like she was a long-lost friend."

She waved me off. "Bev and I speak the same language, that's all." She stopped the fidgeting. "Does she sew a lot?"

"Honestly, I don't know." I shrugged. "I didn't even know she'd taken up sewing. I don't remember her talking about it." I left out the part about being unaware of anything Beverly had done in the last several years.

Was that another hole in our relationship? When would I get to know the real Beverly?

"The point is, Virgie, no one at the office bites. And our clients are people just like us. You'll be much more than a receptionist—we need your computer skills. But if you take the job, you'll be the first person they see. I intend to help with that part of it, too, because rolling out the 'welcome wagon' is part of the appeal of a small town firm."

As Virgie took in my words, I saw her become calmer, more open to talking about what the move to Wolf Creek would entail. Finally, she flashed a grin and said, "At least I know I have the perfect clothes."

With that, we said goodnight. I lingered only long enough to prepare the coffee pot for morning.

When I went into the kitchen the next morning, Virgie was already at the table sipping coffee. She'd declined my offer to make a full breakfast, agreeing only to a Biscuits and Brew blueberry muffin. She didn't want a ride over to the Square either. I grabbed a piece of paper and drew a map showing the route from my house to the Square. Its simplicity made us both laugh.

"I'll be there on time, Georgia," Virgie said, "maybe even a little early to show them just how interested I am."

"It's a big day for you, but I know you'll do fine." I went to her side and gave her a hug. "If you agree join us over at our little firm, we'll be very happy. And so will you. I promise—it's a really good place to work."

Then I left. On the way to the office, it occurred to me that I'd never had a chance to be nervous or excited. I had the job before I'd even driven into Wolf Creek, and Nathan and Jack needed me to pick up where Miles had left off. I'd been lucky that way.

Just as she'd said, Virgie walked into Country Law

ten minutes before her scheduled 10:30 appointment. I was occupied talking over documents Jack needed for an afternoon meeting with an out-of-town client. But I'd heard the bell jingle and looked up as she nodded my way. Everything about her fit. New hair, crisp shirt, slim pants, low-heeled sandals, all set off with the deep jewel colors of the vest. If Jack hadn't been watching, I'd have given her a thumbs-up sign.

I walked from behind my desk to greet her. "Welcome to Country Law." Carrying herself a little taller than she had when she came in the first time, I watched her scan the reception area and my work area.

Her smile changed slightly when she saw Jack, likely guessing who he was.

I put my hand on her back and gave her a little nudge forward.

"Jack, meet Virginia Saunders, better known as Virgie."

Jack extended his hand and said, "We're glad you're here." With a wide grin, he added, "Hang on to that vest for dear life. My wife is likely to steal it the first chance she gets."

Virgie smiled at me. "Funny, Georgia said the same thing. Just say the word, and I'll make one for her."

"Really?" Jack narrowed his eyes, deep in thought. "I need a special gift for Liz."

When the phone rang, I walked away from them to answer it, but they soon took off down the hallway to Jack's office. I relaxed, knowing Jack would ease into the interview. No one wanted help in the office as much as he did—except for me, perhaps.

Minutes later, I turned to the sound of footsteps in the hallway. There was Toby, making a beeline to my desk.

"Hi, Georgia. I go to Sally's today. Want to come with me?" Toby couldn't get the words out fast enough.

His voice revealed no apprehension about being with other kids at Sally's daycare. Nathan had made sure Toby was comfortable about going and Sally knew about Toby's illness and the need to protect his arm.

"Oh, that sounds like fun, Toby, but your dad has lots of

work for me here."

I heard the familiar thud of Nathan's briefcase that he let drop to the floor of his office. A second or two later, he passed my desk on the way to the coffee maker and brought the carafe back with him to fill my cup.

"Can you take him to Sally's?" he asked, quickly followed by telling me he'd watch the phone. "And what about Virgie? Is she here?" He looked at the clock.

"She's with Jack now," I said, wondering what had made him so anxious. "She wants this job, Nathan."

"That's good, but we'll see. I need to talk to her first," he said, still talking a mile a minute. "I'll stop in Jack's office shortly." He turned to Toby. "Have a good day, kiddo. I'll pick you up after lunch."

"Dialy today." Toby held up his arm with the bandage for me to see. He looked at me with those dark blue eyes and a smile crossed his face. "Maybe candy would taste good when I'm done."

I nodded and he opened the drawer to choose from a new selection of bars I'd put in recently.

"Only one." Nathan's soft voice was a gentle reminder for Toby. He gave the boy a shoulder squeeze, and then ducked back into his office, coffee mug in hand.

At times, I still had trouble understanding Nathan's willingness to entrust the boy to me after I'd let Toby be adopted.

Toby picked up his Superman back pack and put the miniature bar in a side pocket. "Ready."

"Me, too." I grabbed my purse and we stepped outside to walk the short distance to Sally's, beyond Farmer Foods and just off the Square. I hoped to see Elliot when we passed the store windows, but only the checker was visible through the window. Still no return call.

By the time I returned to the office Virgie had moved into Nathan's office and Jack was sitting at my desk.

"Maybe I should apply for this job. I seem to be at this desk more than my own lately."

"So, what do you think about Virgie?"

"Well, she listed her qualifications when I asked for them,

kind of like a robot. When I asked about working directly with clients, she hesitated and admitted she'd had little, if any, contact with clients for quite a while now."

My heart fell. Jack didn't sound very encouraging, but he hadn't said no.

"Gottcha." He laughed, long and hard. "No worry. I told her the job was hers if Nathan agreed."

I grabbed the straight-back chair by my desk and sat. "I don't know what I would have said to her if you didn't like her. She'll be here for the whole week!"

Jack flashed an impish grin.

We both turned to the sound of Nathan and Virgie's voices as they approached my desk. Virgie tried to contain her smile. She failed.

"The newest employee of Country Law needs to find a place to live." Nathan said, looking proud of himself for being so clever about announcing his approval of Virgie joining our little office.

Still grinning, Virgie said, "I can stay with Georgia's sister until I find a place of my own."

"Beverly's?" My voice croaked.

"Uh huh. We talked about it Saturday at the fabric store."

What else did my friend and my sister talk about? Suddenly, I wondered what they said about me. A little paranoid, maybe, but I was curious all the same.

She turned her attention to Nathan and Jack. "But I do need to give M and K—oops—Merkel & Kline notice. My apartment building manager, too."

"Well, I figured if Georgia thought her friend wanted to work for us I needed to make a phone call," Jack said. "I didn't want to wait a month or two before you could be here."

Jack now had a rapt audience of three.

"So I called Peter Merkel and explained our situation."

"You know Mr. Merkel?" Stunned, Virgie said, "I've never even seen him."

"We worked a case together a couple of years ago," Jack said, "so no, we're not social friends, but he owed me a favor or two. There is no exit process or timeline for you.

You can work for us starting tomorrow if you like." Jack chuckled. "I told him he made a mistake letting you leave so easily."

"But my apartment, my things?"

"Merkel & Kline will sub-lease your place, but you only have 'til the end of the month to vacate."

"You've been a busy man." Nathan smiled his appreciation and thrust out his hand for Jack to shake.

Jack sure knew how to make things happen.

"Hey, I'm tired of answering the phone and not knowing the answers to the questions people ask. And Liz is tired of me bringing work home." Jack stood and walked away from the desk when the phone rang. "Ha! Someone else can get that."

"Thank you very much for this opportunity, Mr. Pearson, Mr. Connor."

"That's Jack, thank you."

"And Nathan."

With Virgie standing a little behind me, I forwarded a call to Nathan's office and handed Jack the file for clients that had arrived. Business as usual.

"Welcome to Country Law," I said to the new clients, two sisters. "Would either of you care for a beverage—coffee, tea, water?" Jack's clients declined so I walked them down the hallway to his office.

When I came back, Virgie sat in my chair with her hands on top of my desk. She reminded me of myself sitting at Miles' desk when Jack asked me to work in that office. With both men and the clients out of sight, Virgie and I did a high five and agreed to dinner at Crossroads.

"I can't wait to meet Lily. Beverly told me she was excited to have her daughter home again."

Excited? I was seeing a new Beverly unfold.

Virgie left with a plan to visit a few shops on the Square, her new shopping zone she'd called it. Her last stop would be Styles before heading home. I'd given her a key so she could come and go as she pleased.

"I'm on a roll, Georgia. Maybe I'll have luck there, too." She flapped the front of her vest in proud style.

***

The day wasn't through delivering surprises.

Less than ten minutes after Nathan left to pick up Toby, Lily rushed in. "Is Nathan here?"

I shook my head.

"Darn. I wanted to go to dialysis with him and Toby. Nathan told me what happens during the treatment, but I thought if I saw it I'd understand it better."

I dialed Sally's, but Nathan had already left with Toby.

"It's good to hear that Nathan is telling you about Toby."

A light blush covered her face. "He calls almost every day. Or he sends texts. He's even teaching Toby to text me."

When did I move out of that loop? And it seemed Beverly and Virgie had formed a loop of their own.

Lily left after telling me her plan to catch up with Nathan and Toby later.

I watched her cut across the Square and go into Pages. At Miles' funeral, Lily had mentioned a project with Doris, but I never thought to ask either of them about it. Now Lily had whetted my curiosity.

Jack's next clients arrived, a young couple with a baby due soon. They weren't married, and it was my job to keep that information confidential. I'd do my part, but I couldn't help but wonder how they thought they could keep that secret in a town as small as Wolf Creek.

Right on their heels, in came Sarah. Today?

I stood so we met eye to eye. We exchanged greetings, but not as warm or casually as we once had. We still had a ways to go before we were as close as we used to be.

"I met your friend at Styles this morning. After I'd introduced myself to Virgie she mentioned she was a friend of yours. She couldn't keep her news a secret and told me she was moving to Wolf Creek and working with you."

"She's so excited about leaving Milwaukee. I hope she'll enjoy it here."

"The Square will welcome her as we do all newcomers. She sure is an outgoing, friendly lady."

"I hope so." Outgoing? Virgie? Sarah should have seen

her on Friday.

"She mentioned you two were celebrating with dinner at Crossroads tonight."

I nodded, feeling my gut jump a little.

"Uh, would you mind…can I join you?"

"Oh, Sarah, I don't…well, I don't see why not."

Could this day produce anymore situations I knew nothing about? New alliances and friendships forming. I only wished I had prepared a better foundation for myself when I'd come home to Wolf Creek. I'd known what I wanted, but after caring for everyone could I follow my resolution and begin living my own life?

Sarah and I finalized our plan and then she left as quickly as she'd come in.

I forced myself to focus on how I'd go about getting Virgie used to our office routine and introducing her to our clients. This would make extra work for me until she became comfortable handling the day to day responsibilities. But that was okay. I chuckled thinking we might need two coffee pots if Virgie still drank as much coffee as I did.

The day ended with Beverly calling to tell me Virgie had invited her to dinner with us. "Glad you can make it. See you at 7:00." What else could I have said?

After Jack left, I locked the door and turned the Open/ Closed sign around. I needed a few minutes to calm myself from all the excitement this day had brought. And I finally had a minute to call Elliot to tell him the news about Virgie's move to Wolf Creek before he heard it from someone else. I heard the happiness in my own voice when I reached him and pieced all the developments together. Finally, I stopped to take a breath.

"Old news, Peaches."

I laughed. "How is that possible? It's Monday. You never even leave the store on delivery day."

"Small town. News travels fast. Especially when someone new arrives in town—and plans to stay."

I heard him juggle the phone to answer someone's question. "You're busy. I'll call later."

"Later, like tonight?" he asked, his voice tight. "Or later, like maybe when you're sure everyone else is taken care of?"

It was my turn to be terse. So much for good news. "Goodbye, Elliot."

I stared at the phone, panic rising in my chest. Maybe Elliot and I weren't meant to be together after all.

19

Isquelched my fears about Elliot and me and forced a happy face for our foursome dinner. Fortunately, the excitement and happiness of my three companions proved infectious and I didn't need to pretend for long. As long as I stayed focused on the company and the food and didn't let my troubles intrude. We got out of hand, though, when our hoots of laughter got a tad loud and our repartee grew boisterous. Maybe I turned red in the face when Lily showed up at our table acting amused at our antics, but at the same time, asked us to please quiet down.

Were we that loud? With a celebration in progress, reserve was in short supply. And I had to admit that earlier in the day I'd had reservations about Sarah joining us. Yet, here she was, playing her role of Wolf Creek Square's ambassador with great aplomb. She took care not to let on that we'd had our differences recently, and I did the same.

Virgie and Beverly were full of surprises. The dinner plates cleared and slices of Crossroads pie and cups of coffee in their place, Virgie recounted plans she and Beverly had to head to Milwaukee on Friday to pack up her things and arrange for her furniture to be shipped. She'd repeated the steps I'd taken only a few months before in March, prompting me to again wonder if Virgie would find happiness in Wolf Creek like I had.

In a matter of days she had thrown off that neglected, broken woman and replaced her with a confident, hopeful one. M and K had lost a good employee, but we at Country Law were the benefactors.

213

Lily planned to stay at her mom's house while Beverly was gone helping Virgie. Odd that no one had included me in the planning. But wasn't that fine, given my resolution to stay out of other's people's issues, except if asked? I wanted my family and friends to be independent. Didn't I?

Yes, no, maybe. Independent, yes, but not to the exclusion of family—of me. Was I sending mixed messages to everyone? To Elliot? And really, what did I care if others made arrangements without consulting me?

When Sarah pushed back from the table I was focused on Virgie and Beverly's debate about driving one or two cars to Milwaukee. Yes, they could bring more back with individual cars, but they'd enjoy the trip more if they traveled together.

Sarah said goodnight to Beverly and Virgie before lightly touching my arm and whispering, "I'll call soon."

The evening wound down from there, Beverly, Virgie, and I left Crossroads after saying goodbye to Lily and walked out into the light drizzle. It added to the already sultry air that had hung over Wolf Creek for more than a week. No matter how many complaints I heard about summer weather in Wisconsin, I enjoyed the days more than the monotony of winter snow.

Virgie and I had both parked behind Country Law that morning, not a long walk, but Beverly was closer and gave us a ride around the backside of the Square to our cars. We arrived dry and still exhilarated from the day. Once home, I wanted to have a few quiet moments before bed, but that was not to be. Virgie was still deep in celebration mode. She helped herself to a fresh bottle of wine from the rack on the counter and with exaggerated flair opened it and without asking if I wanted any, poured each of us a glass. I frowned at the empty spaces in the wine rack and made a mental note to pick up more of our favorite red.

"My friend, you can't possibly know what these last three days mean to me. Without your offer, I'd have been stuck at M and K forever." She handed me a glass and settled in a chair at the table. "How can I ever thank you?"

"That's easy. Start by taking over the job of answering the phone." Laughing, I sat, too, and tilted my glass to touch hers.

Answering the phone was the bread and butter of our firm. No work without clients, and they contacted us by phone most of the time, even in the cyber age. But I also found it annoying and disruptive when I needed to concentrate on a document or was in the middle of a research project.

"Yes, ma'am."

I flopped back in my chair, sipping the wine and let it do its work of relaxing every muscle in my body. I closed my eyes, enjoying the chance to finally unwind.

"Such a long day," I said. "Exciting, but long. Tomorrow is another busy day at the office for me, so I'm off to bed." I drained my glass and got up and put it on the counter.

"I'm still all wound up," Virgie said. "I'll never sleep if I turn in now." She glanced at the TV. I'll catch some news or a movie, but I'll keep the volume low." She topped off her glass and took it with her to the living room.

"I'm leaving early in the morning, and I'll try to be quiet, too." I was talking to her back, but she waved to me to let me know she understood.

Fortunately, with her plans underway, I didn't worry about Virgie entertaining herself for the next few days. She'd chatted about making lists, mentally deciding what to pack and what to leave behind. Moving from one city to another meant handling one detail after another. She'd already asked about the Wolf Creek Bank and planned to open an account before the end of the week.

I turned off the light on my nightstand, the low hum of voices from the television the only sound. Did Virgie know what program she was watching, or was she lost in her thoughts and plans?

Then it hit me. I'd never called Elliot back. What had hung between us before was still there.

***

The next morning, our two glasses and an empty bottle sat next to the sink. I turned on the coffee-maker and leaned against the counter as I waited to pour my first cup. It occurred to me that Virgie never mentioned calling anyone in Milwaukee to share her news. But I would have been the logical person to call, as I'd done when I decided to move. But I didn't want to smother Virgie by asking too many questions and offer more help than she needed. As it was, she had leaned on Beverly, so I wasn't the only person who could lend a hand in Virgie's move.

Wednesday turned out to be a particularly troublesome day at Country Law. Too many cancellations and other appointments that went too long, and an internet connection that was in and out all day. I was irritable and tired by the time evening rolled around and I had a chance to sit on my porch with Virgie. She'd had her own frustrations dealing with the moving company and learning that storing some of her things was not as easy in Wolf Creek as it was in Milwaukee. And delivery of what she needed to settle in would be delayed, too. For some reason, she'd also run into roadblocks with closing out her phone and utility accounts. "Stop by the office tomorrow and see if Jack can help with the utilities." That was the only solution I could offer.

"If I can't get here on my own what will Jack and Nathan think?" She shook her head back and forth for emphasis. "Anyway, Jack's done more than enough already. No, it's my problem and I'll solve it."

Her resolve reflected the confidence that had come through in the last few days. It would serve her well when Nathan was gone with Toby and Jack and I were busy picking up the slack with our client work.

"Just think, in little over a week I'll have a new address and a new job. I still can't believe it happened so quickly. Can you believe Bev assured me I can rent the room in her home until I'm ready to move into my own place?"

"Right place, right time," I said with a grin. "And I can't thank you enough for taking the job." I threw my head back and groaned. "Nothing could appeal to me less than interviewing a bunch of applicants. And I can tell you Jack and Nathan didn't want to either."

Virgie frowned in thought. "It's all been odd in a way. I thought Nathan and Jack would ask such different questions than they did."

That whetted my curiosity. "Hmm…I might have to interview for some other job in the future, so if you don't mind my asking, what kinds of questions did they ask? And whatever you say, it stays between us."

Virgie laughed. "Since you asked, Jack wanted to know if I could answer the phone and produce documents on the computer. Ha! You know, serious stuff."

She laughed, and I joined her.

"Off the record," she said, her voice serious again, "Jack asked if there was someone special making the move with me."

I nearly jumped out of my chair. "He can't ask that!"

She held up her hand to stop my reaction. "He knew that, Georgia. He even laughed as he asked it. But then he explained that his wife's happiness was part of his decision to join forces with Nathan. He said Marianna, you know, Liz's friend from the quilt shop, was already in Wolf Creek, so she was happy to move. But he said it takes both people to agree if there is a major move and the change is going to work out."

"I never thought of it that way," I conceded, "but still, that's really none of his business."

"True, but I hadn't thought of it Jack's way either, so I didn't mind." She smiled coyly. "Who knows? Maybe someday I'll find someone special."

Elliot's face flashed in my mind. Another day had passed. I hadn't called him, but he hadn't called me, either.

I forced my attention back to Virgie, who was talking about her sewing machine as item number one on her packing list. I couldn't relate to that, but agreed that whatever she needed to be happy, she should bring. "We all need our special things," I said. "You know, comfort stuff."

She nodded. "Absolutely."

We brought sandwiches out to the porch and watched dusk fall over the Square. Somehow, all those little annoyances slipped away.

20

My joy of seeing Toby on Thursdays never diminished. He burst into the office, always running, always smiling. He always brought something to show me, or he had a story to tell, or a joke to repeat—I rarely understood those. Without the tell-tale bandage on his arm, he'd be like any other little boy whose energy bubbled over and filled a room.

"Nathan said we're moving Saturday. Are you going to be here?"

"I'm not sure. What do you think I would do?"

Nathan emerged from the kitchen area with a full cup in his hand. "Put the kitchen in working order."

Did he really mean that as a question to a friend or was it really a request to an employee. "I suppose I can do that."

"I'm going to be the doorman like before." Toby had worked his way around my desk to the candy drawer and helped himself. I was surprised he remembered holding the door open when Charlie and his crew moved the last of the file boxes from Miles' house to the office.

Nathan scowled at Toby. "Did you ask?"

"It's okay—" I wanted Toby to enjoy getting a small piece of candy from my desk.

"No. He's old enough to know to ask," Nathan said, quiet, but definitely the enforcer-of-the-rules. "And say thank you."

"Please?" Toby hung his head a little lower than before.

I nodded and when he'd chosen one wrapped in foil paper, I heard his soft voice say, "Thank you."

"Good boy, Toby." I gave him a squeeze, but my heart jumped. It had been a couple of weeks since I'd hugged him. I'd had no idea he'd become so thin.

The phone rang and our day began, but the shock over Toby's growing frailness lingered.

Late the next afternoon, I felt like Toby when I chose a piece of wrapped chocolate from my drawer. I needed an afternoon boost. Nathan had taken off with Toby after a quick lunch at the office, and Jack had left a little more than an hour ago. With the office empty, I had a chance to see what Charlie and his crew had done with the large open space. I hadn't been upstairs since I'd blocked off the rooms and offered a few ideas. It had become Nathan's private space now, although I was sure he wouldn't have minded if I looked.

I locked the front door and turned out the lights and then went down the hallway to the back door. The door leading upstairs wasn't locked, and curiosity drew me up the stairs.

Wow—ugly and barren were gone, and the sparkling white cupboards and appliances almost spoke the words "look at me." To my left, three doors stood open. The first was going to be Nathan's room, at least I hoped so, because the taupe colored walls blending with the tweed carpet made it warm and welcoming, but definitely an adult's room. The next room, the bathroom, also had white fixtures, including a stackable washer and dryer built into a corner cabinet. I laughed out loud when I peered into the last room. Charlie knew how to make a child happy. A bed built to look like a race car occupied one corner. The dresser had been painted to look like a vertical tool chest. Even the carpet looked like a race track. I wondered if Toby had seen his room yet, but I doubted it. He'd have told me all about it for sure.

I made my way to the front window overlooking the Square. Beautiful and restful and bright with summer flowers, the orange marigolds and white day lilies, pots of impatiens and petunias dressing up the atmosphere.

Charlie had installed a corner fireplace as I'd suggested— our current hot spell would soon give way to chilly nights. I took a step back and slowly turned around. As much as

I wanted to live in the Owen home, I knew I would be comfortable living in a cozy place like this.

When I got home, Virgie happily put supper on the table. She'd made a simple noodle casserole and fresh fruit salad. I saw that she'd packed only a small bag to take back with her and she'd straightened up the bedroom. Since Lily would stay at Beverly's until the move was complete, I agreed that Virgie could leave many of her things behind.

As we ate dinner, Virgie mentioned that Beverly had taken the entire next week off, using some of her accumulating vacation time.

"She even wants to paint the room I'll stay in," Virgie said. "We'll do it together as soon as we get back from Milwaukee."

I sputtered some remark about how nice that would be. But I kept quiet otherwise, not finishing my mental question about who would benefit—Beverly or Virgie? Yes, Beverly was being generous about her place, but Virgie was paying rent for her room. But I reminded myself that no one had consulted me about their arrangements. They were perfectly capable of making their own decisions.

Virgie and I both went to bed early, and even before my alarm rang the next morning, I heard her leave. She'd tried to be so quiet, too. But, knowing I wouldn't go back to sleep I got up and started the coffee. In a matter of seconds, the aroma triggered a growl in my stomach. I wanted a hearty breakfast, not the muffins I'd been having with Virgie. I stirred a couple of eggs to scramble and put a couple of thick slices of homemade bread from Farmer Foods into the toaster. Then I pulled out the leftover fruit salad. I'd have myself a feast. And I welcomed the silence.

I lingered over breakfast and hurried to work, although we had a slow morning, taken up more with curious visitors than clients. It could be like that on the busy days on the Square. By afternoon the attraction of a new business on the Square subsided, which gave me a chance to go into what had been Miles' office. I sat behind the desk, feeling good. Really good. I never dreamed I'd have an office of my own. I'd always shared my work space with secretaries or other paralegals. Uncle Miles words came back to me. "You're smart enough to be a lawyer yourself, Georgia."

But I'd never believed his faith in me, the reason I'd settled for much less. "I will do my best work for Nathan and Jack," I whispered, "but I sure miss you, Uncle Miles."

I didn't want my thoughts of regret to hang over me, so I walked out of my soon-to-be office and closed the door behind me. With twenty minutes left before closing I stood at the front window and watched a flurry of activity on the Square. I never seemed to tire of watching the visitors pass by.

A young couple captured my attention and held it. For some reason, they intrigued me. Probably because they looked like high school sweethearts. They strolled hand in hand, but then in a flash they took to playfully pushing each other, like kids pretending to spar.

I watched him touch her arm and point one direction, but she was pointing the opposite way. Finally, she gave in and went his way. My shoulders and my mood drooped. Why did that disappoint me so?

A memory picture flashed, so fast it startled me. Elliot and I had done the same little dance, down to holding hands and playfully fighting, and pointing in opposite directions. I'd given in, just as that young teenage girl had, right in front of my eyes.

Even now Elliot and I behaved like the teens. He demanded, I withdrew, he wanted to do one thing, but I had another plan. If we wanted to be together and nurture our relationship and help it grow, we needed to peel back the layers of hurt and be blunt about why we lacked mutual trust. I smiled at the recent memory of us peddling the tandem bike, working together and moving in the same direction. That described what the two of us needed better than words!

Virgie and Beverly were off in Milwaukee and Lily worked long hours on the weekends, so that left the days and nights free for me. Before I changed my mind I picked up the phone and made the call, practicing what I'd say to his voicemail message.

"Hi," he said.

No Georgia, no Peaches.

"Uh, well hello, Elliot. I need to ask…I was wondering. Do you have plans after work tomorrow?"

"Not yet." No playfulness in his tone.

"Would you like to come for dinner?"

"Why?"

My stomach fluttered and beads of sweat formed on my forehead. I took a deep breath. "We need to talk, Elliot, about the past…maybe about the future." My resolve was weakening. If I didn't get a half-friendly response, I'd hang up.

"Okay."

"Okay?" *That's what he said…so talk!* "What about six o'clock. I'm helping Nathan and Toby move upstairs in the morning, but we'll be all done by afternoon and then I'll have time…" I willed myself to stop talking.

"Sure you are."

"What?"

"Of course you're helping Nathan and Toby. That's what I meant."

I had no answer for that. I mumbled something about seeing him Saturday, and quickly hung up. I'd come to count on good 'ol Elliot being funny and warm. That's not the Elliot who'd picked up the phone. But I consoled myself with the thought that he'd said yes. I'd had to work for it, but we'd have our chance to talk.

***

I laughed when Liz opened a box of donuts and muffins from Biscuits and Brew Saturday morning in Nathan's miniature kitchen. She'd already brought in milk and juice in individual serving sizes. It all looked familiar, and here was Liz once again fulfilling her self-assigned task of helper.

I hadn't seen much of either Liz or Marianna lately. So much had gone on over the past few weeks that demanded my attention. And while I had made headway in uniting my family, even bringing Lily back to Wolf Creek to stay, apparently, I'd put various pieces of my life on hold.

Lily's life belonged to her, but maybe she and I could enjoy a Sunday morning breakfast soon. I'd been left hanging about how things stood with Lily and Nathan. Was the guy interested in her, or not? Maybe Nathan's curiosity and intrigue over Lily was merely a figment of Jack's imagination. And how did she feel about him? I'd also never thought to ask her about her project with Doris. Not that I was nosey, but curious, yes.

I left my own concerns behind when the men started bringing in the furniture, turning the empty rooms into a home, from the small kitchen table to the beds and chests to the couches and chairs. The furniture made the apartment appear smaller, but not in a confining way. Liz and I agreed that cozy was the perfect word for the apartment.

Toby had marked the boxes for his room with a big T. He raced up the stairs when the last box had been carried up and he'd been relieved of his job as door man.

He appeared at my side and pulled on my sleeve. "Did you see my room?" He tugged a little harder. "Come see it."

Since I didn't have the heart to tell him I'd already had a look at it, I let him take my hand and lead me to his room. I made all the right sounds of approval as he explained every item. Suddenly, Toby heard a noise and ran past me.

"Lily's here," he shouted back at me.

Lily?

I stepped out of his room to see her stoop down so she was eye level with her son. "Hi Toby. Big day for you, huh?"

"Nathan, too." A big smile crossed Toby's face.

Lily turned as Nathan moved toward them. "Hello," she said. "What a change for you." She spread her arms to encompass the apartment.

"A good change," he said, sounding a little flustered. "No driving, no worries about Toby alone with the babysitter. All good." He stopped talking, but he looked as if he wanted to say more.

I marveled that this confident attorney, precise in his language when talking with clients, seemed at a loss for words. But his eyes never left Lily's face.

I spotted a hint of pink covering Lily's neck and cheeks. Energy and sparks going back and forth could have started a fire. Only a houseful of onlookers prevented that. So, Jack had been on to something after all.

Toby's voice broke the silence and sent excitement rippling through the room. "Grandpa!"

Richard had come up the stairs and now knelt down on one knee to bring Toby into a one-armed hug.

"Here's something for you. It's called a house warming gift." Richard brought his hand from behind his back and gave the box he held to Toby.

All eyes turned to the little boy as he tore the paper off the box and lifted the lid.

"Wow." Toby lifted a perfect model of a NASCAR racer from the box. He looked up at his audience. "It's just like my bed. Come see, Grandpa." Toby took hold of Richard's arm to coax him up.

Richard took a second or two to unfold his body from resting on his knee, but he gamely followed Toby into the room with the special bed.

"Did you?" Nathan asked Lily as he pointed to his father's back.

Lily shook her head. "He said Toby called him. Then your dad called me and asked if I thought it was okay to come." Lily stood face-to-face to Nathan and shrugged. "I said I certainly thought so."

An eerie silence in the room followed.

Finally, Nathan nodded. She laughed and we all sighed in relief. "Be careful what you teach Toby about that phone. You might get a real surprise one day."

"This is a real surprise."

I didn't know if Nathan was speaking specifically about his father participating in the move, and his obvious mixed feelings about it, or that so many of us had stepped forward to welcome him to the Square.

Seeing Charlie and his crew go through a round of handshakes and goodbyes, Sarah's writing about the Crawford family came to mind. They seemed to have been a take-charge kind of family and that trait had been passed on to Charlie. But he always seemed to see what was needed and get right to it.

Speaking of take-charge, after Charlie left, Liz organized the grand unpacking job, pointing to boxes and assigning jobs. In no time, books filled the shelves and pillows added color to the couch and chairs. Liz and I finished settling the kitchen, laughing that Nathan would have to open every drawer and cupboard in search of a pan or dish. Two hours later, the bulk of it was done, and Toby was making a tower out of the empty cartons in the middle of the living room.

We stood back and watched as Toby gave his grandfather specific directions on where to put the next box. The final touch. The tower stood taller than Richard. I wondered if Richard had ever played with empty packing boxes in his life. Maybe, maybe not, but he grinned for Lily's camera when she took a couple of shots of the duo and their creation.

We all grabbed boxes to break down and recycle, knowing the next stop was Liz and Jack's house, where lunch would be Sloppy Joes and chips.

21

My nerves skittered as the time for Elliot's arrival approached. I wanted our meeting to be honest and serious so I'd made a list of what I considered his faults and mine going back as far as high school. Sometimes I approached this analysis with enthusiasm, but at other times, I wanted to throw logic away and let my heart take the lead. And my heart wanted Elliot.

I'd settled on my go-to meal, lasagna, and put it in the oven so it would be ready when he arrived. We could eat first and somehow work our way into the more serious part of our evening. I scoffed at the understatement. Our evening might end up defining our future, together or apart. It was no accident I'd chosen the same menu for this dinner as my evening with Virgie the day she arrived. I patted myself on my back over that. Look how her visit had turned out. All that aside, lasagna was not only convenient, it was one of my main comfort foods and, boy, I needed to feel safe and secure tonight.

I'd even considered using the dining room table as a subtle way to convey the seriousness of this dinner. But, after thinking about it, I decided the kitchen would give us a friendlier atmosphere, and maybe make us less likely to be defensive.

When the clock ticked past six and moved on toward 6:15, I wondered if Elliot had decided not to come. Maybe he was done with our relationship, or perhaps unwilling to relive the past in order to have a chance to go forward.

Lost in memories, I startled when the door bell rang. I put

my hand over my heart as if I could steady it as I approached the door. My heart fluttered when I pulled the door open and saw him on my porch.

I held the door back for him to enter. "Come in."

Elliot had always had a quick greeting ready for me, but not this time. Giving me a nod, he shoved his hands into his pockets and followed me through the house to the kitchen.

"Smells good," he said.

The rich tomato aroma had filled the room. "Lasagna from Crossroads." I had opened a bottle of merlot and held it up in one hand as an offering.

"I like Italian." He nodded toward the glass I was holding in my other hand. I poured wine into it, and he lifted the glass from my hand, but our fingers never touched. He made sure of that.

"I have a large salad to go with it."

"Greens are good."

Good, Lord, such fascinating conversation. Would we get anything accomplished if the dinner menu was all we talked about?

"Have a seat," I said. "It'll be a few minutes yet."

He sat at the end of the table facing the dining room. He looked beyond that room to the front of the house. "The house looks different."

"More messy?" I'd picked up a few things, but didn't want him to think I'd cleaned it up just because he was coming. I sat to his left with the sink behind me.

"Hmm...not messy, just comfortable." He leaned to his right and picked up the cocktail napkin that had fallen to the floor. "You like it here, don't you?"

"Here?" I wasn't sure if he meant Wolf Creek or the house, but the buzzer on the oven rang and I got up to put our meal on the table.

As we ate we talked about safe topics, the changes on the Square, the number of visitors that had stopped in to see Country Law, and the old standby, the weather.

At least Elliot wasn't shy about eating the whole portion of lasagna I'd served and a full bowl of salad. He helped himself to two pieces of French bread when I passed the basket to him.

I joked that maybe he hadn't eaten during the day. I was surprised when he said, "Didn't."

A man of few words. Would I get him to open up eventually?

At a loss for words myself, I got up to refill our glasses of wine. Elliot put his hand over the top of his as I was about to pour, but I went ahead and topped mine off.

"I'll have coffee if you're making it."

"Easy enough," I said, grabbing what I needed to make coffee first and then covering the leftovers and putting them in the fridge. Elliot stayed in his chair, but he was obviously nervous, too. He couldn't stop tapping the table like it was a bongo drum.

As soon as the brewing ended I poured a mug for him and brought it to the table, along with my glass. Then I took my list out of my pocket and set it between us.

"What's this?" He turned it so he could read it.

"Our past. And maybe our future."

I started telling him about the teenage couple I'd seen on the Square the day before and how that had led me to evaluate my relationship with him.

"But you never wanted to do the things I wanted to do." His voice became defensive, tight. "You know, outdoor things—fishing at the lake."

"True, I didn't like the idea of a Saturday night date fishing—having a picnic at the lake, yes, but sitting in a boat with buckets of smelly bait. No way. But you never wanted to do the things that interested me either."

"Dumb things. Like the school clubs I didn't care about."

That stabbed me a little. Maybe it was the thoughtlessness of his choice of words. "See what I mean? You don't value my interests."

"Ah, I was just pulling your leg a little. I know you had stuff you liked to do. I just didn't share it. But all that is kids' stuff. None of it counts now, and it sure doesn't explain why you left town—the first time." He'd leaped to a completely different subject, and the way he turned his cup in circles showed exactly how uncomfortable he was. He didn't look away. His eyes drilled into mine.

"If you haven't figured out why, then it's time you learned."

He drew back his head and tucked his chin. "Oh?"

"Your mother said *I* wasn't good enough for you."

"My mother?"

"That's right," I said, folding my arms across my chest. "Your mother wanted you to marry someone better than me. A *Winters* girl wouldn't do."

"Mary Beth." His voice was low and flat.

"Yes. And look how that turned out." Ouch. I guess my gloating was pretty obvious. But I couldn't resist reminding him that his mother's choice was a big failure.

"But still, you left town."

I lifted my shoulders in a weary shrug. "Ah, Elliot. I was young, and believed my mother when she said I needed to let go of my feelings for you. She urged me to leave Wolf Creek and see the world. That's why I didn't fight for you. For all I knew you agreed with your mother. I imagined you also believed a Winters girl wasn't good enough and never would be." I blinked tears away. I didn't want to get emotional this early in our conversation.

Ignoring my tears, he said, "But you came home and then you left again." He waved his hand back and forth, a fair imitation of coming and going on a whim.

"I know I sound like a broken record, Elliot, but all I can say is that I believed my mother's so-called wisdom when she said I didn't belong in Wolf Creek, especially knowing we didn't have a future. You and I had such a rocky relationship in school and when I came back the first time, you were already married."

He nodded, but the muscles in his face relaxed. "I have to ask this. I don't want to keep guessing. Why do you always put me off to help everyone else?"

I heard longing in his words.

"I need to be clear about why I came back. I had no idea you'd even want to see me or even talk to me. I put that aside in my mind." I stopped to draw in a breath. "I had to come home to redeem myself. I'd done a terrible thing when I let Toby be adopted. And I desperately needed—wanted—to

229

find Lily and tell her what had happened to her son."

He pushed his chair back and went to the sink, where he poured his now cold coffee down the drain. Then he refilled his cup and sat down again.

Like starting over.

He shook his head. "That doesn't answer my question."

I'd never liked having to explain myself to anyone, and I sure didn't like laying out the obvious for Elliot. "Have you considered what's happened to me since I got here? Do you even understand what losing Uncle Miles means to me? I was all alone, Elliot and all you did was push."

His hands flew up. "Whoa. Just a minute. Explain *push.*"

"For starters, you called me Peaches. That's high school stuff. You showed up at my door with flowers. I wasn't sure about myself, and how did I know you wouldn't run away from me once you knew the truth. The truth about Toby."

He got up again, emptied his cup and set it in the sink along with the dishes from our meal. "I know one thing for sure. It's time for you to decide."

"I have decided, Elliot."

He twisted his mouth to the side, communicating skepticism.

"But you need to understand that I'm still reeling from everything that's happened so quickly."

"How long?"

"How long what?"

"When will you be ready for us to be together? How long is it going to take?"

"I can't put a date on that!" My frustration with the direction of our talk boiled over and I bolted out of my chair. "Unlike you, I haven't had a close family for years. I'm trying to reunite my fractured family. Not to mention there are all kinds of twists and crises I hadn't imagined."

"Like Toby?"

"You bet, like Toby," I said, my voice loud. "He's sick, really sick. And I started a plan in motion, before I knew the whole story. I got Lily to come back. Now Nathan knows she's Toby's mother. And then Beverly softened, finally." I let out a little laugh. "And we can't forget Virgie's moving here and taking a job I arranged."

"Oh, come on, Georgia, Virgie's not your family."

"No, but sometimes our friends are like family. Besides, I'll need to spend time training her to take over my job."

"And that's going to mean working overtime every evening?"

He'd backed me into a corner. "See what I mean about you pushing?"

"You're hot and cold, Georgia. You kiss me like I'm the only man for you and then you push me away."

He'd used my word—push—and made it sound trite.

"Yes, I do." It was my turn to be honest with him. "Elliot, I'm over fifty years old and for the first time I finally feel safe and comfortable in Wolf Creek."

"But not because of me."

His accusatory tone threw me. "That's not true. I couldn't have gotten through Miles' funeral without you."

"Tell me about your mother's funeral."

Another change in the direction of our conversation. "You know very well we didn't have one."

"Why?"

"Because she'd asked us not to. That's why." The snippiness in my voice sounded juvenile, but Elliot had me jumping from topic to topic. We didn't finish one train of thought before he started another.

"So why didn't you just tell everyone that? Why the secrecy?"

Resting my forearms on the table, I exhaled a heavy sigh. Maybe he'd let me finish this one thought. "It was because of Toby. Beverly and I decided he needed a better home than we could give him. It wasn't exactly something we wanted to shout from the rooftop."

"Surely you knew food and shelter aren't as important as love."

"How would you know? You've never done without either."

"Because I love you, always have. I didn't know how to tell you that before and, obviously I still don't."

He stood up and put my list in his pocket. "Goodbye,

Georgia."

"What? *Goodbye.* See what I mean? *We* didn't decide to end this conversation, *you* did."

He walked out of the kitchen to the front of the house.

"Come back, Elliot. Please."

"What for?"

"Because I love you, too."

"Ah, Peaches." He walked to me with his arms open.

I thought he would stay a while, but he didn't. The things our conversation touched on were too raw for him, but at least I'd communicated well enough that when he left, he understood that he'd been taking my actions personally. And as rejections or ambivalence. But I wondered if he fully appreciated that I wanted family and friends and to keep developing professionally, with the same kind of enthusiasm that drove him to keep expanding Farmer Foods.

After he left I tried to recapture parts of our conversation that were important. Elliot had shared more of himself tonight than he had before. He admitted that he'd known all along that marrying Mary Beth was likely a mistake. He confided that he'd secretly resented his mother for pressuring him.

Our relationship was more honest now. Would it be one without turmoil and misunderstandings? I couldn't say for sure, but I needed time to settle in, deal with Lily and Toby. Elliot needed to decide what kind of relationship he wanted. He seemed to live in a fantasy world, the kind where love really does conquer all. On the other hand, he made sure I knew that I wouldn't have to deal with my worry about Toby alone. If nothing else, he'd always be my friend.

I went to bed after making one promise to myself. I'd try to be much better at making Elliot feel wanted and special. No matter what happened, we and our families would always be part of Wolf Creek—and now the Square. Sarah had a way of reminding me of that.

***

SAM CRAWFORD—Middle Son

The death of Asa Hutchinson devastated the citizens of Wolf Creek. He, and later with his wife, Eleanor, managed the relay station for her father's stagecoach line and it was his vision to establish a small town where an east/west route crossed a north/south road. The town began slowly, but after years of touting its opportunities, it became well established.

Sam had worked for the Hutchinson's for many years both as a driver and a team handler. He enjoyed meeting the travelers and hearing their stories about where they'd come from and where they were going.

His father understood Sam's preference for the stagecoaches over the freight hauling which was a lonely, dangerous job. Not that danger frightened Sam, but he'd always had a soft spot in his heart for Eleanor, too.

"Have you given any thought to the future?" Sam escorted Eleanor home from the cemetery after the funeral. The whole town would be stopping by to give their condolences and share the food the town's women had prepared.

The Hutchinson children, Benjamin, the oldest, and Shawn ran ahead to join their friends. Time for crying had passed. Their daughters, Abigail and Martha, had died shortly after their births.

"No time yet. Haven't been left alone. Father's here. For awhile I suspect."

"Send him home. He'll cause more disrupt than help."

"Yes." She whispered.

Sam turned to face her before they were too close to the house to be overheard.

"Eleanor, I've loved you for many years. So when you're ready, I'll be here."

233

A year later Eleanor stepped off her porch and went to the team of horses Sam was hitching to a coach. "Sam?"

"Yeah?" He tried the clip for a second time, noting its wear. "You need work done on this harness."

"My sons need a man around."

Sam froze.

Two weeks passed. In the church Asa insisted the town build, Sam Charles Crawford and Eleanor Knight Hutchinson were married.

Family stories have the stagecoach business and Crawford Freight Line merging into one ongoing enterprise, but there are few legal documents to support that claim. With Keith away most of the time building roads, Sam became the manager of both.

Sam and Eleanor were blessed with children of their own, two sons and a daughter, Charles, Christopher, and Grace.

Charlie Crawford, owner of the C4 construction company of Wolf Creek, and current resident, can trace his ancestry directly back to Sam and Eleanor.

JACOB CRAWFORD—Youngest Son

Little is known about Jacob Crawford after he quit driving for his family's freight line and traveled to Wyoming to bring back a string of Mustang horses for Sam. He sent the horses back with Wolf Creek resident Tanner Buchanan with a letter telling his family he'd found work on a cattle ranch.

There is a newspaper obituary for Jacob in the Wolf Creek Museum describing his heroism in saving a small child from harm by a runaway horse. He died within days from his injuries asking only that his family be notified.

234

***

A few days later I heard from Beverly and Virgie. Most of the call was taken up with mutual teasing and a lot of laughs. It felt so good to share that mood with Beverly, and with Virgie, too, because she was happier than I'd ever seen her. With Virgie's arrival in Wolf Creek for good, my life would change once again. Even my job would be richer, more focused on law than on running the office. I felt lighter, too, because of Elliot. Somehow, we *would* settle these issues that kept us apart. I was more optimistic than I'd been since I'd heard the familiar voice calling me "Peaches" that day I first arrived in Wolf Creek.

Beverly and Virgie both hinted at a surprise they had for me when they returned to Wolf Creek. For two women who'd known each other less than two weeks, they'd already bonded over their sewing hobby and emerged happier because of it.

The day after they'd come back from Milwaukee, I stopped at Beverly's and found them up to their elbows in paint. Beverly had painted a smiley face on the back of Virgie's T-shirt.

"What's this?" I asked, laughing.

"So, okay," Beverly admitted, "the eyes and smile are a little lopsided, but who's looking that closely?"

That only made us laugh harder. Beverly offered me a brush, but I backed up to keep paint splatters far away. I'd only stopped by to hello anyway. I was on my way to Crossroads. I had a dinner date with Elliot and paint on my clothes was not part of my plan.

August
22

We turned the calendar to August on Virgie's first day at Country Law. She shadowed me in the morning and by afternoon I began to move my things into Miles' office. No, not Miles' office, not anymore. It was mine—Georgia Winters. I showed Virgie my candy stash and I left half the miniature bars in her desk. I wanted Toby to like Virgie, or at least be comfortable around her.

In the middle of the afternoon, Nathan asked me into his office. He shut the door and without fanfare asked if I'd agree to be tested as a donor for Toby. "You're family and it's getting serious."

"How serious?" I asked, a knot in the stomach tightening.

"According to the specialist, the dialysis isn't removing enough of the toxins anymore. But I'm not telling Toby about the transplant yet, so please don't say anything."

"You have my word." I closed the folder he had been using and tucked it under my arm. "Of course, I'll be tested. Just let me know when and where."

Nathan nodded. "I will."

"How's the apartment upstairs working out?"

He laughed. "We should have had diagrams for each drawer. Toby and I laugh when we try to find something. But Toby loves it and he's making friends at Sally's. He's already asking for a sleep over with his friends."

"Nathan, that's wonderful. And Richard? How does he…" My new resolution crossed my mind, it wasn't my place to ask. "Sorry, none of my business."

"Let's just say he's trying," Nathan said, staring at the picture of Toby on his desk. "He told Toby he'd be visiting over the holidays. He's even made reservations at the Inn for Thanksgiving and Christmas. I think he likes Lily."

"And you? Do you like her?" I blurted the words and then slapped my hand over my mouth. "Sorry," I said with a groan. "Don't answer that. Once again, I've blundered into things that are none of my business."

"How about if you ask Lily to answer that?" He rose from his desk and touched my arm. "Lily loves Toby and that's what's important now."

He sat back down. "I'm going to call Beverly and ask her to be tested, too."

Since I didn't know if Beverly would agree, I shrugged noncommittally. Being a donor for a transplant wasn't as simple as having a tube of blood drawn, but first things first. The phone rang and by habit I reached for it. When the ringing stopped I smiled. Virgie was taking care of business. Nathan smiled, too.

"How's the transition going?" he asked.

"She's doing a great job. Asking for more responsibilities all the time. My sister has made her move easier and I think that's helping."

"Lucky lady."

I thought for a moment and realized that Nathan was all alone, too. Richard and Toby were generations apart from him, and if he'd made the decision to be a bachelor, having Toby would have already changed his life completely.

***

I waited for Lily to come home after work. She and Virgie had exchanged rooms and, without a bump, we'd returned to our easy living style. She came in the front door as the late night news began.

"Hi, Georgia. You're up late."

"Waiting for you." I hadn't talked with Lily alone since Virgie had arrived for her interview.

Lily bounced onto the couch. She grabbed a pillow and

held it to her chest. "So how's life?"

"Wonderful. Virgie's doing a great job at the office. Your mom and Virgie are becoming friends. And—"

"And *Elliot?*"

"He's good, we're good." I had no intention of telling her about our conversation. It was between us and would stay that way. To deflect her question I threw one back. "And Nathan?"

She quickly covered her face. "He calls at least once a day or sends a funny text. He tells me what kind of day Toby's had. He loves living on the Square and not driving back and forth to Green Bay every day." She stopped to take a breath. The pillow she'd been holding fell to the floor and she bent over to retrieve it. "He's asked me out…you know, like on a date."

Her voice was muffled. I thought I'd heard her, but I asked her to repeat what she'd said.

"A *date.* I said he asked me to go on a date with him."

"That's wonderful."

"It's too soon, Georgia. I'm scared." She pulled her legs up under her. "Toby doesn't know I'm his birth mother."

"I know. And Nathan must worry a little, since Toby would still remember his, well, his other parents."

Looking down, Lily nodded.

"What does Nathan say about telling him?"

"He wants to wait."

"That's Nathan's call." My resolution to not get involved unless asked was supported by Nathan being a responsible father.

"Yes, it is."

She stared off into space.

"What is it?" I asked. "You seemed to go away."

"Nothing, really. I was just thinking about Nathan. He wants to go to The Wellington in Green Bay on Saturday."

Nothing shabby about that. The Wellington was a fairly upscale steak house in Green Bay. "Will—what's her name—the woman who took your shift when you went to the fireworks? Will she work for you?"

"I haven't asked her, yet."

"Don't you want to go?"

"Sure…but…" She waved her hand to finish the sentence.

"But what?" I pressed.

She stared at her smooth nails, as if examining a manicure. "What if I like him?"

"You already do."

Shocked at my conclusion she punched the pillow with her hand and then threw it at me.

I laughed, tossed the pillow back and wished her a goodnight.

I'd gotten my answer.

***

Nathan came into my office the next morning and asked if I'd stay with Toby while he and Lily went into Green Bay for dinner. Did he think I'd say no? But I wanted to call Elliot, too, and see if he'd like to spend the evening with Toby and me. I mentioned it to Nathan and he laughed. "Elliot just wants to play with Toby's race cars."

Maybe, maybe not. I needed to ask Elliot if he regretted not having children. Whatever regret I'd had years ago was short-lived and long forgotten. When I was young, I wanted Elliot, but I hadn't thought about having a family. But perhaps Elliot had.

The next day I made a quick trip to Green Bay to have blood drawn as the first step in testing to be a transplant donor. Being a more distant relative, genetically speaking, I doubted I would be a match. Maybe, though, as Toby's grandmother, Beverly would be a compatible donor.

On my drive back to Wolf Creek I kept thinking about Toby's father. Who was he? Where was he? Was Lily going to offer information about him? He could be a match. I wanted to ask Lily about him, but would that be overstepping once again? I had to slow myself down. I obviously wasn't the only person to consider that Toby had a father. For all I knew, Nathan and Lily had already talked about him.

Since we had no idea when Nathan would be called away for Toby, I sat in on most of Nathan's appointments, so I'd be able to assist Jack if he needed to take over a particular case. It was possible to make this adjustment because Virgie had quickly caught on to the office routine. Just as I knew she would, she also enjoyed her interaction with the clients.

During our nightly phone call, I shared with Elliot my excitement about having the chance to sink my teeth into the legal issues involved in the cases.

"You should have been a lawyer, honey."

"Miles used to say that all the time, but I love my job now and I'm happy living in Wolf Creek."

Elliot whispered goodnight and my toes curled.

***

After the third evening in a row of talking on the phone to Elliot, it dawned on me that he used my list of teenage hurts and wrong decisions as the subject of our conversations. Strangely, though, the phone gave us a distance from each other so we could talk honestly and relate how our past actions affected our current lives.

"After you left town it was easier for me to be with Mary Beth. I didn't feel so lost, lonely, as I did being alone." Elliot said.

"Did you love her?"

All the relationship articles I'd ever read in magazines claimed that was the number one question never to ask a man. But every now and then it occurred to me that my feelings were butting up against a rival. Could that be true? After all, the way I'd heard it, Mary Beth had walked out on Elliot, not the other way around. On the other hand, I was embarrassed to think that I even sounded like I was preparing for war with Elliot's ex-wife.

"In some ways I probably did, but not the way I loved you, Peaches. It wasn't even fair to her, really, the way I kept comparing her to you." He spoke softly, with a wistful tone coming through. "Even with all that childish stuff and the petty fights, you made me want to live, to make plans for the future."

I shifted in the chair at the table, where I'd taken to

planting myself for these evening conversations. "It makes me sad to hear you talk like that. I regret we didn't have this conversation years ago, Elliot. But we're having it now and we'll build a better future for us because of it."

"Is there a future for us?"

This wasn't the first time he'd asked the question. "Let me say this again, Elliot. I didn't come back to Wolf Creek to be with you. For one thing, I thought you didn't want me. But if we end up with a future, I'll be very happy."

"But I have to share you with family and friends."

This was still an issue for him, and I couldn't figure out why. "Yes, just as *I* have to share *you* with Megan and Eli, not to mention Farmer Foods. And speaking of friends, Beverly and Virgie asked me to come to dinner tomorrow night. They have been hinting at a surprise and maybe I'll learn what it is then."

"They seem to enjoy each other. I saw them in the store the other day talking and laughing. Anyone would have thought they'd known each other for years."

Great observation of the way the two behaved. "I agree. When Virgie talks at the office about settling in Wolf Creek she doesn't know how she'd have done it without Beverly and me."

"Well, Peaches, it's time for bed. Have fun tomorrow night. I'll wait for your call."

"'Night, Elliot."

Yes, I'd call him. Not because he'd asked, but because those two women would be part of my life even if Elliot and I weren't a couple and I wanted to share that with him.

***

Virgie hadn't given me a clue all day about the evening's plans—not even the menu. "Just come when you're ready. And only comfy clothes are allowed," she'd said.

So I stood in front of my closet and tried to find an outfit that would be comfortable now that Wolf Creek was in the "dog days" of August. That's what Mom had called the hot, humid, stifling days when temperatures neared one hundred and the only relief was a blowing fan or a swim in the lake. "It's even too hot for the dogs to play," she'd say. "They just wander off to find a spot in the shade to flop down and wait for a cool breeze."

I really wished shorts and a tunic would suit the occasion. But Virgie hadn't said anything about a picnic or even if they'd have other guests. For some reason, not knowing more about the evening made me nervous. In the end, though, I opted for a cooler seersucker sleeveless blouse to go with my capri pants. I slipped on straw sandals that matched my purse.

I decided to walk the few blocks to Beverly's house, mostly because my body was telling me I needed to move more. Now that I had my own office and wasn't doing the receptionist work, I'd been sitting more. Some days I sat for hours at a time without standing or walking about. No more getting up to greet clients or to fix a new pot of coffee. Virgie did that now.

Predictably, by the time I knocked on Beverly's door I was both parched and sweating. Thankfully Beverly had her air conditioning on and I'd no sooner stepped in the door than she handed me a glass of lemonade.

"What were you thinking walking here on the hottest day of the year?" There was a touch of big sister in her tone.

She was right, but I didn't need her reprimanding me in front of Virgie. Friend that she was, though, Virgie nodded her agreement, but quickly went back to the kitchen.

"Come, sit down. You'll cool off soon."

As I sat on the couch I noticed that the living room looked bright and cheerful, fresh with a new coat of paint. The chair in the corner spot was not the same one I'd seen before.

"Did you paint?" I gestured to indicate something had changed in the room.

"Yup. We enjoyed painting the bedroom so much that we kept moving through the house, room by room, until they were all done." She pointed to the chair. "That's Virgie's favorite chair."

Virgie came into the room with two more glasses and a pitcher to refill my glass. "Did you tell her?" Virgie moved to her chair.

"That's for you to tell."

"Tell me what?" I set my glass on the coffee table and moved to the edge of the cushion.

"Okay, here's the news. Jessica and Mimi ordered twelve one-of-a-kind vests for their store," Virgie said. "And not on consignment, either. They want them before the holiday rush begins." Unable to contain her enthusiasm, her voice rose with each added detail.

"Wow. That didn't take long," I said, clapping my hands in front of me. "And when did they call? Why didn't you tell me?"

"Because I didn't want you to think that the vests are more important than my job at Country Law."

"Can't you do both?"

Virgie smiled knowingly at Beverly, and I caught the message. Obviously, I didn't understand what was involved in making a one-of-a-kind garment.

"Yes and no. It takes time to be creative and draw a pattern, then sew the material and see if it looks anything like you imagined."

"My ignorance is showing here. Sorry."

"Nonsense. You just don't know anything about clothing construction." Virgie glanced over at Beverly. "You tell her. She's your sister."

"Tell me what?" I felt like a parrot.

"I'm going to help Virgie. She'll design, we'll make the pattern together and I'll sew." Beverly's eyes sparkled with enthusiasm.

"I'm speechless!"

Beverly touched my arm.

"We need your help, too."

"My help? I doubt that. I don't know the first thing about sewing."

They both laughed.

"We'd like to set up a partnership or a…" Beverly looked to Virgie for help.

"An LLC," Virgie said, going on to elaborate. "We want this to be a business arrangement. We'll both put in equal money and share the profits. And this time I'll copyright the designs."

"This is quite a surprise." I looked back and forth to both of them. "Are you sure?"

"Yes." They answered in unison.

"Have you talked to Jack or Nathan?" I asked.

"I wouldn't want to bother Nathan with this," Virgie said. "He's got too much on his mind already."

"What about Jack?"

Virgie almost physically withdrew from us.

"What's wrong, Virgie?" I asked.

"Maybe he'll be like that guy in Milwaukee and think it's just a hobby."

"Jack's not that kind of man." I took a swallow of the cool drink to gather my thoughts. "If you're serious about this—both of you—then you need to act like confident business women. Make a list of the provisions you want in the company documents and then make it legal. First, you need a name for the company."

"Virgie's Vests," they said, again in perfect unison.

"We've done nothing but talk about this since we drove home from Milwaukee," Beverly offered.

"And Mimi has a friend in Door County who may want to buy them, too," Virgie said, "but we'll have to hurry if we want them available for the holidays."

"We're going to make the downstairs our studio." Beverly's enthusiasm only added to the surprise. "It needs some remodeling though."

"Call Charlie Crawford," I said. "He did Nathan's apartment and Farmer Foods and other shops and apartments on the Square."

Beverly grabbed a notepad and pencil from the end table and scribbled on it, presumably Charlie's name.

"Marianna told me he's done some remodeling at Quilts Galore, too," I added.

Virgie frowned, suddenly deep in thought. "Yes, the quilt shop. Marianna has wonderful fabrics, Bev. Make a note that we need to see if she has Christmas fabric in yet. You know that patchwork design I showed you."

I sat back in the chair and listened to my friend and sister speak their language of custom sewing.

Suddenly, Virgie laughed. "Oh, my, Georgia. We do get carried away. Sorry."

Odd how thrown I was by their surprise. It truly took me aback. If they were able to forge a friendship and a partnership in such a short amount of time, I would sign on to support any venture they launched.

We continued to talk about their new enterprise and added a few tidbits for Virgie about our family as we ate a simple meal of a summer green salad and cornbread. Beverly talked on about Lily and Toby and how she wanted to build a relationship with them. I hoped she knew that maybe we thought of Toby as family, but Nathan wasn't ready to go beyond the biological connection.

"And Elliot?" Beverly asked, without any warning, bringing a quick change of subject.

"We're good. Getting to know each other again."

"You're blushing, Sis."

"Well, that happens when I think of him and the way he talks about being with me." There was no use hedging my words.

"Ooh, la, la." Beverly apparently couldn't resist a teasing sidelong glance, which took me right down memory lane to our childhood when teasing each other was part of every day.

I didn't stay late and, even over loud objections, Beverly insisted on driving me home. I called Elliot as soon as the tail lights on her car faded down the street.

"They're doing what?"

"They're going to sew vests, and they're creating a business. They want to make their partnership legal because of the money involved—both expenses and profits." I laughed. "More business for Charlie Crawford. I suggested they use him to build the studio they planned in Beverly's lower level."

"Good for them. They know what they want and they're going after it." Elliot chuckled softly. "Like me—us."

"Yes." I whispered. "Now, about this weekend. Are you

off either day so we can go on a picnic?"

"Sorry. It's my weekend to be at the store both days. Lots of locally grown produce coming in now and the Square will be busy."

I heard an odd noise and his voice drifted in and out.

"Oops, I must be so tired I'm fumbling the phone. Can't hang on to it anymore."

"Good night, Elliot. Sweet dreams of...me." I laughed and hit the off button.

I understood Elliot's responsibilities, and how important Farmer Foods was to him. If only he would take me and my commitments as seriously.

23

A raging thunderstorm passing over Wolf Creek woke Lily and me about the time my alarm should have buzzed. My clock face was black and when I turned the switch on the bedside table—click, click—nothing happened.

Lily appeared at the doorway of my room and stated the obvious. "No coffee. No electricity."

"Let's get dressed and go to the Square. Maybe there's power at Biscuits and Brew. If nothing else, Stephanie probably has a generator to keep her refrigeration going. Otherwise, we can drive to Green Bay for breakfast."

My phone rang first. Before I got a full hello out, Nathan said, "There's power on the Square, so come and get your coffee here."

Lily didn't work until later in the morning, but I had to get into the office, so I grabbed my toiletries and slipped into slacks and a blouse. I could only hope that the power would be restored to the house before the end of the day.

By the time I'd driven to the Square the center of the storm had moved east leaving only a light rainfall trailing behind. I detoured to the bathroom and prepared myself to begin another day.

As the time to open approached I wondered if Beverly and Virgie had power or if they were affected at their house. I called Virgie's cell.

"Oh, Georgia, I just woke up. I'm so sorry."

"No problem. The only reason I'm up and about is that I didn't sleep through the thunder and lightning."

"Well, I'll be there in a few minutes. Please tell Nathan

and Jack I'll make up the time I miss."

"Virgie, calm down. You don't work for M and K anymore. I'm here, come in when you're ready."

"We stayed up late making our list of things to talk about with Jack." She sounded breathless.

"Tell me about it when you get here."

A few minutes after ending my call with Virgie, I heard footsteps on the stairs and Nathan stopped at my office door. Not finding me there he came to the reception area.

"Lily and I are going to Biscuits and Brew for breakfast. Want us to bring something back?"

Just then Virgie came in the back door and joined us in the reception area.

"Sorry about being late. No electricity." Virgie hurried to her desk.

"Happens sometimes." He shrugged. "Just check the computers to make sure they're working. Maybe we need to beef up our protection system for them."

I watched Virgie jot down the request. "Consider it done, Nathan."

"Toby is upstairs with his race cars, and he's fine, but will you keep an eye out for him. I'm sure he'll wander down to pay a visit. I told him I'm bringing him back a doughnut. We have doctor's appointment today and he's grumbling about going."

I heard the back door opened and closed again, and Lily joined us.

"Sure, I'll check on him. Don't worry," I said. "Enjoy yourself."

I watched Nathan and Lily cross the Square and then went upstairs to say hello to Toby. This was the first time I'd seen Nathan and Lily together since their date. I'd been eager to hear about it, too. But she'd been private about their evening at The Wellington, other than to comment on the wonderful food. When she left it at that and walked away, I knew I shouldn't pry.

***

Toby didn't run to my desk for a chocolate bar after his appointment. He ran to Virgie's. As much as it pleased me that he was at ease around Virgie, I missed his bright smile and flirty wink. After snagging a bar or two, he ran down the hallway and up the stairs when the bell on the door jingled. New rules for him now that he was living where his dad worked. But so far he'd been fine about scrambling upstairs when clients showed up.

With Toby occupied and out of earshot, Nathan came into my office and closed the door. The depth of his worry was written all over his face. He sat in one of the chairs across from me and rested his head in his hand.

"After our appointment today the doctor met with me alone. Unfortunately, neither you nor Beverly are a donor match for Toby."

That didn't surprise me. "I'm sorry, Nathan. But I have to ask. Have you talked to Lily about Toby's father?"

"All she'll say is that he was a jerk."

Nothing new there. "But, of course, there's Lily herself."

"Uh, well, yes, but I don't want to press," Nathan said, "and Lily is young to, you know, lose a kidney, even if she's a match. A big *if.*"

An odd reaction on Nathan's part, I thought.

"I thought she was having blood drawn about the same time Beverly and I went. I even asked if she wanted to come with us, but she declined. I assumed she made another plan."

Now it was Nathan's turn to be puzzled. He let out a heavy sigh. "I don't want her to be the donor, but I don't get why she wasn't tested. Is something going on with her?" He raised his hand in a questioning gesture. "She avoids the subject and I haven't pressed."

My resolution hit me hard. Was this a place I should intervene without being asked? Nathan needed answers and maybe I could help where Lily was concerned.

"What do you want me to do, Nathan? Do you want me to talk to her? It's your call. You're Toby's dad."

"*Dad.* That sounds so strange to me. Richard is my dad and now I'm a dad whether I know how to be one or not."

"I don't know about that, but there is a little boy who's

counting on you to take care of him." I grabbed a pencil and began turning it end for end. "Just think how scared he is."

Nathan thrust his hands in his pockets and stared at the floor. "At the moment, he's handling all this better than I am."

I reached down into the bottom drawer of my desk and brought out two small chocolate bars and slid them across the top of my desk. "Eat these after supper. Hold him on your lap and read a story to him." Moisture gathered in my eyes, but I managed to keep it at bay. "Tell him we all love him."

"Do you think that might be Lily's problem?" Nathan asked. "Maybe she doesn't think she deserves to be with him? And she doesn't see how she can help him, since she carried the gene that made him sick." Nathan sighed. "As much as I hate to think it, she may be the only person who can help."

"I can't answer that question. I don't know how she feels and, have you considered, maybe she doesn't either? When I came back to Wolf Creek to reunite my family, I had no idea Lily would be confronting her past so quickly. She never had time to prepare for meeting you and Richard, not to mention Toby himself."

Nathan sighed and rubbed the back of his neck. "For a long time I thought I'd never want to get married and have a family of my own, not after the kind of family Chad and I had. Now I want a partner—a wife." He squirmed in the chair, easing his embarrassment. "I haven't said that to anyone else, so please don't repeat it."

"Of course. I couldn't ask for more for Lily." I thought about my next words, but not for long. "Lily has been all over the place—with herself, I mean. I'm sure she never imagined anything like this happening, but I'm also sure she doesn't believe she deserves this kind of good fortune…and happiness."

The phone on my desk rang. Virgie wouldn't interrupt unless it was important. I took the message and immediately passed it on to Nathan. "Long distance for you—New York."

"I'll take it in my office."

With that, he left, but that didn't stop my mind from wandering back to my conversation with Nathan. He hadn't asked me outright to help, but he couldn't have made it any plainer if he had. It was up to me to figure a way to get the conversation going with Lily.

I went home still considering my options and took a glass of iced tea to the porch to sit and ponder for awhile. She surprised me when she bounced up the steps.

"Wow. You're home early."

"Julie wanted to work late tonight so I volunteered to go home." She sat on the summer lounge chair and rested her head back. "Feels good to be off my feet."

I offered her some tea, but she said no. I studied her profile as she closed her eyes. I'd seen her do that before. She held her body very still and willed herself to relax. But relaxed or not I needed, no, Nathan needed, answers.

"Nathan told me I can't be a donor for Toby," I began.

Her body stiffened, but she kept her eyes closed. Like children, I thought, if they can't see you, then you can't see them. She said nothing.

"Beverly can't be either." I kept my voice low and calm. "Have you heard anything yet?"

"I can't help Toby," she whispered.

"Who said that?"

"I did."

"Because you're not a match or because you won't do it?"

She jumped out of the chair. "Don't you think I'd like to help my own son? Even if he doesn't know I'm his mother?" She turned her head away. "I didn't say anything before, but one thing I did learn during dinner at The Wellington was that Toby had a really wonderful mother, loving and kind. His father was the same."

"Oh, Lily," I said, speaking as calmly as I could manage. "Let's talk this through."

"There's nothing to talk about. He had a good mother, but she died." Lily stared into space. "For years, I thought I'd adjusted to what happened. I was stupid and had a baby I couldn't care for. I got on with it. But now I've learned that

I'm the reason Toby is sick. How can I help?"

"Is that what the doctor said?"

"I didn't get tested because I thought, 'why bother'?"

"That's not reason enough. You might just be the one who saves Toby's life."

Lily rubbed her eyes, as if trying to stop tears. "If that's true, then why doesn't Nathan want me tested?"

Huh? What was I missing? I needed to dive into these waters carefully. "What makes you think that Nathan doesn't want you tested?"

"He told me." She swatted the air. "Not in so many words, but up until this morning, he went on about how young I am, and it's too big a risk. *Ha!* Those were just excuses. But now he seemed to have changed his mind. He's suggesting I should get tested. And the next words are something about risk and it's a long shot that I'd be a match anyway."

Okay, those last words matched my understanding of what Nathan wanted. But he sure was all over the map. I decided to ask the question another way. "So, I didn't want you to be a match because of the risk, but you might be the only one who can donate. Is that it?"

She waved off the question. "More or less, but I know what he really means. He doesn't want one of my kidneys in Toby. He thinks *I'm* a danger to Toby. He doesn't care all that much about me."

The mud was settling and water clearing just a bit. I chuckled, a too loudly.

"What are you laughing about?" Lily demanded.

"No, no, honey, I wasn't laughing. There's something ironic here. Something tells me you're confused, because you know Nathan *does* care about you. It seems he cares about you so much he's afraid to put you at risk." I paused and let my suggestion settle in. "Everyone sees that Nathan is attracted to you. So you think you don't deserve Toby, and Nathan's afraid you could be hurt by the surgery, and he's sending mixed messages all over the place."

Lily shrugged. "That's true. One minute he's taking me to the Wellington and we're laughing and talking and the next he's telling me he doesn't want me to be tested. And now, all of a sudden he does."

"You should at least have the option to donate a kidney if you can. Nathan probably came to see that. But let's not get ahead of ourselves. What about Toby's father?"

"He doesn't exist."

I frowned, trying to figure that out. "Want to explain that more fully?"

"There was a party at the lake. I went, and met this tourist guy—here for the summer. We hooked up and spent most of the summer together. He left town in the fall and I was pregnant. I tried contacting him, but the phone number was no longer in service and there is no such town as Appleburg—where he said he lived—in Vermont. I bet his name was fake, too."

I saw self-incrimination all over her face, and though I never knew what she'd gone through on her own I wanted to help her now. The happy-ever-after fairy was on her shoulder and she needed to believe she could help her son.

"So we're back to you being tested. And what have you told Nathan about Toby's father and why you're now refusing to be tested."

"Nothing." She hung her head.

"Don't you believe Toby deserves better?"

"Yes." She hadn't raised her head yet.

"Then call him and tell him what you've told me." I got up and went inside. It was time for me to make my own call to Elliot. It was a difficult conversation, though, because I had to keep so superficial. These developments between Nathan and Lily and her story about Toby's father weren't mine to tell.

A few minutes after I'd turned out my light Lily tapped on the door. "Georgia? Will you go to the office early and give Toby his breakfast? Nathan's going to take me to Green Bay to have blood drawn."

"Come in Lily. No need to talk through the door." I'd turned on my bedside lamp—thankfully the electricity had been restored. The light gave the room a soft glow. "Did you tell him about Toby's father?"

"I'll tell him on the way to Green Bay. I promise." A small smile crossed her face.

"Of course I'll take care of Toby. I'll take him to B & B in the morning."

"'Night." She backed out of my room and closed the door.

I wanted to call Nathan and tell him how Lily wanted to assume all the responsibility for Toby's illness, and maybe I'd try to explain how easily Lily misinterpreted his fear for her. But this was their business and they needed to navigate the baggage their relationship already carried. And it was quite a trunk load. Who would have ever thought it possible that Lily and Nathan would fall in love? Well, at least it seemed Nathan had. I couldn't be sure about Lily.

***

Lily was extra quiet as I drove to the Square in the morning. "Nervous?"

"A little. But Nathan is so easy to talk to. I can't believe we talk every day and don't run out of things to say."

"That's good, isn't it?"

She looked at me like I'd asked the dumbest question in the world. I just smiled, knowing Elliot and I were exactly the same way.

I pulled into a parking spot next to Nathan's SUV. Before I got out and grabbed my tote bag from the back seat Nathan had opened the back door to the office.

He nodded at us as he said, "Georgia, Lily."

I walked straight to my office, but when I looked back to say goodbye to them I saw Nathan give Lily a little kiss. Subtle, but sweet.

My, oh, my. I ducked into my office before they knew I'd seen them. The grin that stayed on my face all day had both Toby and Virgie asking if I was okay. I was better than okay and even more, I was free to share my joy over these developments when I talked to Elliot at the end of the day.

***

When the phone rang that evening I answered the call before checking the caller ID. "Hi, sweetheart. Boy, do I have news for you tonight."

"I hope some man calls me sweetheart before I'm dead."

"Sarah?" I heard a chuckle at the other end of the line. "Oops, sorry. I thought that was Elliot calling."

"That's good, because I sure hope you don't greet everyone that way."

I laughed along with her. Then silence. It occurred to me she'd had second thoughts about calling.

"Oh, Georgia. I owe you an apology." Sarah spoke slowly. "I do want our friendship to continue. I...I..."

"Can I stop you, Sarah?"

Again, silence, giving me a chance to switch the direction of the conversation. "I'm done living in the past. I've said what needed to be said to the people that were affected by my decisions," I said. "Now, I'm moving forward with my life and I'd be very happy if we left the past where it belongs and only look to the future."

"That's quite a change for you. What happened?"

"Here's a short version. Right now, I can see that Lily and Beverly are on their way to the new lives. They were both stuck, but now they aren't. I don't want to be the only one living in the past, so I'm using the old clichés to join the rest of my family. What's done, is done. Water under the bridge. Spilled milk. Whatever...but it all comes down to the same thing. Nobody cares anymore about what happened years ago."

"That's true, but I *care* about you. I *miss* seeing you."

"Honestly, I miss seeing you, too," I said, my voice cracking.

"Well, that's good, because I called to see if you would join me and a couple of my very crazy relatives for dinner."

I didn't hesitate. "Sounds like fun."

We settled on a day in early September. When the call ended I realized I was looking forward to seeing Sarah again. I wanted her to be my friend and although we'd still have some awkward moments, we'd begun the path back to a close relationship again.

I called Elliot and laughingly told him about how I'd answered Sarah's call, but I'd saved the best news for last, Nathan's and Lily's kiss.

"Easy, Peaches. Don't read more into what you saw than what is actually happening."

"How can I not hope that Nathan and Lily would get together?"

"My hope is that we get together."

Me, too. Did I have to spell it out?

***

Every day we waited for the results of Lily's donor sample. The doctor had told Nathan the testing might take at least a week, but he'd ordered a rush considering Toby's condition.

Meanwhile, it was business as usual for Country Law. One afternoon, Virgie asked me to cover for her while she and Beverly met with Jack. Since they needed to buy fabric for the holiday vests and other supplies, neither of them wanted to begin their partnership before they had all the paperwork done that made their business official.

Beverly arrived promptly for their appointment and carried a folder with her. She was smartly dressed in a summer weight paisley blouse and khaki slacks. The smile on her face made my heart sing.

Fortunately we were all in the office when the doctor called. Nathan burst from his office showing excitement on his face that could only mean good news.

"Lily's a match. But…"

We all peppered him with questions he couldn't answer. He held up his hands to quiet the talking. "But she has to go through another set of tests."

"Have you called her?" Jack's voice cut through the rest of us talking over each other.

"She'll be here shortly. She wants to tell Toby about the kidney herself."

I turned from the group when I saw tears in Beverly's eyes. Mine wouldn't be far behind and we didn't need an office of crying women if a client arrived.

Minutes later when Lily bounded in gasping for breath from running across the Square she went directly to Nathan. "Is it true?"

"I wouldn't joke about something this serious, honey."

Honey? The word rolled right off his lips…they must have had some serious conversations in the last few days.

"Let's tell him now." She grabbed his arm and started pulling him toward the hallway. He waved back at us as they went on their way.

Jack still needed documents prepared for a late afternoon appointment so I said goodbye to Beverly and went to my office. When I went to his office to deliver them, he was smiling, too.

"What did I tell you?" he said, looking pretty smug.

"You're right." I hesitated, but only for a second. "Young love—there's nothing quite like it. Except maybe for the middle-aged kind."

"You've got that right," Jack said. "And speaking of love at any age, Liz is going to love these new developments."

"Happy endings and all that," I agreed. "Sounds like Liz's style."

***

The last days of August passed as we waited, and waited. None of us wanted to hope too much if the second set of tests revealed a reason Lily couldn't be a donor, but hope was all we had.

My phone calls to Elliot sounded like a broken record even to me. All I could talk about was Lily and Toby—and now Nathan. They were a trio in my mind and went from worrying about them to being happy for what looked like the start of a new family.

"Enough, Peaches. Plan for the best and prepare for the worst. That's all you can do."

"I can love you."

"I'll be by your side whatever happens. You know that."

"I wouldn't make it through any of this without you being by my side, just like you were when Miles died."

"Seems like a long time ago already."

"We've come a long ways ourselves," I said. "I think we've left our history in the past and we're ready for the future."

"Well, I am."

"Labor Day's next week. Got plans?"

"To be with you."

"My idea exactly. See? We're on the same wavelength."

September
24

Sarah had referred to the ladies as Cousin Clara and Niece Nora to make it easier for me to understand their relationship to her. I understood why. The two could have been sisters, and not just because they looked alike. They bested one another all during our dinner with zany jokes and tales that might have been more storytelling than truth-telling. I don't think even Sara could separate fact from fiction.

Later that evening on the phone, I told Elliot about Sarah's wacky family. "Even Sarah calls them crazy," I said, "but they're definitely not crazy."

I tried repeating two of the jokes they'd told, but the whole exercise felt flat because Elliot didn't understand the punch line of either. But I told him it didn't matter because Sarah and I had probably laughed at the jokes because we'd laughed at most everything. It had been that kind of evening. Boy, that felt good. The group dinner also eased the communication between Sarah and me.

"I don't think you've laughed that hard since you came back home, Peaches. Sarah is a good friend and she showed that by including you."

"You're right, she is." I wiped my damp eyes, damp from laughing. I was sure Sarah and I would continue rebuilding our friendship. Still, Toby, never far from my thoughts, brought me back to a sobering reality.

"Hello? Peaches? You still there?"

"Sorry. I just keep thinking about the days to come. All I

do is worry."

"Wasted energy."

"Spoken like a true man," I quipped. "Men never worry. They just forge ahead."

"Okay. I intend to do just that."

I detected a hesitation in his voice and had learned that meant whatever he said next was important to him.

"Let's go to Door County for Labor Day weekend."

"What? *Now?* With everything up in the air about Toby and Lily?" I caught myself before I did more damage. There was nothing any of us could do but wait—and Lily didn't need me for that. "Elliot, let me start over. Ask me again where you want to go."

"Let's go to Door County for Labor Day weekend," Elliot repeated, his way of letting me know he understood my outburst came from worry and fear for Lily and Toby and not because I rejected his idea. "I know this is a difficult time for you and your family, but Lily and Toby aren't alone. They have many people supporting them through this."

"Where?"

"Just in case you said yes, I called the Landmark Resort in Egg Harbor and reserved one of their two bedroom suites."

"That many bedrooms?" I couldn't stifle my laugh.

"You want to go?"

"Absolutely," I said. "We're close enough that if Toby's condition changes or some other problem appears and we need to come back early."

"Friday. I'll pick you up Friday after work," he said, his voice raised in enthusiasm. "Weather's going to be great. But it doesn't matter what the weather is."

I'd caught Elliot by surprise. He hadn't expected me to let everything else go and take off with him. A weekend, with just the two of us and no interruptions, marked a change in our relationship. All my life I'd wanted this. I'd wanted Elliot.

***

On Saturday morning we sat on our balcony enjoying a breakfast we'd ordered from room service. It was a warm morning, and my light cotton robe was all I needed. Elliot wore shorts, but had chosen to forgo a shirt.

Wedges of quiche, extra high from farm fresh eggs, according to the menu, sat on warmed plates with a carrot muffin and orange slices. When I'd eaten all I could, I passed my plate to Elliot and he happily polished off the last morsels.

Unable to banish worrying altogether, some concerns traveled through my mind. Premature worries at that. If I had to prepare meals for Elliot every day would I need to become a better cook? Did I want to do that?

I put the thought away when Elliot asked if I rode horses.

"Right. Sure. Rodeo Queen Georgia here." I bent over in laughter and rolled my eyes at him. "I'm almost fifty years old and you want me on the back of a horse. Are you crazy?"

"It'll be fun. Put on your jeans and let's go." He popped out of the chair and out the door, on his way to the desk to make reservations for us.

Off we went. It quickly came back to me, too, this riding horses business, at least enough to guide a gentle horse through the woods and onto the beach. Most of the time we rode along companionably, side by side and with no need to talk. Elliot's horse pulled ahead to take the lead on the narrow sections of the trail lined with stands of birches and towering oaks. The warm sun, the cloudless blue sky, the breeze blowing through my hair, plus Elliot's constant smile, combined to bring on the lovely tingling sensation that zipped through me at those special times when everything felt just right.

Even my old horse managed a gallop—sort of—on the beach, the last leg of our ride. Windswept and invigorated, I laughed as I dismounted slowly and stiffly. I hadn't used those particular muscles in a while, so I could barely walk.

Later, we ate our dinner in a room with all-around windows showcasing the waters of the Bay of Green Bay, sparkling in the early evening light. Elliot dug into a steak and shrimp combination meal, and I ate every bite of blackened salmon and roasted vegetables. Too full for dessert, but we ordered coffee so we could enjoy the view a little longer.

Since both of us worked indoors virtually all day, we spent our Sunday morning walking the grounds of the resort and planned to wander through the shops in town all afternoon. Many unique stores were similar to those in our Square. Hand in hand we walked down the tourist-filled streets and browsed the small shops offering one-of-a-kind items.

My mind jumped ahead to Christmas gifts and surprises for my family and friends, so I picked out scented soaps and candles for Lily, Beverly, Sarah, Liz, and Virgie. We didn't have a good source for those items on the Square. For Toby, I bought a one-of-a-kind set of hand-carved wooden racing cars and a set of wooden tracks to go with them. I spotted two or three shops where Virgie's vests would complement the clothing already in stock. When Elliot suggested a walk on the beach, we went back to the resort and ended our day in the glow of the setting sun.

On our drive up on Friday we'd seen some pick-your-own apple orchards. I'd commented that it had been decades since I'd picked apples and suggested we try it one day. Elliot listened, so on the way home on Monday morning after another room service breakfast, Elliot made a turn into the Sharp Family Orchard.

"I've got an in here," Elliot said with a laugh. "We do business with them—they have some of the best Macintosh applies on the peninsula."

He parked the car in the crowded gravel lot and we went inside, where he asked to speak to the manager. I browsed the shelves of homemade jams and pickles, until he waved me over. "I want you to meet Gil Sharp," he said, "who's enjoying one of his busiest days at the orchard."

We shook hands, but Gil shook his head and laughed. "The guy has apples delivered to his door twice a week, but the two of you are going to pick your own. Oh, well, to each his own."

"Only a bag," I said, "maybe two. I haven't done this in many, many years."

"Okay, then, have fun." He handed us a couple of bags

and waved us on our way.

With the trees heavy with fruit we picked more than we'd planned. We laughed when Elliot stretched his long frame to get the large shiny fruit near the top of the trees. We continued on our way home with the sweet aroma of apples filling the car.

Our conversation was easy on the drive home. I began thinking about Wolf Creek and what was waiting for me, both at Country Law and with my family. Elliot seemed preoccupied, too. He'd taken a big step leaving the store on Labor Day weekend. Sure, he arranged for other employees to work his hours and, besides, it was Eli's turn to cover a holiday weekend.

We made good time getting to Green Bay. Neither of us brought up the past or the future—and we didn't talk about Lily and Toby. We laughed about our sore muscles and Elliot suggested we find a riding stable close to Wolf Creek. What do you know? Had Elliot and I found something we both liked to do that didn't involve our work or our families? Did I dare dream that horses might be part of our shared future?

Once past Green Bay, we pulled onto the highway that would take us home. When Elliot's phone rang, it startled both of us. He handed me the phone to answer rather than pulling onto the shoulder of the road to take the call.

"Hello, Eli. Elliot's driving and doesn't want to pull o—"

Eli didn't wait for me to finish.

"Tell Elliot there's a fire at the store."

"Fire?" My voice held a touch of hysteria. "When?"

Elliot put his foot on the brake, slowing down and driving onto the shoulder. The instant we stopped, he grabbed the phone from my hand. "Eli?"

Elliot listened, winced, nodded, groaned, and then disconnected the call. He turned on the blinker, tapping the steering wheel, as he waited for a break in oncoming traffic. The seconds dragged, but finally he was able to merge into the line of traffic heading west.

"What did he say?" I asked, regretting that we hadn't switched places so I could take over the driving. Where would his mind be at a time like this?

"Electrical. They think it started in the cooler," he said, his voice cracking with frustration. "That thing hasn't been working right since the day we installed it."

"How bad?" I'd envisioned the entire building gone, along with all its contents. Maybe even spread to the next building.

"Couple of freezer units and a scorched wall. Mostly foam all over everything from the extinguishers Eli used. More clean up from water and smoke, too."

Elliot had increased his speed, passing slower vehicles on the divided highway at every opportunity.

"But no one was hurt?"

He shook his head. "Apparently not. Eli coughed some, but I don't think he needs to go to the hospital."

We traveled the remaining miles from Green Bay to Wolf Creek in silence. And found the roads into the Square blocked with police cars. Their blue, red, and white lights flashed in that strange disco style of years ago. This was the first time I'd ever seen the Square closed off like this.

Elliot stopped the car and jumped out leaving me to find a parking spot. I made a fast decision to take the car to my house and walk back. Elliot needed my help now. Whether he would accept it or not was another matter.

By the time I returned to the Square only one fire truck was parked behind Farmer Foods. I assumed the fire was out and the firemen were handling reports and taking pictures. Elliot and Eli were likely taking their own set and making calls. They'd need everything documented fast so they could start repairs.

I took a shortcut to the center of the Square by going into Country Law. I was surprised to find the back door open and Virgie at her desk. She answered my question before I asked.

"When Bev and I heard all the sirens we came right over. Bev is with Lily and Toby somewhere out there." She gestured at the window, and when I walked to it, I saw a mass of people standing and looking east toward Farmer Foods.

The excitement subsiding, I saw Marianna and Art among those making their way back to their shops. I was about to go out and talk to them when my family and Nathan entered Country Law.

Toby was first through the door. "Hi, Georgia. You missed the fire. Lots of smoke." His eyes danced as his arms made circles like rising smoke. He couldn't stop moving about. "I'm going to be a fireman when I grow up."

Nathan grinned and nodded. "Good ambition, Toby."

"How bad is it?" I directed my question to Nathan. He didn't know Elliot's family the way the rest of us did, so I figured he'd be less inclined to embellish the facts with emotion.

"Contained. Eli was quick to react." He shrugged. "People were saying there's more clean up than damage. Of course, the produce is ruined. It's going to be a difficult insurance claim. They'll need our help."

Nathan snagged Lily's hand and put his other on Toby's shoulder. "We've done all we can, so we're going out for burgers and ice cream—after a bathroom break. See you tomorrow."

No invitation extended to us. Apparently, they wanted to be alone. Good idea—I approved of them spending as much time as possible together.

Virgie and Beverly invited me to join them for supper at their house, but I wanted to see Elliot and offer my help, or just be there for him. Maybe he'd appreciate a hug more than anything. I also had the set of keys to his car.

After navigating through the dwindling crowd of onlookers I spotted Eli through the glass doors. I waved to get his attention and was surprised when he unlocked the door and motioned for me to enter.

"I'm sorry, Eli. Are you okay? Did you get hurt?" I couldn't control my nervousness around him. "Is the damage bad? Where's Elliot?"

"Georgia, calm down." He reached out to touch my arm. "Everything will be okay. No one got hurt, just the store."

I saw Elliot approaching us and left Eli to run to him. "Oh, Elliot. This is terrible. Is it bad?"

"No. Just a mess. Good food lost. But insurance covers everything."

"Let me help you with the claims. I've worked on many situations like this. I can guide you through it."

Elliot tucked his chin down and a skeptical frown formed.

That hurt. Did he think I couldn't handle an easy insurance claim? "Look, I've spent years doing this kind of work. And if I don't know the answers I'll ask Nathan or Jack. As your attorneys, they'll be involved anyway."

The frown relaxed, but he didn't address what I'd said. "I have to go now. Need to talk to the fire chief."

"I love you." I gave him the ring of keys. "It's parked at my house."

Elliot had withdrawn from me, but I understood. His livelihood had been compromised by a faulty piece of equipment and the shock was evident by how easily distracted he was. He took off to the back of the store—and didn't look back.

Eli unlocked the door to let me leave. "Be around for him, Georgia. He'll want to assume responsibility for this happening. He needs you now."

After relocking the door, Eli, followed Elliot to the back of the store.

Had I heard him correctly? He wanted me to be around for Elliot? What a wonderful gift Eli had given me. I knew Eli and I would build a friendship and provide united support for Elliot. My heart took a grand leap.

25

Tuesday began another busy week at Country Law. During our routine who, what, and when meeting Virgie surprised us by displaying vests she and Beverly had already sewn. They'd worked hard over the weekend. We'd all been involved in Beverly and Virgie forming a partnership and now they were ready to see if their designs would be welcomed in the marketplace. Grateful for our supportive comments, Virgie quickly stashed them out of sight when the clients arrived.

Midway into the morning Nathan came into my office and closed the door. Since it wasn't a planned meeting, I sensed Nathan had something important to say.

"Can I have the keys to your house?"

"Excuse me?"

Nathan flopped in the chair, not characteristic of him at all. He nervously rubbed his hands together, also not typical of the cool Nathan I'd come to know. "I need to talk to Lily. She's a donor match, Georgia," he blurted.

"That's wonderful…oh, my."

He waved me off. "But we've avoided a conversation about her actually being a donor. I've wanted to avoid…it's surgery, Georgia."

"But now you know the truth, Nathan. She's his biological mother. Of course, she'll do it. Especially if…" I held back more words of explanation. I didn't know enough to say for sure what Lily was thinking.

"Lily's life will change if she agrees. There's risk, and I want to talk to her before I tell anyone else."

"Certainly. She might still be sleeping, though. She worked late last night." I reached into my purse and indicated which key opened the front door. "Good luck."

A hesitant smile crossed his face as he left.

More than an hour passed before Nathan returned, with Lily in tow. I was at Virgie's desk talking about a large copying job that involved complex graphics and would need a spiral binding. It was an important job for a new corporate client. But Virgie and I stopped talking when we saw Nathan lead Lily toward us, his hand tucked firmly on her elbow.

Nathan nudged Lily forward and stepped back himself. "You tell her."

"The second test results are in. I'm definitely a match for Toby," she said, tears spilling down her cheeks. "I, we, will have our surgeries soon."

"Oh, honey, that's wonderful." I gave her a hug, then lifted my arms to deliver one to Nathan, too. But I'd have been lying if I'd claimed not to notice the stabs of anxiety deep in my stomach.

Virgie handed the phone to Lily. "Call your mom. She's home today."

We stood with Lily while she gave Beverly the news. When she'd returned the phone to Virgie. "She told me she loves me. She wants to take care of me after the surgery."

Lily knuckled tears away and leaned into Nathan, letting her head rest against his shoulder. "We need to go pickup Toby at Sally's."

"We need to tell him the news," Nathan said. "And I'll need to tell the school." His face clouded over, likely because his list of things to do was growing.

Nathan reached into his pants' pocket and returned my keys. "First, I need to call Jack."

"And then Richard," I added, surprised by the authoritative tone I'd allowed to creep into my voice.

"Yes." He emphasized that with a nod and a faint smile.

They left Country Law by the front door and walked hand-in-hand into a warm autumn day with bright sunshine and puffy white clouds slowly drifting across the sky.

I hurried to my office. I needed to call Elliot and Sarah to share the news. We'd hurdled one worry, getting a donor, but had bumped against new ones, two surgeries and two recoveries.

My family was moving toward reuniting, even more so than I'd dared dream. And without too much drama— at least a major war hadn't broken out. I had endured the embarrassment and guilt over the past and my life was galloping ahead—and at a faster pace than my old horse had managed on the beach.

***

News traveled fast around the Square. Shopkeepers and their employees stopped by Country Law with gifts for Toby and well wishes for the Connor and Winters families. Of course, they didn't know the half of it. Eventually, the whole of our little world would understand the true nature of the miracle.

On Thursday I was in my office covering for Virgie when the bell jingled on the door. I stepped out of my room to greet the visitor. Richard Connor stood in the doorway.

"Hello, Richard. Good news, huh?" I took his extended hand and he held it longer than I was comfortable with. His cheeks turned pink when I ended up pulling away from his grasp.

"I just took a chance," he said, "that you'd be free to have lunch with me over at Crossroads."

"I...I..." I held up one finger to gather my thoughts. Why would he want to talk to me? "Come into my office. Virgie will be back any minute and then we can go."

I'd agreed to leave with him, as if my mouth had a mind of its own and forgot my hesitation about being around Richard. I closed the file folder I was working with and slid it into my drawer. I'd planned to do research for a land dispute case that Jack would be filing next week, but maybe listening to Richard was a better use of my time.

Virgie soon returned and I led Richard to the front door to let her know I'd be at Crossroads with him for lunch. She only raised her eyebrows.

We were seated next to the windows overlooking the Square. I commented about the mums planted in the gardens, a sure sign of fall. The leaves had begun to change color, too, though I didn't mention it and add to the small talk. It was bad enough that Richard had rearranged his silverware on his placemat twice already. Clearly, this wasn't a social lunch, so after we ordered the lunch soup special, I waited for him to begin.

"Nathan said you told him to call me."

"I suggested, yes." Okay, serious understatement.

"Thank you." He took a sip of water. "I can't tell you how good that made me feel." He set—and reset—his napkin on his lap. "I want to be part of Toby's life. And Nathan's, too, of course. But I made a lot of mistakes raising Chad and Nathan and I want my living son to know I don't want a repeat with Toby."

"What do you want from me, Richard?"

Before he answered, our bowls of beef barley soup arrived, giving me time to glance around, disappointed that I didn't see Lily waitressing. But maybe that was for the best. Seeing me deep in conversation with Richard might have seemed odd—not wrong, but strange.

"I want to be a good grandfather to Toby." He reached for the basket of rolls and held it out to me. "And I want to repair my relationship with Nathan."

"Those are two important goals."

"Yes, and I have no clue how to go about making them happen."

"Make it easy for them to love you," I said, the words coming out fast and determined. I shrugged. "I don't know all the answers. You know that as well as anyone. But I've learned the hard way myself to be open and listen, rather than making demands." But I thought about missed opportunities with Elliot so many years ago. "It's so easy to live with misunderstandings that could be unraveled so easily."

Richard studied my face. "You speak from experience, I take it."

270

"Yes. I would have had a different life if I'd learned that lesson earlier." I paused. "But that's the past. Nathan and Toby—and Lily—need our support more than anything now. They'll make mistakes. Lily has sure paid for hers. But, we all have blunders that we have to go back and fix."

His body stiffened. He held his spoon as if to interrupt. Then he laughed. "Yes, you're right. We all have to repair our own damage from time to time."

"Nathan and Toby don't need your money. They need you, Richard. You can't be that busy."

I had no idea how busy Richard was, nor did I care at the moment. He'd asked, I'd answered. I hoped I hadn't sounded too preachy or as if I had all the answers. But then I laughed to myself, thinking of all the damage I'd been repairing these last months.

After taking care of the bill he walked me back to Country Law, and mentioned that he'd planned to be in Wolf Creek for Thanksgiving and Christmas. He turned to leave, but changed his mind. "Do you think Nathan might have time for me to say hello?"

I nodded toward the door. "Step inside and we'll see."

Richard's expression fell when Virgie said that Nathan and Toby were gone for the afternoon.

Saying he'd call them that evening, he walked across the Square and disappeared behind the shops. To get his car, I presumed.

"That was a surprise, huh?" Virgie asked.

"Absolutely. I never expected it."

***

Late Friday afternoon Elliot came into Country Law. I knew that because I heard Virgie's "Hello, Elliot," but he didn't stop to see if I was available because the next thing I knew he was standing in my office and closing the door. This was the first I'd seen him since Labor Day, even though we'd talked on the phone every night. He pulled me out of my chair and kissed me like I was his lifeline. He hung on longer than I expected.

I should have been miffed by the way he commandeered my office. In fact, I was miffed. "Good thing I didn't have a client in my office," I said deliberately terse, "or Nathan or Jack." With that out of the way, I asked what was wrong.

He flopped into one of the client chairs. "Our insurance company is balking at the repair estimates and replacement costs." He raised his hands high in the air. "They refuse to replace the produce. They're claiming it's a perishable commodity."

True, as far as it went, but I kept quiet.

He handed me a fistful of papers, equipment estimates, the insurance policy and an estimate of lost income. Before I gave Elliot any encouragement about receiving compensation I needed to comb through the fine print of the policy and discuss what I learned with Jack on Monday. I explained all that to Elliot and added that I'd call the insurance representative on Monday, too.

"I'll do my best for you. Do you have pictures?"

"Yeah, and so does the fire department."

"We'll need a copy of their report when it's completed." Of course, Elliot knew this, but he was worn out and needed someone else to do this thinking for him. If I left him alone, he'd fall asleep in my chair.

"Go home, Elliot. Sleep. I'll take care of this for you."

Bracing his hands on the arms of the chair he pushed himself up. He murmured his thanks and gave me a quick kiss before he left.

***

Nathan considered doing conference calls when he had news of the upcoming surgeries for Lily and Toby. Events and schedules changed daily, but we stayed on edge, knowing we'd get word soon. And we did. First, we learned the surgeries would be done in Green Bay rather than Madison. A transplant team of doctors from Madison were coming to oversee the team of surgeons at Memorial Hospital and would stay to follow Lily and Toby's first few days of recovery.

I prided myself in staying calm and assisting Jack with his full schedule, and I rescheduled Nathan's client appointments. Jack joked about hiring another lawyer. None of us took him seriously, and I filled in as best I could.

We waited. As days passed...one...two...five...a week. The call came early Friday afternoon. The surgery would be on Tuesday morning, early. Lily and Toby needed to be admitted Monday afternoon.

Over the weekend the entire Winters family, plus Nathan, Richard, Virgie, and Jack and Liz met at Beverly's house. She'd asked us all to be there, surprising me once again.

"Starting today, I'm taking six weeks of vacation. Lily will need help with her recovery and I've talked with her about staying here. Nathan, those stairs are going to be difficult for Toby, and you'll have your hands full trying to juggle everything. So, he can stay here, too, if you'd like. If I'm tending to Lily, I might as well tend to Toby, too."

I closed my eyes, remembering the efficient way Beverly had converted her dining room into a nursery for Toby and a hospital room for Mom.

"Like I told you before, Nathan, I have experience. I took care of my mother for six months."

Nathan exhaled, relief spreading over his features. "Thank you, Beverly. Other than hiring two private duty nurses, one for Toby at my house, and one for Lily, I didn't know how I would take care of both of them. I accept."

Beverly and Virgie had arranged an early fall picnic for us and Liz, in the know about the plans, as usual, had brought a few dishes to round out the meal. Virgie called Elliot to join us, and he arrived about the same time the food hit the table.

"Good timing on my part, huh, Peaches?" He looked better than when I'd seen him on Friday. He told us briefly about the clean up after the fire. "Even after the professional disaster cleanup crew was done, we still had a lot to do. I can't believe how many people have offered to help."

"I'll say it again," Jack said, resting his arm across Liz's shoulder, "Wolf Creek's a great place to live."

In the midst of eating chicken salad and cheese and crackers, we all hovered over Toby. He tired easily, too, and now that he'd become familiar with Lily—and liked her—he crawled into her lap and rested his head against her chest. Nathan dug into Toby's back pack and took out a book she could read to him.

Could any of us have asked for a more beautiful sight? Apparently not, because we all wiped away some tears when Toby slowly closed his eyes and gave into sleep.

***

The nurses tolerated our delaying tactics only so long and Beverly and I had to step back and watch Lily be taken into the surgical suite. We held each other arms for support and slowly made our way to the chairs in the surgical waiting room, a more comfortable environment than I'd expected. I'd brought a book with me, but I doubted I'd be able to concentrate. A few minutes after Beverly and I settled in, Richard followed Nathan into the waiting room. Nathan had been with Toby on the pediatric ward, but he'd assured us we needed to be with Lily. He was Toby's dad, but they hadn't, as yet, told Toby that Lily was his biological mother. There would be time for that later.

The morning passed. We nibbled the muffins and drank the coffee until it was time for lunch. Richard took on that job and accepted Beverly's offer to help. They took off for the cafeteria, soon to bring back an assortment of sandwiches. We were all anxious, though, even though an attendant came out to give us periodic updates. To give Nathan and Richard their privacy, Beverly and I took our sandwiches to a table in the corner of the room. Our little groups were the only ones in the waiting room.

Cupping her chin in her palm Beverly spoke up. "You know, Georgia. I'm getting a second chance to care for Lily. I had no idea how to care for a baby when I had her. After Joe left me Mom criticized me for losing him and never let me forget how proud she was of you doing better than I had."

That was a stunner. Mom knew exactly how hard it had been for me to leave—and how my heart broke over the reasons why. I'd gone away thinking I wasn't good enough for the only boy who'd ever interested me. "Why haven't you told me this before now?"

"Embarrassment, that's why."

"Beverly, that explains so much," I said, putting the sandwich on the plate. I'd yet to take a bite. "I've thought for years that you didn't want Lily around and in your life. That you didn't care about her."

"I suppose that's the way it looked. Especially because Mom took Toby. And I let her, because she made me think I couldn't take care of him."

I took a deep breath. "But did you *want* to?"

She shook her head and stared into her lap. "Of course. Deep in my heart I wanted to do a better job with him than I'd done with Lily. But…"

She didn't finish the sentence because Richard's strong voice carried across the room and drew our attention.

"I *didn't* force your mother to go to an institution," Richard said, loud and clear. "That's the truth. She didn't want you and Chad watching her dying day after day." He slapped the edge of the table, his features grim. Even from across the room, I saw the anger flash in his eyes.

"I tried to keep our family together, Nathan, but I couldn't. She wouldn't tell you the truth and I hid it from you."

Nathan leaned forward and put his head in his hands.

Richard pushed the paper plate with an untouched sandwich to the side. "I never got to tell Chad any of this. And I regret it every day of my life."

"Why now?" Nathan asked. "Why today, when anything could happen to Toby and Lily?"

"Because I'm alone, and feeling desperate. I want to watch my grandson grow up alongside his father." Richard slid his hands across the table to touch Nathan's arm. "I'm so sorry I kept this from you."

I forced myself to stop staring at Richard and Nathan. "Today's not only a new beginning for Toby, but for others as well. I'm glad I'm back in Wolf Creek."

"I'm happy you're here with me," Beverly said. "I'll never be able to thank you for convincing Lily to come home."

"You already have," I said. "Your enthusiasm about Virgie's vests and encouragement about her move to Wolf Creek has already changed her life."

Beverly smiled. "And it's fun."

I picked up my sandwich. "I, for one, am starving. Enough of our serious talk. Let's eat."

Beverly and I had nearly finished our lunch when the surgical teams entered the waiting room still in their blue scrubs. A tall, white haired man stepped forward. Nathan went to meet him. Beverly, Richard and I were out of our chairs, too and gathered behind Nathan.

"Both surgeries were successful," the surgeon said. "No complications. We expect the kidney to function properly in the boy's body."

Another surgeon turned toward Beverly and me. "Are you Lily's family?"

"I'm her mother." Beverly's voice exuded confidence.

"She's doing fine also. She'll be in recovery for a while. I'll have a nurse take you in soon." He shook Beverly's hand. "You have a courageous daughter."

Beverly thanked him, then turned to me. I gathered her in my arms and held her tight while she shed tears of happiness.

***

Following their initial recovery in the Intensive Care Units, adult for Lily, pediatric for Toby, they were moved to private rooms. That meant our restricted two-minute visits ended and we could stay with them longer.

But three days after surgery, Lily spiked a fever.

"No cause for alarm," the head of the medical unit said. "No need to worry."

"That's like telling us not to breathe," Nathan said, his voice flat. He began firing questions at the doctor and the nurse in charge of Lily's care. The rest of us, including Beverly, might as well not have been in the room. We learned that the antibiotic would be changed immediately, but there was nothing else to do but watch and wait.

Nathan raked his hand through his hair. "This is exactly

what I was afraid of all along." He looked at us, his pleading expression begging for confirmation.

"Seriously, Nathan," the nurse in charge of the after-care team said, "this is a common occurrence and more than likely easily treated."

Nathan sighed, and Beverly went to his side, whispering that she understood. She was worried, too.

"I know," Nathan said, lightly touching Beverly's arm, "but I despise 'more than likely' language."

Over the next days, I went back and forth between Green Bay and Wolf Creek, working with Jack and Virgie to keep Country Law running smoothly. Along with Nathan, Beverly insisted on staying at the hospital for two nights. Richard wanted to, but Nathan more or less issued an order that he go home. In between I updated Elliot, and one evening we managed a quick dinner at Crossroads.

Less than 48 hours after the fever shot up, it broke and early the next morning when I went into Lily's room, her smile lit up the world. She and Toby had to spend a few more days in the hospital, so Nathan finally relented and went home to sleep. But over the previous days I'd come to see that Nathan had a network of friends, some of many years duration, in Green Bay. Between Nathan's pals and his new circle in Wolf Creek, neither Toby nor Lily was alone for long.

Lily proved to be a problem in other ways, though. She refused to stay put. With the fever behind her, she took advantage of any alone time she had to sneak off to Toby's room. They became a couple of schemers, which worried the nurses and reassured the rest of us. Clearly, Toby would have no trouble accepting this fun-loving woman as his mom. When the nurses had reprimanded Lily for her antics, she'd smiled like a contrite kid, but according to Nathan, the next time she gave the nurses the slip, she climbed in bed with Toby and they both had a cozy nap.

Meanwhile, Beverly and Nathan were both on missions to have Lily and Toby released. They assured the doctors that Beverly, experienced at this kind of caregiving, had her home set up to care for the pair of patients, with the rest of us filling in where needed.

One evening, I visited with Lily, who, having claimed the bed was too confining, moved to a chair for our visit. A few minutes after I arrived, Nathan burst into the room wearing a happy grin. When he flashed a dramatic thumbs up sign, we all laughed.

"Phase two, home recovery, due to begin tomorrow afternoon," he said.

I clapped along with Lily, who added a hoot and a holler to the celebration.

The next day, Toby and Lily were settled into Beverly's dining room, which now had two hospital beds, one adult size, and the other suitable for a small child. Bedside tables and lamps were also part of the rented equipment.

Charlie Crawford's crew had taken an hour or so of time away from the remodeling work in her lower level to set up the room, which included a couple of comfortable chairs for visitors, along with a table with checkerboard and a television and DVD player. Stacks of books and magazines filled another table.

I stopped in at Beverly's after they'd had time to rest, but I didn't stay long. Toby tired easily and still wasn't quite sure he liked being away from his new room—or not having his dad with him all the time. Beverly remedied that by spending extra time with him when Nathan and Richard weren't around.

The days had flown by, and although I called Elliot with updates, and we'd managed a quick take-out dinner from Crossroads one evening, he warned me about becoming a mother hen, again. His soft voice told me that he understood my concern for my family. "You're a wonderful person, Peaches."

"Well, I think the same about you," I said before sending him out the door.

The next day I was shocked when I saw the note on Beverly's front door listing the times when people could visit her "patients." And that included me, along with Jack and Liz and many other people.

"You can't turn people away if they come," I said when

I went inside.

"Why not? I promised two medical teams I would limit visitors and take care of these two. Lily and Toby need their rest to get well!"

It was hard to argue with that, but still...I wasn't sure I liked being restricted to certain hours. I told myself she'd make an exception for my visits. Besides, none of this would last long, because as the days passed Lily and Toby gradually regained their strength. With every visit Beverly beamed even brighter with pride.

One evening, our conversation turned serious when Beverly confided that she and Lily had spent many hours talking about the past and how their actions had affected their lives.

"Oh, Sis, I think she and I understand each other now. She's done a wonderful thing for Toby. That's a gift enough. But who would have thought we'd see a bright future for her with Nathan and Toby. I have you to thank for that. If you hadn't come back and gone to work for Nathan and Jack, we wouldn't have made these connections."

My plan to reunite the family had worked even better than I could have imagined. The Winters family was not only whole again, it was in the process of expanding.

26

The next time I showed up during Beverly's posted visiting hours, Lily was next to Toby in his bed. Both were resting, as was Nathan who had settled in the soft chair. I gingerly pulled a folding chair next to Toby's bed and sat, but the squeak of the chair woke Lily.

"Isn't he cute?" Lily's dark blue eyes flashed bright and alert. For a second I wasn't sure if she meant Nathan or Toby.

"Which one?" I asked slyly.

"Both, I guess."

Hearing our voices, Toby opened his eyes.

"So, what do you think, Toby? Is your dad cute?"

"Yuck! Cute's for girls." He wiggled a little and scrunched his face.

Nathan, admittedly a wonderful looking man, stretched his arms and shook his head. "I heard that." He finally stood up and walked to the other side of Toby's bed. "If you two are going to embarrass me that way, I'm going home." He stretched across the bed to give Lily a kiss and Toby a high five.

"Don't go away mad." Lily struggled to keep a smile from breaking through.

"Don't want to go at all. That apartment is an empty and lonely place without you guys there."

Lily slipped her hand into his. Their eyes spoke for them and revealed their closeness. This situation had strengthened their bond. Nathan bent forward to give them a three-way hug before checking his watch and taking off for the office.

280

Lily made no move to leave Toby's side after Nathan left. Toby snuggled closer as she gently rubbed his arm.

"What's new for you today?" she asked.

"The Square has changed its face this week and it's beautiful. Summer really has given way to fall. Pumpkins are perched and tucked everywhere and bales of hay are stacked about. Even scarecrows are arranged with pots of colorful mums to edge the walkways."

"I can't wait to see that. They didn't decorate the Square when I was little."

I nodded. This was all new to me, too. "Sarah said there will be orange fairy lights strung in the trees next month for Halloween."

Toby had gone to sleep so Lily slid off his bed and tucked the blankets around him. For safety she lifted the side railings. Partially bent over when she walked, we'd been assured she'd stand taller every day as she healed.

Beverly came into the room with a glass of juice and a small dish containing an assortment of pills. "Time for you to leave, Georgia."

"But…but I just…I mean I've only been here for a couple of minutes."

"Don't try to stretch the rules. I'm this girl's mother and she needs her rest. Out with you." She pointed to the front door. Even Lily looked surprised at her stern voice.

I shrugged. There was no use to fight for more time. I grabbed my purse, gave everyone a hug and left. As I drove home Nathan's words about an empty house made me realize I, too, would be entering an empty house. I'd come to enjoy Lily living with me. I also knew that arrangement would change soon. Nathan and Lily no longer tried to hide their feelings for each other. No reason to hide them, either.

I couldn't take credit for that, could I? No, they fell in love all by themselves.

***

The following week I received a text from Lily asking me to come to Beverly's house on Thursday evening around seven. She gave no clue what she wanted from me and when I text back and asked, her reply came—ULC—you'll see.

Jack and Liz had received the invitation, too. I could only shrug my shoulders when he asked what it was about. Apparently, Liz didn't know, and when Sarah called with the same question, I laughed when I gave her the same answer.

My imagination went wild with speculation. An announcement from her and Nathan? A problem with her recovery? Or Toby's? Maybe she wanted to thank everyone for their support.

Virgie declared she was as surprised as the rest of us to get an invitation. Sure, she lived with Beverly, but she wasn't family.

I called Elliot, but he hadn't received a text from her. That surprised me. Lily had always included him where I was concerned. As we talked, Elliot's soft tone calmed me, almost as if the flurry of the previous weeks was far in the past. I could feel our relationship growing stronger and most days I couldn't wait to talk to him. Today was one of them.

On Thursday evening I drove to Beverly's, apparently the last to arrive because parked cars lined the street. I recognized most of them, but there were a couple I hadn't seen before.

Beverly opened the door as I hurried up the walk. "We've been waiting for you."

I looked at my watch. It wasn't even seven yet. "I'm not late."

"Everyone was too curious to wait." She laughed. "Thankfully, Lily had dressed earlier. She's so excited she's having a hard time not talking about her surprise." Beverly looked behind her, as if checking to see if anyone was nearby. "I don't want her to get overtired."

"Then let's get her started. I promise I won't stay long."

Once inside, I saw the living room filled with people and distracted, I absently took the glass of juice Virgie offered me. I waved to the roomful of people I considered to be my friends, but I stopped when I saw Doris sitting next to Lily and Nathan, holding Toby, on Lily's other side. Beverly directed me toward a pair of folding chairs. As I sat I reconsidered my thought about friends. Some of my friends were here. Even more of the people of Wolf Creek had made me feel that I was part of their tight-knit community and I had Uncle Miles to thank for making my life fuller, richer.

Lily nodded my way and took a small drink from a glass, then passed it to Nathan.

"I want to thank all of you for coming tonight." She swallowed to cover her nervousness. "First, thank you for all your support and well wishes these past few weeks. You were there for us to lean on when the worries and stress became too heavy. And I thank you for your prayers." She reached out and took Nathan's hand. "Now I want to tell you why I called us together."

"When I met Toby at Uncle Miles' funeral and afterward at Georgia's house I saw his joy at getting a truck from Rachel and Thomas. I wanted to get him a toy, too. But the Square had no toy store."

I saw Sarah straighten in her chair and listen more closely to what Lily was saying.

"So I went to Pages to get him a book instead. Being the honest person I am…"

We all chuckled. She looked over at Doris.

Lily released Nathan's hand and put her other one on Doris' shoulder. "When Doris asked if I liked her new window display I told her they were dull and boring. And, being the great business woman she is, she asked me to take one window and create a display. I told her I needed two days to get everything I would use." Lily smiled at Doris before continuing. "I also knew I didn't want to be a waitress the rest of my life. So everything seemed to be coming together at the same time."

She still hadn't told us her plans, but she certainly knew how to keep an audience waiting.

"Doris liked my idea of adding toys and art supplies to the displays. Sooooo…"

She looked at each one of us with a huge smile, her dark blue Owen eyes dancing.

"Doris is renting me a section of her store for toys. We're going to change the name on the building to read 'Pages and Toys`.`"

The room erupted into questions and congratulations.

"Excuse me, everyone." Sarah raised the level of her voice above the rest of the talking. "I want to say that this addition to Wolf Creek Square makes me…"

She hesitated and a hush fell over the room as we all held our breath.

"Excited. Will the toys be here for holiday shopping?"

"Yes," Doris and Lily said in unison, "we have boxes in the storeroom now."

Again, we all laughed.

"I'll be happy to help unpack and price mark the toys," Liz said.

Liz knew why we all laughed yet again, and she responded with a happy shrug. "I know, I don't want to miss a thing."

I grabbed my phone and sent a quick text to Elliot. His idea of expanding the businesses on the Square had happened. He could add one more to his list.

I heard Toby clap his hands and join in the excitement. He probably didn't understand all of what was said, but he picked up on the buoyant mood.

Who would have guessed it? Lily becoming a business partner with grumpy old Doris. I guess I read her wrong, but then, no one else on the Square would have been willing to approach her and suggest expanding her business. But Lily had.

Lily walked around the room and thanked everyone for coming and asking them to spread the news. When she approached Sarah and me I took a step back. I wasn't sure if tonight was the first time Sarah had heard about Lily joining Doris.

When they did a high five I knew Sarah had been privileged with their plans and was part of the evening's revelations.

"We did it, Lily. Even with the delay because of the surgeries," Sarah said.

Lily's hands cupped her pinking cheeks. "Thanks. We're very excited to display our first shipment."

"Call me when you're unpacking," Sarah said. "Liz can't

hog all the fun, and I haven't played with toys in years."

Nathan, carrying Toby, came up behind Lily. "Time for all of us to leave. And that includes me. It's been a big evening for you and you both need to rest now."

"I doubt I'll get much sleep tonight. I'm too excited. Will you take me to Pages tomorrow?"

"Let's see how you feel." He looked over at Beverly, who nodded in approval at his reply.

When Beverly began circling the room and thanking everybody for coming, we got the message. Visiting hours were over. True enough, but nothing spoke louder than Beverly's smile when she watched Nathan and Lily settle Toby into bed.

"Quite a surprise tonight," I said, positioning myself so that everyone else could file out first. "Did you have any idea she was going to partner with Doris?"

"She was very guarded about some papers of hers. You know, hiding them under her blanket or mixing them up with magazines if I came close. But, no, Doris only came once or twice to visit."

"Clever ladies." I leaned in closer. "Seriously, how's Lily recovering? And don't give me the standard answer. I'm family. I want it the whole story."

Beverly stared at her shoes. "The truth? She has good days and bad days—or not so much bad as so-so. As time passes, the days are mostly good, though. The incision itches and annoys her, but the doctors say that's expected. She wants to move around more, but the nurses, specialists in transplants, have convinced her that she'll be better able to take care of Toby later on if she gives herself time to recover now."

"That's good, isn't it?" I asked, mentally thanking those wise nurses.

Beverly nodded. "She seems to know her limits, so I think going to Pages tomorrow for a short visit will be good for her."

"And what about Toby?"

"You should ask Nathan about that."

Wham! It hit me again that even though I was a blood

relative to Toby, Nathan was his legal guardian. Maybe over time, some of those boundaries would ease. I hoped so.

"Let me say goodnight to Lily and then I'll be on my way."

Lily was next to Toby's bed holding his hand and telling him about all the toys he would soon see in the bookstore. I went to her side to give her a hug.

"I miss you not being in my house. It's pretty lonely there now. Come home soon."

Lily smiled and grabbed my hand. "It seems I am home. A house doesn't make a home. It's the people. And look at all the people in my life now. But I miss my room at your house. I'll be there soon."

I needed to remember that Elliot was waiting for me. *Waiting for me*. Those words made me ask why I was waiting.

I left Beverly's and hurried home to call Elliot again. Not a text this time. I wanted to hear his voice.

The days passed. As long as Toby was at Beverly's, still needing recovering time, Lily chose to stay there, too. That meant having Nathan around most of the time.

October
27

The October meeting of the Wolf Creek Square Business Association was short and to the point with only three items on the agenda. I'd come a bit late and found a place to stand along the back wall.

Sarah took charge of the podium and assured everyone she'd be brief. First, she welcomed Lily as a new merchant, and second, she reviewed the weeks' activities on the Square through Christmas, stressing everyone needed to be prepared because they'd be hosting more tour buses than originally announced. "Last, we've finalized arrangements to hold the Harvest Festival dance at the community center this year. That's because we don't have a venue on the Square large enough for the expected crowd. Come when you can, but do attend. We all need to celebrate the harvest and good fortunes of the year."

She turned off the microphone and stepped away from the podium. Someone handed her a glass of deep red wine. I went to join my friend.

Sarah had warned the shop owners about the volume of visitors and bus tours, but no one was prepared for the throngs of people that came each day, and that included all of us at Country Law. Virgie handed out brochures and cards to a steady stream of visitors, a smattering of whom soon called to make appointments.

***

One day mid-week, Lily arrived at Country Law before noon. Her hair sparkled with rain drops from an unexpected shower that had caught her unprepared. With my office door open I heard her ask Virgie, "Is he here?" She didn't have to name the "he" in her life.

The stress in her voice prompted me to step out from behind my desk and go into the reception area of the office. "Something wrong, honey?" For the rest of my life I suspected I'd feel my stomach twist when I sensed Lily's anxiety over something.

"Do you know where Nathan is?"

I looked over to Virgie who was checking the schedule for the day. Lily bounced back and forth on her feet. She appeared distracted.

"He's here. He should be off the phone any minute," Virgie said.

We watched and waited for the light to blink off. It reminded me of waiting for a kettle to boil. The light off, Virgie rang him. "Lily's waiting to see you."

His eagerness to see her was apparent when he raced from his office. "You okay?" He wrapped his arms around her.

She bounced her head up and down. "It came today." She expected him to understand, but his blank face triggered an exaggerated roll of her eyes. "The sign for the front of the shop— "Pages and Toys." She made the quotation marks with her fingers and spoke slowly so Nathan would understand.

"Now? They're putting it up now?"

"Done." She grabbed his hand and pulled him to the front window.

He put his arm around her waist. "I'm so proud of you."

So, she wasn't anxious after all. She was excited. I turned away to let them have their moment alone. I was so happy they were together, but lately, I'd been looking forward to some changes in my own life.

After work, I weaved through the crowd of late afternoon shoppers to see the new sign. My heart soared. Beverly and Lily, united. Each had a brand new business partner, too. Could my plan have worked any better?

I walked into the store, into a child's wonderland, and when I looked closer Lily and Doris had chosen games and toys for not only children, but for adults, too. Lily finished helping a customer who left with a shopping bag filled to the top.

"Hi, Georgia. What brings you by today?"

"Pride. In you and your new life."

"Still scary about investing all my money, but we can't keep up with the sales and replacing stock."

"And books? Are they selling, too?"

"Oh, sure. Some books are sold with a toy. A two for one deal."

"Very clever."

Lily leaned against a book rack. I saw her body slump with fatigue. My take-care-when-asked philosophy held me back from telling her that she shouldn't work so hard before she was stronger. I was sure Nathan had already mentioned it a time or two. Other than the fatigue, though, she glowed.

The bell on the door jingled and before it stopped Toby was by her side. He spun around with his arms out. "Toys, Georgia. Look at all the toys."

"Pretty cool, huh?"

"Way cool." He flashed those dark blue eyes and waved as he ran down another aisle.

"Georgia. Hi, honey." Nathan had come to join us. He bent forward to give Lily a kiss. "Busy day?"

"Very. I need to restock tonight."

Nathan looked around at all the empty spaces on the shelves. "Georgia, are you busy tonight?"

"No plans."

"If you take Toby for supper I can stay and help Lily. We can get her home earlier that way."

His logical lawyer mind was protecting what I'd come to consider as his family—his new family of three.

"Sure, no problem. I'll take him home and you can pick him up there."

"No candy bars," he said.

I raised an eyebrow. That had been my treat for Toby since I first met him.

"Okay, but only *one.*"

I walked down one aisle and moved to the next to find Toby. He was sitting on the floor with a book on his lap.

"It's you and me for supper tonight, kiddo. How about burgers and fries?"

He raised his arms above his head. "Yes!"

We returned the book to the shelf and said our goodbyes, with Nathan adding, "Say please and thank you. Mind your manners."

Toby was a perfect supper partner. We had a small table by the window at Crossroads and I joined Toby and ordered a burger platter and remembered why I enjoyed the old standby dinner once in a while. We talked about living on the Square and the coming of Halloween. Mostly, though the little boy told me stories about Nathan and Lily kissing all the time. He was being eased into a new stage of family life, the kind he hadn't experienced since his parents died. I looked across the table, allowing myself a minute or two to grieve for my family over missing so much of his life, but grieving for Toby, too, and what he must have gone through when he lost the only parents he'd known.

I was drawn back to the present when Toby began describing his silver and black racecar driver Halloween costume.

I let the conversation wander as we ate, He didn't stop talking during the drive to my house, or when I put him on the couch to rest. I laughed to myself. It must have been hard for Nathan not to ask for silence now and then. His eyes soon grew heavy, though, even with my reading light on. I'd started a mystery months before and was determined to guess the villain and finish the book.

Lily and Nathan crashed through the door earlier than expected and laughing loudly like young people in love. Yet, here they were parents to a child whose life had been in question only weeks earlier. I put my index finger over my lips to hush them and pointed to Toby with my other hand.

"You wouldn't believe it, Georgia." Lily tried to whisper, without much success. "He had to play with every toy before he put it on the shelf. Worse than a kid."

"Quality control." Nathan shrugged and grinned. He bent over Toby and lifted him up. But it wouldn't be long before Toby would think he was too old to be carried. Lily opened the door for Nathan, but before he left, he leaned down and kissed her.

Lily sighed, her shoulders sagging a little. "Time to get to Mom's. She's already texted to find out when I'd be home. She'll call out a posse if I don't show up soon." Lily grabbed her purse and the tote bag she carried everywhere now.

"'Night, honey." I watched her get in her car and head toward Beverly's.

I checked the clock to see if it was too late to call Elliot. Love was in the air, and I needed to make sure he knew that included him.

***

The next morning, I called Elliot again, this time to see if he and Eli could stop by around three to go over the generous settlement from the insurance company for the Farmer Foods fire. The two showed up on time and I walked them back to Jack's office, where I pulled up a chair next to the desk.

"Georgia did most of the negotiating," Jack said, nodding to me. "You should know she refused the first offer."

"It was ridiculously low," I added, "truly irresponsible and unacceptable."

"The final settlement covers equipment, of course, but also lost income." Jack handed the check to Elliot who looked at it then passed it onto to Eli.

"More than we thought we'd get," Eli said, relief washing over his face.

Jack shrugged. "You've paid premiums for years— business, home, auto. You deserve compensation when you have a catastrophe."

"All we can do is thank you." Elliot looked directly at me when he spoke. Nothing cute or fuzzy about the comment. He was serious.

"Credit Georgia for this. She worked this case with the

same intensity I'd have done." Jack stood, and that was that. He shook hands with both brothers, saying, "And thanks for trusting Country Law—I know we're the new faces of the firm."

"I'll call you tonight, Peaches," Elliot said as he followed Eli out the door.

Jack had heard that moniker for me for so long now, he didn't even react. But he did extend his hand to me and say, "Nice work, Georgia. Now that Lily and Toby are doing well, I'm going to transfer a couple of cases your way. One is a complex probate case, but you're up to it."

"Ah, yes, families. My favorite topic."

Jack smiled at my tongue-in-cheek remark.

28

With Lily and Toby on the mend, I reconnected with the morning group at Biscuits and Brew. Of course, everyone asked about Lily and Toby. I used superlatives to describe their recovery and turned the conversation to promote Lily's new business. But soon, the women steered the conversation to the really important topic of what they'd picked out to wear for Saturday's dance.

A no-dates-required affair, Megan and Sarah were self-confidant enough to go alone, but they planned to arrive together. I wanted to tell everyone that Elliot and I would be going together, but he hadn't mentioned picking up the tickets. I'd heard they'd been sold out days ago. Had he waited too long to buy ours? I hoped not, because I'd already found the perfect dress at Styles and it hung in my closet waiting for the big night.

Mimi had brought it out from the back room to show me. "I thought of you when I opened the box. I was going to call later to see if you were interested."

And what a dress it was. Sleeveless, with easy-fitting lines, the rust color brought out the highlights in my hair. The iridescent three-quarter length over-jacket sparkled under the bright store lighting. As I moved, colors of rust, yellow, orange, and a touch of blue danced in the light.

I bought a shawl to wear and added crystal blue earrings that matched my eyes. I couldn't have special ordered a more perfect dancing dress.

Mimi had given me a once over, circling around me, adjusting the shawl, tugging a bit at the shoulders of the jacket. Fussing, really. Finally, she declared the dress—and me—stunning.

And with no pretense of false modesty, I agreed. I laughed thinking of Elliot's reaction. Like a teenager counting down the days until the prom, I could hardly wait for the night of the dance to arrive.

***

The community center sparkled with miniature lights woven into the artificial trees in the corners of the room. Bales of hay, like those in the Square, were stacked in groups of two or three and decorated with pumpkins and bowls of gourds. The center of each table had a flickering facsimile candle—they looked like the real thing. Finally, orange tablecloths added another level of rich color to the room.

Because it was Elliot's weekend to close Farmer Foods at the end of the day we arrived when the small band was starting its second set. That was okay, because Elliot immediately whirled me onto the dance floor. The first time we'd danced since we were in high school. It struck me that just like the bicycle and riding the horses on the trail in Door County, we stumbled through the first steps until we found our rhythm. And what a rhythm it was.

After two dances we stopped to get cups of cider and say hello to friendly faces in the crowd. I couldn't count all the people I recognized. Six, maybe seven months ago, I didn't know any of them except Sarah and my sister.

"It's so good to know Lily and Nathan are free to come out tonight," I said. "Talk about a string of miracles. A few months ago I wasn't sure I could coax Lily to come back to Wolf Creek."

"And plenty of people to help with Toby, too."

Virgie had volunteered to stay with him. Not only was he fond of Virgie, she'd helped Beverly tend to him—and to Lily—during their weeks of recovery. Insisting she wouldn't feel left out by staying home, she assured me she'd come next year. "I'll know more people by then and be part of the town. Right now, I'm happy to be with Toby."

I believed her. It was as if Toby had one more great-aunt.

Lily hadn't been able to contain her excitement about the dance and the chance to be out with Nathan alone. It seemed Lily was ready to take her own chance on love. She looked fresh and young, too, in a loose cherry red cocktail dress, with sparkling beaded spaghetti straps, duplicated with a row along the hem. Because of the surgery, she wore black flats, but they didn't detract from the overall effect.

I nudged Elliot when I saw Beverly with Richard at one of the tables. I wanted to say hello to them so Elliot and I began to stroll that direction.

It took almost half an hour before we made our way through the tables and people milling around to get to Beverly's table, but by that time she and Richard had begun dancing to the band's slow rendition of "Moon River."

"They look happy," I said, nodding to Beverly and Richard smiling as they danced around the room.

"Good for them, Peaches, but I'm just getting warmed up. Let's dance until dawn."

"Or until the band stops playing," I said, "whichever comes first." I nestled into his arms and this time we fell into an easy pace, moving to our own beat.

The hours passed and the crowd thinned, but most of the Square crowd was ready to enjoy themselves for awhile longer. We danced a simple polka, tried to follow the leader in a line dance, and shook our bodies to the music of our youth. Elliot and I sang along with "Sweet Dreams (Are Made of This)," maybe because it seemed our old dreams were coming true. We slow danced to "I Want to Know What Love Is," and I couldn't help my mind from wandering to the unfolding story of Lily and Nathan. The band included something for everyone, including some old Beatles tunes, which had everyone on the dance floor, including Jack and Liz. As usual, Liz stood out in the crowd in a dress the color of amethyst and appearing to be having the time of her life.

When the band leader announced the last dance, I turned to Elliot. "Oh, not yet. I'm not ready to quit."

"Me neither," Elliot said, "but we can take this out to the Square and dance to imaginary music."

"You have such good ideas," I said with a laugh.

Out of the corner of my eye, I saw Lily and Nathan. They'd been inseparable for hours, not dancing all the time, but sitting quietly together. Like the rest of us, though, they were dancing to the last song of the evening.

"Don't look now," I said, "but the newest couple of the Square look pretty happy." Other dancers had started to cluster around the couple.

Elliot gave my waist an extra squeeze. "What? I thought we were the newest couple?"

"Okay, the newest middle-aged couple."

Elliot let out a low whistle. "I think I just saw Nathan take an Art&Son Jewelry box out of his pocket."

That brought me to a stop. Sure enough, Nathan opened the blue box and dropped to one knee. The band abruptly stopped playing and a silence fell over the room.

Nathan looked up at Lily with eyes that let his heart shine through. "Will you marry me?"

Lily breathed deeply to still herself in a way I'd seen her do many times before. She hesitated, and a couple of seconds went by. Then she put her fingers in his outstretched hand. "Yes, Nathan. Forever."

Tears of joy immediately rolled down my cheeks as the crowd broke into spontaneous cheers. My family was united, and at last I saw a future for the Owen-Winters family—and now, the Connor family, too.

Through my tears, I turned to Elliot and said, "I'm overwhelmed by how it all turned out. Nathan and Lily found each other in such an unlikely way. And Toby is safe with Lily's kidney. A miracle."

I got close enough to Lily to give her a quick hug and Elliot added his congratulations, too. And then we left.

Elliot was quiet, a certain buoyancy gone. My constant chatter on the drive home overshadowed his silence, though. It was as if my excitement for Lily, Nathan, and Toby took up all the space.

Finally, when he hadn't commented I asked. "What's on your mind, Elliot?"

"Are you leaving Wolf Creek now?"

"What? Why would I leave now? Everything I want is here—these were my dreams. I have family, friends, meaningful work. I'm not going anywhere." I twisted in the passenger seat so I could face him. "And you're here."

Elliot sharply turned the wheel and pulled into my driveway and cut the engine. When we got out of the car, he caught my hand and led me to the porch.

"Let's stay out here for a bit," he said. "It's a beautiful night."

And so it was. I pulled the shawl around me a little tighter, though, in the crisp fall air. We settled in the chairs near the railing.

"Peaches, this may not be the best time, but I can't wait any longer." He put his hand inside his suit coat and brought out an Art&Son blue box.

My heart stuttered. After years of regret and loss could my world become *this* perfect?

His hands trembled as he opened the box and showed me the yellow starburst brooch I'd seen in Art's window in April.

As hard as I tried to prevent it, my face must have fallen just a bit in disappointment. But Elliot smiled. "You like it, don't you? Art said you did."

"It's…it's beautiful, Elliot. I've always… I've so admired Art's designs." I stumbled through my words of appreciation, trying to cover up my letdown.

He reached into his other pocket. "Then you might like this one, too." He opened another blue box. I took in a breath, unable to speak. In its cotton nest, the diamond ring sparkled under the glow of the porch light.

Like my family, Elliot and I had united…at last.

If you enjoyed reading about Georgia's adventure in Wisconsin in **Country Law,** *you may enjoy these books by Wisconsin authors,* **Virginia McCullough** *and* **Mary Grace Murphy...**

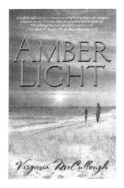

Amber Light

Despite everything, Sarah Whitmore still believes in lucky breaks...

A single act of violence left Sarah pregnant, with her cherished plans for the future in ruins. But she grabs her chance to leave her Wisconsin town behind and create a new life on the South Carolina coast, with help from an aunt and uncle she barely knows. Sarah's new life includes Amber, who Sarah vows will never learn the truth about her violent father.

Over the next years, Sarah includes her job at an island resort another lucky break, along with her unlikely friendship with Woody, who helps her break out of her shell and develop her talent as a portrait artist. But even Woody can't help Sarah believe a relationship with a man is possible for her—*ever.*

Then Sarah meets Barly Rhoads, a dad who fought for the right to be with his child. Barly believes in justice and righting wrongs when he sees them, including fixing his own mistakes. The past refuses to stay buried when Amber's father threatens the safe life Sarah has created for herself and her daughter. Barly proves he will go to any length to protect Sarah and Amber, and in the process exposes some deep wounds of his own. Now Sarah must decide if she's ready for one more lucky break.

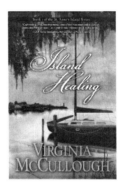

Island Healing

Book 1 of the St. Anne's Island Series

Luke Rawley lives aboard *Midnight*, a classic wooden sailboat, at the dock of St. Anne's Island. Secretly preparing to sail around the world, Luke longs to redeem his father's wasted life and broken dreams. He longs to fulfill this dream with Kevin, his 18-year-old son. With years of hard-won sobriety behind him and bringing hope and stability to Luke's life, he's ready to set sail. Until he meets Geneva…

Geneva Saint returns to her beloved St. Anne's Island, Georgia, leaving her unfaithful husband behind. Back home to stay, she's determined to heal old wounds. Geneva vows to help her brother's troubled family, including her teenage nieces, and her sister-in-law whose health is deteriorating fast. Establishing her one-woman catering company on St. Anne's is all Geneva needs to complete her St. Anne's life. Until she encounters Luke…

About to make his sailing dream come true, Luke wants Geneva to sail with him. Now she's torn between her family and taking a chance on love. With the future on the line, Luke is jolted into facing the truth of his dream, while Geneva wonders if she can ever again trust anyone who claims her heart.

It takes 13-year old Lila to show everyone how a dose of courage brings both hope and healing to every challenge they face.

The Noshes Up North Culinary Mystery Series
by Mary Grace Murphy

Death Nell

Nell Bailey has always suspected food would be the death of her, but never did she consider her relationship with tempting treats would cause her to be a target for murder. After writing an extremely negative review and posting on her blog "Noshes Up North," a blog follower takes issue with her comments and won't let it go. The cyber bullying continues culminating in a gruesome murder. A fellow foodie, coincidentally also named Nell, has been slain in a most heinous manner. Could it be a case of mistaken identity and she was the intended victim?

As Nell wonders how to deal with the situation, her lifetime battle with weight and self image give her no relief. Then she gets help from an unexpected source. Sam, the owner of the restaurant she had torn to shreds in her review. As sparks ignite between them, a chilling question rears its ugly head in the back of Nell's mind. Could Sam possibly be the killer?

Death Knock

Retired teacher Nell Bailey loves her new career as a food blogger and restaurant reviewer. Nell's passion for food is good for the job, but plays havoc on her hips. As she tries to keep her life in balance, she learns that the new man in her life has a questionable past. Adding to her distress, there's a murder at Nell's new favorite local pub. She makes a disturbing discovery while investigating with her "partner in crime," Elena. Could one of their old friends be a murderer?

Acknowledgements

It is difficult to explain to non-writers that "people" talk to me in my head and that story characters become real to me. But my writing friends understand. Plus, these special women: Kate Bowman, Shirley Cayer, Virginia McCullough, and Barb Raffin, are willing to tell me where I need to revise my writing to make it better, stronger. For that trust, I thank you.

For years my family has watched my dreams come true. At the beginning Mom, Muriel Robbins, was there to lead and support. Now, my husband, Gary, has taken on the role of guide and protector. My life would be empty without both of you.

Knowing an entire national organization of writers—the Romance Writers of America (RWA) and the state affiliate chapter, The Wisconsin Romance Writers of America (WisRWA), along with the local Greater Green Bay Area group of WisRWA—are pursuing the same dream makes the journey less lonely. Each group contributes to my success. Thank you.

Brittiany Koren of Written Dreams has put together an exceptional team to transform my words into a book. Your professionalism makes this path rewarding. Thank you.

Gini Athey
March 2015

About the Author

Gini Athey grew up in a house of readers, so much so it wasn't unusual for members of her family to sit around the table and read while they were eating. But early on, she showed limited interest in the pastime. In fact, on one trip to the library to pick out a book for a book report, she recalls telling the librarian, "I want books with thick pages and big print."

Eventually that all changed. Today, Gini usually reads three or four books at the same time, and her "to-be-read pile" towers next to her favorite chair. She reads widely in many genres, but her favorite books focus on families, with all their various challenges and rewards.

For many years, Gini has been a member of the Wisconsin chapter (WisRWA) of the Romance Writers of America and has served in a variety of administrative positions.

Avid travelers, Gini and her adventurous husband live in a rural area west of Green Bay, Wisconsin.

Quilts Galore is the first book in her Wolf Creek Square Series. She is currently writing the third book in the series. Visit her website at www.giniathey.com.

CPSIA information can be obtained at www.ICGtesting.com
Printed in the USA
LVOW11s1439070415

433610LV00001B/29/P

9 781508 978763